A Body in the Bath House

A BODY IN THE
BATH HOUSE

Lindsey Davis

Century · London

Published by Century in 2001

1 3 5 7 9 10 8 6 4 2

First published in the United Kingdom in 2001 by Century
Random House UK Limited
20 Vauxhall Bridge Road, London SW1V 2SA

Random House Australia (Pty) Limited
20 Alfred Street, Milsons Point, Sydney,
New South Wales 2061, Australia

Random House New Zealand Limited
18 Poland Road, Glenfield
Auckland 10, New Zealand

Random House (Pty) Limited
Endulini, 5a Jubilee Rd, Parktown 2193, South Africa

The Random House Group Limited Reg. No. 954009

www.randomhouse.co.uk

A CIP catalogue record for this book
is available from the British Library

Papers used by Random House
are natural, recyclable products made from wood grown in
sustainable forests. The manufacturing processes conform to
the environmental regulations of the country of origin

ISBN 0 7126 8039 X – Hardback
ISBN 0 7126 8150 7 – Paperback

Typeset in Bembo by SX Composing DTP, Rayleigh, Essex
Printed and bound in the United Kingdom by
Mackays of Chatham plc, Chatham, Kent

For Richard, again. This one could only be for you.
With all my love

In Rome

M. Didius Falco	an informer with a nose for trouble
Helena Justina	his partner, who can smell a rat
Julia and Favonia	two sweet and perfect babies
Camilla Hyspale	their sour and imperfect nurse
Nux	a dog, who just smells
Pa (Geminus/Favonius)	a rather ripe householder
Maia Favonia	a 'vulnerable' (not very!) widow
Marius, Cloelia, Ancus & Rhea	her nice (sneaky) children
L. Petronius Longus	a loyal friend, annoying Maia
Anacrites	a dangerous spy, following Maia
Perella	a devious dancer, following orders
A. Camillus Aelianus	a high-class apprentice
Q. Camillus Justinus	a bridegroom on the razzle
Gloccus and Cotta	bath-house contractors, in bad odour
Stephanus	a stinking corpse
Vespasian	an Emperor, footing the bill for:

In Britain

T. Claudius Togidubnus	Great King of the Britons, a makeover fanatic
Verovolcus	a royal facilitator
Marcellinus	a retired designer (with a very nice house)
'Uncle Lobullus'	a contractor, never there
Virginia	a fragrant barmaid

On the New Palace Building Site

Valla, Dubnus, Eporix & Gaudius	more dead men
Pomponius	the project manager (thinks he's in charge)
Magnus	the surveyor (thinks he *ought* to be in charge)
Cyprianus	the clerk of works (just gets on and runs it)
Plancus & Strephon	junior architects (clones of Pomponius)
Rectus	the farting drainage engineer
Milchato	the hard-edged marble mason
Philocles Senior	the short-tempered mosaicist
Philocles Junior	a clone of his father (misinformed?)
Blandus	a seductive painter, with a bad history
The Smartarse from Stabiae	aiming for a good future
Timagenes	gardening in a harsh landscape
Alexas	a medico who mixes a mean draught
Gaius	a clerk who can count beans
Iggidunus	the sniffy *mulsum* boy
Alla	a girl who doesn't snivvle
Sextius	a mechanical statue-seller, moving in on Maia
Mandumerus	the local labour supervisor (a few restrictive practices)
Lupus	the overseas labour superviser (more dogy customs)
Tiberius & Septimus	the universal labourers

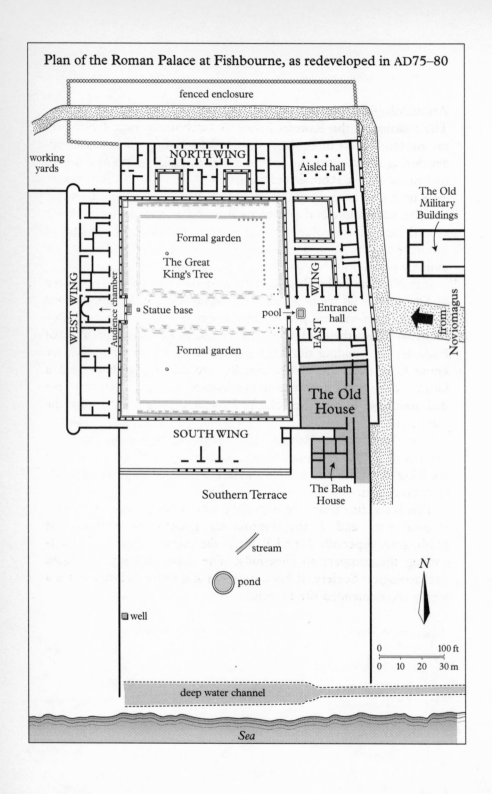

Plan of the Roman Palace at Fishbourne, as redeveloped in AD75–80

fenced enclosure

working
yards

NORTH WING

Aisled hall

The Old
Military
Buildings

WEST WING

Audience chamber

Formal garden

The Great
King's Tree

Statue base

pool →

Formal garden

WING

EAST

Entrance
hall

from Noviomagus

The Old
House

SOUTH WING

The Bath
House

Southern Terrace

stream

pond

N

well

0   100 ft
0 10 20 30 m

deep water channel

Sea

Archaeological Note

The remains of the Roman Palace at Fishbourne, near Chichester on the south coast of Britain, were unearthed by a mechanical digger during the construction of a watermain in 1960. It seemed hard to believe that a Roman building of such wealth and importance *could* be found here. Some of the palace lies under modern houses, but the excavation and preservation of what was accessible owes everything to local volunteers and benefactors. It is still a matter of speculation why such a magnificent building was created in this unlikely place.

If Fishbourne had a Roman name, we don't know it. The palace of Togidubnus (as we now call him), Great King of the Britons, was constructed in various phases. In this novel the Neronian 'proto-palace' is called 'the old house'; it is the grand Flavian expansion that Falco sees at building site stage. I have tried to use only what we know from excavation. Any mistakes are my responsibility and if future work reveals new treasures or leads to new interpretations, we shall just have to say 'they changed the design after Falco saw the plans'.

There were various Roman villas in a similar style along the coast; these were probably homes to local dignitaries, perhaps relatives of the King. That the one at Angmering was built by an architect is my own invention.

This is the first time I have based a story entirely on one archaeological site, and I am enormously grateful to everyone at Fishbourne, especially David Rudkin the current curator, for welcoming the prospect so cheerfully. The palace belongs to Sussex Archaeological Society. It has a museum and other facilities and is a highly recommended site to visit.

ROME AND OSTIA
SPRING, AD 75

B ᴜᴛ ꜰᴏʀ Rhea Favonia, we might have lived with it.

    'There's a *smell*! There's a horrible smell. I'm not going in *there*!'

    I didn't need to be an informer to know we were stuck. When a four-year-old girl reckons she has detected something nasty, you just give in and look for it. My little niece would not go near the bath house until we proved there was nothing horrible in the caldarium. The more we scoffed and told her the hot room was only smelly because of its new plaster, the more Rhea screamed hysterically at bath time. There was nothing visible, and the rest of us tried to ignore it. But the child's insistence unsettled everyone.

    There *was* a faint odour. If I tried sniffing it out, I lost it. When I decided there had been nothing, straight away I smelled it again.

At least Helena and I were able to go home to our own new house. My sister Maia and her children had to stay on there on the Janiculan Hill, in the home that was supposed to be their refuge from trouble, living with that other kind of trouble, Pa. My father, Geminus, and I were in the throes of a house-swap. While I tried to organise decorators to renovate his faded old lair on the bank of the Tiber, he took over the spread on which I had already worked for months, where all that remained for completion was the new bath house.

    The Janiculan house had a highly desirable location – if you worked on the north side of Rome. It suited Pa, with his auction house and antiques business in the Saepta Julia by the Pantheon. My own work required free access to all parts of the city. I was an informer, serving private clients whose cases could take me anywhere. However much I wanted to move out and across the river, I needed to live close to the action. Sadly, this sensible thought had only struck Helena and me after we had bought the new house.

    By chance, father's long-term companion, Flora, then died. He turned into a maudlin romantic, who hated the mansion they had shared. I had always liked the riverside quarter below the Aventine. So we organised an exchange. The bath-house contractors became Father's problem. That was appropriate because Pa had introduced them to Helena in the first place. I enjoyed waiting to see how he would persuade Gloccus and Cotta to finish, a task where even Helena had failed – despite the fact she had been paying their bills. As with all builders, the more unreliable they had become, the more extortionate those bills were.

With Pa, we couldn't win: by some means, he fixed them. Within a week, Gloccus and Cotta had grouted their last wobbly tile and cleared off. My father then possessed a fine domestic outbuilding with a full cold room, tepid room, three-piece sweating-room suite; natty dipping pool; integral changing area with modish pegs and clothes bunkers; separate furnace and log store; de luxe Greek marble basins and a custom-designed sea-god medallion in one newly laid mosaic floor. But while people were admiring his Neptune, they also noticed the odd smell.

In moments when it caught me, that reek seemed to carry hints of decay. Pa knew it too. 'It's as if the room had been locked up with some old codger dead inside for months.'

'Well, the room's brand new and the old cove is still alive, unfortunately.' I gathered Pa must have had some neglected neighbours, in the past life we never discussed. I myself knew about smells like that from other situations. Bad ones.

There came an evening, after a long hot day, when we found we could no longer ignore the stink. That afternoon I had been helping Pa dig over a terrace, Jupiter knows why. He could afford gardeners and I was not one to play the dutiful son. Afterwards, we both sluiced off. It must have been the first time we bathed together since he ran away when I was seven. Next time we met, I was home from the army. For a few years I even pretended not to know who he was. Now I had to tolerate occasional brushes with the old rogue, for social reasons. He was older; he was on his own with that, but I was older too. I now had two baby daughters. I should allow them a chance to learn to despise their grandfather.

As we stood in the hot room that evening, we faced decision time. During the day, I had done most of the heavy work. I was exhausted, yet I still rejected Pa's offer to scrape a strigil down my back. I made a rough job of cleaning off the oil myself. Pa favoured a concoction of what seemed to be crushed iris roots. Incongruous. And on that hot sultry night, nowhere near strong enough to mask the other smell.

'Rhea's right.' I glanced down at the floor. 'Something's rotting in your hypocaust.'

'No, no; trust me!' Pa used the voice he kept for assuring idiots that some piece of Campanian fakery could be 'school of Lysippus', if looked at in the right light. 'I told Gloccus to omit the hypocaust from this room. His quotation was outrageous for underfloor work. I worked out some figures myself, and with that kind of area to heat, I was going to be spending four times as much on fuel . . .' He tapered off.

I eased my foot against the wide instep strap of a bath shoe. Helena's original scheme had involved properly heating the whole warm suite. Once she admitted what she was up to here, I had seen the plans. 'What have you done then?'

'Just wall flues.'

'You'll regret it, you cheapskate. You're on high ground. You'll find it chilly round your rude bits in December.'

'Give over. I work right by the Baths of Agrippa.' Entrance was free. Pa would love that. 'I won't need to use this place except in high summer.'

I stretched slowly, trying to ease the stiffness in my lower back. 'Is the floor solid? Or had they already dug out a hypocaust when you decided against it?'

'Well, the lads had made a start. I told them to floor over the cavity and block off any links to the other rooms.'

'Brilliant, Pa. So there won't be an access point for crawling under this floor.'

'No. The only way in is down.'

Nice work. We would have to break up the mosaic we had only just taken over brand new.

The underfloor space in a usable hypocaust would be eighteen inches high, or two feet at most, with a mass of tile piers to support the suspended floor. It would be dark and hot. Normally they send boys in to clean them, not that I would inflict it on a child today – to face who knew what? I was relieved there was no formal access hatch. That saved me having to crawl in.

'So what do you think about this smell, Marcus?' my father asked, far too deferentially.

'The same as you. Your Neptune is floating on rot. And it's not going away.'

Instinctively we breathed. We caught a definite hum.

'Oh Titan's turds.'

'That's what it smells like, Pa!'

We ordered the furnace slave to stop stoking. We told him to go to the house and keep everyone else indoors. I fetched pickaxes and crowbars, then Pa and I set about ruining the sea-god mosaic.

It had cost a fortune but Gloccus and Cotta had produced their usual shoddy work. The suspended foundation for the tesserae was far too shallow. Neptune, with his wild seaweed hair and boggle-eyed attendant squids, would soon have been buckling underfoot.

By tapping with a chisel, I identified a hollow area and we set to. My father got the worst of it. Always impetuous, he put his pick in too fast, hit something, and was spattered with foul yellowish liquid. He let out a yell of disgust. I leapt back and stopped breathing. A warm updraft brought disgusting odours; we fled towards the door. Judging by its powerful airflow, the underfloor system must never have been blocked off completely as Pa ordered. We were now in no doubt what must be down there.

'Oh pigshit!' Pa peeled off his tunic and hurled it into a corner, splashing water on his skin where the stinking liquid had touched him. He was hopping with disgust. 'Oh pigshit, pigshit, pigshit!'

'Didius Favonius speaks. Come, citizens of Rome, let us gather to admire the elegance of his oratory –' I was trying to put off the moment when we had to go back for a look.

'Shut your lofty gob, Marcus! It's putrid – and it bloody well missed you!'

'Come on; let's get this over with.'

We covered our mouths and braved a look. In a depression that must have been used as the lazy workmen's cache for rubbish, amongst a mass of uncleared site rubble, we had unearthed a stomach-turning relic. Still just recognisably human, it was a half-decayed corpse.

II

I T HAD already been a hard winter. For most of it, Helena Justina had been pregnant with our second child. She suffered more than with the first, while I struggled to let her rest by looking after our firstborn, Julia. As queen of the household, Julia was establishing her authority that year. I had the bruises to prove it. I had gone deaf too; she enjoyed testing her lungs. Our dark-haired moppet could put on a burst of speed any stadium sprinter would envy, especially as she toddled towards a fiercely steaming stockpot or darted down our steps onto the roadway. Even dumping her on female relations was out; her favourite game lately was breaking vases.

Spring saw no domestic improvements. First the new baby was born. It was very quick. Just as well. Both grandmothers were on the spot this time to complicate proceedings. Ma and the senator's wife were full of wise ideas, though they had opposing views on midwifery. Things were frosty enough, then I managed to be rude to both of them. At least that gave them a subject on which they could agree.

The new mite was ailing and I named her in a hurry: Sosia Favonia. In part, it was a nod to my father, whose original cognomen was Favonius. I would never have demeaned myself paying him a compliment if I had thought my daughter would survive. Born skinny and silent, she had looked halfway to Hades. The minute I named her, she rallied. From then on she was as tough as a totter's ferret. She also had her own character from the start, a curious little eccentric who never quite seemed to belong with us. But everyone told me she had to be mine: she made so much mess and noise.

It took at least six weeks before my family's fury at the name I had chosen died down to simmering sneers that would only be revived on Favonia's birthday and at family gatherings every Saturnalia, and whenever there was nobody to blame for anything else. People were now nagging me to acquire a children's nurse. It was nobody's business but Helena's and mine, so everyone weighed in. Eventually I gave up and visited a slave market.

Judging by the pitiful specimens on offer, Rome badly needed some frontier wars. The slave trade was in a slump. The dealer I approached was a creased Delian in a dirty robe, picking his nails on a lop-sided tripod while he waited for some naïve duffer with a poor eye and a fat purse. He got me. He tried the patter anyway.

Since Vespasian was rebuilding the Empire, he needed to mint coinage and had raided the slave markets for labourers to put in the gold and silver mines. Titus brought large numbers of Jewish prisoners to Rome after the siege of Jerusalem, but the public service had snapped up the men to build the Flavian Amphitheatre. Who knows where the women ended up. That left a poor display for me. In the dealer's current batch were a few elderly oriental secretary types, long past being able to see to read a scroll. Then there were various lumps suitable for farm labouring. I did need a manager for my farm at Tibur, but that would wait. My mother had taught me how to go to market. I won't say I was scared of Ma, but I had learned to trot home with what was on the shopping list and no private treats for myself.

'Jupiter. Where do people buy disease-raddled flute girls nowadays?' I had reached the bitter, sarcastic stage. 'How come there are no toothless grannies that according to you can dance naked on the table while weaving a side-weave tunic and grinding a modius of wheat?'

'Females tend to be snapped up, tribune . . .' The dealer winked. I was too careworn to respond. 'I can do you a Christian, if you want to stretch a point.'

'No thanks. They drink their god's blood while they maunder about love, don't they?' My late brother Festus had encountered these crazy men out in Judaea and sent home some lurid tales. 'I'm looking for a children's nurse; I cannot have perverts.'

'No, no; I believe they drink wine –'

'Forget it. I don't want a drunk. My darling heirs can pick up bad habits watching me.'

'These Christians just pray and cry a lot, or try to convert the master and mistress of the house to their beliefs –'

'You want to get me arrested because some arrogant slave says everyone should deny the sanctity of the Emperor? Vespasian may be a grouchy old barbarian-basher with a tight-arsed Sabine outlook – but I work for him sometimes. When he pays up, I'm happy to say he's a god.'

'How about a bonny Briton, then?'

He proffered a thin, pale-haired girl of about fifteen, wilting under

6

her shame as the filthy trader poked her rags aside to reveal her figure. As tribal maidens go, she was far from buxom. He tried to make her show her teeth and I would have taken her if she had bitten him, but she just leaned away. Too meek to be trusted. Feed her and clothe her and the next we knew, she'd be stealing Helena's tunics and throwing the baby on its head. The man assured me she was healthy, a good breeder, and had no claims at law hanging onto her. 'Very popular, Britons,' he said, leering.

'Why's that?'

'Dirt cheap. Then your wife won't worry about you chasing this pitiful thing around the kitchen the way she would with some ogling Syrian who knows it all.'

I shuddered. 'I do have some standards. Does your British girl know Latin?'

'You are joking, tribune.'

'No good, then. Look, I want a clean woman with experience of headstrong children, who would fit in with a young, upwardly moving family —'

'You've got expensive taste!' His eye fell on my new gold equestrian ring. It told him my financial position exactly; his disgust was open. 'We do a basic model with no trimmings. Lots of potential, but you have to train the bint yourself . . . You can win them over with kind treatment, you know. Ends up they would die for you.'

'What — and land me with the funeral costs?'

'Stuff you, then!'

So we all knew where we were.

I went home without a slave. It did not matter. The noble Julia Justa, Helena's mother, had the bright idea of giving us the daughter of Helena's own old nurse. Camilla Hyspale was thirty years old and newly given her liberty. Her freedwoman status would overcome any squeamishness I felt about owning slaves (though I would have to do it; I was middle class now, and obliged to show my clout). There was a downside. I reckoned we had about six months before Hyspale wanted to exploit her new citizenship and marry. She would fall for some limp waste of space; she had him lined up already, I bet. Then I would feel responsible for him too . . .

Hyspale had not approved when Helena Justina abandoned her smart senatorial home to live with an informer. She came to us with great reluctance. It was made clear at our first interview (*she* interviewed us, of course) that Hyspale expected a room of her own in a respectable dwelling, the right to more time off than time on duty, use of the family carrying chair to protect her modesty on shopping trips and the occasional treat of a ticket for the theatre, or better still a pair of tickets so she could go with a friend. She would not accept being quizzed on the sex or identity of the friend.

A slave or freedwoman soon rules your life. To satisfy Hyspale's need for social standing, dear gods, I had to buy a carrying chair. Pa lent me a couple of bearers temporarily; this was just his excuse to use *my* chair to transport *his* property to his new home on the Janiculan. To give Hyspale her room, we had to move in before Pa's old house was ready for us. For weeks we lived alongside our decorators, which would have been bad enough even if I had not been lured into giving work to my brother-in-law, Mico the plasterer. He was thrilled. Since he was working for a relative, he assumed he could bring his motherless brats with him – and that our nursemaid would look after them. At least that way I got back at the nurse. Mico had been married to my most terrible sister; Victorina's character was showing up well in her orphans. It was a rude shock for Hyspale, who kept rushing over to the Capena Gate to complain about her horrid life to Helena's parents. The senator reproached me with her stories every time I met him at the gym we shared.

'Why in Hades did she come to us?' I grumbled. 'She must have had some inkling what it would be like.'

'The girl is very fond of my daughter,' suggested Camillus Verus loyally. 'Besides, I'm told she believed you would provide the opportunity for travel and adventure in exotic foreign provinces.'

I told the excellent Camillus which ghastly province I had just been invited to visit and we had a good laugh.

Julius Frontinus, an ex-consul I had met during an investigation in Rome two years ago, was now suffering his reward for a blameless reputation: Vespasian had made him the governor of Britain. On arrival, Frontinus had discovered some problem with his major works programme, and he suggested I was the man to sort it. He wanted me to go out there. But my life was hard enough. I had already written and turned down his request for help.

III

THE NIGGLE from Julius Frontinus had refused to go away. Next, I was summoned to a light afternoon chat with the Emperor. I knew that meant some heavy request.

Vespasian, who had domestic problems of his own, now lurked frequently in the Gardens of Sallust. This helped him to avoid petitioners at the Palace – and to dodge his sons too. Domitian was often at odds with his father and brother, probably thinking that they ganged up against him. (The Flavians were a close family but Domitian Caesar was a squit, so who could blame them?) The elder and favourite son, Titus, acted as his father's political colleague. Once a wonderboy, he had now imported Berenice, the Queen of Judaea, with whom he was openly conducting a passionate love affair. She was beautiful, brave and brazen – and thus hugely unpopular. It must have caused a few spats over breakfast. Anyway, Berenice was a shameless piece of goods who had already tried making eyes at Vespasian during the Jewish War. Now that his mistress of many years, Antonia Caenis, had recently died, he may have felt vulnerable. Even if he could resist Berenice, seeing his virile son indulging her may have been unwelcome. At the Palace Titus also had a young daughter who by all accounts was growing up a handful. Lack of discipline, my mother said. Having brought up Victorina, Allia, Galla, Junia and Maia – every one a trainee Fury – she should know.

Vespasian notoriously distrusted informers, but with that kind of private life interviewing me may have seemed a peaceful change. I would have welcomed it too – intelligent chat with a self-made, forthright individualist – had I not been afraid he would offer me a bum task.

The Gardens of Sallust lie in the northern reaches of the city, a long, hot hike away from my area. They occupy a generous site on both sides of the valley between the Pincian and Quirinal Hills. I believe Vespasian had owned a private house out there, before he became

Emperor. The Via Salaria, still his route home to his summer estates in the Sabine Hills, runs out that way too.

Whoever Sallust was, his pleasure park had been imperial property for several generations. Mad Caligula had built an Egyptian pavilion, packed with pink granite statues, to commemorate one of his incestuous sisters. More popularly, Augustus displayed some giants' bones in a museum. Emperors have more than a clipped bay tree and a row of beans. Here some of the best statues I had seen in the open air marked the end of elegant vistas. As I searched for the old man, I strolled under the cool, calming shade of graceful cypresses, eyed up by basking doves who knew exactly how cute they were.

Eventually I detected various shy Praetorians lurking in the shrubberies; Vespasian had taken a public stand against being protected from madmen with daggers – which meant his Guards had to hang around here trying to look like gardeners weeding, instead of stamping about like bullies, as they preferred. Some had given up pretending. They were sprawled on the ground playing board games in the dust, occasionally breaking off to gulp from what I gently presumed were water flasks.

They had managed to corral their charge into a nook where it seemed unlikely any deranged obsessive with a legal grievance could burst through the thick hedge. Vespasian had piled up his voluminous purple drapes and his wreath on a dusty urn; he did not care how many snobs he offended with his informality. As he sat working in his gilded tunic, the Guards had a fairly clear view of his open-air office. If any high-minded armed opponent did rush past them, there was a massive Dying Niobid, desperately attempting to pluck out her fatal arrow, at whose white marble feet the Emperor might expire very tastefully.

The Praetorians tried to rouse themselves to treat me as a suspicious character, but they knew my name was on an appointment scroll. I waved my invitation. I was not in the mood for idiots with shiny javelins and no manners. Seeing the official seal, they allowed me through, making the gesture as offensive as possible.

'Thanks, boys!' I saved my patronising grin until I had marched into the safety of Vespasian's line of vision. He was seated on a plain stone bench in the shade while an elderly slave handed him tablets and scrolls.

The official name-caller was still flustering over my details when the Emperor broke in and called out, 'It's Falco!' He was a big, blunt sixty-year-old who had worked up from nothing and he despised ceremonial.

The boy's job was to save his élite master from any perceived rudeness if he forgot eminent people. Trapped in routine, the child whispered, '*Falco, sir!*' Vespasian, who could show kindliness to minions (though he never showed it to me), nodded patiently. Then I was free to go forward and exchange pleasantries with the lord of the known world.

This was no exquisite little Claudian, looking down his thin nose on the coinage like a self-satisfied Greek god. He was bald, tanned, his face full of character and heavily lined after years of squinting across deserts for rebellious tribes. Pale laughter seams ran at the corners of his eyes too, after decades of despising fools and honestly mocking himself. Vespasian was rooted in country stock like a true Roman (as I was myself on my mother's side). Over the years he had taken on all the snide establishment detractors; shamelessly grappled for high-level associates; craftily chosen long-term winners rather than temporary flash boys; doggedly made the best out of every career opportunity; then seized the throne so his accession seemed both amazing and inevitable at the same time.

The great one saluted me with his customary care for my welfare: 'I hope you're not going to say I owe you money.'

I expressed my own respect for his rank. 'Would there be any point, Caesar?'

'Glad I've set you at your ease!' He liked to joke. As Emperor, he must have felt inhibited with most people. For some reason I fell into a separate category. 'So what have you been up to, Falco?'

'Dibbling and dabbling.' I had been trying to expand my business, using Helena's two younger brothers. Neither possessed any informing talent. I intended to use them to lend tone, with a view to wooing more sophisticated (richer) clients: every businessman's hopeless dream. It was best not to mention to Vespasian that these two lads who ought to be donning white robes as candidates for the Curia were instead lowering themselves to work with me. 'I am enjoying my new rank,' I said, beaming, which was as close as I would let myself come to thanking him for promoting me.

'I hear you make a good poultry keeper.' Elevation to the equestrian stratum had brought tiresome responsibilities. I was Procurator of the Sacred Geese of the Temple of Juno, with additional oversight of the augurs' chickens.

'Country background.' He looked surprised. I was stretching it, but Ma's family came from the Campagna. 'The prophetic fowl get pesty if you don't watch them, but Juno's geese are in fine fettle.'

Helena and I had plenty of down-stuffed cushions in our new home too. I had grasped equestrianism rapidly.

'How is that girl you kidnapped?' Had the disapproving old devil read my thoughts?

'Devoted to the domestic duties of a modest Roman matron – well, I can't get her to weave wool traditionally, though she did commandeer the house keys and she is nursing children. Helena Justina has just done me the honour of becoming mother to my second child.' I knew better than to expect a silver birth-gift from this skinflint.

'Boy or girl?' Helena would have liked the even-handed way he offered both possibilities.

'Another daughter, sir. Sosia Favonia.' Would it strike Vespasian that she was partly named after a relative of Helena's? A dear bright young girl called Sosia, who had been murdered as a consequence of the first mission I undertook for him – murdered by his son Domitian, though of course we never mentioned that.

'Charming.' If his eyes hardened briefly, it was impossible to detect. 'My congratulations to your –'

'Wife,' I said firmly. Vespasian glowered. Helena was a senator's daughter and should be married to a senator. Her intelligence, her money, and her child-bearing ability ought to be at the disposal of the halfwits in the 'best' families. I pretended to see his point. 'Of course I explain to Helena Justina continually that the cheap appeal of an exciting life with me should not draw her from her inherited role as a member of patrician society – but what can I do? The poor girl is besotted and refuses to leave me. Her pleas when I threaten to send her back to her noble father are heart-rending –'

'That's enough, Falco!'

'Caesar.'

He flung a stylus aside. Watchful secretaries slid forward and collected a pile of waxed tablets in case he dashed them to the ground. Vespasian, however, was not that kind of spoiled hero. He had once had to budget cautiously; he knew the price of tablet wax.

'Well, I may want to put space between you two temporarily.'

'Ah. Anything to do with Julius Frontinus and the Isles of Mystery?' I pre-empted him.

The Emperor scowled. 'He's a good man. And he's known to you.'

'I think highly of Frontinus.'

Vespasian ignored the chance to flatter me with the provincial governor's opinion of me. 'There's nothing wrong with Britain.'

'Well, you know I know that, sir.' Like all subordinates, I hoped my commander-in-chief remembered my entire personal history. Like most generals, Vespasian forgot even episodes he had been involved with – but given time, he would recall that he himself had sent me to Britain four years ago. 'That is,' I said dryly, 'if you leave out the weather, the total lack of infrastructure, the women, the *men*, the food, the drink and the mammoth travelling distance from one's dear Roman heritage!'

'Can't lure you with some boar hunting?'

'Not my style.' Even if it had been, the Empire was packed with more thrilling places to chase wildlife across ghastly terrain. Most of the other places were sunny and had cities. 'Nor do I cherish a visionary wish to implant civilisation among the awe-struck British tribes.'

Vespasian grinned. 'Oh I've despatched a bunch of lawyers and philosophers to do that.'

'I know, sir. They hadn't achieved much the last time you sent me north.' I had plenty more to say about Britain. 'As I recall, the pasty-faced tribes had still not learned what to do with the sponge on the stick at public latrines. Where anybody had yet built any latrines.' Goose-pimples ran across my arm. Without intending it, I added, 'I was there during the Rebellion. That should be enough for anyone.'

Vespasian shifted slightly on the bench. The Rebellion was down to Nero, but it still made all Romans shudder. 'Well, somebody has to go, Falco.'

I said nothing.

He tried frankness. 'There is a monumental cock-up on a rather public project.'

'Yes, sir. Frontinus let me into his confidence.'

'Can't be worse than the troubles you sorted in the silver mines.' So he did remember sending me to Britain previously. 'A quick dash over there; audit the slapdash buggers; nail any frauds; then straight home. For you, it's a snip, Falco.'

'Should be a snip for anyone then, Caesar; I'm no demigod. Why don't you send Anacrites?' I suggested nastily. I always liked to think Vespasian reined in the Chief Spy because he distrusted the man's abilities. 'I am desolate to disappoint you, Caesar, though honoured by your faith in me—'

'Don't blather. So you won't go?' sneered Vespasian.

'New baby,' I offered as a let-out for both of us.

'Just the time to nip off.'

'Regrettably, Helena Justina has a pact with me that if ever I travel, she comes too.'

'Doesn't trust you?' he scoffed, clearly thinking that was probable.

'She trusts me absolutely, sir. Our pact is, that she is always present to supervise!'

Vespasian, who had met Helena in one of her fighting moods, decided to back off. He asked me at least to think about the job. I said I would. We both knew that was a lie.

IV

JUPITER, JUNO and Mars – I had enough to do that spring.

The house move was complicated enough – even before the day when Pa and I smashed up the bath house floor. Having Mico under my feet at the new riverbank place constantly reminded me how much I hated my relatives. There was only one I would have liked to see here, my favourite nephew Larius. Larius was a fresco painter's apprentice in Campania. He could well have repaid all my kind treatment as his uncle by creating a few frescos in my house, but when I wrote to him there was no reply. Perhaps he was remembering that the main thrust of my wise advice had been telling him that painting walls was a dead-end job . . .

As for that feeble streak of wind Mico, it was not just that he left plaster floats in doorways and tramped fine dust everywhere; he made me feel I owed him something, because he was poor and his children were motherless. Really, Mico was only poor because his bad work was notorious. No one but me would employ him. But I was Uncle Marcus the sucker. Uncle Marcus who knew the Emperor, flash Uncle Marcus who had a new rank and a position at the Temple of Juno. In fact I bought the rank with hard-earned fees, the position was literally chicken-shit and Vespasian only asked me over to the Gardens of Sallust when he wanted a favour. He saw me as a sucker too.

At least, unlike Mico, Vespasian Augustus did not expect me to buy rissoles all round as an end-of-week treat for his horrible family. With gherkins. Then I had to keep a pot handy, because gobbling the gherkins made Mico's awful toddler Valentinianus sick in my newly painted dining room. All Mico's children owned top-heavy names, and they were all villains. Valentinianus loved to humiliate me. His chief ambition currently was to vomit over Nux, my dog.

I now owned a dining room. The same week it was redecorated, I lost my best friend.

Petronius Longus and I had known each other since we were eighteen. We served together in the army – in Britain. We were naïve lads when we joined up for the legions. We had no idea what we were taking on. They fed us, taught us useful skills and trained us to be well up in connivery. They also subjected us to four years in a faraway, undeveloped province that offered nothing but cold feet and misery. The Great Rebellion of the Iceni came on top of that. We crept home no longer lads but men, and bonded like a laminated shield. Cynical, grimmer than the Forum gutter tykes and with a friendship that should have been unshakeable.

Petro had now spoiled everything. He fell for my sister, after her husband died.

'Petronius hankered for Maia a long time before this,' Helena disagreed. 'He was married, so was she. He played around but she never did. There was no point in him admitting how he felt, even to himself.' Then Helena paused, her dark eyes sombre. 'Petronius may have married Arria Silvia in the first place *because* Maia was unobtainable.'

'Cobnuts. He hardly knew my sister then.'

But he had met her and seen what she was like: attractive, independent and subtly dangerous. Such a good homemaker and mother (everyone said) – and what a bright girl! That double-edged remark always implies a woman may be on the lookout. I myself liked a hint of restlessness in a woman; Petronius was no different.

Around the Aventine he was held up as a model of steady fatherhood and virtuous hard work; no one spotted that he liked to flirt with risk. There were girlfriends in passing, even after he married Silvia. He settled down to look like a good boy, but how real was that? I was supposed to be the feckless bachelor, an endless worry to my mother – so like my *father*! So *un*like my brother, the dead hero (though our Festus had been a wreck, with a chaotic life). Meanwhile, Petronius Longus, diligent enquiry chief of the Fourth Cohort of the Vigiles, flitted quietly among the pretty flowers on the Aventine, leaving them happy and his reputation unbesmirched, until he tangled with a serious gangster's daughter. His wife found out. It all became too public; Silvia felt this disgrace was too much. She had seemed utterly dependent but once she threw Petro out, she was off. She now lived with a potted-salad seller, in Ostia.

Petronius might have accepted this, had not Silvia taken their three daughters. He had no wish to enforce his custody rights as a Roman father. But he was genuinely fond of the girls, and they adored him.

'Silvia knows that. The damned woman flounced off to Ostia out of spite!' I had never liked Arria Silvia. It was not simply because she loathed me. Mind you, that was relevant. She was a prissy little piece; Petro could have done better with his eyes closed. 'Her loathsome boyfriend was quite happy selling his cucumber moulds in the Forum; she put him up to moving, to make the situation impossible for Petro.'

He was in a rotten position, though for once he refused to talk to me about it. We had never discussed Silvia anyway; it saved trouble. Then things grew worse. He started to face up to his attraction to my sister; she even began to notice him. Just when Petro thought they might make something of it, Maia suddenly stopped seeing him.

I had cursed when I found one of my sisters wanting to berth alongside my dearest crony. That can damage a male friendship. But it was far more uncomfortable when Petro was dumped.

He must have taken it hard. Helena had to tell me his reflex action: 'Marcus, you won't like this. Petronius has applied for a transfer to the vigiles cohort at Ostia.'

'Leaving Rome? That's madness!'

'There may not be a job there for him,' Helena tried soothing me.

'Oh rats, of course there will! It's an unpopular posting – who wants to be stationed downriver at the port, outwitting customs diddlers and duck-billed cargo thieves? Petro's a bloody good officer. The Ostia tribune is bound to jump at him.'

I would never forgive my sister.

'Don't blame Maia,' said Helena.

'Who mentioned Maia?'

'Your face speaks, Marcus!'

Helena was suckling the baby. Julia was sitting at my feet, repeatedly headbutting my shins, annoyed to be no longer the sole object of attention in our house. That was certainly true; I ignored the little darling steadily. Nux chewed at one of my bootstraps.

'Don't be such a hypocrite,' Helena enjoyed pretending to be a serene mother, rocking the new baby to sleep in her arms. It was an act; she was placidly thinking up ways to slate me. 'Own up. You hated the idea of Petronius and Maia growing close. He was your friend and you refused to share him.'

'And she's my sister. Her husband had died suddenly; she was vulnerable. As her head of household' – we never counted Pa – 'I did not want her messed about.'

'Oh you admit Petronius has a bad record!' Helena smiled.

'No. Never mind his other women. He has been Maia's dogged follower, while my sister turns out as fickle as a flea.'

'So what do you want?' Helena was easily roused by causes. 'That Maia Favonia should move straight from one husband to another, simply because an interested man is available and it is socially convenient? Shall she have no time to readjust after losing the husband we all pretend she loved?' Helena could be very dry – and strikingly honest. Loving that tipsy loser Famia had been out of the question; I laughed harshly. Julia whimpered; I reached down and tickled her.

'No, Maia deserves time to reflect.' I could be reasonable, even when it hurt. 'She is well suited to working in Pa's warehouse – and it's doing her good.' Maia was keeping Pa's records – more truthfully than he did – and learning about the antiques business.

'*Pius Aeneas* graciously approves!' Helena was sneering. She took a tough line with traditional Roman values.

'I do approve.' I was losing, but I stuck to it doggedly. Any head of household tries to stand up to the witch who ties him up in knots.

Plenty of women at our level of society ran businesses. Most started out in partnerships with husbands, then as widows some chose to stay independent. (Independent widows with fears of being cheated were good news for informers. Their children brought in fees too – afraid the widows were planning remarriage with bloodsucking gigolos.) 'If Maia does make herself financially independent, she might still want a man in her bed –'

'And dear Lucius Petronius,' said Helena wickedly, 'with all that practice, would be adequate!' I decided against commenting. Helena had a warning look in her eye. 'I think Maia will want a man in her *life*, Marcus. But not yet.'

'Wrong. Last I saw, Petronius was hanging back. At the Festival of Vertumnus, Maia tried throwing herself at him.'

'Petronius was afraid of being hurt. Maia misjudged that. And she herself may be confused, Marcus. For one thing,' Helena suggested, 'she had been married a long time, and may have lost her confidence.'

'Marriage makes you forget the arts of love?' I scoffed.

Helena Justina looked up at me, straight into my eyes, in a way that was intended to make me wish I had not asked. Both the children were with us; I had to let that pass.

I was sure Maia had not simply mishandled her relationship with Petro. She knew how strongly he felt. She was a straight dealer. She had been all set to start something serious – then she completely backed off. Something made her do that.

Helena and Maia were good friends. 'What happened?' I asked quietly.

'I'm not sure.' Helena looked troubled. She had an idea – but she hated it.

I considered the situation. There was one possibility. Before my sister so briefly became interested in Petronius, she had an abortive friendship with another man. *'Anacrites!'*

Well, she had sunk low there.

Maia deserved better in life than the dice she had shaken out for herself. First as a young girl, she had opted to marry Famia. He may have looked amiable, and even stayed friends with her in his dozy way. Anyone connected with Maia would be stupid to give up on her. But Famia was a low proposition. He was a horse doctor for the Green charioteer faction and he drank continually. In his defence, he allowed Maia a free hand to run their household and bring up their children respectably – which she could have done twice as well without his presence.

Maia was finally widowed and, newly unattached, she took on the traditional role of flighty piece. Her first foray was to adopt a male friend of stunning unsuitability, as widows like to do. Her chosen companion was Anacrites, the Chief Spy. Spies are never reliable lovers, due to their life of risk and their lying natures. Anacrites was also my sworn enemy. We had been forced into occasional shared work for the Emperor, yet I never forgot that Anacrites had once tried to have me killed. He was shifty, jealous, vicious and amoral. He had no sense of humour and no tact. He never knew when he should keep to himself. And I reckoned he took up with my sister just to get back at me.

A woman would have to be cracked to hitch up with a chief spy – *any* spy – but Maia always believed she could handle anything. Anacrites knew our family not only because he had worked with me; he had lodged with my mother. Ma thought he was perfect. I presumed my sister knew that our parent had a blind spot about men (well, dear Mother had married our father, for one thing). Maia also knew how I saw Anacrites. Anyone who looked that plausible had to be fake.

Eventually even Maia sensed a dangerous imbalance in their friendship. Anacrites was too intense for her. She told us they had parted. She would have been tactful. She was even a little upset. If I could see it, he must have known too. He should have withdrawn gracefully.

It was for the best. But would that maggot agree to let go? At last I understood the problem. 'Helena, are you saying Anacrites is harassing Maia?'

Helena usually shared her worries with me, though sometimes she hugged them to herself for a long time first. Finally she burst out, 'I am frightened for her. She changed so suddenly.'

'The children are very quiet.' Still, they had lost their father less than a year ago.

'Have you spoken to Anacrites lately, Marcus?'

'No.' I had thought it might be embarrassing. I expected him to plead with me to intercede with Maia. In fact, he had never addressed the point.

If it hurt him to be rejected, he could react very nastily. Maia would not change her mind. So then Anacrites might do anything . . .

Being the man he was, of course he did.

V

M Y SISTER must have discovered what had happened in the late afternoon. After a normal day working with Pa at the Saepta Julia, she collected the children from my mother's house and returned home. By chance, I came along shortly afterwards. There was never any hope of her hiding the situation. Even before I went into the house, I had sensed the disaster.

As I strolled up the road where they lived, I had seen Maia's three youngest children. She had left them waiting outside; that was unusual. The two girls and Ancus, the nervous one, were clinging together in a group on the pavement, opposite where they lived. Marius, the eldest, was missing (in defiance of his mother, I learned later, he had raced off trying to find me). Maia's street door was open.

This was one of the Aventine's few good locations. People would think it rude to form a nosy crowd. Even so, frowning women were standing in their doorways. Men at foodshop counters were staring this way. There was an ominous stillness. My instincts said something terrible had happened. I could hardly believe it; Maia's home was always well run. No oil lamps fell over, no braziers flickered near to door curtains. No unlocked shutters let in thieves. And she never left her children out in the road.

I approached Cloelia, the maternal nine-year-old, who had her arms around her younger sister, Rhea. Ancus was holding his brother's oversized puppy; Nux, my own dog, slunk past ignoring her offspring as usual, then waited for me snootily as I took stock of the children. They all looked white, staring up at me with shocked, beseeching eyes. I drew a painful breath. I turned towards the house. When I saw the open door properly, the nightmare started. Whoever came here earlier had advertised their atrocious deed: a girl's wooden doll had been hammered to the door, with a great nail through its head.

Beyond, the short corridor was almost blocked. Possessions and shattered furniture were in chaos. I crashed over the threshold. My heart pounded. As I glanced into rooms, there was nothing worse to find. Well, there was nothing left. Every item that belonged to Maia and her children had been torn apart. *Where was she?*

Nothing left. Everything destroyed.

I found her, on the small balcony area they had always called their sun terrace. She stood amid the ruin of cushioned loungers and graceful side tables, with more smashed toys at her feet. Her back was to me; whitened fingernails gripped her bare arms as she rocked slightly to and fro. She was rigid when I took hold of her. She stayed rigid when I turned her round and held her. Then agonised tears came, silently.

Voices. I tensed, ready for intruders. I heard urgent footsteps, then shocked obscenities. Young Marius, the eleven-year-old, had brought Petronius Longus, some vigiles too. After an initial commotion came quieter murmurs. Petronius arrived behind me. I knew who it was. He stood in the doorway; his mouth moved as he cursed silently. He stared at me, then his gaze covered the destruction in near disbelief. He pulled Marius against him, comforting the boy. Marius gripped a splintered chair arm, like a spear to kill his enemies.

'Maia!' Petro had seen plenty of horrors, but his voice rasped. 'Maia Favonia – who did this?'

My sister moved. She spoke, her voice hard. 'I have no idea.'

A lie. Maia knew who it was, and so did Petronius, and so did I.

It took us time to gently persuade her to shift. By then, Petro's men had brought transport. They realised we must get her away. So we sent Maia and all the children with a vigiles escort to my father's house, out of town, on the Janiculan. There they would have space, peace, perhaps some safety. Well, at least Pa would give them decent beds.

Either something else would happen, or nothing. Either this was a statement and a warning – or worse.

Petronius and I cleared everything that night. We spent hours tearing the innards from the house, carrying out the smashed belongings and just burning them in the street. Maia had said wildly that she wanted nothing. Little could be salvaged, but we did keep a few items; I would store them, and let my sister see them later if she changed her mind. The house had been rented. I would terminate the lease. The family never needed to come back here.

Everything material could be replaced. Maia's spirit would revive. Restoring courage to the children might be more difficult. Bringing back peace of mind to Petronius and me would never happen.

After we finished at the house, we plotted. We were at the vigiles' patrol station. Neither of us wanted to start drinking in a caupona.

'Could we have stopped this?' I wondered grimly.

'I doubt it.'

'So much for recriminations! Best to get to the strategy, then.'

'There are two questions.' Petronius Longus spoke heavily, in a dull voice. He was a big, quiet man who never wasted effort. He could see straight to the heart of trouble. 'One: what will he do now? Two: what shall we do to him?'

'You can't wipe out the Chief Spy.' I would have done for Anacrites years ago, if it were feasible.

'Unsafe. Yes.' Petro continued to talk and plan in a far-too-level voice. 'We'll be known to have a grudge. First suspects.'

'There must have been local witnesses.'

'You know the answer to that, Falco.'

'Too scared to talk. So what? We lay a complaint against him?'

'No proof.'

'Visit him mob-handed?'

'Dangerous.'

'Suggest that he desists?'

'He will deny responsibility.'

'Also, he'll know he's had an effect.' For a moment we were silent. Then I said, 'We'll do nothing.'

Petronius breathed slowly. He knew this was not capitulation. 'No. Not yet.'

'It may take a long time. We'll keep her safe. Keep her out of his sight. Let him think he has won, let him forget about it.'

'Then –'

'Then one day there will be an opportunity.' It was a fact. I was not emotional.

'True. There always is.' He smiled faintly. He was probably thinking the same as me.

There had been a man in Britain, during the Rebellion, who betrayed the Second Augusta, our legion. What happened to that man afterwards was subject to a communal pact of silence. He died. Everyone knows that. The record says he fell on his own sword, as an officer does. Perhaps he did.

I rose to leave. I held out my hand. Petronius grasped it without speaking.

First thing next day, Helena went over to my father's house to find out what she could. Pa was hovering at home; he kept the children out of the way while Helena comforted my sister. Maia was still in shock and, despite her previous reticence, the story all came out.

After Maia had told Anacrites she no longer wanted to see him, he seemed to take it well. Then he kept reappearing on her doorstep as if nothing had happened. She never involved me because she immediately realised it would do no good. Maia was stuck.

He had hung around openly for a couple of months, then she started dodging him. He shadowed her more secretly. After the first few weeks he stopped approaching her. Nothing was said. But she knew he was there. He wanted her to know. She dreaded his presence all the time. The oppressive situation took over her life. He intended that. He wanted her to be frightened. Isolated with the problem, even my courageous sister became extremely scared.

Maia kept hoping someone else would catch his eye. There was no reason why not. Anacrites could be pleasant. He was tolerable to look at; he earned a good screw. He had prestige. He owned property. He could take a woman to elegant receptions and private dinner parties – not that he had done so with Maia. Their relationship had been far more casual, just neighbourly. They never formally went about the world together. I don't believe they even went to bed. They never would do now, so his obsessiveness was pointless. Men who stalk victims cannot see that. This was Maia's predicament. She knew she would not shake Anacrites off. Yet she knew it was going nowhere. He had nothing to gain. But she had everything to lose.

Like many women in that situation, she tried enduring her torment alone. In the end, she actually went to his office at the Palace, where for two hours she had tried reasoning with him. I knew how dangerous that could have been, but being Maia she got away with it, apparently unscathed. She appealed to Anacrites' intelligence. Anacrites apologised. He promised to stop hounding her.

Next day, thugs violently trashed her house.

That night, talking grimly about our predicament with the spy, Petronius and I had sworn to be sensible. We would leave him alone. We would both be watchful and patient. We would 'do' Anacrites, together, when the time was right.

But I knew each of us was quite prepared, if a chance arose, to take separate steps to deal with this.

Helena knew it too. Maia herself was a quick-witted girl – but Helena's mind worked even faster. Those great dark eyes saw at once what was likely to happen, and how any move against Anacrites could rebound dangerously on us. I should have realised that while Petro and I were plotting men's action, Helena Justina was constructing deeper plans. With the quiet logic of a cautious, clever woman, *her* plans were designed to take as many as possible of the people she loved well out of the way of trouble.

VI

IT WAS at this dark moment – and because of it – that Pa and I turned up that corpse his treasured builders had left behind.

Maia had gone to live on the Janiculan, swearing it was temporary (hating the whole of idea of moving in with our father). Her children were terrified; she herself was now desperate. Maia Favonia tried to give them all ordered lives. She stuck to normal mealtimes and bedtimes – and since facilities were there, she insisted that her children were clean. Then little Rhea became hysterical every time she was led to the bath house. And eventually we smashed a hole through to the disgusting grave.

I knew what would happen.

As we recovered outside in the fresh air, Pa managed an aggravating prayer. 'Well, thank you, Jove! You have given me a son in a useful profession – Marcus, I rely on you to sort this.' He did not need to tell me he had no intention of paying fees.

I stalked off, telling him to send for the vigiles, so he just had a slave fetch Petronius. I watched my crony curiously to see how he would approach it. 'Geminus, stick this one up your arse.' Good lad! 'It's no use asking me. The vigiles only deal with crud inside the city boundary. Call in the Urban Cohorts. Give those sleepy wastrels something that stinks.'

'Oh come on, boys,' whined Pa. 'Don't wish the bloody Urbans on me . . .'

He had a point. I felt us weakening. The three Urban Cohorts were the inferior rump of the Praetorian Guard. In theory they had a remit to solve serious crimes within a hundred-mile radius of Rome – but their expertise (I mean their lack of it) made us weep. The Urbans were a bandits' charter. Towns in the Campagna and Etruria that were seeking law and order quietly made their own arrangements. Most could produce some ambitious magistrate who wanted to gain fame by cleaning pickpockets off streets. If not, they had the sophisticated alternative: many bandits are available for hire as protection, often at quite reasonable rates.

Petronius relented slightly. 'You'll have to dispose of the body, Geminus. You won't even get an undertaker to face this – I'll send up a man we use for clearing obscene remains. I warn you, he's not cheap.'

'The bill belongs to Gloccus and Cotta, surely,' I said. Then I had a rethink. 'Unless this *is* Gloccus or Cotta . . .' A pleasing idea.

None of us wanted to go close enough to check. In fact, I would not have been able to identify our two useless contractors anyway. They believed in site management from a distance; I had cursed them for months, yet never seen either face to face. Their workforce had been depressing enough: the usual string of inadequates called Tiberius or Septimus who never knew what day it was – all irritating drips who had problems with hangovers, backaches, girlfriends and dying grandfathers. The two things that united the labour force were feeble excuses and a complete lack of building skills.

If you think I sound harsh, just you sign a contract for extending your workshop space or refurbishing your dining room. Then wait and see.

Pa did eventually report the corpse to the Prefect of the Urban Cohorts. They wandered out to his house and first tried their usual trick: since the victims and presumed suspects were Romans, Pa should pass the problem to the city vigiles. Pa stamped on that idea, and Petronius was there to state the case with real authority. Authority was a new concept to the Urbans, who caved in and borrowed lights. Inspecting the burial after nightfall was a great help.

Acting as if they had never seen a corpse before, they took note of the fact that a man (even they could tell that) had croaked and been dumped under a new mosaic floor. Petronius steered them into working out that someone stove in his head with a building tool. 'That might be a spade,' he explained rudely. 'Or a heavy pick, maybe.' The Urbans nodded wisely.

Their corpse was of average age, height, weight and appearance. As far as they knew, there were no missing persons reported with that description. They thought themselves very clever for noticing the dead man had been bearded and was barefoot.

'Someone stole his boots after they topped him,' suggested my father (it was the kind of thing he would have done).

The Urbans then stumbled about the garden in the dark, looking for clues. Surprise! They found nothing. The contractors had been gone a couple of weeks now. One thing they had done really well was to sweep clean the site before they left. 'That must have surprised you!' I commented to Pa. He laughed grimly. We knew now why they were so careful.

The dumb cohort boys caused themselves a lot of confusion when they discovered the tools Pa and I had been using earlier in his garden. After a bit of arguing, we managed to deflect them from that little byway, then they lost interest. They convinced themselves they knew who had killed the man. I pointed out that while somebody working on the bath house *might* be responsible, there was no proof. They saw me as a troublemaker, and ignored that. They sauntered off into the night, believing this one was easy.

Two days later a sad officer called on Pa at the Saepta Julia. By now the Urbans were greatly miffed that no solution had been dropped into their laps by the gods. All they knew was that Gloccus and Cotta had both left Rome. While this seemed to confirm their guilt, it meant no arrest. Were we surprised? What do you think?

The Urban Prefect wanted to clear up the case – and the situation was even worse for me. Pa expected me to take over when the real investigators feebly dropped out.

Well, at least it could be a training exercise for my bright young assistants.

Young, yes; bright, perhaps. Assisting – no chance. I got more help from Nux. The lads were an unlikely pair for informing. Friends of mine thought they would quickly tire of me. I reckoned I would soon be dumping them.

Helena Justina had two well-brought-up patrician brothers: Aulus Camillus Aelianus and Quintus Camillus Justinus. When I first knew her, both had looked promising citizens – Justinus, the younger, especially. He and I shared some foreign adventures; I liked him and although he could behave like an idiot, I was impressed by his abilities. I never expected to work much with him because he seemed cut out for higher things.

Aelianus, two years the elder, had been on the verge of standing for the Senate. To look respectable, he became betrothed to an heiress from Baetica, Claudia Rufina. A nice enough girl, with *extremely* nice financial assets. Then Justinus stupidly eloped with Claudia. They were in love when they ran off, though probably not now.

The abandoned Aelianus felt a fool and refused to go through with the Senate election. He had a point. The family had already survived a political crisis when an uncle tried some dangerous plotting. Now public scandal gathered again. All the chalk-white robes in Rome could not really make Aelianus look a pristine candidate, one with illustrious ancestors and blameless modern relatives.

Deprived of his expectations and in retaliation, while Justinus was away marrying the heiress in Spain, Aelianus wormed his way in with me. He knew Justinus was planning to come home to work with me, and hoped to steal the position. (*What position?* sceptics might well ask.)

Justinus reappeared in Rome early that spring, not long after my daughter Sosia Favonia was born. Claudia had married him. We had all thought she might lose interest (mainly because Justinus already had), but they were both too stubborn to admit their mistake. Her rich grandparents had bestowed *some* money on the pair, though Justinus told me privately it was not enough. He appealed to me for support, and since he had always been my favourite, I was stuck.

I did escape one hairy proposal: Helena had talked about Justinus and Claudia coming to live with us. But their first visit on their return to Rome coincided with one of our nursemaid's days off. While Hyspale was gallivanting on yet another shopping trip, Julia was racing about our new home's corridors with Nux. My dog thought being 'good with children' meant pretending to savage them, so that was noisy. Nux smelt too. Mico's Valentinianus must have rubbed bits of gherkin into her fur. At the same time, the baby – who picked up tricks very quickly – had just learned how to turn herself blue with hysteria. Dear Favonia was well tended, but an unkind father might say babies produce as many smells as dogs. So our newly-weds backed out of sharing accommodation rapidly. I'm sure I would have begged them to reconsider, if I had thought of it.

Over the job, however, Justinus refused to give way to his brother. So now I had both lads at my tunic tails. It was a misery to their parents, who had already lost their daughter to the low-life Didius Falco; now both their noble boys were coming to play in the gutter as well. Meanwhile, I had to keep the jealous pair apart.

I gave them the bath house incident to experiment with. They had been hoping for more impressive clients than Pa. For instance, ones who would pay fees.

'Wrong,' I explained harshly. 'This man is excellent to start with. Why? Now you learn about clients. As informers, you must always outmanoeuvre the devious crook who commissions you: weigh him

29

up *first*! My father, whom you know as Didius Geminus, is really called Didius Favonius – so right from scratch, you're facing a fake name. With a client, this is typical. He has led a double life; he runs a shady business; you can't believe a word he says; and he'll try to duck out of paying you.'

My two runners gazed at me. They were in their mid-twenties. Both had dark hair, which like aristocrats they left to flop annoyingly. Once a few derisive barmaids had pulled it, they would learn. Aelianus was thicker set, a little more untidy, a lot more truculent. Justinus, finer featured and better mannered, had more of a look of Helena. They were entitled to wear white tunics with purple bands to show their rank, but they came to work, as I had instructed, in subdued clothes and nothing fancier than signet rings. They still sounded so well-spoken I winced, yet Justinus at least had an ear for languages, so we could work on that. Unobtrusive behaviour would help. If ever they got in deep trouble, they had both been through army training; even as junior staff officers, they knew how to put in the boot. I was now sending them to Glaucus, the trainer at my gym; I had told him to slaughter them.

'So,' Aelianus condescended to address his younger brother. 'We have learned today that our mentor, Marcus Didius, holds his papa in traditional respect!'

'It sounds,' Justinus said to me, grinning, 'as if we should look at your father as the most likely killer.'

Even I had never thought of that. But with Pa, yes: it was a possibility.

VII

'AULUS,' I instructed, addressing Aelianus by his personal name in an attempt to make him feel inferior. Pointless. If one thing had qualified that blighter for the Senate, it was his inborn sense of divinity. 'Your job is to root out background on our suspects. We have a couple of leads: Pa gave me an address for the yard out of which they are supposed to operate, also a name for the winery where they were regulars. That's where he used to meet up to commission them for work — "work" being a euphemism with these fellows. Then here's a possible home address for Cotta. It's an apartment by a foodshop called the Aquarius at the side of Livia's Portico.'

'Where's that?' asked Aulus.

'On the Clivus Suburanus.'

A silence.

'That runs into town from the Esquiline Gate,' I said calmly. Senators' sons were bound to be ignorant. This pair would have to start drawing themselves street maps. 'If the apartment location is right, someone there should be able to send you on to Gloccus.'

'So if I find them —'

'Not likely. Unless they are very stupid' — which was a possibility — 'they will have fled as soon as their man died. That's whether they topped him personally, or merely had the killer on their payroll.'

'What would they be afraid of if they are innocent?' *Innocent*, that was a sweet word. Was our thickset, sullen Aulus a closet romantic?

'They would fear being tortured by the vigiles,' I corrected him. 'The dead man had been deliberately hidden under their floor — so they are at least accessories.'

'Oh.'

'Just pump their associates for clues about where they have run off to — and physical descriptions would help.'

Aelianus looked less than impressed with his task. Tough.

Both brothers were beginning to feel that working with me was not glamorous. For starters, we were gathered at my new house on the

31

riverbank, eating a very rapid breakfast. A bread roll and a beaker of warm water each came as a shock. They had expected four-hour dalliances in wineshops.

'What can I do?' nagged Justinus plaintively.

'Plenty. Solve the identity of the corpse. Go to the contractors' yard with your brother. Hang about after he leaves and talk to the other workmen.' I knew Aelianus would be rude to the men; then Justinus would be more friendly. 'Make them list whoever was on site during Pa's bath house job. Again, obtain descriptions. If they co-operate—'

'Which you don't expect?'

'Oh I expect the goddess Iris to glide down in a rainbow and tell us everything! Seriously, find out who is missing. If you get a clue, visit wherever the missing man lived and take things on from there.'

'If nobody tells us who he was,' Justinus said, frowning, 'how can we proceed, Falco?'

'Well, you're big boys,' I said unhelpfully.

'Oh go on!' scoffed Aelianus. 'Don't throw us in and leave us to sink.'

'All right. Try this: Gloccus and Cotta were the main contractors. But half the fancy fittings were supplied, and sometimes fixed, by other firms. See the marble-bowl supplier, the mosaicist, the plumber who laid the water-pipes. They don't want to be blamed. So they may be less inclined to conceal the truth. Ask Helena which importer sold her that monster splash basin in the tepidarium. Ask my father's slaves for names of men who tramped mud through the kitchen fetching water for their mortar mix.'

'Were workmen allowed in the main house?'

'No.'

'That wouldn't have stopped them?'

'Right. If you want a really irritating experience, try talking to Pa himself.'

'Then what?'

'Just do the jobs I have suggested. Then we'll reconvene and pool ideas.'

They looked sulky. I kept them back a moment. 'Get this straight. No one forced you to come in with me. No anxious parent begged me to find you a position. I could use someone street-smart instead of you two amateurs. Never forget, I have a queue of my own relatives who need the work.' The Camillus brothers were naïve; they had no idea how much my relations despised me and my work – nor how crudely I loathed the feckless Didii. 'You both wanted this. I'm allowing it as an idealist. When you bunk off back to the high life, I'll just know that two pampered patricians have acquired practical knowledge through me.'

'Oh noble Roman!' Justinus said, smiling, though he had lost his rebellious attitude.

I ignored it. 'Campaign orders: you accept that I am in charge. Then we work as a team. There is to be no showing off on solo escapades. We meet up every morning here, and each man turns in full details of what he has found out so far. We discuss the next course of action together – and in the case of disagreement, my plan takes precedence.'

'And what,' demanded Aelianus caustically, 'are you intending to do on this case, Falco?'

I assured him I would be hard at work. True. My new house had a wonderful roof terrace, where I could waste hours playing. When I grew tired of planning herb troughs and realigning rose trellises, then the kind of dalliance in a wineshop that I had denied to the boys would suit me fine. If they guessed, neither knew me well enough to complain.

Taking both into the business brought me the benefit of their competitiveness. Each was determined to better his brother. Come to that, both would have been happy to put me in the wrong.

They played at being diligent. I amused myself wondering what the hair-plastered labourers made of them. Eventually we summed up progress: 'Quintus, shoot the first spear.'

Justinus had learned in the legions how to give intelligence reports to brusque commanding officers. He was relaxed. Looking deceptively casual, he surprised me with some useful gen: 'Gloccus and Cotta have been partners for a couple of decades. Everyone speaks of them as famously unreliable – yet they are somehow accepted and still given work.'

'Custom of the trade,' I said gloomily. 'A standard building contract contains a clause that says *it shall be the contractor's responsibility to destroy the Premises, abandon the agreed Drawings and delay the Works until at least three Festivals of Compitalia have passed.*'

He grinned. 'They do cheap house extensions, incompetent remodelling, occasional contract work for professional landlords. Presumably the landlords' fees are larger, so the incentive to turn up on site is greater.'

'And landlords employ project managers who flay slackers,' Aelianus suggested. I said nothing.

'Half their clients are in dispute with them for years afterwards,' Justinus continued. 'They seem to live with it. When it looks like becoming a court case, Gloccus and Cotta cave in; they will sometimes bodge repairs, or a favourite trick is to hand over a free statue plinth as supposed compensation.'

'Offering a half-price rude statue that the client doesn't want?'

'And thus squeezing even more cash from him! How did you know, Falco?'

'Instinct, my dear Quintus. Aulus – contribute?'

Aelianus squared up slightly. He was slapdash by nature, but a generous superior would say he might repay the effort of training him. I was not sure I called him a worthwhile investment. 'Gloccus lives by the Portico of Livia with a skinny drab who yelled at me. Her hysteria seemed genuine – she hasn't seen him for some weeks.'

'He left without warning and without paying the rent?'

'Astute, Falco!' Could I bear this patronising swine? 'She described him rather colourfully as a fat, half-bald slob spawned by a rat on a stormy night. Other people agreed he's paunchy and untidy, but he has a secret charm that no one could quite identify. They "can't see how he gets away with it", seems the consensus.'

'Cotta?'

'Cotta lives – or lived – alone in a third-floor set of rooms over a street-market. He's not there now. No one locally ever saw much of him, and no one knows where he's gone.'

'What's he like?'

'Skinny and secretive. Regarded as a bit of an odd case. Never really wanted to be a builder – who can blame him? – and rarely seemed happy with his lot. A woman who sold him cheese sometimes on his way home in the evening, said his older brother is something in the medical line – an apothecary perhaps? Cotta grew up in his shadow and always envied him.'

'Ah, a thwarted-ambition story!' That sort of tale always makes me sarcastic. 'Doesn't your heart bleed? "My brother *saves* lives, so *I'll* smash in people's heads to show I'm a big rissole too . . ." How do their workmen view these princes?'

'The labourers were surprisingly slow to insult them,' marvelled Justinus. Perhaps it was his first experience of the mindless loyalty of men in trade – men who know they may have to work with the same bastards again.

34

'Subcontractors and suppliers?'

'Buttoned up.' They, too, stick with their own.

'Nobody would even tell us who's missing,' Aelianus said, scowling.

'Hmm.' I gave them a mysterious half smile. 'Try this: The dead man is a tile-grouter called Stephanus.' Aelianus started to glance at Justinus, then remembered they were on bad terms. I paused, to show I had noticed the reaction. 'He was thirty-four, bearded, no distinguishing features; had a two-year-old son by a waitress; was known for his hot temper. He thought Gloccus was a turd who had diddled his previous week's wages. On the day he disappeared, Stephanus had gone to work wearing a worn, but still respectable, pair of site boots which had black thongs, one with a newly stitched repair.'

They were silent for only a moment. Justinus got there first. 'The waitress found out that you were working on the murder, and came to ask about the missing father of her son?'

'Smart boy. To celebrate, it's your turn to buy the drinks.'

'Forget it!' Justinus exclaimed with a laugh. 'I've a bride who thinks it's time we stopped living with my parents – and I've no savings.'

The senator's house at the Capena Gate was a spacious spread – but having many rooms to flounce off to only created more opportunities for quarrels. I knew Aelianus thought it was time that his brother and Claudia moved out. Well, he would. 'We are not going to earn much on this, are we, Falco?' He wanted Justinus to suffer.

'No.'

'I see it as an orientation exercise,' Aelianus philosophised.

'Aulus,' snarled his brother, 'you are so pompous, you really should be in the Senate.'

I stepped in fast. 'Informing is about days of nuisance work, while you long for a big enquiry. Don't despair,' I chaffed them cheerily. 'I had one once.'

I gave them a few ideas for following up, though they were losing heart. So was I. The best ploy would be to drop this, but to store our notes handily under the bed. One day Gloccus and Cotta would return to Rome. Those types always do.

Whilst my runners pursued our uninspiring leads, I devoted myself to family issues. One joyless task was on behalf of my sister Maia; I ended her tenancy on the house Anacrites had trashed. After I gave the keys back to the landlord, I still used to walk that way, keeping watch. If I had caught Anacrites lurking in the area, I would have spitted him, roasted him, then thrown him to the homeless dogs.

In fact something worse happened. One evening I spotted a woman I recognised, talking to one of Maia's neighbours. I had told a few trusted people that my sister had moved away to a place of safety; I never mentioned where. Friends understood the situation. Nothing would be said to a casual enquirer. Her neighbour was now shaking her head unhelpfully.

But I knew the infiltrator. She had dangerous skills. Her paid task was finding people who were attempting to stay hidden. If she found them – that is, *when* she found them – they always regretted it.

This woman was called Perella. Her arrival confirmed my worst fears: Anacrites was having the place observed. He had sent one of his best operatives too. Perella might look like a comfortable, harmless bundle who was only after female gossip. She was past her prime; nothing would change that. But under the dark frumpy gown she had the body of a professional dancer, athletic and tough as tarred twine. Her intelligence would shame most men; her persistence and courage frightened even me.

She worked for the Chief Spy. She was damned good – and she enjoyed that fact. She usually worked alone. Scruples did not trouble her. She would tackle everything; she was utterly professional. If she had been given the ultimate order, I knew that she would kill.

My solution was easy. Sometimes the Fates must have a drop too much to drink; while they lie down groaning with a headache, they forget to screw you.

A let-out arrived the same evening, when I reached home. The lads and I had arranged to hold a final consultation about the missing builders. Aelianus and Justinus had discovered something that day which made them think we should call off our search.

'Gloccus and Cotta are way out of reach.' Aelianus used a nasty smirk sometimes.

I was too upset by Perella; I just rambled, with half my mind on it: 'So where are they? A yurt in darkest Scythia? While some tradesmen dream of retiring to a tasteless southern villa, with a pergola that a Babylonian king would envy, do bath house contractors opt for being smoked to oblivion with filthy drugs in exotic eastern tents?'

'Worse, Falco.' Suddenly I knew what was coming. Still too full of himself, Aelianus continued, 'There is some large project overseas – building specialists are being sent from Rome. It is regarded as a hard posting, but we were told it is surprisingly popular.'

'High rates of pay,' Justinus inserted dryly.

They were trying to be mysterious, but I already knew of a project that would fit.

'Do you want to guess, Falco?'

'No.'

I leaned back, cradling my head. I sucked my teeth. This was normal man-management: I looked supercilious while they looked shifty. 'Right. We'll go there.'

'You don't know where it is,' complained Aelianus, always the first to jump in blindly when he ought to suspect a catch.

'Don't I? They are builders, aren't they?' I knew where all the contractors were rushing off to currently. 'Now. I owe this to your parents: one of you has to stay in Rome and mind the office. Agree between you who wins the chance to travel. I don't care how. Draw counters from an urn. Throw dice. Ask a dirty astrologer.'

They were reacting too slowly. Justinus got there first: 'Falco knows!'

'They've gone to a project known as the Great King's House. Am I right?'

'*How* do you know, Falco?'

'We are looking for two builders. I make sure I know what's being talked about in the building world.' It was a coincidence – but I could live with assistants who thought I had magical powers. 'This is an enormous, glamorous palace being built for an old supporter of Vespasian's. The Emperor takes a personal interest. Unluckily for us, the great one – who has an unpronounceable name which we must learn to say – is king of a tribe called the Atrebates. They live on the south coast. That's the south coast on the wrong side of the Gallic Strait. It's an evil stretch of water, and it separates us from a ghastly province.'

I stood up. 'I repeat: one of you can pack a bag. Bring warm clothes, a very sharp sword, plus all your courage and initiative. You have three days to kiss the girls goodbye, while I finalise our commission.'

'Falco! What commission?'

'One Vespasian has particularly begged me to accept. Our commission from Sextus Julius Frontinus, provincial governor of Britain, to investigate the Great King's House.'

It was horrible – but neat.

I would go; I would have to take Helena; that would mean we took the children. I had sworn never to go back, but oaths are cheap. Gloccus and Cotta were not the only lure. I would drag along Maia, removing her from Rome and from Anacrites' grasp.

I set it all up very quietly. I had to arrange things at the Palace so discreetly that Anacrites would not find out. Only then did I warn Maia.

Being one of my sisters – immune to good sense, careless of her own safety, and thoroughly bloody-minded – Maia refused to go.

VIII

M Y PLAN had been to slip out of Rome quietly. By now the Fates must have woken up with a real hangover. The journey took for ever and it was terrible.

The *first* time I went to Britain, I had the army looking after me. Nothing to worry about, except pondering why in Hades I had ever joined up. It was all easy. Kindly officers planned my every waking moment so there was no time to panic; practised supplies managers ensured that food and every kind of equipment accompanied us; good lads were with me, all wanting their mothers just like I did but not saying so.

The *last* time I went out there, it was me and a one-man travel pack. I prepared it for myself without a kit manual, while others added an imperial pass to see me through and a mapskin showing the long road north. On the way back, it was me and a highly strung, furious young divorcée called Helena Justina. She was wondering what it would be like to go to bed with a brutal, outspoken informer, while I was very carefully avoiding the same thoughts. A thousand miles was a long way, trying to keep my hands off her. Especially once I started to sense that she wanted me to stop trying.

'Seems a long time ago,' I murmured, standing on the quayside in Portus, the main docking harbour at Ostia. It was five years.

Helena still had the art of talking to me privately, even amid a hubbub. 'Were we different people then, Marcus?'

'You and I will never change.' She smiled. The old wrench caught me, and I spread my hands on her, the way that dangerous dog four years ago would have loved to do.

This time, our luggage for the trip to Britain covered half the dock. While Nux raced around barking, Helena and I had skulked off towards the massive statue of Neptune, pretending that the sea of chests and wicker baskets had no connection with us. The two Camilli were quarrelling with each other as they oversaw loading. They had still not decided who was coming on the trip, so both planned to sail to Gaul while they continued to wrangle over who must stay behind at Massilia.

'Massilia!' I grinned, still reminiscing. 'I damn nearly went to bed with you there.'

Helena buried her face in my shoulder. I think she was giggling. Her breath tickled my neck. 'I expect you will do, this time.'

'Be warned, lady.' I spoke in the tough voice I used to put on – the one I once supposed had fooled her, though she had seen through it after a week. 'I'm planning to exorcise every memory of places where I let you stay chaste last time.'

'I look forward to that!' Helena retorted. 'I hope you are fit.' She knew how to issue a challenge.

We stood in silence for a time. Wrapped in cloaks against the sea breeze, and closely wrapped up in each other. She must have looked like a tearful wife bidding farewell to an official who was off on a long overseas tour. I must have looked like some fellow who was bravely managing not to seem too keen on the freedom ahead.

There would be no farewells. Ours was a different kind of freedom. We had always enjoyed life on the wing together. We both knew the dangers. We thought about them, even there on the quayside when it was far too late. Perhaps I should have left Helena and the babes at home. But how many careful adventurers make that sensible choice, bum off, survive endless danger and hardship, then return to the Golden City only to find that all their treasures have been wiped out by marsh fever?

There was a virulent strain of marsh fever in Britain. Still, our destination was coastal. Beyond the Great King's picturesque harbour outside his palace would lie windswept open water, not stagnant lakes and fens. Mind you, we had to cross two seas to get there; one was a terrifying stormy strait.

Helena and I thought that life was to be lived together. Private, domestic and shared. Shared with our family: two children, one complaining nursemaid, one scruffy dog. Plus my two assistants, the Camilli. And thanks to the Fates recovering their sense of fun, with the addition on this quayside of my sister Maia and all her children – who were still not coming to safety with us, but who were getting in the way seeing us off. Then there was Petronius. He had tagged along, saying he wanted to visit his daughters in Ostia.

'Got your socks?' I heard him mocking the two Camilli. The word was new to them. When we hit the next ship, crossing the cold and wind-ravaged Gallic Strait, whichever of the two was still with us would work out the point of knitted one-toe socks.

'We could end up with both of them,' Helena muttered quietly.

'Oh yes. Your father thought it worth a formal bet.'

'How much?'

'Too much!'

'You two are incorrigible . . . Father is heading for trouble. My mother ordered both my brothers to stay in Rome.'

'We're taking both, then. That clinches it, sweetheart.'

Now we were both smiling. Helena and I would enjoy watching the lads trying to choose the right moment to confess.

Hyspale was feeling queasy before she was even on the boat. Once aboard, Helena dragged her off to the tiny cabin, taking Maia with them to help calm the woman down. I went below decks with Aelianus, stowing our long-distance baggage. Justinus had the thankless task of explaining to the ship's crew that some items were wanted on the journey. We had a good system of identifier-tags. Regardless of that, someone had mixed up everything. Nothing was missing as far as I could tell, but there seemed to be baggage I knew nothing about.

It is always unsettling, as you wait for a long journey to start. In retrospect, perhaps there was more tension than there might have been. Perhaps people snarled and flustered around more chaotically than usual. There are shouts and bumps as a ship is laden with cargo. The crew do take delight in not bothering to inform passengers what is going on. Casting off seems their excuse to make shipboard visitors panic.

So for once, what happened was not my fault. I was down in the bowels of the vessel anyway. Then I heard the scream.

As I climbed up the rope ladder to the main deck, something worried me. Thudding and rocking had given way to smoother sensations. I felt the change in air movement, then a surge underfoot knocked me almost off balance.

'We're moving already!' Aelianus cried excitedly. Foreboding struck me. A panicky commotion was already telling me the worst: the captain had cast off and sailed out of Portus. Unluckily he did so while Maia was still on-board with us.

My sister was now straining at the rail, ready to throw herself over like a Naiad crazed by too much sun and foam. I had never seen Maia so hysterical. She was shrieking that she had been taken from her children. Only real force from Justinus, who had grasped the situation in his usual quick style and then grabbed Maia, stopped her trying to hurl herself overboard to get back to shore. Like me, she had never learned to swim.

'There's my brother taking a firm hand with the women,' sneered Aelianus.

'My sister knows close-contact wrestling though,' I commented as Maia flung her saviour aside and collapsed weeping on her knees.

As Maia sobbed, something about the quiet way Helena was exclaiming over her in sympathy made me pause. I would have expected my beloved to turn to me and order me to solve this problem before it was too late.

I leaned on the rail and stared back at the quayside. There indeed were Maia's four young children. Marius, Cloelia and Ancus stood in a solemn line together; they seemed to be calmly waving us goodbye. Rhea was held up in the arms of Petronius Longus as if to get a better view of her mother being abducted. An extra small dot must be Marius' puppy sitting quietly on his lead. Petronius, who could have tried commandeering a boat to chase after us, was just standing there.

'My children! Take me back to my children! My darlings; whatever will become of them without me? They will all be terrified –'

The neatly lined-up little figures were all looking quite unperturbed.

Aelianus decided to play the hero; he obligingly rushed to negotiate with the captain. I knew the man would not turn back. Justinus caught my eye and we both stayed where we were, with suitable expressions of concern. I reckon he saw what I was thinking. Perhaps he had even been in on the plot: this was fixed. One reason the captain would not be turning back was that somebody had paid him to cast off quietly – and then to keep going.

My sister was being removed from the reach of Anacrites. Somebody had set this up, whether Maia liked it or not. My guess was Helena. Petronius and even Maia's children might have conspired too. Only Helena could have invented the scheme and paid for it. Maia was unlikely to see the real truth. Once she had calmed down and started to work this out then I, her utterly blameless brother, would end up being blamed.

'Well, let's consider what we can do,' I heard Helena say. 'The children are with Lucius Petronius. No harm will come to them. We shall somehow get you home again. Don't cry, Maia. One of my handsome brothers will be going home from Massilia. You can easily be taken back with him . . .'

Both of her handsome brothers nodded in support – then since neither really intended to turn back at Massilia, they both skulked off out of the way.

Nobody seemed to need me. I got my head down in my work. I tied a long string to my daughter Julia so she could clamber about the deck in safety (and trip up sailors). Nux, a first-time sailor, whined a lot then lay on my legs. I rolled up the new baby in a warm papoose and kept her under my cloak against my chest. Then I sat on the deck with my feet up on an anchor, studying my notes from the Palatine secretariat which administered funds for the Great King's palace.

As usual with official projects, where the client had the highest expectations and the producing agency had the greatest need to shine, the larger were the errors and the higher the costs. Treasury audit had been applied and had nothing good to say. Loss of materials on site had reached epic proportions. There had also been a rash of serious accidents. Even the scheme's architect had submitted a scared report about his fears of sabotage.

Frontinus, the provincial governor, reckoned the programme completion date had not just slipped, it had skidded right into the next decade. He was having difficulties curbing the client's demands and possessed no decent manpower to send in on a rescue mission, due to conflicting needs of the major new works being built in Londinium (that was principally the new headquarters for the provincial governor – himself). Brutal paragraphs in administrative Greek spelled out the worst. The Great King's palace had reached the danger stage: it was all set to be the biggest administrative failure ever.

IX

L UCK IS a wonderful luxury. What could better prove that some are
born under a star of good fortune than the career (and the large,
comfortable home) of the Great King?

'Cogidumnus.' Justinus cautiously tried it out.

'Togidubnus,' I corrected him. This was a provincial of such ripe
insignificance that most Roman commentators never even called him
by the correct name. 'Learn it, please, lest we offend. The Emperor
may be our principal client, but Togi is the end customer. Pleasing
Togi is the whole point of us suffering this trip. Vespasian wants his
house to go up nicely so that Togi stays happy.'

'You had better stop calling him Togi,' warned Helena, 'or you are
bound to slip up and insult him in public.'

'Insulting officials is my style.'

'But you want your assistants to be smoothly oiled diplomats.'

'Ah yes. I have the rough edges – you are a pair of sickly smarm-
pots!' I threw at them.

We had been stuck at some mansio in the drabber parts of Gaul
when we found time for our tutorial. Hyspale had been instructed to
stop moaning about her discomfort (she had the art of making herself
unhappy) and to take care of the children. So Helena was able to shine
as my background researcher. Luckily her brothers (yes, both) were
used to being lectured by their big sister. I myself would never quite
relax when she started explaining things. Helena Justina could always
surprise me by the scope of her sources and the detail they provided.

We had fetched up here after days of weary travel. The children
seemed to be coping better than the rest of us, though Helena and I
had the irritation of disapproval from foreigners. While Gauls were
amazed how strict we were with our daughters, we thought them
slapdash spoilers of their own uncontrollable brats. Some of theirs had
fleas. Ours, swept off into kitchens to be cooed over for their pretty
curls, would acquire them soon. Nux was attacking her Roman ones
vigorously. I had had itches since Lugdunum, though if the creatures

were being carried on my person I had failed to find them. That was because I had rarely had my clothes off to search. Mansios had baths, but if you tarried in the queue to wash, you missed them serving dinner. Afterwards, the water was cold. With ruts in roads and gruesome weather, it added to the fun.

We all sat around a large table in the dingy hall that passed for a communal dining room at the mansio, with my sister hunched slightly to one side. Maia had been sufficiently alarmed by what she saw of the ship's crew who hauled us north past Italy; she refused to go back to Ostia alone. She had never travelled more than twenty miles from Rome before. When we made Gaul, she had no real idea how many dreary miles remained. She still thought she would be going home in a few weeks. We would be lucky even to reach Britain in that time.

Helena had 'found' a letter 'hidden' in her luggage from Marius, explaining that it was the children who had decided to send their mother away to safety. Maia believed Petronius Longus must have helped them, and that it was a ploy to steal her children now his own were with Silvia. Maia sat around the whole journey, planning to poison him with toad's blood. We stopped trying to include her in conversations.

'Our uncle Gaius has sent me some information about the area and the project,' said Helena briskly. 'You two boys have never met him. You have to pretend this is being expounded by a neat, enthusiastic, lifelong administrator who has a huge knowledge of his province and insists on telling you everything –'

Gaius Flavius Hilaris was married to their aunt, a quiet, intelligent woman called Aelia Camilla. He was currently at the end of a long term as financial procurator in Britain. As far as we could tell he had no intention of retiring back to Rome. He had been a provincial, born in Dalmatia, so Rome had never been his home base anyway. He worked like a dog and was absolutely straight. Helena and I both liked him enormously.

'Imagine Britain as a rough triangle.' Helena had a letter in her hand, so well studied she hardly referred to it. 'We are going to the middle of the long south coast. Elsewhere there are high chalk cliffs, but this area has a gentle coastline with safe anchorages in inlets. There are some streams and marshland, but also wooded places for hunting and enough good farming land to attract settlers. The tribes have come down from their hillforts peacefully here. Noviomagus Regnensis – the New Market of the Kingdom Tribes – is a small town on the modern model.'

45

'What makes this different from any other tribal capital?' asked Aelianus.

'Togidubnus.'

'So what makes *him* special?'

'Not a lot!' I grunted.

Helena shot me a mock-severe look. 'Convenient birth and mighty friends.' With her serious air allied to a light-hearted tone, she could make plain facts sound satirical.

'Would he introduce me to his friends?' Justinus said, grinning.

'Nobody with any taste would let you near their friends!' Aelianus snorted.

'Has Togi good taste?'

'No, just top pals and a lot of money,' I said.

'His taste may be exquisite,' Helena murmured. 'Or he may simply employ advisers who know class. He is able to call on all types of specialist –'

'Who charge huge fees and know how to spend lavishly,' I grumbled. 'Then Togi gets our famously frugal Emperor to foot the bill. No wonder Vespasian wants me there. I bet the invoices for this pretty pavilion need scrutinising at arm's length using blacksmith's tongs.'

Helena Justina was a dogged lass. With only a slight rattle of bracelets to reproach me, she tried to reassert sense. Too much tetchy prejudice was rampaging through this group of exhausted travellers. 'Togidubnus straddles the transition where barbarian Britain became a new Roman province. Once, thirty years ago, his tribe, the Atrebates, had an old king called Verica who was under pressure from rivals – the fierce Catuvellauni who were marauding across the southern interior.'

'Fighting fellows.' To the fore in the Great Rebellion when I was there. 'Good haters and encroachers. Boudicca was not their queen, but they galloped after her with panache. The Catuvellauni would follow a dung beetle into battle, if it led them to some other tribe's arable and pasture land – better still, to slicing off Roman heads.'

Helena waved an arm to silence me. 'A huge system of earthwork entrenchments protects the Noviomagus area from raids by chariots,' she continued. 'But in the reign of Claudius there was anxiety nonetheless; Verica called in the Romans to help him fight off trouble. That was when Togidubnus, who himself may already have been singled out to take over as king, met a young Roman commander on his first posting called Titus Flavius Vespasianus.'

'So the invasion landed at this place?' Justinus was not even born when the details of Claudius' mad British venture came flooding back to Rome. I could barely recall the excitement myself.

'One main thrust took place on the east coast,' I said. 'Many tribes who opposed us were grouped around their sanctum, a place called Camulodunum, north of the Tamesis. No question, though; our take-over was facilitated by the Atrebates. It was well before my time, but I guess they may have hosted a second – safer – touchdown base for the landing force. Certainly when Vespasian's legion moved west to conquer the tribes there, he operated out of what is now Noviomagus.'

'What was it then?'

'A bunch of huts on the beach presumably. The Second Augusta would have thrown up solid barracks, stores and granaries – then they began a subtle system of lending Roman builders and fine materials to the tribal chief. Now he wants marble cladding and Corinthian capitals. To indicate his benevolence to subservient peoples, Vespasian is paying.'

'Having a friendly base when your army drops anchor in remote and hostile territory would count for a lot.' Justinus could work things out. He shifted uneasily. Splinters from the crude bench on which we were perched were working their way through the wool of his tunic.

'And Togidubnus was swift to offer beer and bannocks,' Aelianus sneered. 'In the hope of reward!'

'He welcomed a chance to be Romanised,' Helena amended moderately. 'Uncle Gaius doesn't say, but Togidubnus may even have been one of the tribal chiefs' young sons who had been taken to Rome –'

'Hostage?' asked Aelianus.

'Honoured guest,' his sister reproved him. She had all the tact in her family.

'Being civilised?'

'Tutored.'

'Spoiled out of his mind?'

'Exposed to the refining benefits of our culture.'

'Judging by his desire to replicate the Palatine,' I joined in the cynical backchat, 'Togi has definitely seen Nero's Golden House. Now he wants a palace just like it. He does sound like one of those exotic princelings who were brought up in Rome then exported back to their homeland as polite allies, who knew how to fold their serviette at a banquet.'

'Just how big is this fantasy house he's being given?' Aelianus demanded.

Helena produced a rough sketch plan from her uncle's letter. Hilaris was no artist, but he had added a scale-bar. 'It has four long wings. About five hundred feet in either direction – plus pleasure gardens on all sides, suitable outbuilding complexes, kitchen gardens and so forth.'

'This is in the town?'

'No. This is dramatically set apart from the town.'

'So where does he live at the moment?'

Cautious, Helena consulted her document. 'First he occupied a timber dwelling beside the supply base – provincial, though impressive in scale. After the invasion had succeeded, Claudius or Nero showed imperial gratitude; then the King acquired a big, masonry, Roman-style complex to demonstrate how rich and powerful he was. That is still there. Now that he has proved himself a staunch ally in a crisis again –'

'You mean he supported Vespasian's bid for Emperor?'

'He did not oppose it,' I said dourly.

'The legions in Britain were equivocal?' Even Aelianus must have done some homework.

'The Second, Vespasian's old legion' – *my* legion – 'were always behind him. But there was a weak governor and the other legions behaved oddly. They ditched the governor, in fact, then they actually ran Britain themselves with an army council – but we don't talk about mutiny. It was a time of civil war. Afterwards all sorts of peculiarities were scratched out of documents and discreetly forgotten. Anyway, that's the kind of crazy province Britain has always been.'

'If the legions wavered, even lukewarm allegiance from a king was a bonus,' Justinus added. 'For Vespasian, it would have had reassurance and propaganda value.'

'Judging by the size of Vespasian's honorarium, *he* thinks Togidubnus was thrilled to see him as Emperor,' Helena decided. 'They look unlikely friends, perhaps. But Vespasian and Togidubnus were both young men on the make together back in the invasion days. Vespasian has founded his whole political life on his military success then; Togidubnus took over from the ancient Verica. He acquired the status of a respected ally – and by one means or another he obtained substantial wealth.'

'How –'

'Don't ask where the money comes from,' I intervened.

'He is bribed?' Justinus jumped in with the libel anyway.

'When you conquer a province,' his brother explained to him, 'some tribes get catapults hurling big rocks up their backsides – while others are courteously rewarded with ample gifts.'

'I suppose the respective financial benefits have been carefully worked out by generations of palace actuaries?' Justinus still sounded sharp.

I grinned. 'The dear tribes can decide for themselves whether they choose a javelin in the ribs and having their women raped, or cartloads of wine, some nice second-hand diadems and a delegation of elderly prostitutes from Artemisia setting up shop at the tribal capital.'

'All in the name of progress and culture!' Justinus groused dryly.

'The Atrebates *do* see themselves as progressive, so they took the loot.'

'Vespasian is not a sentimentalist,' Helena concluded, 'but he must remember Togidubnus from the special time of his own youth. Now they are both elderly, and old men grow nostalgic. Just wait – all three of you. I hope I'm there to see you all talking about the good old days!'

I hoped she would be. I nearly said that when one day I started mithering and dreaming, the last thing I would want was a dank, frescoed house in Britain. Still, you never know!

Justinus had captured the plan of the King's great new house. He was staring at it with all the envy of a newly married man who was lodged at home with his parents. Jealousy gave way to a more distant look in his dark eyes. Being a cynic, I did not believe our sentimental hero was nostalgic for his Baetican bride of barely a few months, Claudia Rufina.

Claudia had not accompanied us on this trip. She was a game girl, but she had been led to believe Justinus would be returning to Rome. He must have persuaded her to wait behind. I watched him thoughtfully. In some ways I knew him better than his family or friends; I had travelled with Quintus Camillus Justinus on a dangerous mission among barbarian tribes before. I had a fair idea that when he grew nostalgic, there was an unreachable, idealised beauty filling his mind. We would find golden-haired women in Britain who looked like the woman in Germany who still featured in his dreams.

Aelianus, being a bachelor, had the right to enjoy all the amenities of travel, including romantic ones. Instead, he had appointed himself the man of sense who ran our show. So now he was staring in amazement at the mansio landlord's enormous bill.

Helena went upstairs to feed the baby and settle Julia. We were a large enough group to commandeer ourselves a whole dormitory most nights. I preferred to keep my party together, and to exclude mad-eyed thieving strangers. The women accepted shared accommodation calmly, though the boys had been shocked at first. Privacy is not a Roman necessity; our room only needed to be cheap and convenient. We all just fell on our hard narrow beds in our clothes and slept like logs. Hyspale snored. She would.

I stayed behind with a wine flagon now, keeping an eye on Maia. She was talking to a man. I'm no Roman paternalist. She was free to converse. But a woman who distances herself from the party she travels with can be seen by strangers as up for anything. In fact Maia was waiting in tense fury for her nightmare removal from Rome to be over; she seemed so introverted and hostile that people hardly ever bothered her. But she was attractive, seated slightly apart at the end of our bench, a well-rounded piece with dark curly hair in a braided crimson dress. She did have clothes and necessities with her; a packed trunk had been 'discovered' on-board ship and we kept up a pretence that her children had arranged it.

This dress was obviously new – paid for by Pa, who had replenished her wardrobe after Anacrites destroyed everything. Anyone who judged on appearances might think Maia had money.

If Maia acquired a follower, I would not intervene. I was not stupid. Mind you, I would find out exactly who he was, before it went too far.

My back was stiff. I had an old broken rib that played up after hard days in cramped transport. My head was spinning slightly, confused by hours of relentless motion on the road. Half my party had blocked bowels and headaches; the rest were stricken with diarrhoea. Tonight, as I moved awkwardly trying to ease my back, I could not decide which stage my internal works were at. When you're travelling you need to know. You have to plan ahead.

The conversation with my sister looked casual. The man was a lone traveller, dressed serviceably, in trade by the looks of it. He had half-eaten bread on the table in front of him and was working his way down a tall face-pot, containing beer probably. He did not offer anything to Maia.

While he made the running, Maia's response was aloof. The fellow should be glad she was just about pleasant. He spoke diffidently, looking as if he was unsure what to make of her. Talking to him was a gesture of defiance on her part, I knew. I had told everyone to avoid chatting with fellow-travellers but Maia liked rejecting good advice. Flouting her head of household came naturally, and she was setting herself apart from those of us she viewed as kidnappers. On this trip, one wrong move by me and she would become uncontrollable.

Eventually the man went out to brave the cold water in the bath house; Maia departed upstairs without a word. I sat on quietly for a while then followed her.

Next day we saw the stranger, struggling to edge a cartload of large, well-wrapped items out through the mansio gates. Maia mentioned that he was some travelling salesman, with the same destination as us. She said his name was Sextius. I told the lads to help Sextius push his vehicle onto the road. Then I tipped them the nod that one of them had to make friends.

'Aulus, you need some adventure in your life . . .'

When we finally arrived across the Gallic Strait in Noviomagus, I was down to one official assistant. Aelianus had become the rather grumpy sidekick of a man who hoped to interest the Great King in mechanical statues. One day, if he ever turned into a chubby landowner with villas at Lake Volusena and Surrentum, our dear Aulus could purchase his own curiosities in the safe knowledge that he knew how to oil a set of moving doves so they pecked up model corn from a golden dish. I told him to enjoy the disguise – and he told me which obnoxious fate he would like to impose on me.

All I had to do now was fix up Justinus as an ornamental fishpond fanatic, and we should be able to creep up on Gloccus and Cotta from three sides. That is, assuming they were there.

BRITAIN:
NOVIOMAGUS REGNENSIS

High Summer (for what that's worth!)

X

DESTINATION. Day one. An absolutely enormous building site, right on the southern coast.

The clerk of works was busy. But as I waited, he had glanced at me, and I reckoned he would be polite. They usually are. Conciliation is their business; anyone who can stop the hot-headed plumbers tearing the damn fool architect to pieces when he makes them redirect an inlet pipe yet again (but refuses to pay for it) can deal with an unwanted site visitor.

I had already witnessed a pomposity who must be the architect, sneering at a stonemason unpleasantly. That was no surprise.

I had not been allowed anywhere near the plumbers. Still, that would change. Every trade on this site was on my list to be investigated. Not many trades were contributing yet. The 'site' so far only seemed to consist of a vast levelling project.

I had ridden out by mule from Noviomagus that morning. I still felt queasy from the sea crossing. After a mile on a wide shoreline road that obviously led somewhere, I fetched up in dismay at this vast muddy scene.

It was not the kind of venue where a big-city informer likes to operate. The future palace was sited in a low-lying coastal nook between the marshes and the sea. To my left as I rode up lay the harbour approach – a lagoon of sorts where dredgers were languidly messing about in what I knew was intended to become a deep channel. Swans went about their business, unperturbed. On arrival, my road had crossed a bridge over a stream, newly canalised to control it, then petered out into a bald new service track that would run around the extended palace. To my right, just before the bridge, stood some old, military-style buildings. The new palace would stand on an enormous platform which was in the process of being raised to create a firm, drained base. It rose almost as high as me, five feet above the wiry bog plants at the natural ground level.

The torn-up landscape made a desolate scene. Peewits and frantic skylarks vied with the sounds of stone chipping from a depot area. Up ahead there were some existing structures – primarily a stone-built complex on the near side, at present shrouded in scaffolding. Beyond this suite, which must be the Great King's existing residence, the great platform was just a ghastly sea of mud.

I had tethered the mule and made my way onto the site. Cart tracks meandered across haphazardly. I could see a criss-crossing of surveyors' poles and strings, apparently where footings for the new works had already been made up. Unfilled areas between these foundations lay waiting for the unwary to break bones falling in. Mounds of fill stood everywhere. Astounding quantities of clay and rubble were being moved over from the far side and dumped at this end. Large numbers of structural piles were being incorporated in the areas that had not yet been backfilled. So many were being jammed in along wall lines that a whole oak forest must have been sacrificed to provide the heavy timber. Where there had been a little more progress, stacked drains and ashlar blocks were ready for incorporation – though like most building sites, this one had very few labourers incorporating anything.

I had spent an hour wandering about, trying to get my bearings and make sense of the plan, before I was apprehended and asked to explain myself. So far, the site officials thought I was just a curious sightseer on a visit from Rome along with a lady of distinction who was staying in a house in town that belonged to the procurator of finance for Britain. They assumed I had brought the noble Helena Justina to see her uncle Gaius and aunt Aelia, pausing at their house in Noviomagus Regnensis to recover from our long journey before travelling on to Londinium.

The clerk of works found a moment to speak to me. I held back, getting the measure of him. He tried putting me off, saying he had to go to a project team meeting; he said he would like to allow me to wander around, but building sites were dangerous, so a safety edict declared the works out of bounds to unescorted visitors. I was about to show him the governor's introduction. Depending on his reaction to my docket from Frontinus, either I would make him squirm by producing my pass from the Emperor as well – or I'd merely let him know it existed.

He was a lean, middleweight, furrowed man of obvious intelligence. Dark brown eyes darted everywhere. Every time he crossed from his site hut to collect a hot drink from the covered canteen, he was looking for loafers, for errors, for sneak-thieves with their crafty eyes on equipment and materials – and if he had been forewarned to expect the proverbial man from Rome, then he was looking out for me. He oozed competence. And his restrained behaviour meant that whether or not he knew I was being sent to investigate, he would cope well when I came clean. If he was as good as my secretariat briefing had said, he would welcome my presence. If he had been away from Italy too many years, and had grown complacent or actually corrupt, then I would have to watch my back. The reason clerks of works can afford politeness is that apart from the architect, they hold absolute power.

He was called away again, to answer some question about setting-out. He gave me a nod, a gentle hint to leave. Not me. While he got stuck in with the surveyor around the *groma*, I stood where he had left me (so he would not worry what I was up to) but I refused to go, like a crass lad who had no social graces. Someone else then engaged the clerk of works in conversation, as tends to happen, so I tried chatting to the surveyor while he waited to resume.

'It's a prestigious site.'

'All right if you like it,' he returned. Surveyors are unhappy men. Intelligent, shrewd characters, they all believe that were it not for them, disaster would devastate any new construction. They feel their importance is not taken seriously. On both counts they are quite correct.

'Big project?'

'Five-year rolling programme.'

'Big enough to go adrift!' I made the mistake of grinning.

'Thanks for the confidence,' he answered sourly. I should have known that a surveyor would take it as a personal slight. He seemed tense. Perhaps he just had an edgy nature. He gave me a terse 'Excuse me –'

Time to assert myself. I could have produced a note-tablet and written memos. That lacked subtlety. For official missions you need a certain air. I had it. I could cause anxiety just by strolling to the edge of a new wall's foundations, then watching what was going on among the labourers. (They were hand-bedding flints in concrete between a double row of piles. Well, a man and a boy were doing that, while four other men stood by and helped them by leaning thoughtfully on spades.)

As I parked myself with my thumbs in my belt, simply looking in silence, the surveyor smelt audit immediately. I was expecting his half-hidden jerk of the head to warn his crony; the clerk of works reappeared at my side again, with narrowed eyes. 'Anything else, sir?'

I knew as well as he did that it pays to be courteous. But I started as I intended to continue – and it was tough. 'The name is Didius Falco. I did some work for Flavius Hilaris a few years back. There were cock-ups in the organisation of the silver mines. Now they've called me back again.'

He remained non-committal. 'To my site?'

'You hear me.'

'I wasn't told.'

'But you are not surprised.'

'So what's your work here?'

'Whatever is needed.' I made it clear there would be no messing.

He knew better than to resist. 'You have authorisation?'

'From the top.'

'Londinium?'

'Londinium and Rome.'

That caused the right buzz of excitement. 'We have a team meeting about to start – I'll introduce you to our project manager.'

The project manager was bound to be an idiot. The clerk of works clearly thought so; to have no faith in the project manager was the formal specification for his job. The surveyor was laughing behind his hand too, I reckoned.

'Who leads your team?' It can vary between the disciples, particularly on schemes like bridges or aqueducts, with a high engineering content.

'The architect.' The fellow I had seen earlier, being rude. No doubt he would soon be rude to me.

'Any hope that they issued you one who knows his stuff?'

The clerk of works was formal: 'Pomponius has had many years of training and has worked on major schemes.' He deliberately did not comment, *And he buggered up the lot of them.* The surveyor sniggered openly, however. When this surveyor started his career, he would have undergone serious training of his own; some sessions would have been taught by grizzled old *groma*-geniuses who called their task *Stopping the bloody architect ruining the job.*

I had gained a good impression of this pair. 'You mean, Pomponius is the usual mixture of arrogance, sheer ignorance and fanciful ideas?' The clerk of works allowed himself a faint smile.

'He wears Egyptian faience shoulder brooches!' confirmed the surveyor dourly. He himself was the smartest professional on site: crisp grey hair, immaculate white tunic, polished belt and enviable boots.

He carried instruments in a neatly buckled, well-oiled satchel; I would happily grab it off a second-hand stall, even though it had obviously seen a lot of wear.

The clerk of works decided he should lighten the atmosphere. 'Watch out if Pomponius offers you a presentation. It has been known to last three days. The last VIP was carried out unconscious on a stretcher – Pomponius had not even started to show him colour charts and paint samples.'

I smiled. 'Then don't introduce me formally. Just slide me in at the project meeting and I'll make myself known to him at a later stage. I mean, after I've seen just how stupid he is.'

They grinned.

We set off towards some elderly wooden buildings, ancient military hutments that looked as if they dated back to the Claudian invasion. Now they were being used as site huts, but must be earmarked for demolition when the new scheme was complete.

The project meeting would normally have started before this, but had been delayed. Somebody had had an accident.

'Happens all the time,' the surveyor gushed dismissively. Although we had been acting like friends up to that point, he was glossing over an issue.

'Who was it? Is he hurt?'

'Done for, unfortunately.' I raised an eyebrow. The surveyor seemed tetchy and made no further comment.

'Who was it?' I repeated.

'Valla.'

'What happened to him?'

'He was a roofer. What do you think happened? He fell off a roof!'

'Better get along to the meeting,' interrupted the clerk of works. 'Do you have a clerk, Falco?'

We were now entering the old military hutment they were using as the project manager's office. I let the unspoken issue about the roofer fade away, at least temporarily. 'No, I take my own notes. Issue of security.' In fact I had never been able to afford secretarial help. 'My assistants back me up when needed.'

'Assistants!' The clerk of works looked startled. A man from Rome was bad enough. A man from Rome with reinforcements was really serious. 'How many do you have?'

'Just the two,' I said and smiled. Adding for fun, 'Well – until the rest arrive.'

XI

POMPONIUS SPOTTED me at once.

It cannot have been easy. The site meeting was the largest collection of men with tool-holsters and one-sleeved tunics that I had attended. Maybe this explained the problem. The palace project was too big. No one man could keep track of the personnel, the programme and the costs. But Pomponius thought he was in charge – the way men who are losing their grip on a situation usually do.

I took against him immediately. The thick hair pomade gave him away; his vanity and studied vagueness clinched it. He was a distant man, too certain of his own importance, who behaved as if someone had waved a bowl of rotten shellfish under his nose. He had a deliberately old-fashioned way of looping up his toga, which made him seem an oddity. To wear a toga at all set him apart: we were in the provinces, and he was at work. One of his gaudy finger-rings was so bulky it must interfere when he was at the drawing board.

I found it hard to envisage him actually designing plans. When he did, it was a sure bet he would be so busy thinking up expensive décor, he would forget to include stairs.

The team he had assembled was dominated by the decorative trades. Cyprianus (the clerk of works) and Magnus (the surveyor) pointed out in undertones the chief mosaicist, the landscape gardener, the chief fresco painter and the marble mason before they got to anyone as sensible as a drains engineer, carpenter, stonemason, labour supervisors or admin clerks. There were three of the latter, for tracking the programme, cost control and special ordering. Labour was divided between local and overseas, each with a man in charge.

An obvious tribal dignitary, very proud of his torque, had cleared himself a substantial area right at the front. I nudged Magnus, who muttered, 'The client's representative has graced us with his hairy presence!'

Pomponius had decided to bar me. He spoke in a superior accent that increased my loathing. 'This meeting is for team members only.'

Dark heads, bald heads and the one crown of flowing ginger locks on the client's representative all turned my way. They all knew I was there and had been waiting to see how Pomponius reacted.

I stood up. 'I'm Didius Falco.' Pomponius gave no sign of recognition. I had been told by the imperial secretariat in Rome that the project manager would be warned I was coming. Of course, Pomponius *might* wish to keep my role a secret so I could observe his site incognito. That would be too helpful.

I was sure he had been sent a briefing. I could already deduce his irritation with correspondence from Rome. He was in charge; he would give no time to orders from above. Bureaucracy cramped his creativity. He would have glanced at the relevant memo, could not face the tricky issues, so forgot he ever read it. (Yes, I had previous experience of architects.)

He gave me two options: to be sidelined – or to fight back. I could live with an enemy. 'I'll take it that my letter of authority has been mis-filed here. I hope that is not indicative of how this project is run. Pomponius, I won't delay you – I'll spell out the situation to you when you're free.'

Polite but terse, I strode to the front. Apparently leaving, I positioned myself in full view of everyone. Before Pomponius could stop me, I addressed them: 'You will learn this soon enough. My brief is direct from the Emperor. The scheme is behind time and over cost. Vespasian wants lines of communication cleared and the whole situation rationalised.' That implied what I was here to do, without using dangerous phrases like *allocate blame* or *weed out incompetence*. 'I am not setting up a war camp. We are all here to do the same job: get the Great King's palace built. As soon as I'm established on site you will know where my office is—' That made it clear Pomponius had to give me one. 'The door will always be open to anyone with something helpful to say – use the opportunity.'

Now they knew that I was here – and that I felt I had more authority than Pomponius. I left them all to mutter about it.

Right from the start, I had detected a bad atmosphere. The conflict was brewing before I spoke; it had nothing to do with my presence.

With all the prominent team members trapped at their meeting, I decided to inspect the corpse of the dead roofer, Valla. Wondering how to find it, I was able to appreciate the site at a quiet moment. A labourer humping a basket of spoil glanced at me with mild curiosity. I asked him to show me around. He seemed completely incurious about my motives, but quite happy to take time off from his duties.

'Well, you can see we've got the old house there, on the shore side –'

'You're pulling it down?'

He cackled. 'There's a big row about that. Owner likes it. If he gets to keep it, we'll have to raise all the floor levels.'

'He won't be happy when you start infilling his audience suite and he has concrete up to the ankles!'

'He's more unhappy with losing the building.'

'So who says he can't keep it?'

'The architect.'

'Pomponius? Isn't his brief to provide what the client wants?'

'Reckon he thinks the client ought to want what he's told.'

Some labourers are well-built specimens, their muscles and stamina suited to heaving stone and concrete. This was one of the wiry, pasty, strangely feeble-looking types. Perhaps he was happy on ladders. Or perhaps he simply started in the trade because his brother knew a foreman and fixed him up with work cleaning old bricks. Like most building workers he obviously suffered with his back.

'Did I hear you lost someone in an accident?'

'Oh Gaudius.' I had meant Valla.

'What happened to Gaudius?'

'Swiped with a plank, knocked backwards in a hole. Trench wall collapsed and he was crushed before we could dig him out. He was still alive when we started clawing at the fill. Some of the boys must have trod on him as they tried to help.'

I shook my head. 'Horrible!'

'Then Dubnus. Dubnus got stewed one night. He ended up knifed in a bar at the canabae.' Canabae were semi-official bothies, outside military forts normally; I knew them from my army days. There the locals were allowed to set up businesses servicing off-duty needs. This meant the flesh trade, with other offerings that ranged from dangerous drink to hideous souvenirs. It led to disease, birth pangs and illegal marriage – though rarely death.

'Life out here is tough?'

'Oh it's all right.'

'Where are you from?'

'Pisae.'

'Liguria?'

'A long time ago. I never like to settle down.' That could mean he was fleeing a ten-year-old charge for stealing ducks – or that he really was a rootless bird who liked his boots on the move.

'Do the management treat you well?'

'We have a nice clean barracks and decent tuck – it's fine, if you can stand living on top of nine other fellows, some of them right farters and one who cries in his sleep.'

'Will you stay in Britain when the job's completed?'

'Not me, legate! I'm for Italy as quick as you like . . . Still, I always say that. Then I hear about some other scheme. There's always pals going, and the pay sounds rich. I get lured off again.' He seemed content with this.

'Would you say,' I asked narrowly, 'that this site is any more dangerous than others where you have worked?'

'Well, you lose a few fellows, it's natural.'

'I know what you mean. I've heard that outside the army, more men are killed on building sites than in any other trade.'

'You get used to it.'

'So what are the casualty numbers like?'

He shrugged, no statistician. I bet this easy-going lamb was just as dozy over his pay.

No, I didn't. I bet he knew what he was owed to the nearest quarter *as*.

'Know anybody on this site called Gloccus or Cotta?'

He said no.

XII

Directed by the labourer, I found the infirmary where the body of the roofer killed that morning was supposed to lie. This was a small but efficient medical station, set among some site huts on the far side, with a young orderly, Alexas, who tended day-to-day cuts and sprains – of which there were many. I guessed his job also included identifying malingerers. They would have those on a regular basis too.

Without surprise, he showed me the dead roofer. Valla had been a typical site navvy, ruddy-skinned and slightly paunchy. He probably liked a drop to drink, probably too often. His hands were rough. He smelt very slightly of old sweat, though that might only be that he rarely washed his tunic. He would smell worse soon if nobody paid to cremate him; my recent memories of the corpse under Pa's hypocaust were revived unpleasantly.

Valla lay on a stretcher, untended by mourners or flute-players, yet respected. A coarse cloth was pulled back with a gentle hand, ready for my inspection. The orderly stayed with me, as if he took as much care of this dead man as any screaming ditcher with a sickle through his leg. They had standards on this site, apparently.

'Will Valla be given a funeral?'

'It is normal,' said Alexas. 'We get deaths on any project, some perfectly natural. Hearts give out. Disease takes a toll. The workers will have a whip-round, probably, but on a long-distance job, arrangements are made by management.'

'You then ship the ashes home to relatives?' He looked embarrassed. 'Too much trouble,' I agreed calmly. 'I bet half the crew here have never named a blood relation to be contacted.'

'They are supposed to,' I was assured earnestly.

'Of course.' I tapped his chest. 'Have *you* put your wife or your mother on a scroll?'

Alexas began to speak, then paused and grinned back at me. 'Now you mention it . . .'

'I know. We all think anything bad will happen to some other man

64

. . . This one was mistaken, though.'

The body was cool. I was told nobody saw what happened. It looked as though he came off cleanly; there were certainly no signs that he scraped his hands trying to regain a grip. There were no real marks on him. The fatal injuries must be internal. If anybody shoved the poor fellow to make him lose his footing, then they had left no evidence.

'Where did his fall happen?'

'The old house.'

'It's under scaffold, I know. Isn't there some dispute over the building's future?'

'I'm not the man to ask,' Alexas said. 'If they are demolishing any part of it, Valla would have been salvaging tiles.'

'Hmm. So what's your theory?'

'What do you mean?' asked the orderly in genuine puzzlement.

'Is this death suspicious?'

'Of course not.'

An informer gets used to being assured that stabbings and stranglings are 'merely accidents'. I had come to expect lies whenever I asked questions – but maybe a world still existed where people suffered ordinary mishaps.

'Did he let out a cry, do you know, Alexas?'

'Would that be important?'

'If he was pushed, he might have protested. If he jumped, or fell, he might have been more likely to stay silent.'

'Shall I try to find out for you?'

'Not worth it, thanks.' It would be inconclusive anyway. 'The palace project has hardly started – but this is not your first fatality.'

'It won't be the last either.'

'Can I see any of the other bodies?'

He stared. 'Of course not. Long gone in funeral pyres.'

Suspicious as ever, I was wondering about a cover-up. 'Did you inspect the bodies, Alexas?'

'I saw some. "Inspect" is too strong a word. We had a man felled by one of those end finials off roofs –' Alexas went out to his wound-dressing area, rooted under a counter and produced the guilty party: it was a dead-weight lump in the shape of a four-sided arch – a miniature tetrapylon – with a ball on top. He dumped it in my arms and I staggered slightly.

'Yes, that could dent your skull!' I shed it fast, onto the shelf. 'You keeping it for something?'

'Make a nice bird hut.' Alexas grinned. People on building sites are always snaffling materials for their own domestic purposes. I noticed one of the four legs was stained. 'Sparrows won't notice a bit of blood, Falco!'

'Hmm . . . Any other mishaps?'

'A slab of uncut marble flattened someone. The marble supervisor was furious that it got damaged; he said it was priceless.'

'A heartless swine?'

'He reacted without thinking, I suppose. Then another man got swiped with a spade in a fight last week.'

'Unusual?'

'Unfortunately not. Construction sites are always full of tools – and hot-headed men who can wield them skilfully.'

'I came across a spade killing in Rome before I left,' I said, again thinking of Stephanus being swiped and stuffed under Pa's new mosaic.

'I've seen plenty,' scoffed Alexas. 'Axe-deaths. Crane decapitations. Drownings, crushings, leg and arm amputations –'

'All these have happened on the palace scheme?' I was horrified.

'No, Falco. Some have happened. Others may yet.'

'A man was stabbed, I hear? Knife fight. Drink involved.'

'So I believe. I heard it happened in the town. The body was not brought here.' He was patient, but he thought me a time-waster.

'Alexas, don't misread me. I'm not looking for trouble. I just heard that the death count was too high here and it might be significant.'

'Significant of what? Slack management?'

Well, that would do as an explanation until I found a more precise definition. If that was ever possible.

I left him to staunch a workman's blood-dripping finger. I noticed that he carried out the task with calmness – just as he faced everything, including me jumping about looking for scandals.

Now that I had talked to him, I thought I understood him. He was a man in his middle twenties, with drab colouring and a dull personality, who had found a niche as a specialist. He was happy. He seemed to know that in rougher areas of life he would have ended up a nobody. Some lucky chance had brought him to work at the routine end of medicine. He dispensed herbal remedies, staunched blood on straightforward wounds. Decided when a surgeon ought to be sent for. Listened to depressives with a helpful manner. Perhaps once in his career he would encounter a real maniac who needed tying down in

66

a hurry. Perhaps his ignorance killed off a few patients, but that's true of more doctors than doctors will admit. On the whole, society was the better for his existence and that knowledge pleased him.

I suppose it pleased *me* to think that Alexas would regard it as a matter of professional competence to report any irregularity. I would find no clues otherwise. I would have to rely on Alexas for information on the past 'accidents'.

But the situation was covered now: I was here. That should reassure anyone who had the misfortune to be done in in murky circumstances!

When I left the medical post, somebody was hanging about outside in a way that made me look twice at him. I felt he was intending to quiz Alexas about me. When I stared straight at him he changed his mind. 'You're Falco.'

'Can I help you?'

'Lupus.'

Broad-browed and squat-bodied, with a tan that said he had lived out of doors in all weathers for maybe forty years, he seemed familiar. 'And your position is?'

'Labour supervisor.'

'Right!' He had been at the project meeting; Cyprianus pointed him out to me. 'Local or foreign workers?'

Lupus looked surprised that I knew there were two. I just waited. He muttered, 'I do the overseas.'

There were benches outside the bandage house for queuing patients. I sat down and encouraged Lupus to do likewise. 'And where are you from yourself?'

'Arsinoë.' It sounded like a hole at the back of a gully in the desert. 'Where's that?'

'Egypt!' he said proudly. Reading my mind, the loyal sand flea added, 'Yes, yes; it's the place they call Crocodilopolis.'

I took out my note-tablet and a stylus. 'I need to talk to you. Was Valla one of your men? Gaudius? Or the man who died in the knife fight at the canabae?'

'Valla, Dubnus and Eporix were mine.'

'Eporix?'

'A roof feature fell on him.' The heavy finial Alexas showed me.

'And tell me about the knife victim? That was Dubnus, wasn't it?'

'Big Gaul. A complete ass. How he managed not to get himself slaughtered twenty years before this, I'll never know.'

Lupus spoke matter-of-factly. I could accept that half his workforce were madhats. Almost certainly they came from poor backgrounds. They led a gruelling life with few rewards. 'Give me the picture.' I left off the stylus to look informal.

'What do you want?'

'Background. How things work. What are the good and bad aspects? Where does your labour hail from? Are they happy? How do you feel yourself?'

'They come from Italy mostly. Along the way a few Gauls are recruited. Spaniards. Eporix was one of my Hispanians. The fine trades get workers from the east or central Europe; they pick up on the orders for materials in the marble yards or wherever, and follow the carts looking for high wages or adventure.'

'Are the wages good?'

Lupus guffawed. 'This is an imperial project, Falco. The men just *think* they will get special rates.'

'Do you have trouble attracting labour?'

'It's a prestigious contract.'

'One which will embarrass people in high places if it goes wrong!' I grinned. After a moment, Lupus grinned back. Dry lips parted slowly and reluctantly; he was a cautious partaker of mirth. Or just cautious. He was at least talking to me, but I did not fool myself. I could not expect his trust.

'Yes, it's rather public.' Lupus grimaced. 'Otherwise, it may be bloody big, but it's just domestic, isn't it?'

'Major engineering is more complex?'

'The governor's palace in Londinium has more clout. I wouldn't say no to a transfer there.'

'Any snobbery because the client is a Briton?'

'I don't care who he is. And I don't let the men complain.'

Most of his front teeth were missing. I wondered how many barroom fights accounted for his losses. He was of burly build. He looked capable of handling himself, and of splitting up any trouble-makers.

'So you have a whole crowd of migrant workers — scores, or hundreds even?' I asked, recalling him to the subject. Lupus nodded, confirming the larger number. 'What sort of life is there for the men? They get basic accommodation?'

'Temporary hutments close to the site.'

'No privacy, no room to breathe.'

'Worse than house slaves at some luxury villas – but better than slaves in the mines,' Lupus shrugged.

'Yours is free labour?'

'Mixture. But I hate slaves,' he said. 'A big site's too open. Too many transports leaving. I don't have time to stop the merry hordes running off.'

'So your men get adequate rations, washing facilities and a roof.'

'If the weather holds, our fellows are out of doors all day. We want them fit and full of energy.'

'Like the army.'

'The same, Falco.'

'So how is discipline?'

'Not too bad.'

'But the high value of materials on site leads to diddling?'

'We keep the risky stuff locked away in decent stores.'

'I've seen the depot with the new fence.'

'Yes, well. You wouldn't think there was anywhere around here to sell the stuff, or any means of moving it away – but some bugger will always manage. I arrange the best watchmen I can, and we've brought in dogs to help them. Then we just hope.'

'Hmm.' That was an area I had to pursue later. 'And how is life out here? The men have leisure time?'

He groaned. 'They do.'

'Tell me.'

'That's where my troubles really start. They are bored. They are thinking they will get large bonuses – and half of them spend the money before we even dole it out. They have access to beer – there's too much, and some are not used to it. They rape the native women – or so the women's fathers claim when they come haranguing me – and they beat up the native men.'

'That's the fathers, husbands, lovers and brothers of their attractive lady friends?'

'For starters. Or on the right night, my lads will take on anyone else who has a long haircut, a strong accent, or funny trousers and a red moustache.' Lupus almost sounded proud of their spirit. 'If they can't find a Briton to abuse, they just beat up each other instead. The Italians gang up on the Gauls. When that palls, for variety the Italians tear into each other and the Gauls do the same. That's less tricky to deal with in some ways than distraught civilian Britons hoping for a compensation payout, though it leaves me short-handed. Pomponius gives me all Hades if too many on the complement are laid up with cracked heads. But, Falco –' Lupus stretched towards me earnestly – 'this is just life on a building site abroad. It is happening all over the Empire.'

'And you are saying it means nothing?'

'It means I have my work cut out – but that's what I'm here for. These are simple lads, mostly. When they start a feud, I can find out what's up by reading the curse tablets they lay lovingly at shrines. *May Vertigius the snotty tiler lose his willy for stealing my red tunic, and may his chilblains hurt him very much indeed. Vertigius is a swine and I don't like him. Also, may the foreman, that cruel and unfair person Lupus, rot and have no luck with girls.*'

I laughed quietly. Then I threw in, '*Are* you unfair, Lupus?'

'Oh I look after my favourites scrupulously, Falco.'

I thought not. He seemed like a man who was as much in control of a slippery situation as he could be. He seemed to understand his men, to love their craziness, to tolerate their stupidity. I reckoned he would defend them against outsiders. I thought only the truly mad among them – and a few real lunatics would be on the payroll – would seriously curse Lupus.

'And how are you with girls?' I asked mischievously.

'Mind your own business! Well, I do all right,' Lupus could not resist boasting.

He was an ugly trout. But that meant nothing. Toothless whippers-in can be popular. He held a position of authority and his manner was confident. Some women will sidle up to anyone in charge.

I stretched. 'Thanks for all that. Now tell me, have you a couple of recent acquisitions from Rome called Gloccus and Cotta?'

'Um – not that I can think of. Do you want to scan my rolls of honour?'

'You keep lists?'

'Of course. Pay,' he explained sarcastically.

'Yes, I'll look through them, please.' They could be using false names. Any pair of tradesmen who had turned up just before me would be worth checking out. 'Just one more question – you control the immigrant labour, but I gather there are British workers too?'

Perhaps Lupus closed in slightly. 'That's right, Falco.' He stood up and was already leaving. 'Mandumerus runs the local team. You'll have to ask him.'

There was nothing in his tone to imply a feud directly, yet I felt he and Mandumerus were not friends.

'By the way, Falco,' he informed me as we parted. 'Pomponius asked me to pass on his apologies; he mistook you for a travelling salesman – we get a lot coming around to bother us.'

'Mistook me, eh?' I sucked my teeth.

'He sent a message – he's found the scroll explaining you. He wants to give you a presentation about the full scheme. Tomorrow. In the plan room.'

'Sounds like that's all of tomorrow taken care of, then!'

He grinned.

XIII

HELENA CAME with me from Noviomagus for the project presentation. On arrival at the palace, we wandered around the scaffolded part and looked at the roof where poor Valla must have fallen to his death.

It was a straightforward case of sending a man aloft, on his own, too high up, with inadequate protection. Apparently.

We had time in hand. Turning back, we surveyed what they called the old house. Togidubnus' palace, his reward for allowing the Romans into Britain, must have stood out in the land of hillforts and forest hovels. Even this early version was a gem. His fellow-kings and their tribesmen were still living in those large round huts with smoke holes in their pointed roofs, where several families would cram in festively together along with their chickens, ticks and favourite goats; but Togi was fabulously set up. The main range of the royal home comprised a fine and substantial romanised stone building. It would be a desirable property if it stood on the shores of the lake at Nemi; in this wilderness it was an absolute cracker.

A double veranda gave protection from the weather, opening onto a large colonnaded garden. It was well tended; someone enjoyed this amenity. Set slightly apart from the living suite for safety, the unmistakable domed roofs of what might well be the only private bath house in this province lay on the seaward side. Gentle smoke from the furnace told us Vespasian did not need to send the King a civilisation-trainer to teach him what the baths were for.

Helena dragged me to explore. I made her take care, for some architectural features were in the process of being stripped by the builders. This included the colonnaded pillars around the garden; they had highly unusual, rather elegant capitals, with extravagant rams' horn volutes, from between which worrying tribal faces wreathed in oak leaves peered out at us.

'Too wild and woody for me!' Helena cried. 'Give me simple bead and dart tops.'

I agreed with her. 'The mystical eyes seem to be an outdated fad.' I gestured at the columns being dismantled. 'Pomponius starts a client's refit by tearing down everything in sight.' I noticed that these columns were coated with stucco, which in some places was peeling as the stone beneath flaked. Weathering had forced hideous cracks in their render. 'Poor Togi! Let down by tacky Claudian tat. See; this apparently noble Corinthian pillar is just a composite – thrown together on the cheap, with a lifespan of less than twenty years!'

'You are shocked, Marcus Didius,' Helena's eyes danced.

'This is no way for the Golden City to reward a valued ally – nasty chunks of old tile and packing material, thrown together and surfaced over.'

'Yet I can see why the King likes it,' said Helena. 'It has been a fine home; I expect he's very fond of it.'

'He's fonder still of expensive fiddling.'

A window flew open. No tat this; it was a tightly carpentered hardwood effort with opaque panes, set in a beautifully moulded marble frame. The marble looked conspicuously Carraran. Not many of my neighbours could afford the genuine white stuff. I felt myself growing envious.

Wild ginger dreadlocks flailed; around a fleshy bull neck I recognised the heavy electrum torque that must be nearly choking its excited owner.

'You are the man!' shrieked the King's representative in stilted Latin.

'*The man from Rome*,' I corrected him firmly. I like to pass on colloquial phrases when I travel among the barbarians. 'Gives a better tone of menace.'

'Menace?'

'More frightening.' Helena smiled. The tribesman let himself be charmed by this refined vision in white; she was wearing earrings with rows of golden acorns and he was a connoisseur of jewellery. There were not many women on site. None would match mine for style, taste and mischief-making. 'His name is Falco.'

'Falco is the man.' We gazed at him. 'From Rome,' he added lamely. Education claimed another demoralised victim. 'You have to come, man from Rome – and your woman.' Leering, he waved an arm, resplendent in checked wool, towards an entrance. We were amenable to the hospitality of strangers. We agreed to go.

It took us some time to find him indoors. There were quite a few rooms, furnished with imported goods and all ornamented strikingly. Blue-black dados had dashing floral designs, painted with a sure hand and dramatic brushwork; friezes were divided into elegant rectangles, set off either with white borderlines or with faux fluted pilasters; a perspective painter had created mock-cornices so well they looked like real mouldings bathed in an evening glow. Floors were restrained black and white, or had those cutwork stones in multicolours – a calm geometry of pale wine-juice red, aqua blue, dull white, shades of grey, and corn. In Italy and Gaul these are considered old-fashioned. If his interior designer was alert to trends, the King would undoubtedly change them.

'I am Verovolcus!' The client's representative had at least mastered that language lesson where he learned to say his name. 'You are Falco.' Yes, we had done that. I introduced Helena Justina, by her full name and with her most excellent father's details. She managed not to look surprised by this ludicrous formality.

I could see Verovolcus liked Helena. That's the trouble with foreign travel. You spend half your time trying to find edible food, and the rest fighting off men who profess extravagant love to your female companions. I'm amazed how many women believe outright lies from foreigners.

This could become embarrassing. I was primed to be a perfect diplomat in Britain – but if anybody laid a hand on Helena, I would sock him in the finer parts of his woad pattern.

I wondered what Maia was up to. She had elected to remain in town, along with Hyspale. Hyspale had just discovered there was nowhere in Noviomagus where she could go shopping. I was saving up the news that there were no decent emporia *anywhere* in Britain. Next time she really annoyed me, I would lightly drop word that she was now completely out of range of ribbons, perfumes and Egyptian glass beads. I was looking forward to seeing her reaction.

'You like our house?' Verovolcus had mastered some playboy's chat-ups. They always do.

'Yes, but you are having a new one built,' Helena responded with a regal smirk. 'The architect is to tell Falco all about it.'

'I will come with you!' Oh Jupiter, Best and Greatest, we were lumbered.

There was worse. Verovolcus led us to a room where a man whose wild hair had paled to grey some years earlier now sat in an upright magistrate's chair waiting for people with complaints to rush in and plead for his benevolent counsel. Since the Atrebates had not yet learned that among civilised people complaining was a social art, he looked bored. Easily sixty, the fellow had been play-acting a Roman of rank for generations. He had the proper way of lounging, all boredom and a nasty attitude: arms apart on the supports, knees apart too, but booted feet together on his footstool. This tribal chief had studied Roman authority at close quarters. He was wearing white, with purple borders, and probably had a swagger stick stashed away under his throne.

Now we were *seriously* lumbered. It was the Great King.

Verovolcus launched into rapid chatter in the local language. I wished I had brought Justinus; he might have made something of it, even though his knowledge of Celtic linguistics derived from German sources. I myself had been in the army, mostly in Britain, for about seven years, but legionaries representing Rome despised native argots and expected all the conquered world to learn Latin. Since most ethnic people were trying to sell us something, this was a fair attitude. Traders and prostitutes soon mastered the necessary verbals to cheat us in our own language. I had been a scout. I should have acquired a smattering of *their* tongue for safety reasons, but as a lad, I had thought that lying under a furze bush in the pouring rain was enough punishment for my system.

I caught the name of Pomponius. Verovolcus turned to us triumphantly. 'The Great King Togidubnus, friend of your Emperor, will come to hear about his house with you!'

'Jolly nice!' I had kept any ruefulness or satire out of my tone, which was just as well. Helena looked at me sharply, but it passed unnoticed. Verovolcus seemed thrilled, but had no time to answer my platitude.

'It would be rather fun to hear a progress report,' replied the Great King on his own account. In perfect Latin.

I thought this man must have something seriously expensive that he wants to sell to Rome. Then I remembered he had sold it already: a safe harbour and a warm welcome to Vespasian's men, thirty years ago.

'Verovolcus is assigned the task of monitoring events for me,' he then told us, smiling. 'Pomponius will not be expecting me.' That, we gathered, would enhance the fun. 'But please don't let me be a nuisance, Falco.'

Helena turned to me. 'King Togidubnus knows who you are,

75

Marcus Didius – though I did not hear Verovolcus telling him.'

'And you are the perceptive, sharp-witted Helena Justina,' the King interrupted. 'Your father is a man of distinction, friend of *my* old friend Vespasian and brother to the wife of the procurator Hilaris. My old friend Vespasian holds traditional views. Does he not yearn to see you married to some noble senator?'

'I don't believe he expects that to happen,' she replied calmly. She had flushed slightly. Helena had a true Roman matron's respect for her own privacy. To be the subject of imperial correspondence made her teeth set dangerously. The daughter of Camillus Verus was considering whether to give the Great King of the Britons a black eye.

Togidubnus surveyed her for a moment. He must have grasped the point. 'No,' he said. 'And having met you, with Marcus Didius, neither do I!'

'Thank you,' Helena answered lightly. The whole conversation had turned. I kept well out of it. The Great King responded by inclining his head, as if her implied rebuke was in fact some tremendous compliment.

Verovolcus shot me a complicitous glance, seeing that his own flirtation had been sidestepped. But I was used to Helena Justina making unexpected friends.

'To my new house!' cried the King happily, wrapping himself in a huge, gleaming toga as casually as if it were a bath-house robe. I had seen imperial legates with pedigrees back to Romulus struggle and need four toga-valets to help them with the folds.

Needless to say, I had not even unpacked my own formal woollen wear. It was quite possible that when I left Rome, I forgot to include it. I had to hope Togidubnus would overlook the slight. Did Romanisation courses for provincial kings include lectures on gracious manners? Putting your guests at ease. Ignoring crass behaviour from brutes inferior to yourself. That stuff my respectable mother dinned into me once – only I never listened.

When he skipped down from his daïs to join us, the King clasped my hand with a good Roman handshake. He did the same with Helena. Verovolcus, who must be more observant than he seemed, quickly followed suit – crushing my paw like a blood brother who had been drinking with me for the past twelve hours, then clinging on to Helena's long fingers with slightly less violence but an admiration that was equally embarrassing.

As we all made our way to see Pomponius, I was starting to see just why Togidubnus had made and stayed friends with Vespasian. They both came up from inferior social situations, but made the best of it by using talent and staying power. I had the glum feeling I would end up with a real sense of obligation to the King. I still believed his new palace was an over-scale extravagance. But, since the taxes of ordinary Romans had been allocated to pay for it – and since the money was certainly going into *someone*'s coffers – I may as well ensure the stylish home was built.

The King had taken over Helena. It reduced me to a cipher husband, trailing with Verovolcus. I could live with it. Helena was no cipher wife. When she wanted me, she would drop the pride of British nobility like an over-hot sardine.

Any woman was bound to be impressed by a fellow who was equipping his house with brand-new floor mosaics throughout. It beats being fobbed off with a new rag rug and the promise that you, her layabout head of household, will replaster the bedroom alcove yourself 'when you can get round to it' . . .

XIV

'YOU'RE LATE, Falco – I can't do you now . . .' In the midst of glaring at Helena, whom he had not expected, Pomponius tailed off. He had seen the King.

'I am *so* looking forward to hearing your current perspective on our project,' declared the royal client. The architect could only seethe. 'Just pretend I am not here,' offered Togidubnus graciously.

This would be difficult, since his portable throne, his entourage and his hairy servants plying him with trays of imported snacks in little shale dishes were now filling most of the plan room. Olives, in rich oil spiced with flecks of herb, had already been spilt on some elevation drawings.

Pomponius sent for a couple of architectural assistants. They were supposed to help with the presentation. That way at least, he ensured himself an admiring audience. Both were ten years younger than him, but were learning all their bad habits from his fine example. One was copying the project manager's hair slick; the other had bought his outsize scarab from a similar fake Alexandrian jeweller. They had less personality between them than a flyblown carrot.

These old hutments must be falling apart. They were more breezy than army tents. The plan room was heated with antique braziers. With so many people crammed in we were already sweating. That would soon dry out the skins on the architect's plans and make them crackle. A map-room librarian would be horrified by these air conditions. I felt ready to warp myself.

An extensive layout drawing had been hung up ready for us – well, ready to impress me. This showed a monstrous four-square complex with innumerable rooms, set around an enormous enclosed garden. It was edged by blue hatching where the sea lapped. Green areas indicated not only the huge main garden in the centre of the four wings, but another vast parkland on the south side running right down to the harbour.

'The new palace,' began Pomponius, addressing me directly as if he

78

could not be expected to concern himself with tribal kings or women, 'is to be the largest, most magnificent Roman development north of the Alps.'

Presumably the governor's headquarters in Londinium would be equally massive. To impress official dignitaries that would need to be glamorous, and to house the provincial administration it would be elaborate. Since I had not seen it, I kept quiet. Maybe my frugal colleague Frontinus had chosen to run Britain from a festival marquis.

Pomponius cleared his throat. He glared at me, thinking I was not paying attention. I smiled, with a flash of teeth, as if I thought he needed reassurance. That put him right off.

'Er – the main approach is from the Noviomagus road, bringing most traffic from the tribal capital and beyond. To greet them, my concept provides for a stunning exterior façade. The monumental east front is the first aspect presented to visitors; it will be dominated by a central entrance hall – externally this has two dramatic pedimented façades, each with six massive columns, twenty feet in height. Internally the spatial content is divided into smaller units such as arcades, first to provide lateral support –'

'The roof weighs a bit?' It sounded more facetious than I meant.

'Obviously. Second, design features will draw people forwards to establish a flow-through into the interior –'

'Grand!'

Pomponius thought I was being insulting. Perhaps I was. I grew up in overcrowded apartments, where the people flow-through was provided by Ma, wielding a broom on dawdlers' buttocks.

'Planned benefits include fine statuary and a dramatic marble-edged pool with a significant fountain feature,' the architect warbled. 'My intention is to dramatise the scale and the fine quality fittings without oppressing occupants, at the same time emphasising the sight-line through the hall to the formal gardens beyond. This is a superior concept – cultured patrician living for a discerning, high-class client.'

Togidubnus was munching an extremely juicy apple that took all his concentration, so the half-hearted flattery was lost.

'Also included in the east wing is a semi-public assembly hall. En suite private rooms, fitted out to a good standard and with their own closed-access courtyards, are designed with peace and relaxation in mind –'

'Won't they be rather noisy if they are located so near the main entrance?' asked Helena, rather too politely.

Pomponius stared at her. Arty types can manage tall girls with patrician accents and taste, but only as their own subjugated mistresses. He would have allowed her to hand round dainties at a soirée, but in any other context Helena Justina was a threat. 'These are guest rooms for lesser officials, on temporary assignments.'

'Oh Falco! I am looking forward to your next assignment in Noviomagus,' Helena cried archly. (There was no way I intended to come back.) Immediately she urged Pomponius on again: 'You mentioned the formal gardens?'

'The central court will combine visionary elegance with serene formality. A spectacular hedged walkway, forty feet in width, transports people to the audience chamber opposite. To the left and right, balanced harmonious parterres of extravagant size contribute grandeur tempered with the tranquillity of open space. Rather than stark lines, this main thoroughfare will be given a treatment of sculpted greenery, probably box: alternating topiary arcs and squares in grave dark foliage colourings – a reference to the best Mediterranean tradition.'

'Why,' I asked, 'is there a single tree marked up there?' A large specimen was marked in the north-west area of the formal lawns. It was in a rather strange position.

The architect flushed slightly. 'Indicative, only.'

'Have you a nasty drainage tank to hide?'

'The tree will relieve monotony!' put in the King. He sounded curt. He certainly understood his site layout. 'When I come out of the audience chamber and stand looking to my left, a mature tree will relieve the bleak horizontal lines of the north wing –'

'Bleak? I believe you will find,' Pomponius humphed, 'the elegant repetition –'

'There should be another tree balancing this one in the opposite quartile, to shield the south wing similarly.' Togidubnus interrupted coolly – but Pomponius was ignoring him.

'Urns,' he rattled on, 'will provide handsome talking points; fountains are being assembled to provide aural delight. All footpaths will be defined by triple hedges. Plantings are to be set within geometric sculpted beds, again with topiary surrounds. I have asked the landscape gardener to aim for sophisticated species –'

'What – no flowers?' Helena giggled.

'Oh I insist on colour!' snapped the King at Pomponius. Pomponius looked set to launch into a hot defence of textured leaf contrasts – then thought better of it. His gaze flickered to me. He was irritated that I had noticed the tension between the King and him.

'You may want to ask the landscape gardener to consult your own people about pests,' Helena suggested blithely to Togidubnus. She was either diffusing the bad atmosphere – or being mischievous. I knew which I thought.

'Pests!' intoned the King at his man, Verovolcus. He was really enjoying himself. 'Make a note of that!'

'Slugs and snails,' Helena elaborated to Pomponius. 'Rust. Insect damage –'

'Bird nuisance!' contributed the King, with an intelligent interest. Between them, Togidubnus and Helena were winding Pomponius into fits of frustration.

'So tell me more,' I interrupted: Falco, the voice of reason for once. 'Your monumental entrance to the east wing clearly starts a series of impressive effects?'

'A breath-taking promenade,' agreed Pomponius. 'A triple succession: awe-striking physical grandeur as one walks through the entrance salon; next, the surprising contrast of nature in the formal gardens – completely enclosed and private, yet created on a stupendous scale; then, my visionary design for the west wing. This is the climax of the experience. Twenty-seven rooms in exquisite taste will be fronted by a classic colonnade. At the centre is the audience chamber. It is made the more imposing by a high stylobate base –'

'Don't stint your stylobates,' I heard Helena muttering. Stylobates are stone block platforms giving height and dignity to colonnades and pediments. Pomponius was a man who seemed to place himself on an invisible stylobate. I cannot have been the only one who would have liked to shove him off it.

'The whole west wing is raised five feet above the level of the garden and other suites. A flight of steps against this platform fixes the eyeline on the massive pedimented front –'

'Have you chosen a statue to stand before the steps?' asked the King.

'I feel . . .' Pomponius did hesitate, though not as awkwardly as he might. 'A statue would detract from the clean lines I have planned.' Once again, the King looked annoyed. Presumably he had wanted a statue of himself – or at least of his imperial patron Vespasian.

Pomponius rushed on: 'Climbing the steps, gazing upwards, the visitor will be confronted with theatrical majesty. The royal audience chamber is to be apsidal, lined with benches in elegant contemporary woods. The floor will be created by my master mosaicist, supervising both construction and design in person. A stunning twenty-foot-wide semi-dome crowns the apse, with a vaulted ceiling, stuccoed, white ribs picked out in regal hues – crimson, Tyrian purple, richest blues. There, visitors will encounter the Great King of the Britons, enthroned in the manner of a divinity . . .'

I glanced at the Great King. His expression was inscrutable. Still, I reckoned he was game for it. Impressing folk with his power and wealth would be all in a day's work. If civilisation meant he had to pretend to be a god enthroned among the stars – rather than simply the most accurate spearman in his group of huts – then he was all for climbing up on his plinth and arranging constellations around himself as artistically as possible. Well, it beat squatting on a wobbly three-legged stool, with chickens pecking your boots.

Pomponius was still droning on. '. . . My perception of the four wings is that each should be linked in style to the others, yet distinct in conception. The strong west wing/formal garden/east wing axis forms the public area. The north and south wings will be more private – symmetrical ranges with discreet entrances to exquisite room suites, set around locked-in private courts. The north wing, especially, will contain celebratory dining facilities. The south wing is lined on two sides with colonnades, one offering views of the sea. The east wing, with its grand entrance and meeting hall, serves public functions, yet lies *behind* the visitor on his progress forward. Once he enters the interior elements, the great west wing is the heart of the complex with its audience chamber and administrative offices, so that is where I have placed the royal suites –'

'*No!*' This time the King had let out a roar. Pomponius stopped warbling abruptly.

There was a silence. Pomponius had finally hit big trouble. I glanced at Helena; we both watched with curiosity.

'Now we have gone over this before,' complained Pomponius, tight as a tick in a sheep's eye. 'It is essential to the unity of the concept –'

King Togidubnus tossed his apple core onto a dish. Age had not diminished his eyesight. His aim was perfect. 'I disagree.' His voice was cold. 'Unity may be achieved by employing common features of design. Structural details and themed decoration will tie in any disparate elements.' He was wielding the fancy abstract terms with an off-hand flourish – easily the architect's equal.

Helena was sitting extremely still. There was a thin murmur among the King's staff, then they subsided expectantly. Grinning, Verovolcus seemed half bursting with excitement. I reckoned all the Britons had known that Togidubnus had a mighty beef; they had been waiting for him to explode.

Pomponius had been aware of this sub-plot too. He already had the rigid air of one who knew his client spent too much spare time reading architectural manuals. 'Naturally there will be areas where we need to compromise.' Nobody who says that ever believes it.

It was soon apparent what had made the King so angry. 'Compromise? I, for my part, have conceded that my garden colonnade shall be ripped out, its fine rams' horns hacked off with bolsters, and its smashed capitals stacked up haphazardly for reuse as hardcore! I make this sacrifice for integrity of form in the new complex. *That* is as far as I will go.'

'Excuse me, but including the old house is a wasteful economy. Remedying the levels –'

'I can endure that.'

'The disruption would be intolerable – but my point,' argued Pomponius in a taut voice, 'is that the approved scheme envisages stripping the entire site for a clean new build.'

'*I* never approved that!' The King was dogged. Approval is always a problem when a project is to be paid for by the Roman Treasury yet constructed a thousand miles away for local occupation. Scores of liaison meetings routinely produce deadlock. Many a project founders on the drawing board. 'My current palace – which was an imperial gift to symbolise my alliance with Rome – will be incorporated into your design, please.'

The 'please' was simply terse punctuation. It marked the end of the King's speech, nothing more. The speech was meant as an order.

'Your Majesty may not appreciate the finer –'

'I am not a fool.'

Pomponius knew he had patronised his client. That did not stop him. 'Technical details are my sphere –'

'Not exclusively! I shall live here.'

'Of course!' It was already a hot quarrel. Pomponius tried wheedling. He ruined everything. 'I intend to convince Your Majesty –'

'No, you have failed to convince me. You must honour my wishes. I had an equitable relationship with Marcellinus, your predecessor. Over many years I would appreciate his creative skill, and Marcellinus in turn knew that his skill must be allied to my needs. Architectural drawings may look beautiful and be admired by critics – but to be good, they have to work in daily use. You, if I may say so, seem to be

83

planning only a monument to your own artistry. Perhaps you will achieve such a monument – but only if your vision is in harmony with mine!'

With a flick of his white toga, the Great King was on his feet. Gathering his entourage, he swept out of the plan room. Servants scampered in his wake as if well rehearsed. Verovolcus, who probably spent much useless effort trying to advance his master's views in project meetings, shot the architect a triumphant glare then strode after the King, clearly well satisfied.

I might have guessed what would happen next. As his two assistants (who had previously let him suffer unaided) now swarmed up to mutter their sympathy, Pomponius turned on me. 'Well, thank you, Falco,' he snarled with bitter sarcasm. 'We were in quite enough trouble before you caused all that!'

XV

HELENA AND I walked out into the air. I felt subdued. This client/project manager conflict was one of the problems I was supposed to clear up. It would not be easy.

Pomponius had rushed out ahead of us, supported by one of his junior architects. The other happened to leave later, while we were still getting our breath.

'I'm Falco. Sorry, you are . . . ?'

'Plancus.'

'That was a bitter little scene, Plancus.'

Troubled by the tension, he seemed relieved to be approached about it. He was the one with the flash scarab. It was pinned on a tunic he had worn too many times. Crumpled, yes; probably stained too. I preferred not to check. He had a thin, bristly face, with elongated arms and legs to match.

'So does this happen all the time?' I asked quietly.

It met with embarrassment. 'There are problems.'

'I was told the project is behind time and over budget. I assumed it was the old problem – the client kept changing his mind. But it looked today as though the Great King's mind is too firmly made up!'

'We explain the concept, but the client sends along his representative, who can barely communicate . . . We tell him why things must be done one way, he seems to agree that, then later there is a huge fight.'

'Verovolcus goes back and talks to the King, who sends him back to you to argue?' Helena suggested.

'It must be a diplomatic nightmare keeping things simple – I mean, cheap!' I grinned.

'Oh yes,' agreed Plancus weakly. He did not strike me as hot on cost control. In fact, he did not strike me as more than lukewarm on any subject. He was as thrilling as a flavoured custard that had been left on a shelf growing green fur on its skin. 'Togidubnus demands endless impossible luxuries,' he complained. That must be their clichéd excuse.

'What, like keeping his existing house?' I reproved the man.

'It's an emotional response.'

'Well, you can't allow that.'

I had been inside enough public buildings to know that few architects owned or could appreciate emotions. Nor do they understand tired feet or wheezy lungs. Nor the stress of noisy acoustics. Nor, in Britain, the need for heated rooms.

'I saw no hot-air specialist on your project team?'

'We don't have one.' Plancus was probably intelligent in some ways, but failed to apply his brain to wondering why I had asked. It ought to be a professional issue. He ought to see my point immediately.

'How long have you been out here?' I asked.

'About a month.'

'Take my word then, you need to mention it to Pomponius. If the King has to use naked fire braziers all winter, your unified concept with the fine sight-lines is likely to go up in grandiose flames.'

Helena and I walked slowly, hand in hand, across the spacious site. Seeing the plans had helped. Now I was finding my way around better; I could appreciate how the different ranges of rooms had been laid out. The neat footings ended feebly near the old house; this had been left as 'too difficult'. We found Magnus, the surveyor I met yesterday, pottering there. His *groma* was plunged in the ground, a long metal-tipped stave with four plumb bobs hung from two metal-cased wooden bars; it was used for measuring out straight lines and squares. While one of his assistants played with the *groma* for practice, he himself was using a more complicated gadget, a *diopter*. A sturdy post supported a revolving rod set in a circular table, marked out with detailed angles. The whole circle could be tilted from the horizontal using cogged wheels; Magnus was underneath, tinkering with the cogs and worm screws that set it. Some distance away, another assistant waited patiently beside a twenty-foot-high sighting rod with a sliding bar, ready to measure a slope.

The chief surveyor squinted up at us, then looked around longingly at the unbroken ground; he badly wanted to set out the last corner of the new palace, where the south and west wings would meet – and where the disputed 'old house' stood.

I told him about the scene we had witnessed between architect and client. Crawling out from his gadget, leaning away so as not to disturb the setting, he stood upright. He reckoned the animosity was normal, confirming what Plancus had told me. Pomponius had not dared to ban King Togidubnus from meetings, but he kept him at arm's length. Verovolcus came along instead and blustered, but he was a third party, with language problems. Pomponius took no notice of anything he said.

'Who was Marcellinus?' I enquired.

Magnus scowled. 'Architect for the old house. Worked here for years.'

'Know him?'

'Before my time.' I wondered if he had paused slightly. 'He was halfway through planning his own rebuild when Vespasian approved this complete redevelopment.' Magnus pointed out where areas of the site contained unfinished foundations for some vast buildings, not in the current design. 'The Marcellinus scheme stopped dead. I can't work out what his plans involved. But his foundations are hefty – a real menace to our own west wing. Not that we let a dirty great outcrop of unfinished masonry get in our way! Ours is just slapped on top . . .'

'Togidubnus seems to have been on good terms with Marcellinus. What happened to him? Dismissed? Died?'

'Just too old. He was retired. I think he went quietly. Between ourselves,' muttered Magnus, 'I've got him down as an evil old bastard.'

I laughed. 'He was an architect, Magnus. You would say that about any of them.'

'Don't be cynical!' quipped the surveyor – in a tone of voice that showed he shared my view.

'Did Marcellinus go quietly?'

'He's not entirely gone,' grumbled Magnus. 'He keeps niggling at the King about our plans.'

Helena had been gazing around. I introduced her. Magnus accepted her with much better grace than had Pomponius.

'Magnus, is it feasible to incorporate the old house in the way the King wishes?' she asked.

'If it is decided at the outset, it's perfectly possible – and will save money!' He was a problem-solver, who happily set about proving his point to us. 'You understand that we had a serious problem of levels here? The natural site slopes with a big gradient to the west – plus another tilt south towards the harbour. Streams feed into the harbour. In the past there have been drainage problems, never really solved. So, our new scheme raises the ground base in the lower-lying areas, hoping to rise above the damp.'

'The old house will then be left stranded too low?' I put in.

'Exactly.'

'But if the King accepts the disruption of having all his rooms infilled . . .'

'Well, he knows what a building site is like!' Magnus laughed. 'He enjoys change. Anyway, I sketched out a drawing myself to see if it's do-able. His garden courtyard would be sacrificed –'

'For schematic unity?' Helena murmured. She had listened well.

'Integrity of concept!' Magnus quipped back. 'Otherwise, Togi can keep pretty well the same room layout, with new floors – which he will *love* choosing – new ceilings, cornices, et cetera, and redecorated walls. Oh, and he preserves his bath house, handily at the end of his domestic corridor. With the Pomponius plan, Togi would have to live way across the site – traipsing around in a loincloth with his oil flask whenever he wants a scrape down.'

'Hardly regal,' said Helena.

'No fun during an October gale!' I shuddered. 'With an equinoctial wind howling in off the Gallic Strait, you could feel as if you were right among the breakers, shaking hands with Neptune. Who wants sand in his privates and sea spray messing up washed hair? So,' I asked lightly, 'is the bath house to be rebuilt at all?'

'Upgraded,' replied Magnus, perhaps a little shiftily.

'Oh! Pomponius is making a concession, then?'

Magnus was turning back to his *diopter*. He paused. 'Stuff Pomponius!' He glanced around, then told me in a low voice, 'We have no official funding for a bath house. Pomponius knows nothing about this. The King is organising the bath house refurbishments himself!'

I let out a breath.

'Have you been involved, Magnus?' Helena asked with cheerful innocence. She could ask brazen questions as if they just came to her coincidentally.

'The King asked me to walk the area with him,' Magnus admitted.

'You could hardly refuse!' Helena sympathised. 'I have a particular interest,' she continued. 'I just had a terrible time with some bath builders in Rome.'

'Gloccus and Cotta,' I put in, sounding bitter. 'Notorious!' Magnus showed no reaction.

'Togi is lucky to have your advice,' Helena flattered him.

'I may have made one or two technical suggestions,' reported the surveyor in a neutral tone. 'If anyone accuses me of drawing up his specification on my off day, I'll deny everything! So will the King,' he added firmly. 'He's a game, determined sod.'

'I presume he's paying. What contractors is he using?' I ventured.

'Oh don't ask me, Falco. I don't get involved with bloody labour, not even for a nice old king.'

'The wild garden is coming along, if you like greenery,' Magnus called after us, guessing well. Needing to clear our heads of nonsense, we both leapt at the invitation.

It was a peaceful haven. Well, it had a sea view as we had been promised – though the shore was taken up with a jetty where a ship was unloading stone very noisily.

A sea inlet ran through the area. Water features must be popular. The wild garden also had a significant pond site; mucking out of a disgusting kind was in hand. Herons from the landward and gulls from the seaward sides stood around, hoping for excavated fish among the muddy silt. Apart from the deep channel that was being created out in the harbour, the beaches were low along this coastal reach, and riddled with water courses and creeks. It made everywhere brackish and damp.

Once again, we were on an artificial terrace, three hundred feet of it, providing eventual occupants of the south wing with an informal vista, against which lapped the waves – now controlled by a mole and gates lest Oceanus should behave *too* naturally. Behind the westward range of the palace a new domestic-services complex was already going up, including an obvious bakehouse and a monster grinding stone. Once the palace itself rose to its full height, those buildings would be hidden; the observer would only see artificial parkland sloping away to the sea and well-tamed woods beyond the inlet. The concept was strongly reminiscent of the 'urban countryside' devised by Nero when he filled the whole Forum with trees, lakes and wild animal parks, for his extravagant Golden House. The effect here, in rural Britain, was somewhat more acceptable.

Gardeners were toiling away. Since this was to be a 'natural' landscape, it required elaborate planning and constant hard work to keep it looking wild. It also had to remain accessible to those who wished to stroll here while lost in contemplation. Random specimen shrubs struggled listlessly against the salt and surf. Ground-cover plants rampaged healthily across the paths; sea–holly scratched our ankles. Grottos were being cemented; they would be delightful once shrouded in violets and ferns. But their fight against sea, and marsh, and enduring bad weather, had given the workers an air of desperate fatality. They walked in the slow way of men who did a great deal of leaning against the wind.

To demand of these poor locals a 'natural' plot was a grim trick. They must now have gardened for Togidubnus for several decades. They knew too well that nature would forge its own way past fenced boundaries, slithering over walls, sprouting with giant weed fronds against their tender Mediterranean specimens, gobbling up precious slips and undermining exotic roots. It was all too wet and cold, and made us long for Italy.

We met the landscape specialist I had glimpsed at the project meeting. He confirmed the craziness.

'It won't be too bad in the formal courtyards. I'll plant them out three times a year with colour; prune the permanents in spring and autumn; then just turn over the lot to be mowed, hoed and trimmed. No need to touch it otherwise.'

He shouted instructions to men who were hoisting a heavy rope about, using its sluggish bends to devise an attractive layout for a winding path.

'But this is hard work.' Helena waved an arm, then chilled, she pulled her stole closer around her, tucking back loose strands of hair that had been freed by the wind.

'Misery, frankly.' He was a bowed, brown, shaven-headed man, whose apparent gloom hid real enthusiasm. 'We don't get to stand at ease with the sun on our faces, like in Corinth or New Carthage – we're battering back nature wherever it raises its head. Scything it down, slashing it through, scratching it with hooks and flattening it with spades as it scuttles across the soil. The soil is horrible, of course,' he added with a grin.

I was intrigued by his geographical references. 'What's your name, and where are you from?'

'I'm Timagenes. Learned my stuff on an imperial estate near Baiae.'

'You're not just a trowel-wielder,' I commented.

'Certainly not! I am in charge of the people who supervise the trowel-wielders' gang leaders.' He was half mocking his status – yet it mattered. 'I can spot a slug – but basically, I'm the man who devises the glamorous effects.'

'And they will be glorious,' Helena complimented him.

'Pomponius has been describing your scheme for us.'

'Pomponius is a deluded snot,' replied Timagenes helpfully. 'He's all set on ruining my creative vision – but I'll get him!'

There seemed to be no hard malice in his words, yet for him to be so open was instructive.

'Another feud?' I enquired mildly.

'Not at all.' Timagenes sounded quite comfortable. 'I hate him. I hate his liver, lungs and lights.'

'And hope he has no luck with girls?' I was remembering Lupus, the overseer, describing angry curses laid at shrines by his labourers.

'That would be too cruel.' Timagenes smiled. 'Actually, there's no girl around here who would look at him. Girls are not stupid,' he opined with a polite salute to Helena. 'We all suspect he prefers boys – but the boys in Noviomagus have better taste too.'

'What has Pomponius done to upset you?' Helena asked.

'Far too obscene to mention!' Timagenes bent down and gripped a small blue flower. 'A periwinkle. These do well in Britain. They peg their dark mats into dank spidery places, with strong glossy leaves that you hardly notice, until suddenly at the end of April they push up their sturdy blue stars. Now that's gardening out here. The startling discovery of some bright, defiant thing –'

The poetic foliage-forager pulled at the blossom, yanking so violently he presented Helena with a stringy rope two feet or more in length. There were very few flowers, and white roots dangled in unpleasant clumps. She took the offering gingerly.

'So what did Pomponius do to you?' I insisted laconically.

Ignoring the question, Timagenes only turned up his face to sniff the air, then answered, 'Summer is here. Smell it on the wind! Now we're in real trouble . . .'

Whether he meant horticulturally or in some wider sense, we could not tell.

XVI

As helena and I later made our way back to the Noviomagus road and our transport, we came across a slow wagon trailing up to the site.

'Stop laughing, Marcus!' Luckily, there was nobody around to spy on our meeting. It would have been rude of me to guffaw at strangers the way I did now. But one of this mournful party was only disguised as a stranger. His grumpy scowl was all too familiar.

The scene was bright. Summer had come, as Timagenes observed. A fiercely cold morning with a lacerating wind had now developed into an afternoon of incredible mildness. The sun broke through the racing clouds as if it had never been away. It gave notice that even this far north, without any noticeable transition, there would be extra hours of light lengthening both ends of the day.

This spirit of renewal was wasted on the miserable young man we had met. 'Don't even speak to me, Falco!'

'Hail, Sextius!' I greeted his companion instead. 'I trust our dear Aulus is proving useful to you. He has some truculence, but we think well of him generally.'

The man who sold moving statues hopped down to gossip. Helena's brother turned away with even greater bitterness. Still in his role as an assistant, he began foddering a lanky horse who pulled the cart of stoneware samples. Helena tried to kiss his cheek in sisterly affection; he shook her off angrily. Since we had kept all his luggage, he was wearing the same tunic as when we left him in Gaul. Its white wool had acquired a dark, greasy patina which some ruffians would take years to apply to their working gear. He looked cold and glum.

'Is that a suntan or are you utterly filthy?'

'Oh don't worry about me, Falco.'

'I don't, lad, I don't. You are a repository of republican virtue. Nobility, courage, steadfastness. Let's face it, you're the kind of virtuous cur who really likes suffering –'

He kicked the wheel of the cart. It lurched, causing a sound of crashing stone.

'Oi!' protested Sextius, horrified.

As the statue factor clambered up to investigate, Aulus turned to me grimly. 'This had better be worth it! I can't tell you what a time I've had . . .' He did lower his voice. If he offended Sextius, Sextius could easily shed him, which would not help me. 'I'm bruised and bashed, and sick to the teeth of hearing about wonderful Heron of Alexandria's inventions. Now we have to slog here, find some completely uninterested buyer, then try to fib him into believing he needs a set of dancing nymphs worked by hot air, whose costumes fall off –'

'Whoa!' I stopped him, grinning. 'I had a crazy great-uncle who adored mechanical toys. This is a new variation on an old favourite. When did the famous dancing nymphs shed their dresses?'

'A modern twist, Falco.' Aelianus was displaying a prim streak. Hating popular taste, though he clearly understood it, he growled, 'We give our buyers what they want. The more pornographic the better.'

'Don't tell me *you* devised the striptease?' I chortled admiringly. 'Great Jupiter, you're really taking to this. My uncle Scaro would love you, boy! Next thing you'll have one of Philon of Tyre's dip-in-me-all-ways inkwells.' Scaro had told me enough about Greek inventors to see me through this banter.

'Gimbals!' snarled Aulus. Thus proving that he had heard all about Philon's magic octagon, the executive toy every scribe wants as his next Saturnalia present. 'Don't interrupt when I'm raving,' Aulus carried on. 'I'm sick of this. Why me? Why not my devious brother?'

'Justinus is younger than you and he's delicate,' Helena reproved. 'Anyway, I promised dear little Claudia that I would look after him.'

'Quintus is quite hardy – and no one promised Claudia anything; she thought her darling bridegroom would be going home from Ostia. I always get the short measure. I already know I'll be eating rancid broth, and sleeping at the side of the cart, under an awning alongside the horse.'

'There are canabae,' I told him, with a grain of pity.

Sextius overheard me as he jumped down again beside us. 'That's for me!' he cried. 'Lucky I've got you, lad. I'm not taking this stuff anywhere it might get pinched, young Aulus. You'll have to stop with the cart and mind the goods. I'm going to find myself a drink and maybe a tasty wench tonight.'

Aelianus was about to spit with frustration. Then we all pulled up. A voice which at least Helena and I recognised was calling my name excitedly. 'Man from Rome!'

We turned to greet him as one, like a set of well-oiled but slightly guilty automata. 'Verovolcus! Does your sophisticated king like moving statues?'

'Greek athletes he likes, Falco.'

'I think that means classical art, not oily boyfriends,' I explained to Sextius. 'I don't know what's on offer, Verovolcus. I just met these interesting salesmen for the first time. They are trying to find out the procedure for getting an appointment to show off their wares —'

'They have to see Plancus.'

'The assistant architect? But he's an idiot,' I wheedled.

'Plancus — and Strephon who works with him,' Verovolcus repeated dismissively. He seemed like a native comedian, yet the response was so brisk I looked twice at him. He knew how to rebuff foot-in-the-door men. Suddenly I could visualise him taking a hard line in other situations.

'Look, we know you must get canvassers all the time —' Aelianus began.

'If Plancus and Strephon let them see Pomponius — then *he* turns them down!' roared the King's representative. It was a huge joke.

'Oh go on — how about a bird that guards her fledglings from a snake!' wheedled Sextius.

'With wings that really make her fly up and hover,' added his assistant wearily. Aelianus must have suffered endless rehearsals somewhere. 'In the direct tradition of the marvellous technician Csetiphon —'

'*Ctesiphon!*' hissed Sextius.

'Of Tyre—'

'Of *Alexandria*!' Alexandria must be awash with eccentrics building gadgets.

'We can show you the latest in talking statues — worked by a speaking tube. I operate the display model,' Aelianus explained, 'but I can easily train a slave of yours in the technique. Then we offer a mechanism for opening your palace doors as if by an invisible hand — you would need to dig a pit for the water tank, but I see you have labourers on site here and it's simplicity to use once you're set up properly. Consider a self-regulating oil-lamp wick —'

Sextius dug him in the ribs for rushing the script.

'See Plancus — see Strephon.' Verovolcus waved them aside, so he could address Helena and me with his errand. 'Man from Rome! My king invites you and your lady to the old house. It has many rooms, all beautiful. You can stay with us.'

'But we are travelling with two very small children, their nurse and my sister-in-law . . .' Helena demurred shyly.

'More women!' Verovolcus was thrilled.

'I cannot allow myself to socialise, I'm afraid,' I said warily.

'No, no. My king says you must be left to do your important work.'

Helena and I consulted quickly.

'Yes?'

'Yes!'

My girl and I don't muck about.

The idea had obvious attractions. Flavius Hilaris was lending us a decent house in Noviomagus, but nothing like a palace. I would see more of Helena if she were living with me on site than if I had to leave her in the town while I worked out here. Assuming she wanted it, she would see more of me.

'Hmm.' She made a show of reconsidering the practical disadvantages. 'I'll have to stop the little ones tumbling into deep trenches while you have fun solving the project problems.'

'Organise however you like, fruit. You can audit the project, and I'll play with the infants, if you like.'

So while Aelianus seethed in silence, thinking of his outdoor lodging in the rain and cold, his sister and I made our arrangements to live in luxury with the King.

XVII

WHILE CAMILLUS AELIANUS was being toughened up on the open road, his little brother had been enjoying life. I was keeping Justinus under wraps in Noviomagus, in case I found a role for him where he must look unconnected with me. He was finding life dull at the Procurator's town house.

'I'm bored, Falco.'

'Tell yourself it could be worse. Aulus can't have washed for a week. He has a filthy horse as a pillow, while in his dreams he tries to puzzle out how to fix a drive-wheel up an iron dove's arse. Want to swap?'

'He gets all the pleasure!' Justinus whined satirically.

My sister sniggered. I was glad to see Maia cheer up, if only briefly. She continued to mourn the absence of her children, and to resent all of us. I had not warned her yet that the King's man Verovolcus was just looking for a sophisticated Roman widow on whom he could practice Latin.

I sent Justinus out to find somebody who would hire us a luggage cart. He looked hopeful. 'So I'm coming with you to this palace?'

'No.'

'Are you staying in town?' he then asked Maia. They seemed to be getting on well.

'She comes with us!' I snapped. The idea that Helena's brother might start mooning over my sister – and that she might allow it – filled me with irritation.

While Helena fed our screaming baby in private and our eldest hurled her toys about, I had told Hyspale to start repacking. 'But I have only just *un*packed everything!' she wailed.

I gazed at her. She was a small chubby woman, who thought herself attractive. Which she was, if you liked eyebrows plucked so heavily they were little more than snail trails on her white-leaded face. Where my idea of beauty involved at least a hint of responsiveness, hers stopped short of intelligence. Talking to her was as monotonous as threading a mile-long string of identical beads. She was a self-centred, snobbish little property. If she had been good with our children I might have forgiven her.

She could have been good with children. We would never know. Julia and Favonia failed to arouse her interest.

I folded my arms. I was still staring at the freedwoman. This dough-faced treasure had been given to us by Helena's mother. Julia Justa was an astute, efficient woman; had she wanted to pass on a household trial to us? She knew Helena and I would tackle anything.

Helena normally dealt with Hyspale because of the family connection. I tended to hold back – but had we been in Rome, I would be sending Hyspale straight home to the Camilli without apology. Broaching that delicate issue must wait. Best not even discuss it now. I was tough – yet not so harsh that I could ditch a pampered unmarried female in the wilds of a brutal new province. Still, my grim face should be telling her: the contract for her services had an end date.

Hyspale failed to take my point. I was a working informer. She was the favoured freedwoman of a senatorial family. Equestrian status and an imperial commission would never be enough to impress her.

'Stuff everything back in the bags,' I said quietly.

'Oh Marcus Didius, I can't face all that again straight away –'

My jaw set off-line. My daughter Julia, more sensitive to atmosphere than the freedwoman, looked up at me anxiously then threw back her little curly head and started crying loudly. I waited for Hyspale to comfort the child. It did not occur to her.

With a swift glance at me, Maia scooped up Julia and carried her off elsewhere. On the whole, Maia was refusing to involve herself with my children on this trip, as a punishment for being wrenched away from her own. She pretended that mine could scream themselves unconscious and all I could expect from her was a complaint about the racket. But when she was on her own with them, she let herself be the perfect aunt.

Hyspale enraged her. Maia, leaving, ordered her angrily: 'Do what you are told, you half-hearted, slapdash scut!'

Perfect. It was the first time Maia and I had shared an opinion since we left Rome.

Justinus arranged our transport, then returned to the house and hung about looking dissatisfied again.

'You're bored. That's good,' I said.

'Oh thanks.'

'I want you *really* bored.'

'I hear and obey, Caesar!'

'Try making it more obvious.' He thought the remark was sarcastic. 'I have a job for you. Don't mention Helena Justina; don't mention me. If you meet Aulus or his companion Sextius you can speak to them but don't show that Aulus is your brother. Otherwise, you can play this in character. You're the bored nephew of an official, trapped in Noviomagus Regnensis when you'd rather be out hunting. In fact, you want to be anywhere except where you've been dumped. But you have no horses, no slaves and very little money.'

'I can certainly act that.'

'You're on your own in a dead-end British town, looking for some harmless thrills.'

'With no money?' Justinus jibed.

'It won't get stolen off you that way.'

'The thrills in Noviomagus Regnensis had best come *very* cheap.'

'You can't afford their sleazy women, that's for sure. So I can face your beloved Claudia with a clear conscience.'

He made no comment on his beloved Claudia. 'So what am I after, Marcus?'

'Find out what's here. I heard they have the usual canabae – bound to be dire, but unlike your brother you can at least come home to a clean bed. Watch yourself. They use knives.'

He gulped. Justinus had plenty of bravery, though he rationed it. On his own, he would never venture into bad situations. I had been out with him in Germany, in his patch as a tribune in the First Adiutrix legion; he had stuck to the approved military drinking dens, which he left discreetly when the gamblers and guzzlers started duffing people up. He knew how to cope in worse places too; I had taken him to a few of those. 'Am I looking for Gloccus and Cotta?'

'We all are, all the time. In between, I want to discover the story on a dead Gaul called Dubnus. He was stabbed in a drunken fight recently. And look out for people going out the back of bars to buy pinched materials from the building site. Or bent subcontractors who might be offering stolen goods to the site managers. I also want to identify any disaffected workmen.'

'You know such people may exist?'

'Apart from Dubnus, it's guesswork. Mind you, I've seen the amicable atmosphere on site! Most of them dislike each other, and they all loathe the project manager. And I was briefed in Rome that the scheme is rife with corrupt practices.'

Justinus bit his thumb. He was probably excited at his task. Cocky about it, even. But those deep brown eyes, whose warm promise had lured Claudia Rufina from Aelianus almost without either brother noticing what was on her mind, were now pondering how to approach this. He would be planning his wardrobe and rehearsing his script as a disaffected young aristocrat far from home. He was weighing risks too. Wondering whether he dared take a weapon – and if so, where to hide it. He realised that once he wandered into the local canabae on a gloomy British evening, there would be no simple escape route and no handy officials he could call upon for help.

As I sat alone with him now – especially without his bickering brother – I was remembering how secure I always felt when I worked with Justinus. He had excellent qualities. Quiet good sense, for one thing.

He needed that. What I had just asked of him was no idle game. Time was, if anyone had to infiltrate the dark hovels of a native cantonment, there would be no option: I would go myself. Sending a lad in my place would never have occurred to me.

Perhaps he could see my thoughts. 'I will take care.'

'If in doubt, retreat.'

'That's your motto, is it?' A smile flashed easily.

There was one good reason for sending him instead of me. I was middle-aged nowadays, with the air of a well-married man. Justinus was about twenty-four; he carried his wedded status lightly. He might not think of himself as handsome, but he was tall, dark, slim and very slightly self-deprecating. He struck strangers as easy-going; women found him sensitive. He could talk himself into anyone's confidence. There would be naïve teenage barmaids queuing up to talk to him. I knew, and I was certain he remembered, that the golden-haired women of the northern world would readily let themselves be persuaded that this grave young Roman was wonderful.

How my conscience would square *that* next time I saw his Claudia (a shy brunette, incidentally) could be dealt with in due course.

Much more difficult was how I would handle Helena, if anything should happen to her favourite brother.

XVIII

WHEN I STUCK my head around the door of his site hut, the mosaicist looked up from his steaming mug of *mulsum* and immediately rapped out, 'Sorry. We're not taking anybody on.' He must think I wanted work.

He was a white-haired man with a trimmed white beard and face whiskers, who had been talking quietly to a younger fellow. Both wore similar warmly layered tunics, belted in and with long sleeves; presumably, they could grow shivery as they spent hours crouched at their meticulous work.

'I'm not looking for employment. I have enough intricate puzzles of my own.'

The chief mosaicist, who had seen me earlier at the site meeting, started to remember me. He and his assistant were each leaning their elbows on a table, holding hot mugs between their hands. The same look of detached wariness occupied both faces. It seemed to be routine, not caused by me especially.

'Falco,' I explained myself to the assistant, inviting myself in. 'Agent from Rome. Troublemaker, obviously!' Nobody laughed.

I found a place on the opposite bench. Between us lay sketches of Greek keys and elaborate knots. I could smell the low-grade mulled wine, its vinegar base mildly spiced with aromatics; none was offered to me. The two men were waiting for me to take the initiative. It was like facing a pair of wall plaques.

We were in a fenced-off area of site offices, outside the main plot, in the north-west corner near the new service buildings. Today I was tackling décor. The mosaicists neatly inhabited one of a double set of temporary hutments, the other of which was the chaotic province of the fresco painters. Here they could all work on drawings, store materials, try out samples and – while they waited for the builders to give them rooms to decorate – they could sup beverages and think about life. Or whatever interior designers fill their brains with when the rest of us would be forgetting work and dreaming of home makeovers.

In the other hut, the painters had been having a loud argument as I passed. I might have barged in, hoping this was evidence of problems on the site, but I could hear it was all about chariot racing. I left the raucous painters for later. I was feeling limp, after the effort of moving my family here at short notice yesterday. Halfway through unpacking last night, Verovolcus had dropped in on us; he was aiming to inspect my women but they knew how to vanish and leave me to entertain him. Now I was nursing a headache, just from weariness. Well, that was my story.

Inside here, the mosaicists' quiet refuge, all the wall space was hung with drawings, some overlapping haphazardly. Most were mosaic designs in black and white. Some showed complete room layouts with their interwoven borders and tiled entrance mats. Some were small trial motifs. They went from the simplicity of plain corridors with straight-line double edgings, to numerous geometric patterns composed of repeated squares, cubes, stars and diamonds, often forming boxes within boxes. It looked simple, but there were elaborate crenellations, interlinked ladders and latticework such as I had never seen before. The profusion of choice argued huge talent and imagination.

The plan was for every room in the palace to be different, although there would be an overall style. Two large floor designs stood out as special, prominently nailed up in clear wall space. Among the few in colour, a preliminary mock-up had a fabulous complex guilloche of intertwining threads, which formed a centre roundel. That was currently blank. No doubt some handsome medallion was planned – with the King's choice of mythological subject still to be supplied. Within the twined border ran a ring of rich, autumn-tinted foliage, eight-petalled rosettes and elegant tendrils of leaf predominantly in browns and golds. Outside, the corners were infilled with alternate vases and, for some reason, fish.

'North wing,' said the chief mosaicist. Bleating so expressively almost finished him. He did not explain the marine life. I was left to theorise that it was to decorate a room for fish suppers.

The other grand design was fully worked out. This was black and white, a stunning carpet of dramatic squares and crosses, some of its patterns devised from arrowheads, compass rosettes and fleurs-de-lys. The images had been put together so the effect was three-dimensional, but I realised that irregularities made the patterns seem to shift. As I moved position, the perspective changed elusively.

'His "flickering floor", said the assistant proudly.

'North wing,' grunted the chief mosaicist again. Well, skilled repetition was his art.

'People will love it,' I flattered them. 'If you run out of work here, you can come to my house!' Being slow men, whose lives ran at the restrained pace of their work, they did not quip back the obvious retort. I said it for them: 'I don't suppose I can afford you.'

Nothing gave.

I tried again: 'Not a lot for you to do around here at present.'

'We'll be ready when they are.' The chief spoke dourly.

'I can see you're a cut above the average. This client won't be fobbed off with apprentice work and a few preformed panels, cut in at the last moment.' Again, he did not deign to comment.

'Your most important activity takes place before you're even on site,' I mused. 'Creating the design. Choosing the stones – I assume it's to be mostly stone here, none of those glass fragments or sparkly gold and silver particles?'

He shook his head. 'I like stone.'

'Me too. Solid. Cut well, there will be plenty of light reflected back. You can achieve a gleam without gaudiness. Do you make the tesserae yourself?'

'When I have to.'

'Done it in your time?'

'I use a team now.'

'Your own? You trained them?'

'Only way to get good colour matches and consistent sizing.'

'Do you lay your own screeds?'

He scoffed. 'Not any more! Those days are behind us.'

He had put down his beaker. His hands dipped automatically into the baskets of tesserae that littered his table, running the matt miniature tiles through his fingers like embroidery beads. He didn't know he was doing it. Some of these samples were minute, at least ten to the inch. Setting them would take for ever. He had a trial block in front of him, with a band of tight interwoven border in four colours – white, black, red and yellow – executed exquisitely.

'Audience chamber.'

This was a fellow who saved himself. He let time pass by calmly; he would live long – yet his joints would go, despite the use of padded kneelers, and his eyes must be doomed.

The younger man must be his son. He had the same body weight, face shape and manner. These were archetypal craftsmen. They passed their skills from generation to generation, developing their art to suit the times. Their world had a tight circle. Theirs was solitary work. Limited by a man's private concentration, constrained by the reach of his arm.

These were workers who, in the course of their daily life, rarely looked up at what was going on nearby. Apparently they lacked curiosity. They had an air of ancient, honest simplicity. But I already knew from my study of this oversized building scheme, the mosaic workers were a bugbear. They wasted time, kept no proper records of supplies and overcharged the Treasury more relentlessly than any other trade. The chief knew I was on to it. He defied me silently.

I, too, examined a bunch of black stones. I let them clatter slowly back into their basket. 'Everyone else I have interviewed so far told me who they hate. So who annoys you?'

'We keep to ourselves.'

'You come along at the end of the job, the last finishing trade – and you know nobody?'

'Nor want to,' he said complacently.

Loud guffaws sounded through the thin walls from the volatile fresco painters. I was starting to think they would be more fun. 'How do you get on with them next door?'

'We work it out.'

'Tell me – when a room has an elaborate floor, something like your "flicker" design, then it needs quiet walls. You want people to admire it without distraction. And vice versa: when there is flamboyant painting – or the occupants plan on using a lot of furniture – the floor needs to be restrained, in the background. So who chooses the primary design concept each time?'

'The architect. And the client, I suppose.'

'You get on with Pomponius?'

'Well enough.' If Pomponius had kicked him in the privates and stolen his lunch-basket, this buttonmouth would never get excited about it to me.

'When they pick a style, do you have any input?'

'I show them layouts. They choose one, or a general idea.'

'And is there conflict?'

'No,' he lied.

If he completed his floors to the fine standard in his artwork, he was a high achiever. That did not alter the fact, this man was as surly as they come.

'Have you come across anyone called Gloccus or Cotta?'

He thought about it, taking his time. 'Sounds familiar . . .' He shook his head, however. 'No.'

'What line are they in?' enquired the son. The father glared, as if it were a rash question.

'Bath-house construction.' Pa's wonkily tiled Neptune had nothing in common with the cool sophistication that had been ordered up for the palace. 'They do lay floors – sub-contracted – but nothing of your quality.'

Reluctant to say that the last time I stood on a new floor mosaic, I had put a pick through it and then my father squelched his tool into a corpse, I ended the interview. It had hardly advanced my knowledge. Still, I had formed some thoughts about how I would like my dining room at home relaid.

One day. One day when I was really rich.

XIX

W HEN I CAME out from seeing the floorers, the fresco painters'
hut next door now lay silent. I looked in.

It was the same kind of chaos, though more crowded since their
best friend was a trestle. It had been given a home where the table
would have been if these lads had been proud housekeepers. Instead,
they ate squatting on the floor (I could tell from the mess) and had
upended the table against a window, to give them more access to wall
space. They wanted lots and lots of free area to cover with their sheer
brilliant brushwork.

The last painters I had dealings with were a mad crowd of crooked,
aimless semi-criminals from a winebar called the Virgin; they wanted
to bring down the government but had no money for bribes and no
charismatic charm to fool the plebs. Most of the time they could
hardly remember their own way home. They were connected with
my father. Enough said.

These loud characters here were probably layabouts too. All
gambling, drink, and high ideals about betting systems. What they
possessed in abundance was talent. All over their hut were fantastic
examples of mock-marble scumbling. Dainty purple flecks on red,
with trickles of white. Wandering orange streaks. Two shades of
grey, sponged in layers. A blank square patch of wall was satirically
labelled 'LAPIS BLUE HERE', presumably because the jewelled paint
was too expensive to waste in experiments. All other surfaces were
daubed. Every time they came in for a break and a barney and a bite
to eat, they must flick new paint around just for the joy of seeing
different colours and effects. When they were feeling even more
obsessive, they produced elaborate bands of wood-graining so
perfect it seemed a tragedy that this crude hut with their experiments
would one day be pulled down and burned.

There were paint pots everywhere, mostly with great wet glops
sliding down them. Paint rings stained the floor. I kept well outside.

'Anyone home?'

No reply. I did feel saddened.

XX

As I left the site huts, my heel slipped in a barrow rut. I landed flat out. Wet mud attached itself down the full length of my tunic. I had badly jarred my spine. When I stood up again, cursing, pain shot all up my back and into my head, to score a direct hit on a grumbling tooth that I was trying to ignore. I would be walking stiffly for days.

I planted my feet apart, getting my breath back. This part of the palace grounds was in general use at present. The official hutments were fairly smart and arranged in a regular pattern. Scattered tents belonging to hangers-on and hobos had been pitched in an untidier camp. Smoke wreathed from untended cooking fires. The smell of dank leaves harboured duskier odours that I chose not to identify.

Pyramids of enormous sawn logs, mighty oak trunks from some nearby forest, had been piled at the track-side. In other rows, square stacks of bricks and roof-tiles waited, layered with protective straw. Somewhere not far off, I could smell caustic smoke, probably lime being burned off for mortar. Here, heavy delivery carts, many still with their contents, were parked in a rough line, their oxen and mules unhitched and hobbled. If there was supposed to be a watchman, he had gone off for a pee in the woods.

One of the carts belonged to Sextius. I limped over to it. I found Aelianus, looking heavily unshaven and distinctly grey. He was curled up awkwardly, in a cramped space in the back of the cart, fast asleep. The senator would approve of his son's endurance – though Julia Justa, who favoured her truculent middle child, would produce a more tart response.

Seeing a rough hide cover, I manhandled it free and gently laid it over him. I was careful. Aulus did not wake.

I leaned for a moment on the cart wheel, rubbing my sore back. Then I heard noises. Instinctively, I felt guilty lurking there alone. It made me cautious how I emerged into public view.

I must have crept like a mouse sneaking out from a skirting. A man who was atop a nearby wagon failed to see me at first. A flash of his extremely white tunic caught my eye. I had a good view of him. He was dragging up old sacks that covered the cart contents and peering underneath. He could have been the owner searching for something – or a thief. He looked furtive, not legitimate.

In fact I knew him. It was Magnus, the surveyor. I was so surprised to find him leaping about these transports on his own, I must have moved abruptly. He glimpsed me and tried to change position. Then he fell off.

Wincing myself, I hopped over there as fast as possible. He lay on the ground, but was making enough noise to prove that parts of him were undamaged. Obscenities came thick and vivid.

'Stuff you, Falco! What a start you gave me –' I helped drag him to his feet. He roared and shifted to and fro, pretending he had to rejig his limbs in their joint sockets. His fall must have been so unexpected he had stayed limp and that saved him. Basically, he was unhurt.

He had noticed my own filthy tunic, so I said, 'Now there's two of us stiffening up like planks – I took a tumble myself a minute ago. What were you up to, Magnus?'

'Checking a marble consignment,' he breezed off-handedly. 'And you?' Considering *he* had been behaving oddly, he was looking at me hard.

'I've been trying to squeeze more than two words at a time out of the mosaicist.'

'Philocles? Oh, he's all gab!' Magnus laughed.

'Right. *He* didn't even tell me he was called Philocles. What about the other – his son, is it?'

'Philocles Junior.'

'Surprise!' Why waste imagination thinking up a different name?

We had started to walk slowly towards the main site. Magnus had been battered by a far worse shock than me, but he was recovering. He must be in general good shape. Refusing to be put off, he insisted, 'Going back to your office by the scenic route?'

I reflected wryly that he sounded like me, harassing some suspect.

There was no need to connect myself to Aelianus, so I told Magnus how the previous day I had met the man with moving statues to sell; I played up Great-Uncle Scaro's interest in automata and just said I was curious. 'The fellow isn't there. Must be making his pitch to Plancus and Strephon.'

'Good luck to him.' Magnus grinned. 'Yes, I found his cart myself.'

Now I did have to check. 'And the snoring assistant?' I felt unease at someone else inspecting Aelianus without his knowledge. 'Looks a rough character!'

'Oh I don't think so, Falco,' replied Magnus demurely. 'Rather odd, I thought – did you not notice? He was wearing a very good quality tunic and has manicured hands.'

'Oh dear!' I had been right to worry. I tried to pass it off. 'One of the playthings they hawk about, is he? Maybe Sextius uses him to model moving parts.'

Somehow I managed to manoeuvre the conversation onto delusional statuary. We ended up discussing Homer. That was another shock. According to Magnus there was a scene in the *Iliad* where the underworld god Hephaistos appeared, complete with a set of three-legged bronze tables that moved around on wheels. 'They follow him like dogs, dogs who will even turn round and go home by themselves at his command.'

'Sounds like a good set of nesting-tables for drinks parties.'

'When your guests have had enough, you can whistle and the tables remove themselves.'

I liked Magnus. He had a sense of humour. But I was surprised to find that he read Homer, and I told him so.

'Surveyors take an interest in the world. Most of us are well read,' he bragged. 'Anyway, we spend time alone. Other people think we're tricky sods.'

I made no comment. I had moved Magnus onto my list of men to watch. For one thing, checking important deliveries ought to be done by Cyprianus, the clerk of works. And I would expect marble to be kept not in some unsupervised encampment full of oddball hawkers and interlopers, but safe in the well-fenced site depot.

Covered with mud, I was hardly impressive. I went back to the old house and stripped off. Helena discovered me rootling through a chest of clothes. 'Oh Marcus, what happened?'

'Fell down.' I sounded like a sad little boy.

'Did somebody push you?' Helena was not being maternal; she worried about me getting into serious fights.

'What, some big rough bully? No, I fell down all on my own. I was dreaming and not looking where I put my feet. I'd been looking at work by some fresco artists; I must have been thinking about Larius.'

Larius, my favourite young nephew, had bunked off to learn to be a painter in the Bay of Neapolis, where the rich had their fabulous villas and there was top-class work. It was three years since I had seen him. I tried luring him to Rome to help me decorate Pa's Aventine house, but my letter went unanswered. Larius had always been a businessman, too sensible to commit himself to unpaid favours. Besides, in Rome he had his appalling parents. Galla and her ghastly husband were enough to drive any son to a remote apprenticeship.

'Hmm . . . So that's where it is!' Helena brushed past me suddenly to seize on a dress of hers. It was a cream affair, with wide bands of blue on the hems. Although simple, it had cost a sackful; the material was a gorgeous weave shot through with silk. As she lifted it out with a seductive rustle and held it by the shoulders, she caught me looking sceptical. 'Hyspale keeps trying on my clothes. There's no point. I am far too tall so they bunch on her.' I said nothing. 'Yes, she does it to annoy me.'

Another problem with the damned nurse. I sighed. 'You know –'

'I know!'

I held my peace.

'When we get home,' promised Helena. 'I'll tackle her in Rome. Mother will take her back.'

'And she won't be surprised.'

Helena looked at me. 'Are you sniping at my mother?'

'No.'

It was true. She might be my mother-in-law, but I had observed the Camillus family enough to know she had had a strong influence on Helena's development. I paid the proper respect to that. When a senator omits to divorce his wife after she has given him the correct number of children and he has used up the dowry, it generally means something too. I did not mess with Julia Justa.

'Oh your undertunic's mucky too, Marcus. You'll have to take it off and bathe.'

I was already halfway through the motion of peeling down to bare skin when I realised that Hyspale had come into the room.

Helena flushed. 'Hyspale, do knock, please!' I made sure I stayed decent. I can stand admiration from the wider public, but I rather liked Helena Justina deciding my body was her personal territory. She was shaking out the cream and blue dress. 'Did you move this? Can we understand something, Hyspale – I would not allow my sister, my *mother* even, to borrow my clothes without asking me.'

Hyspale glared at me as if she believed I had caused her reprimand.

'Where are the children?' I asked coldly. Hyspale stormed out. Actually, I had already seen the children safe in the doting care of fair-haired, fair-skinned women from the King's household, who were entranced by my daughters' dark eyes and foreign good looks. The baby was asleep. Julia always behaved perfectly for strangers.

Helena and I looked at each other. 'I shall deal with it,' she repeated. 'At least she's not beating or starving them. We just reached the stage where our servants are other people's useless gifts. Next, we shall choose our own – no doubt bungling it through inexperience. Then at last we shall move on to exactly what we want domestically.'

'I'd like to miss out some stages.'

'You like to rush everything.'

I grinned salaciously.

I found my oil flask and strigil, selected clean clothes and went out to explore the King's baths. Helena then scurried after me, growling under her breath and needing to relax in the steam. In a private bath house owned by a royal master there is always hot water. At off-peak times, you can virtually guarantee no one else will turn up to be shocked by mixed bathing.

We found the bath suite was high quality. To one side of the entrance lay a room with a cold swimming pool. None of your shallow paddling puddles; this was more than waist deep with plenty of space for a good thrash, as Helena vigorously proved. I had never learned to swim. She kept threatening to teach me; a freezing pool in Britain did not encourage me to start lessons. I sat on the pink mortared bench and watched Helena for a while, though even she was gasping at the temperature. Slightly chilled, I wandered off to enjoy myself in not one but three different hot rooms, each of increasing temperature. She stopped showing off her stamina and joined me.

'You found the fresco painters this morning?'

'I found their hut. I saw the mosaicist.' My solemn lack of logic had Helena giggling.

'Don't play up, Falco.'

I gave her a cheeky smile.

Helena languidly went to a basin where she used a dipper to splash water over her shoulders. It ran down . . . well, where gravity was bound to take it. She came back to sit by me. That gave me the chance to trace the water streaks with my fingers.

'So,' she asked me doggedly, 'what stage have you reached?'

'Are you supervising?'

'Wouldn't dare.' Untrue. 'We consult, don't we?'

'You consult and I confess . . .' She kicked me to encourage honesty. I sobered up to save my shins. 'I've got the measure of the project architecturally. It's a good structure and the planned finish treatments are striking. I'm eyeing up the personnel; that's ongoing. Now I have to find an office –'

'I have sorted out a room near our suite for you.'

'Thanks! That's good – not too close to the site managers. So next I take all the project documents into my new office and lurk there auditing. I know what scams I'm searching for. When I'm ready, I'll pull in your brothers to help. Meantime, both are placed in good spying positions.' I omitted their seamy conditions. Their loving sister might storm off and rescue them.

Within the thick walls of the bath house, we were cut off completely from the outside world. Nobody knew we were here. Naked and peaceful together, able to be ourselves. Once you have children, such private moments are rare.

I gazed at Helena quietly. 'Britain.' I took her hand, winding my fingers among hers. 'Here we are again!' She smiled slightly, saying nothing. I first met her in this dismal province – both of us at a low ebb at the time . . . 'You were a snooty, angry piece and I was a sour-faced, hard beggar.'

Helena smiled more, this time at me. 'Now you're a snooty but mudstained equestrian and I'm . . .' She paused.

I wondered if she was content. I thought I knew. But she liked to keep me on edge. 'I love you,' I said.

'What's that for?' She laughed, suspecting bribery.

'It's worth saying.'

I felt sweat trickling slowly down my neck. I had a vague scrape with my strigil. I had brought my favourite, which was bone. Firm, yet comfortable on the skin . . . like many fine things in life.

When I complained about the pain in my wrenched back, Helena eased it with some interesting massage. 'Toothache as well,' I whimpered pathetically. She leaned round from behind me and kissed my cheek gently. Flattened by the steam, her long straight hair fell forwards, tickling parts of me that decidedly liked being tickled.

'This is nice. No one using these smart facilities but us . . . Maybe we should take full advantage, sweetheart . . .' I pulled Helena closer.

'Oh Marcus, we can't –'

'I bet we can!'

We could too. And we did.

XXI

ONCE YOU have servants, even rare moments of privacy are at
risk. I fooled the woman, though. By the time Hyspale sought
us out at the baths, Helena Justina was in the changing room, drying
off her hair. I was coming out through the porchway, newly clad in a
clean tunic. With a mother like mine, I had long ago mastered the art
of looking innocent. Especially after a hot dalliance with a young lady.

'Oh Marcus Didius!' Our freedwoman's podgy face glowed with
satisfaction at disturbing me. 'I've been looking for you – somebody
wanted you!'

'Really.' I was in a good mood. I tried not to let Hyspale dissipate
that.

'I should have sent him here to you . . .'

She was determined to follow the cliché that men of affairs use the
public baths to socialise with their lawyers and bankers, all dull creeps
seeking dinner invitations. Not my style. In Rome, I patronised
Glaucus, my trainer. I went to get my body fit. 'I don't take the
conservative line. When I'm at the baths, Camilla Hyspale, it's for
cleanliness and exercise.' All types of exercise. I managed not to smirk.
'I don't want to be found.'

'Yes, Marcus Didius.' She was an old hand at using people's names
as insults. Her meekness was a front. I had no faith in her to obey.

Helena came out behind me. Hyspale looked shocked. And she
only thought we had been bathing together.

'Who was it?' I asked calmly.

'What?'

'Looking for me, Camilla Hyspale?'

'One of the painters.'

'Thanks.'

With a terse nod to the women of my household, loved and loathed,
I strode off to be a man of affairs in my own way. The one I loved blew
me a kiss suggestively. The freedwoman was even more shocked.

I returned to the site.

I had a feel for it now. In some ways, it reminded me of the four-sided walled complex of a military fort. With the same, slightly rectangular layout, the palace would be almost half the length and breadth of a full legionary base. They house six thousand men, two-legion bases double that. Like a small town, a permanent fort is crammed with magnificent buildings, dominated by its Praetorium, huge administrative headquarters and the commandant's home. The King's new palace was about twice the size of a standard Praetorium. It, too, was designed primarily to impress.

Activity in a far corner caught my interest. I made the diagonal route march over there. Pomponius, the project manager, was in heavy debate with Magnus, Cyprianus the clerk of works, and another man, whom I soon deduced was the drainage engineer. In this part of the site, where the level was natural, labourers had gone ahead with the stylobate platforms that would front each wing. They were laying the first courses of supporting blocks on which colonnades would stand.

The planned extra height of the dramatic west wing with its audience chamber posed a problem the designers must always have known about – how to link it aesthetically to the colonnades of adjoining wings; where they abutted at the corners they would be much lower. Now Pomponius and Magnus were having one of the long site discussions where such matters are thrashed out, feeding each other with suggestions – then each finding insurmountable difficulties in any idea that was put forward by the other man.

'We know we have to step the colonnades,' Magnus was saying.

'I don't want any variation in the visuals –'

'But you're losing five foot, off twelve foot, max. Unless you raise the ceilings, only dwarves will be able to walk in the ends of these wings! You need graded head space, man.'

'We lift the colonnades, in gradual stages –'

'Bitty. Much better to employ single flights of steps. Vary your roof line if you want. Let me tell you how –'

'I have made my decision,' Pomponius asserted.

'Your decision's crap,' said Magnus. He was frank, yet given that surveyors tend to be hot-headed know-it-alls, he spoke amiably enough. He was only concerned to explain the good solution he had devised. 'Listen – at each end, put in steps to move the people up to the west wing. Then, don't just run the lower colonnades along level until they bump into the big stylobate. Put in one taller column on each wing. Raise the colonnades at top height.'

'No, I'm not doing that.'

'These columns will need thicker diameters,' Magnus pressed on, deaf to the objection. 'It gives better proportions – and if you tidy off with roof features, they'll be carrying more weight.'

'You're not listening to me,' complained the architect.

'You're not listening to me,' the surveyor answered logically.

'The point is,' piped up Cyprianus, who had been listening to both patiently, 'if we go with Magnus, I need to put in our order for the over-height columns now. Those in your main run are twelve foot. You'll be going up to fourteen, fourteen and a half, for the larger ones. Specials always take longer –' Not even Magnus was listening to him.

It was clear they would be wrangling over the corner design for hours yet. Days, possibly. Weeks, even. Well, be realistic; call it months. Only when the builders reached the point of no return would this design feature be settled. My money was on the Magnus plan. But Pomponius was, of course, in charge.

Seated on a great limestone slab, from time to time the engineer put in, 'What about my tank?' No one so much as acknowledged him.

From its placing, the slab under his backside seemed to be part of a preliminary mock-up of one of the colonnaded walks that would line the interior garden. I deduced it was part of a gutter that would lie at the foot of the stylobate and catch the run-off from the roof. Its deep hollowing at least provided a shaped perch while the engineer waited to be heard.

Pomponius and Magnus moved off slightly, still going endlessly over the same points. This probably often happened. Delaying the decision might allow time for new ideas to form; it could prevent expensive mistakes. They were not exactly quarrelling. Each thought the other was an idiot; each made that plain. But this seemed to be a perfectly routine conflab.

'*Finials!*' cried Magnus loudly, like an exotic obscenity. Pomponius only shrugged.

I parked on another slab of limestone and introduced myself to the engineer. His name was Rectus. He must suffer from cold feet, for he wore knitted grey ankle socks in his battered site ankle boots. But his wide body must be tougher; he had only a single tunic, with short sleeves. Bushy eyebrows flourished above a big Italian nose. He was the type who always saw disaster coming – but who then without despair attacked the problem practically. Gloomy in aspect, he was a doer and solver. But he never gained the self-confidence to cheer up.

'So you have a problem with a tank?' I sympathised.

'Nice of you to notice, Falco.'

'I'm here to apply bandages to this project's wounds.'

'You'll need a few rags.'

'So I'm learning. Tell me about your tank.'

'My tank!' said Rectus. 'Well, I just need to remind those fart-arses to build it before they get any further with their farting stylobates. It sits on a stone base, protruding into the garden, for one thing. I want a cavity dug out and the base laid. The sooner they put the tank in the happier I shall be. Never mind the farting levels of their fancy colonnades.'

I glanced at the sky – a typical British grey all over. 'So what is this pet tank?'

'Settling tank for the aqueduct.'

'*Aqueduct?*'

'Oh we have all the amenities here, Falco. Well, we will do.'

'Right!'

'I got approval for the aqueduct from the governor himself, during his state visit.'

'State visit?'

'Came to introduce himself to the Great King.'

'Fun?'

'Believe it!' he marvelled. 'We had to build a new latrine, in case the governor wanted a shit.'

'He must have been delighted! Is this my pal Frontinus?'

'He spoke to me!' exclaimed Rectus excitedly. Frontinus was extremely down to earth.

'Frontinus enjoys the company of experts. And,' I said, grinning, 'he was commissioner of waterworks in Rome. He does like aqueducts.'

'It will only be a small one.' Rectus subsided into embarrassed diffidence.

'Still, you got your aqueduct . . . I know it has to have a settling tank. Otherwise your pipes would clog – so what's the problem, Rectus?'

'Not included in the budget. Should have been a provisional sum.'

'A what?'

'Notional costing. The aqueduct itself is to be funded as a provincial amenity.' I had wandered into the picturesque byways of Treasury bureaucracy. 'But the collection tank is on our site, so it's our baby. Cyprianus can't arrange the work for me without a pig's pizzle docket.' Bureaucracy had summoned its own range of swear words. 'Since it was never allowed for, Pomponius has to issue me a variation order first. He piddling well knows he has to do it, but the bastard keeps putting it off.'

'Why?'

'Because that's the kind of fart-arse bastard Pomponius is.'

We fell silent. Rectus was still waiting for his talk with the architect. I had no firm plans.

I was looking at the place where the workmen had begun building up the great base for the spectacular west wing. 'That platform base will be five feet high, am I right? With its colonnade sitting on top of it?'

'Revetted,' said Rectus. 'Towering like a bloody great bulwark on a frontier fort.'

'With a massive blank wall facing the garden, won't the overall look be extremely bleak?'

'No, no. Same thought struck me. I've been talking to Blandus about that.'

'Blandus?'

'Chief fresco artist.' Possibly the mysterious visitor who missed me when I was bathing. 'They want to paint it – naturalistic greenery.'

'A mock-garden? Can't they have real flowers?'

'Plenty. When you look back towards the east wing they are going to install flowering trees on trellises, and beds full of colour will camouflage all the lower stylobates. But all the internal walls behind the colonnades are to be painted, mostly picked out discreetly. This big wall has its own design. It will be a spread of bold dark green creepers, through which,' said Rectus, pretending to mock although he seemed to like the concept, 'you can peep at what seems to be another part of the garden.'

'That's some thought!'

I was intrigued by Rectus. Some of the workers here seemed to inhabit closed compartments. They only knew about their own craft, had no clue about the overall scheme. He took notice of everything. I could imagine him spending his lunch-break wandering into the architects' offices in the old military complex, to gaze at site plans just out of curiosity.

'So . . . you know Frontinus!' He seemed fascinated by my famous contact.

'We worked together once,' I said gently. 'He was the consular,

117

enthroned; I was the runabout at gutter level.' It was not quite true, but passed off the connection graciously.

'Even so – *working* with Frontinus!'

'Maybe people will be saying to you one day *"working with Falco!"*, Rectus.'

Rectus considered that; saw it was ludicrous; stopped being in awe of my prestigious friends. He then told me sensibly about his discipline.

Scale was his main challenge. He had to cope with enormously long pipe runs, both to bring fresh water in along the various wings, and take away the rain outfall, which would be of huge volume in bad weather. Where his water pipes and drainpipes had to pass under buildings, it was essential to ensure they were completely free of leaks, their joints stopped tightly and the whole length surrounded by clay, before they became inaccessible under the finished rooms. Domestic needs were only part of his brief. Half the paths in the garden area would be laid over pipes to supply fountains. Even the wild garden by the sea, so richly supplied with streams and ponds, still needed a delivery pipe at one point for watering plants.

He was a real expert. When we were talking about how he planned to drain the garden, he told me that on one run the drop would be barely one in one eighty-three. That's a virtually invisible slope. Measuring it accurately would take patience – and brilliance. The way he talked convinced me Rectus possessed that skill. I could envisage that when everything was up, water would be gushing away down this near-horizontal conduit quite satisfactorily.

Pomponius had finished wrangling with Magnus. We saw Magnus stumping off with Cyprianus, both shaking their heads. Now the architect came wafting over to us, clearly intending to have a go at Rectus. The high-flown bully was transparent. He had failed to impose his will on the experienced surveyor and clerk of works, so he was now planning to shower scorn on the drainage scheme.

Rectus had dealt with Pomponius before. He rose from his block of limestone looking nervous, but he had his speech ready: 'I don't want a fight, but what about my farting tank? Look, I'm telling you now, in front of Falco as my witness, the tank needs to be programmed in this week.'

I was remaining neutral. I stayed seated. But I was there. Maybe that was why Pomponius suddenly backed off. 'Cyprianus can write out a docket and I'll sign it. Fix it up with him!' he ordered curtly. As clerk of works, Cyprianus was in charge of allocating labour to the task; he also had the authority to call up the right materials. Apparently that was all Rectus needed. He was a happy man.

Pointless tension evaporated.

Elsewhere things were not so calm. In the daytime the site was always noisy, even when little seemed to be happening. Now, shouts that sounded far more urgent than normal rang across the open area. I jumped up and stared over, towards the south wing. It looked as if a fight had started.

I set off there, running.

XXII

EN HAD flocked to the scrimmage. More labourers than I had
been aware of that day on site popped out of trenches and
rushed to watch, all yelling, in various languages. I was soon in a
crowd, jostled on all sides.

I pushed to the front. Jupiter! One of the protagonists was the elder
Philocles, the white-haired mosaicist. He was going at it like a
professional boxer. As I burst through the crowd, he knocked the
other to the ground. Judging by his paint-spattered tunic, the man
who fell had to be a fresco artist. Philocles wasted no time in
exploiting his advantage. Astonishingly, he leapt up in the air, drew
his knees up, then crashed down on his opponent, full in the stomach,
landing with both boots and all his weight. I sucked in air, imagining
the pain. Then I fell on Philocles from behind.

I thought others would help drag him off. No luck. My
intervention was just a new phase in the excitement. I found myself
tussling with this red-faced, white-haired, violent old-timer who
seemed to have no sense of danger and no discernment over
whom he attacked – but only a furious temper and wild fists. I could
hardly believe it was the tight-mouthed man I had met that
morning.

As I tried to prevent Philocles causing more damage, to me
especially, Cyprianus turned up. When the stricken painter struggled
to his feet somehow and for no reason threatened to join in fighting
me, Cyprianus gripped his arms and pulled him backwards.

We held the mosaicist and painter apart. They were both madly
struggling. 'Stop it! Cut it out, both of you!'

Philocles had gone crazy. No longer the taciturn drone who held
himself aloof, he was still thrashing like a beached shark. He swung
madly. Caught out by mud underfoot yet again, I skidded. This time
I managed to stop falling, at the expense of another jarring of my back.
Philocles lurched the other way, hanging like a deadweight so he
pulled me over. We rolled on the ground, with me grinding my teeth

but clinging onto him. Being younger and tougher, eventually I hauled him back upright.

He broke free. He swung around and took a swipe at me. I ducked once, then I clipped him hard around the head. That stopped him.

By now, the other man had realised just how painful being jumped on felt. He doubled up, collapsing to the ground again. Cyprianus bent over, holding him. 'Get a plank!' he yelled. The painter was barely conscious. Philocles stood back, clearly reconsidering. Suddenly he was worried. His breath came fast.

'Is that Blandus?' I asked Cyprianus. The man was being stretchered onto a board so people could carry him. Alexas, the medical orderly, squeezed through the press to examine him.

'It's Blandus,' Cyprianus confirmed grimly. He must be used to settling disputes, but he was angry. 'Philocles, I've had just about enough of you two and your stupid feuds! You're going in my lock-up this time.'

'He started it.'

'He's out of it now!'

Pomponius arrived. All we needed. 'Oh this is ridiculous.' He rounded on Philocles, shaking his finger furiously. '*For the gods' sake!* I have to have that man. There's nobody to touch him within a thousand miles. Will he live?' he demanded of Alexas, as peremptory as could be.

Alexas looked worried but said he thought Blandus would live.

'Put him in your sickbay,' ordered Cyprianus roughly. 'Keep him there until I say otherwise.'

'Tie him to the bed if you have to! I look to you, Cyprianus,' declared Pomponius in a mincingly superior tone, 'to keep your workforce under some control!'

He stormed off. Cyprianus glowered as he watched him leave, but somehow refrained from all the optional rude sounds and gestures. He was a standard clerk of works: first class.

The crowd melted away fast. Managers tend to have that effect. Blandus was carted off, with Alexas running alongside. Philocles was manhandled away too. Among the mutters as the mêlée dispersed, I heard one provocative jeer in particular. It was aimed at Lupus, the foreign-labour supervisor, by a sinister, bare-armed tough nut who was covered in woad patterns.

'Don't tell me,' I muttered to Cyprianus. 'That's the other gang leader – the local workers' chief – I see *he* has a feud with

Lupus?' They had gone off in opposite directions, or it looked as though another fight would have occurred. 'What's he called – Mandumerus?' Cyprianus said nothing. I took it I was correct. 'All right – so what's with Philocles and Blandus?'

'They hate each other.'

'Well, so I see. I'm not reduced to reading with a concave spyglass yet. Tell me why?'

'Who knows?' replied the clerk of works, quite exasperated. 'Jealousy, say. They are both leaders in their field. They both think the palace scheme will collapse without them.'

'So will it?'

'You heard Pomponius. If we lost either of them, we would be pushed. Try persuading any craftsman with serious talent to come this far north.' We were now standing alone together in the middle of the bare site. Cyprianus relieved himself of a rare bitter harangue: 'I can manage to find carpenters and roofers without too much trouble – but we're still waiting for my chosen stonemason to decide if he will unclench his bum from his comfy bench in Latium. Philocles brings his son with him everywhere, but Blandus only has some daft new lad working on his team. He praises him, but . . .' He had gone off into a secondary path, then returned to the main tirade in a final flush: 'All the fine finishes are a nightmare. Why should they travel to this hole? They don't need it, Falco! Rome and the millionaires' villas in Neapolis offer much better conditions, better pay and a better chance of fame. So who wants Britain?'

My recently changed tunic was now filthier than the previous one. Once more, I went back to my quarters to swap garments.

'Oh Marcus – *no!*' Helena had heard me. She could tell my step at half a stadium's length. Nux had wuffed too. 'I seem to have *three* small children—'

'Wonder if I can claim voting privileges?'

'Put laundry bills on your expenses sheet anyway!'

I had worked through my white and my buff-coloured outfits. Now I was down to the blueberry thing that had been re-dyed twice, with streaked results. I changed my boots as well this time. You can't win. In the city, hobnails sent you on your back when they skidded on stone pavements. On site, studs were useless and plain leather had no grip at all. I might be forced into wooden pattens, like those the workmen wore, or even to tie on nasty sacks.

'Sorry; I couldn't help it.'

'Maybe you should sit indoors quietly doing office work,' suggested Helena.

'It will soon sponge off,' I reassured her as she sprang past me and got her hands on the newly grubbied buff garment. I had bundled it up carefully, but she threw it out flat to see the worst. She screamed and pulled a face. Mud does have a habit of looking like fresh oxdung from a beast with bad diarrhoea.

'Ugh! At least when we lived in Fountain Court Lenia's laundry was on hand. Now keep out of trouble, please.'

'Of course, my love.'

'Oh shut up, Falco!'

I did stay in the office for a while. Then she let me come out for lunch.

I was glad she cared. I would hate to think we ever reached the point when my presence made her blasé. I preferred it when she still came suddenly to find me, as if she missed me when I was absent for an hour or two. And when she looked at me, abruptly still. Then if I winked at her, she would say, 'Oh grow up, Falco!'

And turn away, in case I saw her blush.

She made me go back and work in the office all afternoon. One of the clerks brought over more documents, shuffling in, believing I was safely out on site and would not confront him. I sat him down, ignoring his terrified look, and took this chance to get to know him. He was a spare, thin-featured fellow in his twenties, with short dark hair and a line of beard that was less successful than he must have hoped. He looked intelligent and slightly wary; perhaps he was worried by me.

Part of the problem with costs on the project quickly became obvious. They had changed the major records system.

'Vespasian wants to run things tightly. What's been altered? A few accounting tweaks?'

'New docketing. New logs. New everything.'

I threw back my head and blew out air in frustration. 'Oh don't tell me! Complex new bookkeeping, redesigned from scratch. It probably works perfectly. But you hated to abandon the system you knew – then when you tried the unfamiliar version, it didn't seem to work . . . I bet you started the palace project with the old system, then swapped halfway through?'

The clerk nodded miserably. 'We're in a bit of a mess.'

I realised what had happened. He was now using two different

123

accounting strategies at once. He could no longer tell how much muddle he was in. 'This is not your fault.' I was angry and that worried him. He thought I was berating him personally. 'The Treasury fly boys have set up a Corinthian-columned record scheme – but none of the elevated brains who devised this fancy thing would ever dream of training you clerks!'

'Well, we only have to operate it, after all.' This clerk was not as subdued as I had thought. He had worked in government service for maybe a decade, acquiring a dry wit to sustain himself. He was scared of *me*. But I wanted that.

'Did they send you out a new rule book?'

'Yes.' He looked shifty.

I knew how things worked. 'Anyone snipped the ribbon and opened the scroll yet?'

'It's on my desk.' I understood that euphemism.

'Fetch it,' I said. At my feet, Nux looked up curiously.

The costing clerk seemed bright enough; he must have been selected for this crucial project because somebody thought well of him. So as he slunk to the door I called out kindly, 'You and I will get to grips with it together. Bring all the old site orders and invoices right from the start. We'll rewrite all the bookkeeping from day one.'

I could send to Rome for an official to come here and train people. That would waste months – even if he ever arrived. Vespasian employed me for my dedication and my willingness to knuckle down. So I would sort it: *I* would read the rules. Knowing little of the old ones, I would not be flummoxed by changes. So long as the new rules worked, as they were likely to, then I would teach the clerks.

Some informers lead a life of intrigue, plunging into the dark seams of society, amazing people with their enquiry skills and their deductive talent. Ah well. Some of us have to earn our fees pondering who had put *thirty-nine denarii for hardcore on the Ides of April* in the wrong column.

At least if this site had any hardcore fiddles, I would trace them.

Grow up, Falco. There's no money to be made from hardcore. Any fool knows that.

(*Thirty-nine denarii?* Exorbitant! There was one slip of the stylus to be corrected right away.)

The clerk and I were soon getting along nicely, sorting flint requisitions into baskets on his side and work-sheets for the boy who brought round beakers of hot *mulsum*, which I spiked to the table with my dagger, on mine.

'Tell this boy to include us in his rounds now. Mine's half wine, half water, not too much honey and no herbs.'

'He never remembers orders. You get it as it comes.'

'Oh nuts! That means cold, weak and with funny floating things . . .'

'There's a good side, Falco: only half a cup. He spills most as he comes across the site.'

We worked all afternoon. When the light faded too much for figurework and I decided we could stop, the clerk had relaxed somewhat. I was not so cheerful; I now saw the full scale of the job, and its boring qualities. And my bad tooth hurt.

'What's your name?'

'Gaius.'

'Where do you normally work, Gaius? Where's your nook?'

'Alongside the architects.' I had to stop that.

'Over in the old military block? Tell you what – it will be easier if you work in my office from now on.' I softened it: 'At least so long as I'm here on site.'

He looked up and said nothing. He was bright. He knew my game.

As he said goodbye, my new friend commented, 'I like your tunic, Falco. That colour is really unusual.'

I would have growled a stern response but inevitably, now that we were packing up, the *mulsum* boy arrived. That's life in an office. You wait all afternoon, then the refreshments finally appear, just as you are pulling on your cloak to go home. We asked politely if we could have our drinks slightly earlier tomorrow.

'Yes, yes.' He scowled. He was a stroppy runt with a tray he could hardly carry, unable to wipe his snotty nose on his sleeve because he was holding the tray. Perhaps it was because he worked out of doors in the cold British air that his nose was *very* runny. It dripped. I put my beaker back on the tray. 'I'm only a bit late. I have to tell everyone the news, don't I? Then people asks questions.'

'So may I ask a question, please?' I was calm. The *mulsum* boy should never be rushed, crushed or otherwise offended. You need him on your side. 'What news?'

'Give me a chance, legate – today's big thriller is: Philocles just died.'

XXIII

'DON'T YOU mean Blandus?' I corrected the *mulsum* boy. 'He was in the fight earlier.'

'All right. Blandus, then.' All he cared was that he had one less beaker to brew.

'He got stamped on very badly – so, what's happened?'

'I went in with his *mulsum*. He jumped up for it. Next minute he was falling down dead.' Spleen, I thought. Internal bleeding, anyway.

'Wasn't Alexas watching him?'

'Alexas wasn't there.'

I lost my temper. 'Well, he damned well should have been! What's the point of taking people to the medical hut if they just lie on their board and die?'

'It wasn't in the medical hut,' protested the *mulsum* boy. I lifted an eyebrow, restraining myself. 'He was in the lock-up.'

I would have ground my teeth, but was treating the sore one tenderly. 'In that case it is Philocles.'

'That's what I said! *You* told me it was Blandus, chief.'

'Well, I don't know what I'm talking about, obviously . . .'

I got him to take me to the lock-up. It was a small, solid lean-to where the clerk of works held bloody-minded bingeing drunks for a day, or if necessary two days, while they sobered up. The interior looked as if it had been well used.

Alexas was at the scene now. Cyprianus must have sent for him.

'You seem to have more corpses than live patients,' I said.

'It's not funny, Falco.'

'I am by no means laughing.'

Philocles was lying on some grass outside. He was dead all right. They must have towed him into the fresh air. Too late. As Alexas continued to rub his limbs and shake him, just in case, I looked over the orderly's shoulder; I could see a few bruises but no other marks. 'It was Blandus who took the worst punishment. Philocles seemed fine.' I bent and

126

turned his skull, inspecting where I hit him. 'He was fighting mad. I had to crack him one.'

Alexas shook his head. 'You've confessed – sleep easy. Don't trouble your conscience over hitting his head. The way the boy described it, his heart stopped. Excitement won't have helped, but this would have happened anyway.'

The *mulsum* boy did a dramatic show of clutching his side, staggering, then falling by stages to the ground. 'Very good.' I applauded him. 'I look forward to seeing you play Orestes at the Megalensian Games.'

'I'm going to be a cart driver.'

'Good idea. Much better pay, and you don't have to fight off swarms of adoring girls.' He shot me a disgusted look. He was about fourteen, a lad in a man's world, growing up fast. He was old enough for girls, but money matters did not yet trouble him. Still, the girls would see to that.

As the mosaicist's body was carried away, with Alexas in train, Cyprianus shook his head. 'I'd better tell Junior that his father has died.'

'Ask him if he knows what the fight was about.'

'Oh we all know that!' Cyprianus snapped irritably.

'Jealousy, you said.' I watched him.

'They had a war going back decades.' Now Cyprianus spoke in a tired voice, telling me the sour site secrets he had previously tried to keep private from the Emperor's man. There was no point sheltering Philocles Senior now, and for joining in the fight Blandus must take his chance. 'Most sites, the rule was if you employed Blandus, you had to forget Philocles – and vice versa. This was the first time for years they had been on the same project.'

'This being Britain, where your choices of craftsmen are limited, because nobody wants to come out here?'

'Yes.' Cyprianus spoke with rueful pride. 'And being the Great King's palace, where we want the best.'

'Were these two warned before they came that they might meet up?'

'No. Of course *I* warned them, when they got here, that I would not allow trouble. Pomponius had hired them. He awards the special sub-contracts. He either did not know they hated each other – or he didn't care.'

'Personal relationships are not his strong point.'

'Tell me!' Cyprianus sighed wearily. 'So now Philocles Senior is on his way to Hades, and Junior will probably walk out on us. Blandus is laid up and who knows if or when he'll be on his feet again . . .'

I thumped his shoulder. 'Don't let it depress you. What I still don't see is what it's all about?'

'Oh you know painters, Falco!'

'Light-fingered?' I guessed.

'Fingers everywhere, you mean. Randy little beggars, the lot of them. Why do you think they become painters? They go into people's houses, with access to the women.'

'Ah! So Blandus . . . ?'

'Screwed the wife of Philocles Senior. The husband discovered them.' I winced. 'But don't tell Junior,' Cyprianus pleaded. 'He's a bit slow. We all think that he doesn't know.'

A thought struck. 'Blandus is not by chance his real father?'

'No. Junior was a baby.' Cyprianus had thought about it too. Then he chuckled. 'Well, I think he was . . . Let's pretend we're sure. He'd be torn whether to carry on floor-laying, or to take up marbling walls instead!'

'You need him piecing in the tesserae – I'll keep mum.'

For a moment Cyprianus did gaze at me. 'There's nothing else for you to do about this, Falco.' He was either checking my opinion anxiously, or seeking to influence my actions if I wanted to cause trouble.

'Why should there be?' I answered him. 'It's death from natural causes. He left us his creative work. Either Philocles Junior or some other humourless floor fixer will eventually lay those designs. Otherwise, it's Fortune. This happens all the time. You curse their timing, comfort any relations, fix up a funeral – then you move on and forget them.'

Maybe Cyprianus thought me harsh. That was better than him thinking I would hold an enquiry. And, even though his work on building sites was dangerous, maybe I had seen more sudden deaths than he had. I was tough. Mind you, I could still get angry.

While the clerk of works went to break the bad news to the chief mosaicist's son, I tried to see Blandus. Alexas let me in to where he was lying, but he was snoring. He had been in so much pain the orderly had drugged him.

'Poppy juice?'

'Henbane.'

'Careful!'

'Yes. I'm trying not to kill him,' Alexas assured me sombrely.

XXIV

THIS ENQUIRY was making more demands than I expected. Today I had had a fall and a fight, then been involved in accidental death. I was shaken both mentally and physically. That's without counting toothache, hard work in the office, or personal matters that had more pleasantly drained my strength.

I was glad I had brought Helena and the others here, so I did not have to face an evening donkey ride before I found dinner and solace. Anyway, it was clear I now needed regular access to my clothes chest. During a case, I liked a change of venue. The trouble with provincial assignments was always the same: the place and the personnel stayed with you day and night. There was no escape.

I was missing Rome. Back there, after any long day working, I could lose myself in the Forum, the baths, the races, the river, the theatre and thousands of street gathering points – which hosted many kinds of edibles and drinkables to take your mind off trouble. I had been here three days and I was already homesick. I missed the tall, teeming buildings in the slum areas just as much as the high temples, glinting with bronze and copper, which crowned those famous hills. I wanted hot streets full of cracked amphorae, wild dogs, fishbones and falling window boxes; itinerant sausage-sellers peddling lukewarm meats; line after line of washed tunics, hung between windows where ninety-year-old hags leaned out and cackled their disgust over girls who were flashing too much leg at slippery bath-oil salesmen who were probably bigamists.

Nobody could collect several wives in Noviomagus; in this sparse population everyone would know him. Any be-torqued no-good boy would be found out and marched back to his own hut. I longed for a city where deception flourished and there was some hope for sophisticated guile. I yearned for a whiff of perversion among sweet scents of frankincense, pine needles and marjoram. I was ready to accept a garlic-tasting kiss from a seditious barmaid or to let a slimy Lycian sell me an amulet made from some exotic sexual organ, imperfectly embalmed. I wanted stevedores and garland girls, librarians and pimps, snobbish financiers in luxurious purple togas, their overheated wool rich in that foul dye from the shores of Tyre that stinks so expressively of the shellfish it is squeezed from. Dear gods, I missed the familiar noise and stress of home.

Three days in Britain: I could hardly wait to leave. But so soon after coming out here, the thought of the endless journey back to Italy was almost unbearable. Before we faced that, I might have to take us for a quick boost of city life up in Londinium.

Anyone who has been there will see that's a joke.

It must be June. At home there would be blue sky. We had missed the great flower festival; they would have gone on into heroes and gods of war.

Here it was pleasant; well, I could pretend. People sat out of doors on a fine evening, we Romans with mantles slung around our shoulders. Today casual food trays had been brought to us by the King's servants and we ate where we were in the garden. Camilla Hyspale spent her time ostentatiously shivering, which made others of us determined to enjoy the open air.

The baby was restless. I tried dandling her. It never works in company. Babies know you would like to impress people with your magic touch; they stop niggling to fool you – then wail louder.

'Another twenty years and she'll be really good,' Maia sniggered. Nux crept under Helena's skirt, whining softly. Helena, looking tired, whined back.

I tried that trick of standing up and pacing slowly. My mother could always do it. Once, when Julia had been screaming for about three days without a break, I saw Ma quieten her in about five strides. Favonia was not fooled by my efforts.

Further down the large garden, near the King's own quarters, we could see Verovolcus. He was with a small group of other Britons. They had been served at the same time as us, and were now dawdling through the food dishes, drinking too. It all seemed subdued, though perhaps would not stay so quiet. Verovolcus kept looking our way. Instinctively we avoided contact, keeping our group domestic. The last thing I wanted was to establish a pattern of heavy international socialising every night.

'He seems to be taking to heart the King's instructions to keep back and let you do your work,' Helena remarked in an undertone. She knew how I felt.

I jiggled Favonia. She decided to stop crying. A bubbling hiccup reminded me this was a choice she could retract at any moment.

Julia, who was crawling around on the grass, now noticed the silence and released a piercing yell. My sister Maia leaned down and waved a doll at her. Julia smashed it aside, but she did shut up.

'Bed?' threatened Maia.

'*No!*' Dear little poppet. It had been one of her first words.

I glanced over at Verovolcus, watching him the same way he watched us. 'I don't like to be antisocial, but –'

'Perhaps it works the other way.' Helena smiled. 'Here we are – all smart clothes, loud Latin and showing off our love of culture. Perhaps our shy British hosts are smitten with a fear that ghastly politeness will force them to mingle with a bunch of brash Romans.'

We were silent. She was right of course. Snobbery can work two ways.

The fine rooms of the old house lay between the courtyard garden and the perimeter road. This meant the garden was peaceful, sheltered from traffic noise by the main structure. But on a still summer night we were aware of constant movement on the road behind. Voices and footsteps told their story: groups of men were making their way off site. Most were on foot by the sound of it. They had eaten, and were heading for their evening entertainment. Their destination could only be downtown Noviomagus, to the low haunts that offered women, liquor, gambling and music – the seedy delights of the canabae.

As the unseen irregular procession passed, I looked forward to the early hours, when they would all be returning. Helena read my thoughts. 'I was too exhausted to notice last night. No doubt they creep back to their barracks like discreet mice.'

'Mice make a damned racket!' In Fountain Court I had once lived with a rodent infestation who were all kitted out with army boots.

We were favoured with visitors that evening. From the camp beyond the site huts came Sextius; someone else must be minding his cartload of goods because he brought Aelianus. I let them sit down and talk. We gave them beakers, though not food-bowls. It would look fairly natural; we were all outsiders, who came over from Gaul together and who had palled up. Sextius and his sidekick might have taken us seriously when we issued that old clichéd invitation, *do drop round for a drink some time* . . . When of course we really meant, *please don't!*

I was still carrying the baby, an informal touch.

Sextius fixed his attention on Maia, though he sat at a distance; he hardly spoke to her and made no overt move. She was still moping. Except when she wanted to insult someone, Maia kept to herself. Normally my sister was a cheerful soul, but when she moped, she intended the world to notice. Any one of my sisters in a bad mood could depress a whole family party; Maia, whose mood was usually the sunniest, now reckoned she was owed some deep gloom.

Hyspale dropped to her knees and for once started playing with Julia. That way, she too could distance herself. As a freedwoman, she was part of the family; we allowed her – indeed encouraged her – to join in when we conversed together generally. Her senatorial roots were showing again. Having to share space with a couple of statue-sellers horrified her. It took her some time to notice that the malodorous assistant was Camillus Aelianus, the spoiled darling of her previous refined home. Suddenly she squeaked with recognition. I did enjoy it.

He ignored her. She was the daughter of his childhood nurse. Aelianus was as much a snob as anyone around here. He was a thankless lout too.

He had rejected a seat then roamed about, helping himself to leftover food from any bowl he could reach. Helena watched, taking note that I had let her brother almost starve. She would have fetched him a feast, but Aelianus was gorging on his own account. That's the joy of a patrician background: it stuffs young lads with confidence.

'How did you get on with the architects?' I asked Sextius.

He shook his head. 'They won't see me.'

'Ah well. Keep trying.'

Plancus and Strephon might well reject his tiresome novelties, so I hoped he would not try too hard. If he left Noviomagus, spurned, I would lose my handy plant. I wanted to keep Aelianus in the field.

Eventually the voracious lad stopped snacking. Equipping himself with a large beaker of undiluted wine, he sauntered closer to me.

'Falco!'

I rocked the baby, nuzzling her sweet-smelling head as if lost in purely paternal thought. 'Any news?'

'Nothing much. I did see one of the managers having a big row today. Couldn't get near enough to listen, but he was laying into a carter roundly.' From his subsequent description, I thought it could be the surveyor, Magnus.

'Hmm. I saw him poking about the delivery wagons this morning. Was he neatly dressed, smart boots, maybe a shoulder bag?' Aelianus shrugged uselessly. 'What was in the cart?'

'Nothing; it looked empty. But the cart seemed to be what they were arguing about, Falco.'

'Is it still there?'

'No. Drove away later.'

'Heading where?'

'Umm . . .' He tried to remember. 'Can't be sure.'

'Oh that's helpful! Keep looking. This could be part of some materials racket. Any time you are on your own near the parked-up wagons try inspecting them surreptitiously, will you.'

He scowled. 'I was hoping I could finish skulking.'

'Tough!' I said.

Not long after that, Favonia was sick on my shoulder – a good excuse to break up the party and retire for the night.

'Oh it will sponge off!' jeered Maia as we went to our rooms. I was too experienced to be fooled. I had run out of tunics too.

The workmen who had been out to the canabae started coming home just as I nearly fell asleep. They rambled back in dribs and drabs, mostly quite unaware they might be disturbing people. They probably thought they were really quiet. Some were happy, some obscene, some full of loud animosity for the group in front. At least one found that he needed an extremely long pee, right against the palace wall.

Way into the hours of darkness, their noise finally ceased. That was when little Favonia decided to wake up and cry non-stop until morning.

XXV

*M*ULSUM SERVED on a building site is disgusting. Unpalatable beverages must be provided to labourers deliberately, to discourage them from taking time off for drinks. To troops, stuck at the back end of nowhere, marching a long road through a dense forest or trapped in some windswept frontier fort, even sour wine seems welcome – whilst in an emperor's Triumph, when the army returns home to Rome in splendour, they are awarded real *mulsum*. That's four measures of fine wine mixed with one of pure Attic honey. The further you go to the outposts of the Empire, the less hope there is of an elegant wine or genuine Greek sweetener. As nourishment deteriorates, your spirits droop. By the time you reach Britain, life can get no worse. Not, that is, until you are sitting on a building site and the *mulsum* boy arrives.

Refreshed by my night's rest (that's another bitter quip), I had crawled to my office. Bleary-eyed, I set to, peering at some wages bills in case I could find Gloccus or Cotta listed. I had been first up in our household. There was no breakfast. So I fell on my beaker cheerfully once the sniffing boy arrived. A mistake I would only make once.

'What's your name, boy?'

'Iggidunus.'

'Do me a favour – just bring me some hot water next time.'

'What's wrong with the *mulsum*?'

'Oh . . . nothing!'

'What's wrong with you, then?'

'Toothache.'

'Want do you want water for?'

'Medicine.' Cloves are supposed to dull the pain. They did not work on my dying molar; Helena had tried me on cloves for the last week. But anything would taste better than the *mulsum* boy's offering.

'You're an odd one!' Iggidunus scoffed, bumming off in a huff.

I called him back. My brain must be working in its sleep. I had not found Gloccus and Cotta, but I had spotted an anomaly.

I asked whether Iggidunus served a brew to everyone, the entire site. Yes he did. How many beakers? He had no idea.

I told Gaius to provide Iggidunus with a waxed tablet and a stylus. Of course he could not write. Instead, I showed the boy how to create a record using five-barred gates. 'Four upright sticks, then one across. Got it? Then start another set. When you finish, I can count them.'

'Is this some clever Egyptian abacus trick, Falco?' Gaius grinned.

'Do one round of the site, Iggidunus.'

'I only do one. It takes all day.'

'That's hard on the people who miss you.'

'Their mates tell me. I leave their cup with a tile on top.'

'So there's no escape! Count every *mulsum* cup you serve. Also, put down a stick for anyone who should get a beaker but who says no thanks. Then bring the tablet back to me here.'

'With some hot water?'

'That's right. Boiling would be nice.'

'You are joking, Falco!'

Off Iggidunus went. I placed my beaker of *mulsum* on the floor for Nux. My shaggy hound took one sniff, then stalked off to the clerk's side of the office.

He stared at me. 'Gaius, can you find me the tallies for the caterer's regular food order?'

He shuffled around, identified them, heaved them over to me. Then he leaned across, so he saw which records I was already working on and the notes I had scribbled. It took him no time to make the connection. 'Oh rats!' he said. 'I never thought of that.'

'You see my point.' I was cradling my cheek gloomily. 'Nothing matches, Gaius. The wages bill is high. Money drains away through a sieve – and yet look at these food invoices. The quantities of wine and provisions brought in don't marry up for those numbers of men . . . I'd say the supplies quantities are about right for those I've seen on site. It's the labour figures that are suspect. If you look around outside, we have hardly any of the trades, other than basic heavies who can dig trenches.'

'The workforce is low, Falco; that's proved by the way that the programme keeps slipping. The clerk who keeps the programme doesn't care, he just plays dice all day. The project team explained it as "delays due to bad weather" when I queried it.'

'They always say that.' Trying to employ Gloccus and Cotta back in Rome had taught me the system. 'Either rain threatens to spoil their concrete – or it's too hot for the men to work.'

'None of my business anyway; I'm here to count beans.'

I sighed. He had tried. He was just a clerk. He had so little authority everyone ran rings round him.

'It's time you and I counted heads, not beans.' I took him into my confidence. 'Here's my theory: it looks like at least one of our merry supervisors is claiming for a phantom labour force.'

Gaius leaned back with his arms folded. 'Whew! I like working with you, Falco. This is fun!'

'No, it's not. It's very serious.' I could see a black hole opening up. 'It may explain why Lupus and Mandumerus are at odds. There could be a turf war for control of the labour fiddle. That's bad news. Whichever of the supervisors is running the racket, Gaius, listen: take great care. Once they know we've found out, life will become extremely dangerous.'

Gaius then continued with his own work rather quietly.

I slipped out later, to look into another aspect. I had been thinking about Magnus and his peculiar behaviour yesterday around the delivery carts. He had claimed he was 'checking a marble consignment'. I thought it unlikely – but clever frauds often deceive you not with lies but with cunning half-truths.

I wanted to find the area where marble was being worked. I was led there by the screeching and scraping noises of saw-blades. With Nux at my heels, I made my way into the fenced enclosure. Men were preparing and squaring up newly delivered irregular blocks, using hammers and various grades of chisels. Nux ran off with her tail down, alarmed by the din, but I could only put my fingers in my ears as I hung around, inspecting various upright slabs.

Four men were pushing and pulling a multi-bladed saw to split a blue-grey block into pieces for inlay. The untoothed iron blades were supported in a wooden box frame, its progress lubricated by pouring water and sand into the cuts. By a slow and careful process, the men were slicing through the stone to produce several delicately fine sheets at once. From time to time they lifted the saw, resting their hands. A boy then moved in to brush away the damp powder produced by their labour, the marble 'flour', which I knew would be collected and used by the plasterers, mixed into their topcoats to give an extra fine glossy finish. The boy then fed new sand and water into the saw grooves to provide abrasion, and the sawyers resumed their cutting.

The resulting slabs would then be stacked vertically according to their thickness and quality. Lying around haphazardly were also a number of broken blocks, which must have shattered under the saw. Elsewhere fine sheets had been laid out on benches and were now being smoothed to a high finish with ironstone blocks and water.

As I wandered around, I was amazed by the colour and variety of the marble being worked on. It all seemed a little premature, given that the new building was only at foundation stage. Perhaps that was because the materials were coming from far-flung places and needed to be acquired well in advance. Preparation on site would take a very long time, in view of the huge scale of the proposed palace.

The head marble mason found me watching. He dragged me into his hut. There I readily accepted the offer of a hot drink – since he had despaired of Iggidunus and was brewing up his own on a small tripod.

'I'm Falco. You're – ?'

'Milchato.' They were a cosmopolitan bunch here. Who knows where he hailed from with a name like that? Africa or Tripolitania. Egypt, possibly. He had grizzled grey hair, but his skin was dark; so was his narrow beard. His origin must be somewhere the web-footed Phoenicians left their mark. Or raking up old sores, let's call it somewhere Carthaginian.

'Worth the fire risk.' I grinned, as he blew on the charcoal burner, heating up wine in a small bronze folding saucepan. A man who tolerated life in a temporary camp by bringing his own battery of comforts. It reminded me, with a pang, of my efficient friend Lucius Petronius. Britain was where he and I served in the army. I was seriously missing Petro. 'I've been looking at your stock. I thought most of the planned decoration on the palace would be paint – but Togidubnus seems to like his marble too. I'm staying in the old house; there's quite a range there. Surely it's not local?'

'Some.' He sprinkled dry herbs in two beakers. 'You'll see a bluey-coloured British stone. Slightly rough.' Ferreting among the clutter, he tossed me a piece of it. 'Comes from down the coast to westward. And what else has the old fella got? Oh, there's a red from the Mediterranean – and some brown speckled stuff from Gaul, if I remember.'

'You worked on the old house?'

'I was just a lad!' he grinned.

Like the other craftsmen, he had a vast array of samples scattered around him. Irregular pieces of multicoloured marble lay everywhere. A few had tablets pegged under them, with what must be firm orders for the new scheme. Leaning casually against the hut's doorframe, used as a doorstop, was a superb finished panel of inlaid veneers with a pentagon set in a circle. I picked up a delicate moulding with a seductive shine. It looked like a dado rail or a border between panels.

'Fillets!' exclaimed Milchato. 'I like a few carved fillets.'

'This is exquisite. And I've rarely seen so many types of marble in one place.'

Milchato demonstrated offhandedly. They came from places far apart: the blue stone, plus a similar grey, from Britain and then crystalline white from the central hills of distant Phrygia. He had a fine green and white veined type from the foothills of the Pyrennees, a yellow and white from Gaul, more than one variety from Greece . . .

'Your import costs must be staggering!'

Milchato shrugged. 'That's why there will be quite a lot of paintwork – including mock-marbling.' He seemed relaxed about it. 'They've brought a lad over to do it; naturally it's not his field, he's really a landscape specialist –'

'Typical!' I sympathised.

'Oh . . . Blandus knows him. Jobs for the guild, you know. Some smartarse from Stabiae – it's no problem; I can train him in what marble really looks like. The young fellow's all right, quite bright really – for a painter.' Milchato drained his beaker. He must have a throat that could swallow hot bitumen. 'My contract is big enough to keep me busy and believe me, Falco, I can buy what I want. Free hand. Authority to draw on resources from anywhere in the Empire. Can't ask for more than that.'

But could he, though? Was he somehow topping up his salary? I would have to check how much stone was being imported and whether it was all still here.

'I'll be frank,' I said. 'You know I am here to look for problems. There may be diddling with the marble.'

Milchato gazed at me, wide-eyed. He was giving his most careful attention to this theory of mine. If he studied it any more seriously, I would think he was mocking me. 'Whoops! Do you think so?'

'I wouldn't insult you by claiming it, otherwise,' I replied dryly.

'That's terrible . . . surely a mistake.' He ran one hand over his beard, which rasped as if he had tough hairs and a dry skin.

'Do you rule it out?' Only an idiot rules out fraud anywhere on a building site.

'Oh I wouldn't say that, Falco.' Now he was being open and helpful. 'No, it's entirely possible . . . In fact, you may well be right.'

This was easy. I always like that. 'Any ideas?'

'The sawyers!' cried Milchato at once, almost eagerly. Yes, it was very easy. Loyalty to his labour force was not his strong feature. Still, I was the man from Rome; he would feel even less respect for me. 'Bound to be them. Some of them deliberately use too coarse a grain of sand when they're cutting. It wears away more than necessary of the slabs. We have to order more material. The client pays. The sawyers split the difference with the marble supplier.'

'Are you sure of it?'

'I have had my own suspicions for a while. This fiddle is famous. Oldest trick in the book.'

'Milchato, that is extremely helpful.' I rose to leave. He came to the door with me. I slapped him around the shoulders. 'I'm glad I called on you. This will save me days of work, you know. Now I'm going to leave you with it for a while; I want you to look out for the trick, and see if you can put a stop to it. I could order the bastards to be sent home again, but we're really stuck out here. I can't lose them. Obtaining new labour for a specialism is too difficult.'

'I'll jump on it, Falco,' he promised gravely.

'Good man!' I said.

It was time to leave. He had another visitor. An elderly man in a Roman tunic, wrapped in a dramatic long scarlet cape and with a travelling hat. He acted as if he was somebody – but whoever it was, I was not introduced. Though Milchato and I parted on good terms, I was sure the marble master waited deliberately until I left the area. Only then did he greet his next visitor properly.

It was decent of him to admit the fault. If all the supervisors with scheming workmen came through so well, I would soon be going home.

On the other hand, when any witness in an enquiry owned up too readily, my habit was to look around to see what he was *really* hiding.

Iggidunus brought his five barred gates late that afternoon. They started off large, then became smaller as he ran out of space on his tablet. I could see at once that if his count was vaguely accurate, my fears were correct.

'Thanks. Just what I wanted.'

'Aren't you going to tell me what it's for, Falco?' Out of the corner of my eye, I could see Gaius, head down over his work, looking apprehensive.

'Auditing pottery,' I decreed smoothly. 'The storekeeper isn't happy. Seems we've had too many beaker breakages on site.'

Iggidunus, thinking he would get the blame, scurried off hastily.

Gaius and I at once grabbed the tablet and started to set our official labour records against the numbers who were actually here on site according to the *mulsum* round. The discrepancy was not as bad as I had expected, but then they were still digging foundations and the current complement was low. When the walls of the new palace started rising, I knew Cyprianus was due to take on a very large tranche of general masons, plus stone-cutters to shape and face the ashlar blocks, scaffolders, barrow boys and mortar-mixers. That would be any day now. If we acquired non-existent workers in the same proportions, our numbers would at that point be out by nearly five hundred. In army terms, someone would be defrauding the Treasury of the daily cost of a whole cohort of men.

The clerk was extremely excited. 'Are we going to report this, Falco?'

'Not straight away.'

'But —'

'I want to sit on it.' He did not understand.

Discovering that a fraud exists is only the first step. It has to be proved — and the proof has to be absolutely watertight.

XXVI

I WHISTLED TO Nux and took her on a walk. She wanted to go home for her dinner, but I needed the exercise. As I plodded along, lost in thought, she looked up at me as if she thought her master had gone crazy. First I dragged her on a frightening ship, then an immense journey overland, and finally I brought her to this place where there were no pavements and the sun had died. Half the human legs she sniffed were clad in hairy woollen trousers. Nux was born a city dog, a sophisticated Roman layabout. Like me, she wanted to be kicked at by the bare-legged bullies of home.

I took her to the painters' hut, hoping to ask the assistant about Blandus' progress. There was no sight of this lad everybody talked about. I did see more of what must be his work. In the blank space where someone had previously written 'LAPIS BLUE HERE', that note was now scrawled out and a different hand had added 'POMPONIUS TOO MEAN: BLUE FRIT!' Perhaps that was the assistant. Some deep blue paint was mixed in a bucket, no doubt ready to obliterate the graffiti before the project manager saw it.

Since I was last here, someone had tried out new types of marbling. Blue and green paints were smeared together in an artistic technique he had not quite mastered, with pairs of symmetrical patches like the mirrored patterns of split-open marble blocks. Endless squares of better-executed dull pink and red veining had been added to the chaos. There was a landscape panel, a stunning turquoise seascape, with finely touched white villas on a shore that looked exactly like Surrentum or Herculaneum. No; it was Stabiae, of course – whence the smartarse had been fetched.

Light seemed to dance off the waves. With a few competent brush-strokes the artist had created a haunting miniature holiday scene. It made me long for the Mediterranean . . .

The fresco assistant had loafed off somewhere. Given what Cyprianus said about painters, he might be after some woman. It had better not be one of my party.

In the hut next door I did find the bereaved mosaicist, Philocles Junior.

'I'm sorry about what happened to your father.'

'They say you hit him!'

'Not hard.' The son was obviously all fired up. 'Keep calm. He was going mad and had to be restrained.'

The son took after his father, I could see. It seemed best not to hang about. I had too much to do; this was no time to start making myself a slow-burning, brooding enemy. If Philocles Junior wanted a feud in his late father's mould, he must look elsewhere.

I led Nux past the parked wagons, hunting for Aelianus. He was lying in the statue cart not quite asleep today, but looking bored. Recognising him, Nux jumped on him happily.

'Ugh! Get it off me.'

'Not a dog-lover?'

'I spend half my time hiding from the guard dogs from the secure compound.'

'Fierce?'

'Man-eaters. They bring the pack out once a day, looking for human flesh they can train them with.'

'Ah, British dogs have a tremendous reputation, Aulus.'

'They're gruesome. I was expecting them to howl all night – but their silence is worse, somehow. The handlers can hardly hold them. They snake around, virtually towing the men, searching for someone who's stupid enough to try running away. It's clear they'd kill anyone who did. I think the handlers bring the dogs out so would-be thieves see them and are too terrified to break in.'

'So you're not going over the fence to pick up a new fountain bowl for your father's garden?'

'Don't joke.'

'All right. I don't want to have to tell your mother I found you with your throat torn out . . . Anything to report?'

'No.'

'I'll be off, then. Stick with it.'

'Can't I stop doing this, Falco?'

'No.'

Nux and I set off to our elegant royal quarters for dinner, leaving Aelianus out in the damp woods. As I started walking back, I wondered how his brother was, and when Justinus might manage to send me word of his activities. My assistants and I were too scattered.

I needed a runner. At home I could have brought in one of my teenage nephews; here there was no one I could trust.

Nux was rootling. This was better. She had learned that in Britain there were at least ways of getting her hair full of twigs and her snout earthy. Maybe the guard dogs had left fascinating messages as they passed this way. She spent long pauses with her nose in the leaf litter at the side of our track, then she tired of that and rushed crazily after me, dragging a large branch and barking hoarsely.

'Nux, let's show the barbarians some forum manners, please – *don't roll in that!*' Too late. 'Bad dog.' Nux, who had never grasped the finer points of reprimands, wagged her tail frenetically.

Why had I taken in a reckless street mongrel with a taste for dung as an unguent, when other Romans acquired sleek lapdogs with long pointed noses to appear in the stone plaques they commissioned? Father togate and serious with a scroll, mother matronly and bestoled, infants tidy, slaves respectful, moneybags flaunted – and clean pet gazing up at them adoringly . . . I should have known better. I could at least have let myself be picked by a dog with short hair.

Mine was happy now she stank. She had simple taste. We walked on. Gloomily, I pondered the possibility of taking Nux through the Great King's bath house. It could have raw consequences. Ever since the official insensitivity that led to Boudicca and the Great Rebellion, all Romans who came to Britain were required to conduct themselves with clean-hands diplomacy. No rape; no plundering inheritances; no racial abuse; and absolutely no cleaning muck off your dog in a tribal king's domestic plunge bath.

I was trying to call her back to me, with a view to attaching a rope to her so she did not rush indoors before I had had a chance to sluice her down, when Nux found new excitement. A pile of rough-hewn tree trunks had slipped. I could see that, because some were spilt across the track. Nux dashed up the remaining pile, scrabbling.

'Get down from there, Stinky! If they roll again, I'll leave you crushed in the woodpile –'

Nux obeyed me enough just to lie rigid with her muzzle in a crack between two tree trunks, whining. I put my boot up beside her and craned to peer at her discovery. For some reason, I thought it might be a dead body. You get like that. Something whimpered. I could now see cloth, which turned out to be a child's clothing. The child was still inside the dress, alive luckily. She was not herself trapped under the timber, but her skimpy gown had been caught so securely she could hardly move. She was scared – mostly that she would be in trouble.

I wedged a couple of stones under the bottom of the pile and then heaved up the top log just enough to free her. I lifted her down then caught her just before she ran away. Upset by her fright, though bravely not crying, she glared. We had rescued a tough eleven-year-old girl called Alla who knew how to lie but who finally admitted she had been warned by her father several times not to play on the stacked logs. It emerged, after a fierce extraction process, that her father was Cyprianus, the clerk of works. I grabbed her hand and took her back to the site to find him.

'This little loner is yours, I think? I don't want to snitch, but if it were one of mine, I'd like to be aware she had had a scare today.'

Cyprianus made as if to swipe her. She nipped behind me. If he meant it, he had a terrible aim. She pretended to bawl her head off, but this was done purely on principle. He jerked his head at her; she stopped crying.

I got the picture. Alla was bright, bored and mostly unsupervised – an only child, or the only one to have survived infancy. She roamed about, mainly content with her own company. Cyprianus, with his own busy concerns, had to ignore the fact she was at risk. There was no mention of a mother. That gave two possibilities. Either the woman had died – or Cyprianus had joined up with a foreigner in some other exotic territory and now she stayed out of sight. I imagined her in their hut stirring stockpots, having little in common with him or the places he brought her to – and probably bemused by their solitary, highly intelligent, Romanised offspring.

'Want something to do? You could come and help me,' I suggested.

'Your dog smells.' My dog had saved her from a night in the open, maybe worse. 'What would I have to do?' she deigned to ask.

'If I provide a donkey, can you ride?'

'A *donkey*?' I was in the land of the horse.

'A pony, then.'

'Of *course*!' She was a bareback terror by the sound of it. Her father stood back and let me negotiate. 'Ride to where?'

'Into Noviomagus sometimes to see a friend of mine. Can you write, Alla?'

'Course I can.' Cyprianus, who had to be both literate and numerate, must have taught her. As she boasted, he was looking on with a mixture of pride and curiosity. They were close. Alla probably knew how much you had to pay per day for first-class plasterers and how long new roof-tiles should be left to dry out at the clamps where they were made. One day she would run off with some layabout scaffolder, and Cyprianus would be heartbroken. He already knew it would happen, if I were any judge of him.

'Are you a good girl?'

'Never – she's terrible!' Cyprianus grinned, cuffing his roughneck fondly.

'Come and see me in my office tomorrow, then. I'm Falco.'

'What if I don't like you?' Alla demanded.

'Yes you do. It's love at first sight,' I said.

'You think a lot of yourself, Falco.'

She might have been brought up entirely in a series of foreign provinces, but little Alla had the pure essence of any scornful Roman sweetheart at the Circus Maximus.

Back at the old house we ate outside again. I can't say it was warm, but the light was better than indoors. Tonight's food was lavish; apparently the King had visitors and the royal cooks had made a special effort.

'Oysters! Ugh. I like to know where my oysters come from,' mouthed Camilla Hyspale.

'Suit yourself. British oysters are hymned by poets, the best you'll ever taste. Give yours to me then –' I had my arm out to snaffle the rest when Hyspale decided she might try one after all. Thereafter she hogged the serving dish.

'That painter was here looking for you again, Marcus Didius.'

'Wonderful. If it's the assistant from Stabiae, I was at his hut looking for him. What's he like?'

'Oh . . . I don't know.' I had not yet trained Camilla Hyspale to provide a witness statement. Instead, she blushed slightly. That was clear enough.

'Watch him!' I grinned. 'They are notorious for lechery. One minute they are chatting to a woman harmlessly about earth colours and egg-white fixers, the next they have fixed her up in quite a different way. I don't want any lout in a paint-stained overtunic getting the better of you, Hyspale. If he offers to show you his stencil-stumping brush, you say no!'

While Hyspale was spluttering in confusion, some of us wondered hopefully if we could pair her off. Helena and I were die-hard romantics . . . And leaving the nursemaid in Britain would be bliss.

The royal party must have dined formally, but afterwards some of the usual group with Verovolcus among them brought their wine, beer and mead into the garden. We never saw the King in the evening; his age must have condemned him to an early-night routine. When we had finished eating, I went over to the Britons to broach with Verovolcus the subject of the King's bath-house upgrade.

Before I mentioned it, I noticed a stranger. He seemed well at ease in company with the King's retainers, but turned out to be that evening's guest. I could hardly miss him because, unlike anyone else in this province, he was wearing a two-piece formal Roman dining suit – a synthesis: loose tunic and matching overmantle the same shade of red. Nobody I knew ever made themselves look foolish with an old-fashioned twinset, even in Rome. Only rich-boy partygoers of a certain eccentricity would bother.

'This is Marcellinus, Falco.' Verovolcus had at last stopped calling me the man from Rome with every breath. However, if he did not need to tell Marcellinus who I was, my role must already have been discussed. Interesting.

'Marcellinus? Aren't you the architect for this palace, the "old house"?'

'The *new* house, as we called it!'

I remembered now that I had seen him before. He was the elderly cove who had turned up that morning to see Milchato the marble chief. He made no mention of it, so I held my peace too.

Like many in artistic professions, he cultivated a stylish air. His unusual clothes were outlandish in a casual setting, and his élite accent was agonising. I could see why he chose to stay an ex-patriot. He would have no place in Vespasian's Rome, where the Emperor himself would call a wagon a dung-cart – in an accent that implied he once knew how to shovel manure. With a grand Roman nose and gracious hand gestures, this Marcellinus stood out above the commonplace. It did not impress me. I find such men a caricature.

'I admire your superb building,' I told him. 'My wife and I are greatly enjoying our stay here.'

'Good.' He seemed offhand. Put out, perhaps, that the scheme to which he must have devoted many working years was now to be superseded.

'Have you come to see the new project?'

'No, no.' He cast down his eyes demurely. 'Nothing to do with me.' Was he disgruntled? I felt he deliberately distanced himself – but then he made a joke of it for my sake. 'You must wonder if I am interfering!' Before I could answer, he continued charmingly, 'No, no. Time to let go. I retired, thank goodness.'

I don't allow autocratic men to brush me aside. 'Actually I thought you might be here to mediate. There are problems.'

'Are there?' Marcellinus asked disingenuously. Verovolcus, like a gnarled Celtic, tree-stump god, leaned forward with his elbows on his knees, watching us.

'I feel the new project manager misjudges things.' Falco the frank orator outfought Falco the man of guarded neutrality. 'Pomponius is a narrow official. He sees the project as an imperial commission only – forgetting that there would be *no* commission without its very specific British client. No other tribes are to be provided with a full-scale palace. This scheme will far outlive our generation – yet it will always be the palace that was built for Tiberius Claudius Togidubnus, Great King of the Britons.'

'No Togi, no palace. So what Togi wants, Togi should get?' His use of the crude diminutive in a serious discussion – in front of the King's servants – jarred. Marcellinus was supposed to be on good terms with the King. His lack of deference sat poorly with the affectionate way Togidubnus had spoken of *him* in my hearing.

'I like a lot of what the King suggests. But who am I to comment on architecture?' I smiled. 'But I suppose it is nothing to do with you nowadays.'

'I finished my task. Someone else can carry the burden of this great project.'

I wondered if he had ever been considered as project manager for the new scheme. If not, why not? Was being replaced by a newcomer a surprise to him? And did he accept it? 'What brings you back today?' I asked lightly.

'Seeing my old friend Togidubnus. I don't live far away. I spent so many years out here,' Marcellinus said, 'I built myself a delightful villa down the coast.'

I knew some provinces could win the hearts of their administrators, but Britain? That was ridiculous.

'You must come and see me,' Marcellinus invited. 'My home is about fifteen miles east of Noviomagus. Bring your family for a day. You will be made very welcome.'

I thanked him and made off back to my loved ones before I could be forced to arrange a date.

XXVII

WE HAD another bad night. Both the children kept us awake. Camilla Hyspale was indisposed by a violent stomach upset. She blamed the oysters, but I had eaten plenty and was perfectly all right. I told her it was the penalty for flirting with the young painter. That caused more wailing.

Next day I felt jaded. Staring at figurework held no appeal. Now I knew that Gaius was capable of flogging on through the records revision without me, I thought I would give the office a miss. I had requisitioned a pony for sending Alla to see Justinus, but I decided to take things easy and check up on him myself. I had something else to keep my runner busy. I introduced Alla to Iggidunus and told them I had decided it was time that the *mulsum* round was reappraised.

'You are both bright young people; you can help me sort this out. Iggy, today when you are taking round the beakers, I want Alla to come with you; she can write things down. Speak to every one of your customers personally, please. Tell them we are conducting a preference survey. You give Alla their names – Alla, set each one out neatly. Then list what kind of *mulsum* they like, or whether they don't have any.'

'But I done the counting yesterday, Falco!' Iggidunus protested.

'Yes. That was brilliant. Today we are on a different exercise. This is an organisational method study to straighten out the refreshment rota. Modernise. Rationalise. Revolutionise . . .'

The young persons fled. Management twaddle can always clear a room. The door closed behind them just in time, as Gaius the clerk collapsed in a fit of giggles.

Verovolcus saw me riding off. I had selected a small pony, thinking Alla would be riding it. My boots were almost scuffing the dust. Verovolcus burst out laughing. I was causing happiness all round today. I just grinned feebly. We Romans are never keen on horseflesh.

I was perfectly happy knowing I could apply a brake by just putting my feet on the ground.

I hit Noviomagus about midday. It seemed distinctly quiet. Maybe this was not the best time. Either I had missed the busy hour – or else there never was one.

I had been here when we first landed, but was then exhausted and disorientated after the weeks of travel. This was my first real chance to look around. It really was a new town. I already knew that the kingdom of the Atrebates had had to restore its fortunes when Togidubnus took over. Prior to his reinstatement at the Roman invasion, fierce Catuvellauni from the north had pushed in and raided the territory of this coastal tribe, nibbling into their farmland until they were squeezed back right against the salty inlets. The Romans rewarded Togidubnus for his support with the gift of increased tribal areas. He called this 'the Kingdom', as if other British tribes and their royalty did not count.

At that time, he must have adopted a new tribal capital. He had to build it too – but then he did love building. Being Romanised himself, he had probably found it natural to use the legionaries' supply base as his starting point. So the 'New Marketplace of the Kingdom' lay here, part enclosed by the curve of a small river, a little way inland. Perhaps abandoning the old settlement (somewhere on the coast?) had symbolised the King's affinity with the new way of life that would come with Britain's status as part of the Roman Empire. Perhaps the old settlement just fell into the sea.

Noviomagus showed how flimsy Romanisation was. I knew there were towns which had developed from military forts, often with legionary veterans forming the main body of citizenship. Queen Boudicca burned several, but they had been rebuilt now. They were utterly provincial, though solid and thriving. Unlike them, Noviomagus Regnensis had barely acquired any decent masonry properties or a population worth counting. Even though it was the headquarters of the most loyal British leader, this was still backwoods country. Wattle-and-daub remained the building style in the narrow streets, where only a few house-dwellers and businesses had so far ventured.

Main roads came in from Venta, Calleva and Londinium. At a central point they met the inbound track used by market traders. The crossroad had a large gravelled area which masqueraded as a forum. There was no evidence of use for democratic purposes, or even for gossip. It did provide stalls for selling pensionable turnips and pallid spring greens. There were a couple of dark little temples, a piss-poor set of baths, a faded sign to the out-of-town amphitheatre and short row of brooch-shops producing ethnic enamel ware.

Togidubnus had a house here, and so did Helena's uncle, Flavius Hilaris. His boasted hot air flues and a very small black and white mosaic. In his almost permanent absence it was run by a couple of wimpish slaves who were apparently out at market today. Lovely. Turnip soup was the gourmet speciality they would provide for Camillus Justinus, their honoured Roman guest. Ma would say, if we gave this province nothing else, people would thank us for the turnip . . .

Justinus was still in bed. I found the rascal still asleep. I hauled him out, poured cold water into a washing bowl, handed him a comb, found a scrunched-up over-tunic on the floor under his bed. He had shaved – though not since I last saw him. According to my calendar, that was two days ago. He looked rough – yet to do the job I had given him, he was passable.

Someone appeared to have seen through his act: he had a black eye.

'I notice you are going into this task thoroughly. Lying in all morning with a terrible hangover – and sporting shiners.'

He groaned.

'Oh *very* good, Quintus. You do have the art of sounding half dead. Do you want your belt, or would firm support around the midriff be too much to tolerate?'

With a huge yawn, Justinus took the belt and wound it half-heartedly around himself. Fastening the buckle was too complicated. I tightened it for him as if he were a dreamy three-year-old. The belt was a splendid effort in British tooled leather with a silver and black buckle – though I could tell from the elongated prong holes it was not new.

'Second-hand?'

'Won it.' He grinned. 'Game of soldiers.'

'Well, take care. I don't want to find you sitting here naked next time because some trickster has cleaned you out playing strip draughts!' Helena would be horrified. Well, his darling bride Claudia would. 'Shall I reel you back in for safety – or are you doing good work?'

'I'm having a delightful time, Falco.'

'Really! Who hit you?'

Justinus touched his eye gently. I found a bronze hand mirror among his kit and showed the damage. He winced, more at the marring of his looks than the pain.

'Yes,' I said calmly. 'You are a big boy now. Looks like you've been playing with some older boys that your mummy would disapprove of.'

My assistant was not in the least discomfited. 'He was young, actually.'

'Just stupidly drunk, or hated your accent?'

'Slight disagreement about a young lady.'

'You are a married man, Quintus!'

'So is he, I gathered . . . I was squeezing her for information – while he was just squeezing her tits.'

'Marriage has made you very crude.'

'Marriage has made me –' He stopped, on the verge of some enormous sad confession. I let it pass.

As I pulled him to his feet and carried him off to the kitchen for sustenance, I kept him talking lest he fall asleep again. 'So, you compared notes with your assailant? That would have been when you became blood brothers in a heart-rending reconciliation, over jugs of British beer?'

'No, Falco. We are two homesick Romans stranded here. When the disloyal girlie went off with someone else, he and I found a quiet wineshop where we shared a very decent Campanian red and a civilised platter of mixed cheeses.' Justinus had the knack of telling an unbelievable story as if it were entirely true.

'I bet.' I shoved him to a bench by a table. Someone had been chopping onions. Justinus went green and put his head in his hands. I moved the bowl away smartly.

'It was civilised,' he vowed again weakly.

'I don't like the sound of that.' I put some bread in front of him. 'Eat, you beggar. And keep it down. I will not clear up a mess.'

'What I really fancy is some nice traditional porridge . . .'

'I'm not your adoring grandmother. I've no time to pamper you, Quintus. Stuff in the bread, then tell me what you've found out.'

'The nightlife,' declared my disreputable agent, through a mouthful of stale crust, 'is almost non-existent here. What there is – well, I've found it!'

'I can see that.'

'Jealous, Falco? When the troops were here thirty years ago, they must have quickly taught the natives what tough lads needed in the way of a brothel and a couple of dingy drinking dives. You can get several colours of imported wine, not well-travelled, and dried-up whelks as appetisers. In very small dishes. Second-generation hostesses and tapsters run those places – people, I'd say, with half or quarter Roman blood in them. The Second Augusta – that was your legion, wasn't it? – must be well represented in their pedigrees.'

'Don't look at me. I was based at Isca.'

'Anyway, you were a shy boy, weren't you, Falco?'

Truer than he knew. 'Innocence is more normal than most boys admit.'

'I believe I remember it myself . . . Falco, the canabae hosts speak with a bastard Esquiline twang and can part you from your cash as quickly as any caupona keeper in the Via Sacra.'

I caught his drift at once. 'You are getting no more money.'

'On expenses?' he wheedled.

'No.'

He sulked, then carried on reporting. 'Men from the palace site come into town most evenings. They walk here and back.'

'It's about a mile. Easy when you're sober and not impossible when drunk.'

'Once they arrive, they tend to divide up. The foreign labour drinks in one area, near the west gate, which is the first part of town they come to. The Britons venture further and favour the south-gate end. The road there goes out to a native settlement, on a headland at the coast.'

'What I'd expect. There are two gangs, with two different supervisors. The supervisors don't like each other,' I told him.

'And nor do the men.'

'Is there much trouble?'

'Almost every night. From time to time they hold a running street battle and throw bricks at shuttered windows to deliberately annoy the locals. In between, they just arrange one-to-one punch-ups. And knife fights – that was what happened to that Gaul you asked me to find out about.'

'Dubnus?'

'He fell foul of a gang of the British. Insults were traded and when the Britons scattered, he was lying there dead. He had been alone at the time, so his mates don't know who to take vengeance on – though they think it was brick-makers.'

'Is this tale common knowledge?'

'No, but I had it from a rather common source . . .' Justinus leered. 'I discovered it in confidence from the young lady I mentioned. Her name,' he said, 'is Virginia.'

I gave him a look. 'Sounds a regular flower to cultivate! But then what about your fighting friend?'

'Oh.' He grinned. 'The painter and I can share her!'

'He's a *painter*? Well, if he's the new assistant then I've been looking for him, and word has it he wants to talk to me. Hyspale wouldn't say no either – she thinks he's a cute prospect.'

Justinus was grimacing. 'Hyspale's our freedwoman. Can't have her smooching the pig's-bristle boy!'

'So *you* will drink and fight with this fellow, but your womenfolk are off-limits to him? Let's have no snobbery. He can take her, if his wife will let him,' I retorted with feeling. 'Anyway, tell your boozing mate, he's known on site as "the smartarse from Stabiae".' I paused. 'But don't tell him that you know me.'

Justinus was bored with eating. He slowed down, looking as if he wondered when the next drink and fight might come along. 'So I can carry on? It's exhausting me, having such a good time –'

'But you will be brave and uncomplaining?' I rose to leave him. I gave him a very small allowance in cash. 'Your commendatory gold medal is being moulded. Thanks for suffering.'

'It's a tough assignment, Falco. Tonight I am off to my favourite den of iniquity where if the rumour is correct, a *really* interesting female from Rome will come in to entertain the lads.'

I was halfway back home on my pony when for some reason his remark about the female entertainer bothered me.

XXVIII

I HAD GROWN depressed.

'One of my assistants wants to be a playboy; the other simply doesn't want to play.' I was moaning to Helena. She adopted her usual method of showing sympathy – a heartless expression and burying her head in a poetic scroll. 'Here I am, trying to re-impose order on this huge chaotic project, but I'm a one-man arena orchestra.'

'What have they done?' she murmured, though I could see the scroll was more interesting than me.

'They have done nothing; that's the point, sweetheart. Aelianus lies in the woods with his feet up all day; Justinus goes on the town drinking all night.'

Helena looked up. She said nothing. Her way of staying silent implied I was leading her brothers astray. She was the eldest and she cared about them. Helena had a habit of diligently loving wastrels; that was what had made her fall for me.

'If this is what it means to be an equestrian,' I told her, 'I would rather be half starved at the top of a tenement. *Staff* –' I spat the word out. '– staff are no good to an informer. We need light and air. We need space to think. We need the freedom – and the challenge – of working alone.'

'Get rid of them, then,' said the loving sister of the two Camilli callously.

When Aelianus called on us that evening, still complaining sulkily about his conditions, I told him he ought to be more placid and even-tempered, the way I was. I felt much better after mouthing this hypocrisy.

He lay on some grass with a beaker balanced on his stomach. The whole Camillus family seemed to have a drink problem on this trip. Even Helena was diving into the wine tonight – though that was because baby Favonia was crying endlessly again. We sent Hyspale into our room with both children and told her to keep them quiet.

154

Nux followed her to supervise. After that I could see Helena all keyed up, expecting trouble indoors. I was listening out for it myself.

'What's the matter around here?' scoffed Aelianus. 'Everyone is growling like unhappy bears.'

'Falco has toothache. Our children are niggly. The nursemaid is moping after a fresco artist. Maia is plotting alone in her room. I,' maintained Helena Justina, 'am complete serenity.'

Being her brother, Aelianus was allowed to make a rude noise.

He offered to tie a string to my tooth and slam a door on it. I said I had doubts that the door furniture installed by Marcellinus in the old house would survive. Aelianus then passed on some horror story Sextius had told him, about a dentist in Gaul who would drill out a hole and stick a new iron tooth right in your gum . . .

'Aaargh! Don't, don't! I can unearth buried corpses or change a baby's loincloth, but I'm too sensitive to hear anything that teeth-doctors do . . . I'm worried about my sister,' I diverted him. Maia had slunk off indoors by herself; she often did. Most times, she wanted nothing to do with the rest of us. 'We got her away from Anacrites temporarily, but it's no real solution. Some day she will have to go back to Rome. In any case, he's a Palatine official. He will learn that I am on a mission to Britain. Suppose he guesses that Maia came with us – and sends someone after her?'

'In a province like this,' Aelianus soothed me, 'a trained spy will stand out rather.'

'Nonsense. I'm a professional myself and I meld in.'

'Right.' He chortled. 'If anybody comes to get Maia Favonia, we are here. She is more closely protected than she would be in Rome.'

'And in the long term?'

'Oh you'll sort something out, Falco.'

'I don't see how.'

'Deal with it when you need to.' Aelianus was sounding like me these days. He lost interest in my problems. He sat up. 'Well, I want to do something, Falco. And I'm not going back to mind those damn statues. Sextius can mollycoddle his own junk.'

'You are going back right now.' I had to keep this trooper in line. Anyway, I had a plan. 'I am coming with you.' There had been the usual tramping of booted feet all evening as the labour force marched off into town. 'By the sound of it, they have all gone to see the wondrous female entertainer Justinus mentioned. Bare flesh, bad breath, leather knickers and a ratty tambourine – while the labourers are trying to paw her bikini strings, the coast is clear for us. You and

I are going to have a look in some of those delivery carts. Something's going on.'

'Oh I know what it is!' Aelianus amazed me by saying as he scrambled to his feet. 'It has to do with them sneaking materials off site. A new cart came in today; all the drivers looked at me, and said loudly, *"Here's the stolen marble; don't let Falco find out!"* nudging each other.'

'Aulus! I should have been told about that hours ago – you're a lot of use.'

As I went to fetch light, boots and outer wear, the baby started wailing again plaintively. Helena jumped up and suddenly said she was coming with us.

'Oh no!' cried her brother. 'Falco, you can't allow it.'

'Hush; be calm. Someone has to hold the lantern while we search.'

'What if we run into trouble? What if someone discovers us?'

'Helena and I can fall down on the ground in a passionate clinch. We'll be two lovers having a tryst in the woods. Perfect alibi.'

Aelianus was outraged. He could never cope with the thought of me making love to his elegant sister – least of all because he rightly sensed that she liked it. Publicly I gave him credit for some experience and he of course played the worldly type, yet for all I knew he was a virgin still. Nice girls of his own age would be chaperoned, he would be scared of disease if he paid for his fun, and if he ever eyed up his mother's matronly friends for a little adultery across the generations they would only tell his mother. Senators' sons can always jump on their household slaves – but Aelianus would hate having to meet their eyes afterwards. Besides, they would tell his mother too.

He became extremely pompous. 'And where does that leave me, Falco?'

I smiled gently. 'You are a pervert, spying on the legover from behind a tree, Aulus.'

XXIX

Rome has its deep areas of darkness at night. Nothing quite like the open country, though. I would have felt safer in narrow twisting alleys, unlit courtyards and colonnades where any lamps had been doused by passing burglars. There even seemed to be fewer stars in Britain.

We took the service road around the palace, going up carefully on the eastern side then along the north wing, past the secure depot. Walking on the metalled road was easier than tripping across the site, with its mud and fatal pitfalls. A young fox let out a blood-curdling scream from nearby undergrowth. When an owl hooted, it sounded like a human wrongdoer signalling to lurking friends. Noises carried alarmingly.

'We are mad,' Aelianus decided.

'Quite possibly,' whispered Helena. She was unperturbed. We could hear that my supposedly sensible lady was now thrilled to be up and at an adventure.

'Face it,' I told her brother. 'Your sister never was the docile type who would happily fold tablecloths while her men went out to spend, bet, feast and flirt.'

'Well, not since she noticed Pertinax doing all those things without her,' he conceded. Pertinax had been her short-lived first husband. Helena hated to have a failed marriage, but when he neglected her she took the initiative and issued a divorce notice.

'I saw her reaction, Aulus, and I learned from it. Whenever she wants to play outside with the boys, I let her.'

'Anyway, Falco,' Helena murmured silkily, 'I hold your hand when you're scared.'

Something quite large rustled away in the undergrowth. Helena grabbed my hand. Perhaps it was a badger.

'I don't like this,' Aelianus whispered nervously. I told him he never liked anything, then I led my companions silently past the specialist finishers' huts.

The mosaicist had his window shuttered tightly; he probably still mourned his dead father. From the fresco painters' hut came a smell of toasted bread; someone inside was whistling loudly. We had already gone by when the door was flung open. I sheltered our lantern with my body; Aelianus instinctively moved closer to help block the light. A cloaked figure emerged and, without a glance our way, skipped off in the opposite direction. He was a fast, confident walker.

I could have called out and initiated a deep argument about crushed malachite (which is *so* expensive) as against green earth celadonite (which fades), but who wants to start libelling 'Appian green' with a painter who is known to thump people?

'Your Stabian, Falco?'

'Presumably. Toddling off to thump your brother again.'

'Or serenade Hyspale?'

'I bet he hasn't even noticed her. He and Justinus are on a promise with a winebar-dainty called Virginia.'

'Ooh, I can't wait to tell Claudia!' Aelianus sounded as if he meant it, unfortunately.

Helena gave me an angry shove. I moved on.

We found the line of carts. Poking about strange transport wagons in pitch darkness, when the owners of the wagons may be waiting there to jump you, is no fun. An ox sensed our presence; he started lowing with a mournful bellow. I could hear the tethered mules stamping. They were restless. If I had been a carter here, I would have come to investigate. No one moved. With luck, that meant no one had stayed here to watch the wagons. Not that we could assume anything.

'Helena, we'll explore. Listen out for anyone coming.'

Not long after we first started searching, Helena thought she heard something. We all hushed. Straining our ears, we did hear faint movement, but it seemed to be retreating away from us. Had someone spotted us and gone for help? It could have been horses or cattle nosing about.

'Pretend that like rats and snakes *they are more scared of us than we are of them . . .*'

I ordered Aelianus to resume, but told him to hurry. With our nerve almost going, we hopped from vehicle to vehicle. The empty carts were no trouble. We checked them for false bottoms, feeling fools as we did so. We found nothing so sophisticated. Other carts were carrying goods for sale – wicker chairs, hideous mock-Egyptian side tables and even a batch of soft furnishings: ugly cushions, rolls of garish curtain material and some ghastly rugs – all made to lousy standards of workmanship, in what was thought to be provincial taste by people who had none themselves. Other cheapjack entrepreneurs like Sextius must have made their way here on the off-chance. If they failed to find a buyer in the King, they then drove into town and tried to flog their merchandise to the townspeople. In exchange, the canny Britons probably tried to palm off the sellers with fake amber and cracked shale.

Not wanting to leave signs that we had searched, we had problems with these carts. Still, we poked beneath the merchandise to our best ability. One of us would heave up the crude produce, while the other quickly scrabbled underneath. It would have helped if Aelianus had bothered to prop things up as he was supposed to, instead of letting a lady's armchair crash down on my bent head. Woven basketware is damned heavy.

'Steady on! Some tribal spearsman's daughter is going to find her new bedroom seat covered with my blood –'

Luckily I only had a sore noddle. The scent of blood was the last thing we needed. Because just at that moment a crowd of men rushed from the darkness, yelling at us – with the unleashed depot guard dogs baying ahead of them.

We had nowhere to go. It was a thousand yards back to the safety of the King's old house.

I pulled Helena up onto the furniture cart, shoved her right down among the wicker chairs and told her to lie still in this fragile *testudo*. Aelianus and I jumped to the ground and scattered, trying to draw off the dogs. I never saw where he went. I took the one open route in front of me.

I got a brief clear run to the campsite. Crashing through undergrowth, I burst into the clearing where various outcasts lurked on the fringes and no doubt preyed on the building site. Some had quite decent tents with ridge poles, some had nothing but branches bent over and covered with skins. A group of bonfires burned listlessly. It was all I could hope for out here. I grabbed myself a burning branch, stirred up the nearest blaze and as the sparks flew, light illuminated the clearing. I managed to pick up a second lit brand. Then I turned to face the guard dogs as they raced towards me through the trees.

XXX

HEY WERE big, fierce, black-haired, long-eared angry curs. They hurtled heavily towards me at full pelt. As the first reached me, I leapt back right over the bonfire, so his pads must have been singed as he jumped over. He felt nothing, apparently. I made wild feints with the live brands. Snarling, he sought to dodge the flames but still snapped at me.

Startled heads had popped out from some of the bivouacs. Other dogs careered up and attacked the tents. This was hard on the occupants, but distracted the other dogs from chasing me. I was left with my lone attacker. I roared and stamped. You have to outface them, someone had once told me . . .

My attacker was barking ferociously. Men arrived, shouting. The blanket-wrapped lumps who lived in the benders had come to – I glimpsed pans and staves being whacked around violently. Then I stopped looking as the terrifying dog launched straight at my throat.

I had crossed the fiery brands in front of me. Ends out, I rammed them at his mouth. It did at least make him miss his aim. He crashed onto me; we both bowled over backwards, and I kept rolling. I hit a hot cauldron. The pain seared my arm, but I ignored that. I grabbed its two loop handles, tore it from its hanging hooks and flung the whole thing at the dog as he squirmed around. Either the heavy vessel hit him or the boiling liquor scalded. He turned tail for a moment, whining.

A second's grace was all I needed. I was on my feet. When he leapt again, I had wrapped my cloak around my hand and torn down a spit that was roasting a rabbit over a fire. I speared the dog with it; he expired at my feet. No time for shame. I ran straight at the group of men who had brought the dogs as they tried to round up the others. They were too surprised to react when I kicked them aside. While they milled about, I broke free of the campsite.

Back in the woods, I took a new direction. Stumbling, skidding and cursing, I ran headlong. Bushes tore at me. Brambles clawed my clothes. Desperation gave me more courage and speed than any pursuers. The ground underfoot was deeply treacherous and I was in darkness. A few near invisible stars served to show my orientation but offered no light. I lurched free of cover, and knew from the noises and the smells of dung that I had somehow reached the tethered beasts. I dragged a mule around by the head and cut his rope with the knife I keep in my boot. Judging direction from memory, I rode past the parked carts.

'*Helena!*'

She popped up, still holding the lantern. What a girl. Wasted as a senator's daughter. Perhaps even wasted on being my girl. I should have let this Amazon deal with the dogs. One look from those scathing dark eyes and they would have cringed into submission. Me along with them.

Hoiking her skirts and tucking the loose folds of cloth well into her girdle, she stepped off the cart sideways, sliding behind me onto the mule's back as if trained in a circus act. I felt her arm around my waist. With her free hand she held out the lantern to glimmer faintly on the track ahead of us. Without pausing, I geed up the mule and set off back to the old house.

'Wait – where's Aulus?'

'I don't know!' I was not uncaring, but I had to save Helena. She was worried stiff about her brother, but I would sort him out later.

Helena groused, but I kept the mule heading homewards. Security flares on the building site soon lit our way more safely. We arrived at our dwelling-place, shed the mule and bundled ourselves indoors. We were both shaking.

'Don't tell me –'

'You are an idiot, Falco. So am I,' confessed Helena with fairness as she shook out her skirts.

I was wondering how in Hades I could find Aelianus, when Maia and Hyspale both appeared. We told them nothing was the matter, so they knew something was wrong. Anyway, they would have realised when we were then disturbed by violent hammering at the outside door.

I opened up. I did it cautiously, sneaking a quick look out for dogs. Magnus and Cyprianus, the surveyor and the clerk of works, were standing there. They both looked furious.

'What a surprise at this time of night, lads!'

'Can we offer refreshments?' asked Helena weakly. I hoped I was the only one who would see from the light in her eyes that she was nearly laughing with mild hysteria.

They were not here to socialise. 'Have you been out just now, Falco?' Magnus demanded.

'A gentle stroll . . .' My scratched arms and legs and Helena's wide eyes must have given us away.

'Have you been by the delivery carts?'

'I may have ambled that way . . .'

'Intruders were disturbed by the guards from the depot.'

'What? Your dog-keepers? How lucky they were on hand to prevent trouble! What do these intruders say for themselves?'

'That's what we have come to ask you,' growled Cyprianus. 'Don't mess about, Falco. You were there; you were recognised.'

I reminded myself I was the Emperor's envoy and had every right to investigate anything I wanted. Guilt undermined me, nonetheless. I had been wrong-footed. Now I had a burned arm, canine teeth had ripped my tunic, I was hot and breathing hard. Worse, in my search I had found nothing. I hate wasted effort.

'I don't have to answer you tonight,' I said quietly. 'I have imperial authority to skulk – I could ask, what were *you* doing out there with a bunch of savage dogs?'

'Oh why are we arguing?' raged Magnus suddenly. 'We are all on the same side!'

'I hope that's true!' I scoffed. 'We can't have it out at this time of night. I suggest a site meeting with Pomponius tomorrow. Now it's late, I'm tired – and before you go, there was somebody else on the prowl near the carts. What have you done with that young man who accompanies the statue-seller?'

'We never got him. What's he to you?' demanded Magnus.

I kept up the pretence that Aelianus was a stranger. 'He looks wrong. He hangs about. He seems to despise the artwork that Sextius is supposed to be selling – and if you must know, I don't like the colour of his eyes!' Neither Magnus nor Cyprianus looked fooled. 'I want him found, and I want to interrogate him.'

'We'll have a look for him,' Cyprianus offered fairly helpfully.

'Do that. But don't beat him up. I need him in a condition where he can still talk. And I want him first, Cyprianus: whatever his game is, he's mine!'

It did no good. I found out next day they had looked half the night for him. There was no trace of Aelianus anywhere.

I went out myself at first light, trawling all around the site. There was flattened undergrowth everywhere, but Aelianus had vanished. By then I had realised that even if Magnus and Cyprianus had found him, they would never have handed him over to me until they had knocked out of him anything he had to say. They would extract more than that too. They would want him to incriminate himself – whether he was guilty of anything or not.

At least if he was dead in a ditch, none of us had pinpointed the ditch. Only as the site came alive in the morning did I make myself reluctantly try the last place where he might be. Slowly, I dragged myself to the medical hut and asked Alexas if anyone had brought him a new corpse.

'No, Falco.'

'Relief! Thanks for that. But will you tell me if you get one?'

'Someone in particular?' the orderly asked narrowly.

There was no point pretending any longer. 'His name is Camillus. He's my brother-in-law.'

'Ah.' Alexas paused. I waited, with my heart sinking. 'Better look at what I have in the back room, Falco.' That sounded grim.

I whipped aside a curtain. My mouth was dry. Then I swore.

Aulus Camillus Aelianus, son of Camillus Verus, darling of his mother and dutifully loved by his elder sister, Aulus my sullen assistant was lying on a bunk. He had one leg heavily bandaged and a few extra cuts for emphasis. I could tell by his expression as his eyes met mine he was bored and in a bad mood.

XXXI

'Look who's here! – What happened to you?'
        'Bitten.'
'Badly?'
'To the bone, Falco. I am told it could go seriously septic.' Aelianus was dismal. 'Men have died from less, you know. Alexas patched me up. I have to keep off this leg for a while – but I'll be kicking people with it soon!' I could tell who he wanted to kick.
'You're just angling to be sent home to your mother.'
'I am damn well not! I'm in enough pain.'
'Helena will come over and sort you out. She can bring you to the palace. Camilla Hyspale can nurse you.' Aelianus shuddered. 'No, all right. You are suffering enough. Helena will tenderly care for you. I'm so relieved to see you, I may even straighten your bedcovers.'
        I sat on his bunk. He shifted away petulantly. 'Leave me alone, Falco.'
'I have been searching everywhere for you,' I assured him. 'The thought that you had died on me was heart-rending, Aulus.'
'Shove off, Falco.'
'Everyone has been scouring the site. So how did you get here?'
        I was the only entertainment available. Aelianus sighed and gave in, prepared to talk. 'You went off one way and I headed back up the track. The mosaicist ignored me when I banged on his shutter. I had legged it as far as the painters' hut when some of the dogs caught up. I just managed to scramble inside, but one got his damned teeth into my shin. I shook the fiend off somehow, and slammed the door closed. Then I sat with my back jammed against that door and my knees braced hard, I can tell you!'
'I'm sorry I couldn't come for you. I was rescuing Helena.'
'Well, I hoped you had her.' The way he said it meant, *on the other hand – stuff you, Falco!* 'In the end the dogs were called off and taken away. I heard that mosaicist lambasting the men outside for the noise the dogs made. He was giving them a real earful – so nobody looked

in the painters' hut, thankfully. I was not prepared to venture out again. I thought I wouldn't make it anywhere anyway. I must have drifted off into oblivion – then the painter lad came home.'

'Your brother's pal?'

'He was completely out of it.'

'Drunk?'

'Lathered.'

'So no use?'

'Oh I was just glad to have human company. I told him what had happened and he listened blearily. He passed out. I passed out. Eventually we both woke up. It was at that point we noticed how much I had bled.'

Aelianus told this tale with rakish fluency. He could be a prude over women, but I knew that as a young tribune in Baetica he was one of the crowd. Even in Rome, with his fond parents watching, he had been known to roll home at dawn uncertain of how he had spent the previous night.

'The painter brought you to be bandaged?'

'It was still very early; no one was about. So he hitched an arm around me and I hopped here. We told Alexas not to mention me to anyone.'

'The painter could have let me know.'

'He wanted to go back to sleep in his hut. He was not a well boy.'

'Alexas could have given him a draught.'

'Alexas said he wouldn't waste good medicine.'

'Does this fine toper know you are connected to your brother?'

'He knows that Quintus *is* my brother.'

'Then he knows everything by the sound of it.'

'He's all right,' said Aelianus, usually no fan of anyone. He must have felt really lonely in that hut last night until the painter joined him.

He closed his eyes. Shock had taken its toll. Dog bites hurt badly too. I patted his good leg. 'You've done enough. Have your sleep. I am truly sorry you were wounded to no purpose.'

Aelianus, who had propped himself up when I first entered, lay down again on his back. 'Shall I tell him?' he asked the low ceiling. 'Yes I will! He treats me like shit, he abandons me to die and he jibes at me. But I am a person of honour, with noble values.'

'You are warped.' In fact he sounded like his sister. It was the first time any likeness to Helena had revealed itself. 'Yet in a crisis you act responsibly. Spit it out then.'

'The painter lad has a message from Justinus which – were they not a pair of reprobates – they would themselves be telling you urgently. Instead, my brother merely informed this adolescent painter, about whom we know absolutely nothing, and *he* deposited the vital facts with *me,* a drugged-up invalid. He did seem to think you would find me, Falco,' Aelianus mused with some surprise.

'I'm glad someone has faith in me . . . What's the word?'

'You're in big trouble.' Aelianus always gained too much pleasure from telling bad news.

I glared. 'What now?'

'When Justinus and his friend were drinking in their favourite piss-hole in Novio last night, they overheard some men from the site. Have you had a bunch of urchins collecting names and writing up a chart?'

I nodded. 'Iggidunus and Alla. Checking up who really works on site – as opposed to the inventive wages records.'

'The men started out laughing about it. Thought you a real clown, wasting time on official nonsense. I hear there were jokes, some cruder than others. I was not given details,' Aelianus said with regret. 'But then one labourer who must have a sliver of brain saw the implications.'

'They realise I am counting them?'

'You reckon there is a numbers diddle?'

'And I'm planning to stop it.'

'That's what they worked out,' warned Aelianus, no longer mischief-making. 'So be on your guard. Justinus heard them making serious plans. Falco, they are coming after you.'

I wondered what to do. 'Has Justinus had his cover blown?'

'No, or he would be here, petrified.'

'You underestimate him,' I stated curtly. 'What about you?'

'The painter says they all regard me as your spy.'

'Well, donkey's dingalings, you must have been really careless!' For jeering at his brother, he was due some insults back. 'I'll move you over to the palace as quickly as possible. We should have the King's protection in the old house. I'll ask Togidubnus to supply me with a bodyguard.'

'Can you trust him?' Aelianus asked.

'Have to. The working presumption is that as Vespasian's friend and ally, he represents law and order.' I paused. 'Why do you ask?'

'The labourers who are after you are the British gang.'

'Oh brilliant!'

Whether I could trust the King when British tribesmen were against me was indeed an unknown quantity. Would his decision to be Roman override his origins? Would completing the project take precedence?

Suddenly it looked as if my personal safety might depend on just how much the royal homeowner wanted his new house.

XXXII

THE BRITISH involvement was confirmed by a quick trip to my office. Alla and Iggidunus had handed in their list of named workers there last night. The clerk Gaius had already worked through it. The non-existent men to whom Vespasian was paying wages all belonged to the local group who were managed by Mandumerus.

'You may like to know,' Gaius said heavily, 'Iggy refuses to have any more to do with you; he won't even bring us *mulsum*. And Alla has been kept at home by her father. She won't be helping you again either.' Fair enough. I had no intention of placing the young people in danger.

'How about you?' I scoffed dryly. 'Want to bunk off school as well?'

'Yes, I tried to get a sicknote from my mother. Trouble is – she lives in Salonae.'

'And where is that?'

'Illyricum – Dalmatia.'

'She won't get you off, then.'

Gaius stopped bantering. He spoke lightly, but underneath it he was tense. 'I've never exposed a fraud before, Falco. I take it those involved won't like us now?'

'Us? Thanks for aligning yourself with me,' I said. 'But you'd better say in public, "I know nothing about it; I'm just the clerk." Let me be the one who exposes the fraud.'

'Well, you are paid more than me . . .' He was angling to find out how much. Any clerk would want to know. I did not frighten him by saying that if I died here I would not be paid at all.

I took a chance. There was no real alternative. I found Verovolcus and without giving reasons I told him that my position had become hazardous: in the name of the Emperor, I wanted the King's protection for me and my party. Verovolcus was not taking me seriously – so with reluctance I mentioned the labour scam. He said at once that he would tell the King – and fix bodyguards. I then

168

confessed that the culprits were the British group. Verovolcus' face fell.

I might be surrounding myself with more trouble. But if the King was serious about Romanisation, he would have to abandon his local loyalties. If Togidubnus could not do that, I would be in deep trouble.

I was now overdue at the site meeting – the one I had called. As I walked briskly to the ramshackle military suite where Pomponius had his work area, I was aware of a sinister new mood on site. It confirmed the message from Justinus. The workmen had previously ignored me as some fancy management irrelevance. Now they took note. Their method was to stop work and stare at me in silence as I passed them. They were leaning on shovels in a way that had nothing to do with needing a breather – and all to do with suggesting they would like to beat those shovels over my head.

Remembering the battered corpse Pa and I had discovered back in Rome, I felt chilled.

Pomponius was waiting for me. He was too much on edge even to complain that I had kept him waiting. Flanked by his twin caryatids, the younger architects Plancus and Strephon, he sat chewing his thumb. Cyprianus was there too. Verovolcus turned up unexpectedly just as I arrived; I guessed the King had sent him speeding here to see what happened. Magnus followed a minute later.

'We don't need either of you,' said Pomponius. Verovolcus feigned not to understand. Magnus, strictly speaking, had no direct management role. Of course he did not accept that definition. He was seething.

'I would like Magnus to be present,' I put in. I was hoping we would find time today to discuss the delivery-cart problem, whatever that was. 'And Verovolcus already knows what I have to say about our labour problems.'

So Pomponius and I were daggers drawn right from the start.

Pomponius took a deep breath, intending to chair the meeting. 'Falco.' I held back. He was expecting me to want to lead, so that floored him. 'We have all heard what you have discovered. Clearly we should review the situation, then you will send a report to the Emperor.'

'We need a review,' I agreed tersely. 'Reporting to Rome would take over a month. That's time we don't have – not with so much slippage already in the programme. I was sent to sort things. I'll do that, here on the ground. With your co-operation,' I added, to smooth his pride.

So long as I took any blame for problems, Pomponius had enough arrogance to seize this chance to act independently of Rome. Plancus and Strephon looked excited by their leader being decisive. I felt it could work out badly.

I outlined the situation. 'We have a phantom labour force being charged to imperial funds.' I was aware of Verovolcus listening hard. 'My research, I'm afraid, indicates that the problem is with the British group, the one Mandumerus runs.'

Pomponius leapt in: 'Then I want all the Britons off the site. *Now!*'

'Not possible!' Cyprianus had spoken up quickly while Verovolcus was still swelling with outrage.

'He's right. We need them,' I agreed. 'Besides, to run a prestigious construction site in the provinces without any local labour would be most insensitive. The Emperor would never allow it.' Verovolcus kept quiet, but he was still simmering.

I had no idea how Vespasian would really react to widescale fiddling by a bunch of tribal trench-diggers. Still, it sounded as if he and I had shared hours of discussion on the fine points of policy.

'Right.' Pomponius came up with a new idea. 'Mandumerus is to be replaced.'

Well, that was sensible. None of us argued.

'Now this dodge has come to light,' I said, 'we have to stop it. I suggest we stop paying the supervisors in the current way. Instead of group rates based on their reported manpower figures, we'll make them each submit a complete named roll. If either can't write Latin or Greek, we can provide him with a clerk from the central pool.' I was thinking ahead to how other scams might develop: 'Rotating the clerks.'

'On a random basis.' Cyprianus at least was working on the same lines as me.

'Cyprianus, you will have to become more involved. You know how many men are on site. From now on, you should always countersign the labour chits.'

That meant if the problem persisted, the clerk of works would be personally liable.

I wondered why he had not spotted anomalies previously. Perhaps he had. Possibly he was crooked, though it seemed unlikely. I bet he just felt nobody would back him up. Judging him to be sound at base, I left that unpursued.

'I would like to know why you keep the two gangs separate,' I said.

'Historical,' Cyprianus replied. 'When I came out here to set up the new project, the British group were already on site as the palace maintenance crew. Many have worked here for years. Some of the old 'uns actually built the last house under Marcellinus; the rest are their sons, cousins and brothers. They had formed established, tight-knit teams. You don't break those up without losing something, Falco.'

'I accept that, but I think we have to. Amalgamate the groups. Let the British workers see that we are angry; let them know we have formally discussed whether to dismiss them. Then split them up and re-allocate them among the foreign sector.'

'No, I won't have that,' Pomponius interrupted haughtily, with no logic. He just hated to agree anything that had come from me. 'Leave this to the specialists, Falco. Established teams are a priority.'

'Normally yes. But Falco has a point –' Cyprianus began.

Pomponius brushed him aside rudely. 'We shall stick with the present system.'

'I believe you will regret it,' I said in a cool tone, but I let it rest. He was the project manager. If he ignored good advice, he would be judged on results. I would report to Rome – both my findings and my recommendations. If the labour bill then stayed too high, Pomponius was for it.

A wider issue struck me. With Verovolcus present, raising it was tricky: I wondered whether King Togidubnus had known all along about the phantom labour. Had it been a regular arrangement for years? Were previous Emperors, Claudius and Nero, each overcharged? Was this fiddling routine – never detected by Rome, until new Treasury vigilance under Vespasian brought it to light? And so had the King knowingly *allowed* the fraud as a favour to his fellow Britons?

Verovolcus glanced at me. Maybe he read my mind. He was, I thought, intelligent enough to see that whatever had gone on under the old regime, the King now had to operate my package of reforms.

'We shall have to deal carefully with Mandumerus.' I was still trying to impose physical order. The last thing we wanted was an outbreak of sabotage. 'If Mandumerus has been sharing his proceeds with his men, they are bound to feel sympathy for him if he's arrested – not to mention their grief for lost income. It could lead to revenge "incidents".'

'What do you suggest, then?' snapped Pomponius.

'Hold him liable for the lost wages. I recommend taking him under guard to Londinium. Get him right away from here –'

'Not necessary.' Pomponius reacted with daft bias yet again. 'No, no; this is where we can show our magnanimity. A gesture to local sensitivities. Diplomacy, Falco!'

Diplomacy my arse. He just wanted to cut across me. 'You cannot have him staying in the district as a focus for disruption. The men go drinking in Noviomagus every night. Mandumerus will be sitting right there, inciting them –'

'Nail him up, then!'

'*What?*'

Pomponius had had another wild idea. 'Put up the man on a crucifix. Make him a direct example.'

Dear gods. First this clown ran a completely lax site, then he became a scourge.

'That's an overreaction, Pomponius.' This was serious. We had the brooding presence of Verovolcus – no longer the comic figure, but a hostile witness whose knowledge of these mad Roman machinations could do us great harm. 'Crucifixion is a punishment for capital offences. I cannot allow it.'

'I run this site, Falco.'

'If you were a legionary commander in a full war situation, that might pass for an excuse! You answer to the civil powers, Pomponius.'

'Not on my project.' He was wrong. He had to be wrong. Pained silence from Magnus and Cyprianus confirmed that Pomponius might get his way. Unluckily my own brief did not extend to locking up the project manager. Only Julius Frontinus could authorise such a major step – but the governor was sixty miles away. By the time I could contact Londinium it would be too late.

'What tribe is Mandumerus?' I asked Cyprianus.

'Atrebates.'

'Oh, well done, Pomponius!'

This would have been bad enough in any province. Exposing locals as corrupt had to be handled with great delicacy. Of course there must be a public scapegoat – but would he be a scapegoat for decades of royal complicity and Roman mismanagement? His punishment had to reflect any ambivalence.

Pomponius smiled serenely. 'All issues of design and technical competence, welfare, safety and justice are mine. We endure quite enough pilfering. Organised fraud will be drastically punished . . .'

'Why don't you keep a bunch of man-eating leopards in the depot

172

along with the guard dogs? You could throw wrongdoers to the beasts in your own little arena, with you daintily dropping a white kerchief to initiate the fun – but you cannot do that.' I knew I was right. 'Only the provincial governor has praetorian power. Only Frontinus is invested with the Emperor's authority to execute criminals. *Forget it, Pomponius!*'

He leaned back. He had taken up position today in a folding seat, the symbol of authority. He put the tips of his fingers together. Light flashed off his enormous topaz ring. Arrogance flowed around him like a general's overweight crimson cloak. 'I shall adjudicate, Falco – and I say the man dies!'

Verovolcus, who had stayed significantly silent, rose swiftly and left the meeting. He made little fuss. But his reaction was clear.

'Straight to the King,' Cyprianus muttered.

'Straight in the shit for us,' growled Magnus.

In Britain, where memories of the Great Rebellion were set to last for ever, the causes ought to have been fixed in the architect's mind: high-handed Roman violence by minor officials who had had no feeling for the tribes and no judgement.

The Atrebates here in the south had not joined Queen Boudicca. When Rome was nearly swept out of Britain, the Atrebates had supported us as usual. Romans fleeing from massacre by the Iceni had been welcomed, comforted and given refuge at Noviomagus. Togidubnus had again offered our beleaguered armed forces one safe base in the enflamed province.

Now a member of that loyal tribe had committed fraud, perhaps with official connivance. We had to keep it in proportion: the fraud had resulted only in financial loss, not real damage to the Empire. The damage would be caused if we handled the situation badly.

How could Pomponius be blind to the implications? If he executed Mandumerus, we were verging on an international incident.

I was so angry I could only jump up and storm out. I strode away so furiously I had no idea whether the sycophants all stayed with Pomponius, or whether other people followed me.

XXXIII

NOBODY WAS working on the site. Of course they all knew what was happening.

Verovolcus had gone ahead and disappeared from view. I strode to the old house. At the King's quarters I was turned away. Not wanting to create a scene, I headed for my own suite.

A couple of warriors were lounging outside in the garden. Seeing me, one of them stood up slowly. My heart sank. He was only saluting. These must be our bodyguards. I managed to find a smile for him.

I stormed indoors, disturbing a scene of domestic peace. The children were being good for once. Maia and Hyspale were using hot rods to frizzle their hair into rows of formal curls. Helena was reading. Then she read my expression. Seeing I had a real crisis, she abandoned the scroll.

As I told Helena what was up, Maia listened in, grim-faced. Finally my sister burst out, 'Marcus, you said you had brought me from Rome for safety! First last night's trouble – and now more problems.'

'Don't worry. His work is always like this.' Helena tried to make light of it. 'He rampages about as if the gods had him under a murderous curse – then he clears everything up. Next minute he's demanding when is dinner . . .' She tailed off. It was doing no good.

The way Maia was standing very stiffly made me drag my concentration round to her. She met me with a hard stare.

'Everything's fine.' I dropped my voice soothingly. Reassurance failed to work. Maia had learned to be suspicious of men pretending to be affectionate.

'I have been talking to Aelianus,' Maia retorted. Helena must have fetched him here while I was at the site meeting. Deeming him at least innocent of the conspiracy to bring her away from Rome, Maia volunteered to nurse him. 'He says his brother goes drinking in the town.'

'Yes, it's a ploy. Quintus is on watch for me. Drinking is what young lads do on a night out... Look, Maia, I have an issue that needs quick thinking. Unless this is important –'

Maia said in an accusing voice, 'There is a dancer, Marcus.'

'A dancer. Yes. Luring good men from their mothers.'

'A dancer – here in Noviomagus.' Maia was not recommending a good night out to improve our social lives. What had caused only vague unease in me was a source of terror for my sister. 'You knew it – and you failed to tell me!'

'Maia, the Empire is stuffed with grimy castanet girls –'

The bluff failed. Maia already knew why the dancer might be a threat to her: 'This one comes from Rome – and she is special, isn't she?'

'Justinus did tell me the woman was causing excitement – some young chit who takes off more of her clothes than usual, no doubt –'

Maia simply glared at me.

'What is it, Maia?' Helena asked in a troubled voice.

'Anacrites has a dancer who works for him.' Maia was stony. 'He once told me he has a special agent who works for him abroad. He said she is highly dangerous. Marcus, she has followed me. He has sent her to get me.'

My sister had a right to be angry. And frightened too. I threw back my head and breathed slowly. 'I doubt if this is her.'

'You know all about her, then?' Maia shrieked. Wide-eyed, Helena had now caught on.

'Oh yes.' Did that make me sound efficient, or just devious? 'Her name is Perella. I met her in Baetica. Helena and I both met her. As you see we survived the experience.'

Perella, it had turned out then, had not been in Baetica looking for me. But I did remember how it had felt while I had thought I was her target. She and I had had a wrangle afterwards, when I stole the credit for a job she had wanted as her own commission. Our relationship since had been professional – but she was no real friend of mine.

It did not help that when I mentioned Perella, Helena hugged her arms around herself and shivered. 'Marcus, why would Perella be here?' she asked. 'Why would she know anything about Maia?' I tried not to answer. 'Marcus! Has Anacrites really sent her?'

'If it is Perella, I can't say what Anacrites has told her to do.' Helena knew, as I did, Perella would simply follow orders. She would assume it was state business.

'Tell me the truth!' Maia ordered. She tossed her dark curls contemptuously.

She had a right to know. 'All right. This is the situation: Perella was seen in Rome, hanging around your old house. That's why some people wanted you to leave.'

'*What? Who* saw her?'

'I did.' Naturally, Maia was furious. Helena, too, looked annoyed that I had kept it secret.

My sister's next question slightly surprised me. 'Did Petronius Longus know all this?'

'Yes. I'm sure that's why he helped your children with their scheme to extricate you –'

'And what about extricating my children?' seethed Maia. 'It hasn't worked, has it? I am still being chased by this woman, while my poor children –'

'Are with Petronius,' Helena interrupted. It was in effect her confession that she had been involved. 'They are safe.'

'What is he intending to do with them?'

'Let them be seen in the neighbourhood for a while, so it looks as if you are still in Rome –' I could easily see that going wrong. My anger at Petro for not talking to me about the plan redoubled. 'Then of course he will take care of them in the safest way. Don't worry about them,' Helena insisted. 'Lucius Petronius knows what to do.'

All Maia's old fear of Anacrites had returned. I was none too happy myself. 'I'll go and look at this dancer,' I offered gently. 'Don't worry about it, Maia. I shall know if it's Perella or not. As soon as I have sorted out this site problem, I'll go and check.'

XXXIV

THAT WAS a hiccup that I could have done without. Perella! Dear gods.

Sorting the labour problem would be a time-consuming enterprise, thanks to Pomponius. Luckily we had a short reprieve: Mandumerus must have heard we were on to him. When I made enquiries, I was told the rogue supervisor had left the site.

The other workmen now gathered in groups, muttering. I thought it unlikely they would go for me, at least not openly. When I approached, most pointedly turned their backs. One man with a barrow of spoil came straight at me and tried to push me into a deep trench. Soon afterwards, as I walked under scaffolding against the old house, a sandbag which had been used for weighting a pulley suddenly fell off and crashed right beside me. It missed, or the deadweight could have killed me.

There was nobody in sight above. It could have been an accident.

I might extract information from the one man who seemed to be at odds with Mandumerus – Lupus, the other supervisor. But when I asked after him, he was unavailable. Pomponius had now called a site meeting, with the leaders of all the trades – like the gathering from which he had debarred me on the day I arrived. Whether today's was to discuss general progress or to make specific changes following my revelations about the labour scam I did not know. He did not invite me to attend.

I worked in my office with Gaius all afternoon, trying not to feel demoralised.

Just before we packed up, someone threw a large rock through our open window. Gaius and I spent half an hour discussing whether to ignore this vandalism or stress ourselves reacting publicly. We chose to feign indifference.

Regular hard work lost its interest. Instead, Gaius said, 'I did look out for Guttus and Cloaca, those pipe-benders you were asking about.'

'Drippy and Drainage? Finding Gloccus and Cotta could be too much excitement at present, Gaius.'

'Neither is here,' he assured me. 'I checked all through the lists when I was doing the comparisons and, Falco, they don't feature.'

'False names.' I grimaced despondently. 'Like their fake workmanship.'

'Does Lupus know anything about them, Falco?'

'He says no.'

'Mind you, Lupus is the worst liar I've come across,' Gaius beamed cheerfully.

I groaned. 'How unusual!'

'They could be anywhere, you know, Falco. Some of the trades come out here on contracts – but a lot of men just turn up. Chances are they will be taken on if they can show a good pedigree from Italy or anywhere else that sounds civilised. We are making demands that Britons are not used to – unfamiliar materials and sophisticated techniques. A craftsman who says he has handled fine marbles, say, will be at a premium.'

'But plenty of cities in Gaul and Germany are being restored or expanded – so there is big competition for craftsmen, Gaius.'

'Right. Even in Britain, towns are throwing up temples to the imperial cult, or fancy public baths.'

'It's baths that interest me. And my information is that Togidubnus has a private plan to renovate his facilities here.'

'He has a firm lined up, I think,' Gaius told me. 'Some crew that Marcellinus, the old architect, recommended.'

'Do you know them?'

'I've been told nothing about it.'

'Is Marcellinus involved with the King's bath refurbishment?'

'That creep Marcellinus would like to be involved with everything,' Gaius grumbled.

'He's ex. Is he a problem?'

'We can't winkle him out. He's always hanging round the site. He really irritates Pomponius.'

'Don't most people?' I laughed.

The afternoon site meeting must have broken up at exactly the time I dropped my pretence of working and emerged. Most people scattered, but I caught up with Blandus, the chief painter. I had wanted to speak to him ever since I saw him being injured in the fight with Philocles. He was walking slowly, perhaps still in discomfort. When the others saw me, they scurried on, heads down; he could not hop away so fast, so was lumbered.

'Glad to see you about again!' He grunted. 'I'm Falco. A painter's looking for me. Is it you?' He grunted again, apparently a negative. Conversation was not his strong point. Hard to see how he had such notorious success with women. Maybe he achieved his wicked way using those old Roman standbys: a noble profile and suggestive winks.

His profile was nothing to talk about, in my opinion.

'It must be your assistant, then.'

'I know nothing about that,' muttered Blandus grumpily. 'He does what he likes. I've been laid up.'

I gave him a dry look. 'Yes, I was there. Tough about Philocles Senior! I hear Junior is cut up over losing his papa.'

Blandus, who had caused the trouble by seducing Philocles' wife all those years ago, refused to react. Still, I felt better for pointing out someone other than me had made enemies around here.

Maia was making it plain she supported the men who were throwing rocks at me. So instead of having dinner with my dear ones in our private suite, I took one of my British bodyguards and sloped off on a pony to see Justinus instead. I wanted him to take me to see the famous dancer – but he knew she was not appearing that night.

'Day off, Falco. The owner of the winebar plays it cleverly. He lets the lads grow keen, then as word spreads, he only offers performances at intervals.'

'Saves paying the damn woman every night.'

'He's even cleverer. The actual appearances are never publicised until the last minute.'

'So how do you know, Quintus?'

He grinned. 'Private source: dear little Virginia.'

'What a treasure. So while the curmudgeon who runs the bar is pretending he never knows when his artiste will agree to flirt her stuff, the luscious Virginia sells drinks to the crowds anyway? The keen ones still keep coming?'

'The owner claims that after a break, the dancer is fresh.' Justinus grinned. I ignored his leer.

'What's her name?'

'Stupenda.'

I winced. 'Her stage name, presumably! Tell me, please, that she's just a busty teenager.'

'Mature,' Justinus disagreed, shaking his head wisely. That was bad news. '*Experienced!* That's the fascination. You start out thinking

"This is a raddled hag" – then you find she has enchanted you . . .'

'Oh Jupiter.'

This was what Perella liked to do: station herself near her quarry, working as a dancer in some sour dive. There she would listen, watch, make herself known in the district until nobody thought twice about her presence. All the time she was planning her move. Eventually she would vanish from the dancing venue. Then she struck. I had seen the results. When Perella found her victims she took them out, fast and silently. A knife across the throat from behind was her favourite method. Without question, she had others.

Next came another disappointment: Justinus was not seeing the young painter that evening. 'We felt we could benefit from a night off drinking water.' Justinus had the grace to look sheepish.

I told him how Aelianus, fleeing the dogs, had met his friend the night before.

'So you got my message about the British workmen?' He did not ask about his brother's welfare.

'Yes, thanks. The men are now making their mood all too obvious – I don't know whether to keep looking upwards in case a loose scaffold board falls as I walk underneath, or to keep my eyes pinned to the ground looking for big deep thatch-covered holes they have set up as mantraps.'

'Olympus.'

'The Britons' leader is called Mandumerus. He's a thickset, woad-tattooed mental defective whom I would *not* like to meet in a narrow lane. I'm telling you that for a reason. He vanished from site this morning after I exposed the labour fraud – so I want you to look out for him in the canabae, please. Send word at once if he turns up.'

Justinus nodded. He seemed sober today. He was probably listening, though he looked rather vague.

'Don't approach Mandumerus on your own,' I reiterated.

'No, Falco.'

He fed me, courtesy of his uncle's placid house slaves. We both drank water with our dinner. Justinus needed to cure his hangover. I wanted a clear head too.

I collected my bodyguard, who had been eating where he could watch the street outside, and we picked our way carefully back to the palace along the mile or so of road. I felt glad that I had taken the precaution of covering up in a mantle and a large hat. Travelling a coastal road at night can be eerie enough. A buoyant wind wafted around us, smelling of seaweed and surf. Expecting any moment to pass groups of hefty, hostile labourers, my ears were alert for the slightest sound behind us or ahead. Even with a bodyguard I felt very exposed. For all I knew, this silent Briton in the red and yellow cloak who rode alongside might be Mandumerus' brother-in-law.

On the other hand, that might ensure his loyalty. Judging by how I felt about my own sisters' husbands, if he loathed Mandumerus he would look after me with due diligence.

We hit the palace again before I was expecting it. I had travelled this way enough times now for the road to shrink. Lights showed. I tensed. It was the same here as in Rome. Never relax when you seem to be in sight of safety. That can be the most dangerous moment.

I was jumpy. As we rode in under the dark scaffold that shrouded the King's quarters, a dangling rope brushed against me; I nearly fell off my mount. Its saddle was Roman, with high front pommels that you gripped with your thighs, and I managed to stay put. The bodyguard grinned. I returned his mirth manfully as we rode around to the courtyard garden. There I was preparing to swing down to ground level when we heard urgent running footsteps. Someone came haring around the outside of the building towards us.

If this was an attack, it was damned obvious. But an ill-executed ambush by idiots can be even more dangerous than a skilled operation.

Dim flares lit the courtyard. It was dark, so nobody was sitting out here. I was armed with a sword, which I drew quietly. The bodyguard grasped a long spear; he looked as if he knew what to do with it. Moving to a pool of light, we remained mounted. That gave us the best chance to manoeuvre. I hoped my companion did not realise I was keeping one eye on him in case he was planning a double-cross. With the rest of my attention I was watching to see who arrived.

One man, on foot.

Stark naked! White torso, deep brown arms and legs. Wild eyes. Oblivious to his daft predicament.

I relaxed somewhat, laughing. The bodyguard dismounted with a disbelieving grin. He hitched his horse and my pony to a column, bringing up one of the flares to shed more light. I skewed sideways and jumped down, then faced the ludicrously nude man. He was startled by my drawn sword as he arrived.

It was the clerk of works. Red-faced, he fell against the back of a garden bench, gasping so hard he looked ready to expire. His clothes were in a bundle, which he dropped. The bodyguard was casting a careful eye around the vicinity, so I was able to concentrate on helping Cyprianus calm down. I grabbed at his clothes bundle and pulled out a tunic.

Eventually he managed to stop wheezing. He got himself into the dingy blue tunic I was offering. As his head emerged through the neck hole, for a moment he just gazed at me. Whatever was wrong, it must have some magnitude.

He coughed again, bending low to brush grit off his feet and pull on boots. 'You had better come, Falco.' His voice rasped with distress.

'What is it? Or do I mean *who*?'

'Pomponius.'

'Hurt?' Unlikely. Cyprianus would have run for help from the medical orderly, not rushed here for me.

'Dead.'

'No doubt of that?'

A rueful expression crossed Cyprianus' face. 'Afraid not, Falco. Absolutely no doubt.'

XXXV

I LED THE way – taking the indoor route. There was no point attracting attention until I had seen for myself. We went into the old house via my suite, enabling me to drop off my outer clothes and collect a flare. Helena appeared, but I shook my head in warning and she withdrew, calling Maia and Hyspale after her. My grim face would have told Helena there was something wrong. Then we made our approach through the secluded inner corridor.

Cyprianus had found Pomponius in the baths. At least this corpse would be fresh. It was only that morning I was arguing with him. The thought crossed my mind professionally that I was glad I had an alibi tonight.

I went in alone. I grasped the torch in one hand, my sword in the other. Neither was much use for dispelling fear. When you know you are about to see a dead body your nerves tingle, however many times you have done it before. The flaming brand caused wild shadows on the pink stuccoed walls and my sword gave no reassurance. I have no truck with the supernatural, but if the architect's ghost was still whistling around the hot rooms, it had only me to haunt.

The entrance and changing room were faintly lit with oil lamps at floor level. Most were running out of fuel. Some had already burned down to nothing; a few guttered madly, their flames lengthening and smoking before their last moments. A slave would have poured fresh oil when dusk first fell. People normally bathe before dinner; the big rush would have been some hours ago. Only the fact that this was a large community, one with possible latecomers who might have some rank, would cause the bath house to be kept working late. In palaces and public buildings, men who have been held up by professional duties or newly arrived travellers have to be provided for.

In one of the clothes lockers sat folded garments. Rich cloth in vibrant colours – turquoise contrasted with brown stripes. All the other cubbyholes were empty. Nothing hung on any of the wooden cloak pegs. A few discarded linen towels scattered the benches.

There were no slaves present. A stoker must keep the furnace alive to power the hot-water boiler, but his access to the stoke-hole would be outside. Since there were no entrance fees and anyone could use the communal oil flasks, attendants were unnecessary. Cleaners would mop floors early in the morning and perhaps from time to time during the day. The towel supply would be replenished. At this hour, there was normally no staff activity.

The enclosed rooms, with their massively thick walls, were hushed. No splashing of dippers or slapping of masseurs' fists disturbed the dead silence. I glanced in at the swimming-pool area to the left of the entrance. The water shimmered with slight movements, but not enough to create lapping sounds. No one had disturbed the surface recently. There were no wet footprints around the perimeter.

Cyprianus had told me where to look. I had to go to the hottest steam room. Treading carefully in my leather-soled outdoor boots, I crossed the first room, entered the second, then checked the large square tepidarium with its plunge bath. There were lingering odours of cleansers and body oils, but the room had begun to cool and the scents were now growing faint. An abandoned bone strigil caught my eye, but I thought I had seen the same one there before.

There seemed nothing unusual. Nothing any late arrival has not witnessed at any commercial bath house where the ticket woman has already left and the hot water has cooled down. And most private baths would be like this after the stoker went to dinner. You could rush through and still end up clean enough, but there would be no real comfort for your bones.

Even in the ascending heat of the sweat rooms, the floor and flue convection was now fading slowly, although bare feet might still need the protection of wooden-soled slippers. I went into the third steam room. The body was lying on the floor. There was no sign of life. Cyprianus was right about that.

At about the time I found the corpse, I heard noises: someone behind me in the outer regions was now wedging open heavy doors to cool the inner rooms. Sensible. Sweat was pouring off me. Fully dressed, I felt damp and unhappy. My concentration was slipping, when I needed to be alert. I put my sword down and wiped my face roughly with my arm.

Take notes, Falco.

I had no tablet or stylus but memory was always my best tool. Well, Hades, I can still see the scene today. Pomponius was lying face down.

His hair was wet, but its colour and florid style made him recognisable. He was turned slightly, partly on his left side, facing away from me; his knees were slightly drawn up so the posture was a curve. One arm, the left, was under him.

Someone with poor eyesight might suppose he had fainted. I spotted at once that a very long thin cord was wound tightly around his neck. Several times. A loose end was caught under his right arm; it trailed backwards, then meandered over the floor towards me as I stood near his feet. He was wearing slip-on bath clogs. If there had been a struggle, they would probably have come off. A modesty towel encircled the body, loosened yet still more or less in situ around the waist.

A small pool of pallid, watery blood was near his head. Cyprianus, horrified, had warned me what that was. He had pulled up the body, ready to turn it over. Shocked by what he saw, he had let the corpse fall back.

I braced myself. I steadied my foot against the centre of the dead man's spine to stop him sliding across the floor, and pulled his upper arm hard. He was slippery with sweat, steam and oil, so I had to change my hold and grasp the wrist more firmly. In one strong movement I hauled him right over onto his back.

Then I looked. One of his eyes was gouged right out. I stood back. I managed not to gag, but a hand came up over my mouth involuntarily.

Cyprianus now came in behind me. He had brought spare towels to dry the running sweat off our faces.

'Aargh . . . there's something about eyes.'

'He's been stabbed too.' My voice sounded dull. Maybe it was due to the acoustics in here. 'You probably didn't notice –'

'No,' he admitted. 'I just ran.'

In the throat and on the naked torso there were wounds, made with something that caused extremely small entrance and exit cuts. Cyprianus pulled a face. 'What caused such wounds, Falco?'

'It's curious. They are almost bodkin-sized. Could a woman be responsible?' I pondered, looking around for inspiration. The weapon was no longer in the room. Little blood had escaped. These stabbings could well have been done after death.

A bodkin? Would a woman have had the strength to strangle Pomponius, apparently without him fighting back? The towel that must have been tucked around his midriff as he bathed was the usual useless napkin that you have to tighten up every five minutes. It would have fallen off straight away if he did anything energetic – even if he tried twisting around quickly. Could it have been placed back over him after the killing? Probably not. It was not just lying on the corpse; before I moved him, and although Cyprianus had made an attempt, the linen cloth was still wrapped right under his hips.

It was the strangling that did for him, I was sure of that. Either somebody came up behind him unexpectedly, or he was relaxed in the 'safe' presence of a social acquaintance. Most people sit in steam rooms on the side ledges, facing inwards to the room, backs to the wall. So coming up from behind was less likely.

Suppose this: Pomponius, bathing in the normal sequence, had reached the hottest room. After a hard day, irritating me and others, he had been full of torpor. Someone he may not have liked but whom he knew came in, sat fairly close, alongside maybe. If they had carried any large weapons, he would have seen. So they had a string, coiled up in the palm of the hand perhaps, and a small blade of some kind, also concealed. They whipped out the string and wound it around the architect's neck very fast – they stood up to do that, probably. They were strong enough to hold him still. (Or perhaps they had help – but either way I could see no bruising on his arms.) He stopped breathing. To make sure – or to exact further vengeance, they stabbed him and scooped out his eye. The eye could have been extracted with the same stabbing weapon, pushed in and then turned in a circular movement, like shucking an oyster. Finally, they lowered the body to the floor. My guess was that the whole incident had been very quick.

There could have been more than one assailant. One each side of him? A little too threatening when they first took up position. Say this: one sat beside him, one at a distance. The near one had the string. The second rushed up when the action started. He maybe had the concealed bodkin-like tool.

I bent and made myself unwind the string, jerking it from the folds of flesh into which it had dug so cruelly. Someone really pulled this tight. Loop and tug, loop and tug again . . . If Pomponius sat to relax in the steam the way so many of us do, leaning forward with his elbows on his knees and his head bowed, it would have been easy to collar him. Especially if he expected nothing. Both ends of the string had lain to the left of the head, as if the killer attacked from that side.

When I unwound the string fully, I found a couple of small knots along its length. They were very old, made so long ago that they were now solid and impossible to untie. The string was a firm, tightly twisted type, with no stretch. It seemed to be waxed, and was blackened with ancient dirt. Both free ends were tied in little loops.

While I was bending over, I had noticed the wet floor was muddy from my outdoor boots. Circular footprint smudges, in black watery slurry, marked every step I had taken. Cyprianus, now booted, had made the same mucky trail. There had been no other dirt when I first came in. None I had noticed in the other rooms either.

'Cyprianus, I take it you were bathing when you found him? No clothes? Bare feet?'

'Slip-ons. Why?'

'Look what a mess our feet are making now.'

He nodded. 'The floor was clean. Sure of it.'

'So, whoever it was, when they entered this caldarium they too looked like an innocent bather or bathers. You didn't see anyone?'

'No. I thought I was alone. That made it more of a shock when I walked in here.'

'No one went out past you, as you first entered the baths?'

'No, Falco. Must have been long gone.'

Not so long gone as all that, probably. He may have just missed meeting the killer or killers face to face.

'The next question must be: did they come here on purpose to kill? No question, in fact. Who goes into a bath house equipped with a length of twine and a bodkin?'

'Could a strigil have caused these wounds, Falco?'

'Too big. Snapped and splintered, maybe yes – but these entry wounds are very neat. Whatever made them was smooth, not broken. Like a poultry needle, or something medical.' I made a private note to discover if Alexas had an alibi.

Cyprianus crouched briefly and checked out one of the stab wounds. 'Straight,' he confirmed. 'In and out through the same channel. Not a curved implement.'

Looking around, I found strigils lying right on the water basin. There were three decorative bronze implements with fully right-angled curves, in various sizes. They were clearly made as a set, along with a globular oil flask and dipper, all of which could hang on a fancy ring. I sniffed the oil: rampantly expensive Indian nard.

'I've seen Pomponius scraping himself down with those,' Cyprianus said. The architect's strigils had smooth rounded ends, and were all undamaged. No bloodstains either.

We were both expiring with the heat. We left the corpse and sought fresh air.

XXXVI

Helena had followed me to the bath house. Looking anxious, she was waiting in the entrance, accompanied by Nux and our bodyguard. I asked the Briton to go and tell the King what had happened, then to arrange quietly to close off the baths, leaving the corpse inside for the moment. That way nobody else would discover the dead man.

'It's late; it's dark; half the people from the site are off in town. Let's keep this quiet until morning. Then I'll call a site meeting and start an enquiry. I always like to examine witnesses before they hear what's happened.' The Briton looked worried. 'This is my job,' I said patiently. 'Work I do for the Emperor.'

He gave me a look as if he felt perhaps I caused such tragedies by my very presence. He still seemed not to believe I had an official role, but toddled off to report to the King. Togidubnus would know the position. Vespasian would have told him I was to investigate the rash of 'accidental' deaths. Little did we think that would include the project manager.

'What are we to do now?' Cyprianus groaned. He sat on one of the benches in the changing area. I dumped myself nearby; Nux jumped up on another bench and lay there with her big hairy paws together, taking an intelligent interest; Helena sat alongside me. With the cloak I had earlier discarded pulled tightly around her body, she was frowning. I told her the details rapidly, in a low voice.

I was tired. Shock had worsened how I felt. Nonetheless, I stared hard at the clerk of works. 'Cyprianus, you were on the scene within a short time of the murder; your evidence is crucial. I shall have to ask you to go through it sometime. Let's start now.'

Like most witnesses who sense they have become suspects and must explain themselves, he showed a flash of resentment. Like the intelligent ones, he then realised it was best to accept the situation and clear himself.

'I had a long day, Falco. Meetings, arguments with the men. I stayed on site, pottering. I must have been the last one there.'

'That's usual?'

'I like it. Especially when things are going wrong. You get time to think. You can make sure no bastards are hanging around, up to no good.'

'And were they?'

'Not once they saw me doing my rounds. Most of the types who enjoy plotting had scarpered into town early.'

'Because of the Mandumerus exposure? Do you expect trouble?'

'Who knows? In the end, they want the work. That helps encourage them.'

I sat quiet, wearily.

Helena Justina adjusted her wrappings, turning one end of the cloak back over her left shoulder like a proper modest stole, and tightening the rest around her body so her long skirt flounced from under it, hiding legs that deserved display. 'I heard about the quarrel this morning between Pomponius and Falco,' she said. 'Wasn't there another site meeting in the afternoon?'

Cyprianus looked askance, expecting my support against this feminine intrusion. When I, too, simply sat and waited for his answer, he forced out, 'There was.'

'What happened?' I nudged him myself, so he would get the idea that Helena and I worked in partnership.

'We all went over the same ground again. Magnus lost his temper exactly the way you had, Falco. I managed to hold onto mine, though I was close to dotting Pomponius more than once. Lupus did not want to take the Britons onto his complement, so our plan to reorganise the labour force was soon bogged down.'

'Why is Lupus opposed to it?' Helena asked.

Cyprianus shrugged. 'Lupus likes to do everything his way.'

'So Lupus was angry, Magnus was angry, you were too,' Helena counted off. She spoke quietly and calmly. 'Anybody else?'

'Rectus – the drains engineer – was sounding off. A new consignment of ceramic pipes has walked. They are very expensive,' the clerk of works explained, assuming Helena would have no concept of equipment pricing. He was not to know that far from having a steward to pay all her bills, she carried out that task for me. Helena checked invoices with a meticulous eye.

'What are these pipes?' I asked.

'We are using them in the garden watering system. The garden goes in last; Rectus was a fool to have called them up so early. Still, who else in Britain would have a use for them? I'll have to check the site. The damn things could just have been unloaded in the wrong area, though Rectus says he's looked . . .'

Something bothered Cyprianus. He was worrying over this missing-pipes issue as if there was more to it than routine theft.

Helena was on to it: 'Have you lost expensive materials prior to this?'

'Oh . . . it happens.' Cyprianus clammed up. 'Falco knows the score.' There was at least one problem, with the marble cladding. Milchato had admitted it.

Falco was not taking back the baton yet, however. Falco liked seeing his darling investigate on his behalf.

'Was Rectus *angry*?' she asked next, seeming merely curious.

'Rectus is a flaming comet. He only knows how to curse and rage.'

'What else happened at the meeting?' Helena asked. 'Was anyone else upset?'

'Strephon was agitating about that statue-seller you're friendly with, Falco, the one who wants an interview. Pomponius hates salesmen. Strephon tried him again but he still said no. Strephon can't tell hawkers to march. Strephon is too *nice*. He hates unhappiness.'

'Would Sextius know yet that Pomponius won't see him?' Helena was wondering if Sextius might have a grudge.

'Only if Strephon has been a big boy and passed the information on. But Strephon was sulking the last I saw.'

'What form did his sulk take?'

'Biting his nails and kicking the stool Plancus was sitting on.'

'Was Plancus irritated by that?' I put in, grinning.

'Plancus wouldn't notice if his head fell off. Dim as a duck.'

'How did he get on a prestigious project such as this?' Helena asked. Cyprianus eyed Helena nervously and refused to answer.

'It's a good question. Tell us how!' I insisted.

The clerk of works looked at me scathingly. 'Plancus was Pomponius' boyfriend, Falco. I thought you realised.' The thought had never crossed my mind.

'So Plancus joined the project only because he was the chief architect's favourite – but he's untalented?'

'Coasting. World of his own.'

'Strephon? Is he a pretty boy too?'

'Doubt it. Strephon has a wife and child. As a designer, he shows potential. But with Pomponius ruling everything, it's never been called upon.'

'What are relations between Plancus and Strephon, then?'

'Not close!'

'And is Strephon jealous of the bond between Pomponius – his superior – and the boyfriend Plancus?'

'If he's not he ought to be.'

'It all sounds rather unhappy,' Helena said.

'Normal,' Cyprianus told her gloomily.

There was a thoughtful pause. Helena stretched her feet out, staring at her sandals. 'Did anything else happen that we should know about?'

Cyprianus gave her a long look. He was a traditionalist, unused to women asking questions on professional subjects; that 'we' of hers had raised his hackles. I knew Helena was aware of it. I shot him an inquisitive look myself, and eventually he forced himself to shake his head to Helena's question.

After a moment, he repeated his anxiety when we first sat down here: 'What are we to do now?'

'About the body?' I queried.

'No, about the loss of our project manager, Falco! This is an enormous site. However is the job to continue?'

'As normal, surely?'

'Someone has to steer. Pomponius was a Rome appointment. We'll have to send off for a new man; they must identify someone who's good, persuade him that a remote sojourn in Britain is just the torture he wants, then extract him from whatever he's working on at present . . . We've no hope they can find a good architect who is free at this moment. Even if they could, the poor sod has to get here. Then he must learn his way around someone else's design plans . . .' He tailed off in despair.

'Would you say,' I asked slowly, 'Pomponius had been chosen for this project because he was good?'

Cyprianus considered the proposition, but his answer came swiftly. 'He was good, Falco. He was *very* good if he was held in check. It was just power he couldn't handle.'

'So who can?' I sneered.

Cyprianus and I both laughed. It was a man's joke. Even so, Helena gave a little smile at some amusement of her own.

We heard noises; the King had sent people to lock up the baths as I suggested. I stood up stiffly. 'It was late before; now it's later. Two requests, Cyprianus: keep your mouth shut over this – don't even relate the tale to your friend Magnus, please. And in the morning, can you fix me up another site meeting, with everyone who attended today?'

He said yes to both. I was past caring whether he obeyed the plea for secrecy. This had been a long day and tomorrow was bound to be longer. I wanted my bed.

I don't know what arrangements Cyprianus made for his own security, but I made damn sure that my family's suite was well locked up that night.

XXXVII

M Y BAD tooth had reasserted itself when I arrived at the project
meeting. I was late. I had had a rough night, due in part to the
baby crying. But I absolved Favonia. I can never rest peacefully after
an encounter with a corpse.

Everyone else was already present. My hope for surprise was
thwarted: they all knew what had happened. I wasted no time holding
an inquest. There had never been much chance of keeping things
quiet.

We all crowded into the architect's room, this time with me taking
the chair. I sensed that it did not entirely put me in charge.

The atmosphere was quiet, tense and sour. They were all aware
Pomponius was dead, and they probably knew how.

There had been collusion obviously. Instead of me watching them
for their reactions, they were all staring at me. Informers recognise the
challenge: *well, let's see if you can work this out, Falco!* If I was lucky, they
were just curious to see how clever I was. A worse alternative would
be that they had set some trap. I was the man from Rome. I should
never forget that.

Present was all of the surviving project team: Cyprianus the clerk of
works; Magnus the surveyor; both Plancus and Strephon the junior
architects; Lupus the overseas labour supervisor; Timagenes the
landscape gardener; Milchato the marble mason; Philocles Junior the
bereaved mosaicist, taking his father's place; Blandus the fresco
painter; Rectus the drainage engineer. Absent was anyone representing the British labour now Mandumerus had absconded. Gaius
represented all the clerks. Alexas the medical orderly had joined us at
my request; later I would escort him to the bath house to remove the
body. Verovolcus had added himself, no doubt at the instigation of the
King.

'Should we have carpenters? Roof-tilers?' I asked Cyprianus.

He shook his head. 'I stand in for the trades unless we have a
technical issue to discuss.'

'You wanted all of us from the farting meeting yesterday,' Rectus groused.

'That's right. You had an issue to raise then?'

'Technical hitch.'

He did not know that Cyprianus, while in shock last night, had described the hitch: expensive ceramic pipes missing and Rectus incandescent with fury. 'It's sorted?' I asked innocently.

'Just routine, Falco.'

The drainage engineer was lying – or at least putting me off. It might be significant – or just symptomatic. The team was against me, that was certain.

It was not the first time everyone in a case was hostile, but that was to my advantage. I had professional experience. Unless they regularly arranged murders when life became difficult on site, they were amateurs.

There was not much room in the project manager's packed quarters, and certainly no privacy for individual questioning. I handed them tablets that I had brought for that purpose and asked everyone to write down their whereabouts the previous evening, supplying the names of anyone who could vouch for them. Verovolcus looked as if he thought himself exempt from this after-banquet party game, but I gave him a tablet anyway. I did wonder whether he would be able to write, but it appeared he could.

'While you are doing that, can I make a general appeal for anyone who saw anything significant in the region of the royal bath house?'

Nobody responded, although I thought there were some sideways glances. I realised that when I came to look at these tablets the men were gravely inscribing, they would all fit neatly, each one covered with an alibi and each in turn covering somebody else.

'Well,' I said quietly. 'I don't suppose Pomponius had many friends here.' That did raise a cynical murmur. 'Most of you represent larger groups; in theory, anyone off the site could have born a grudge and done for him last night.' Downcast eyes and silence were now my only reward for this frankness. 'But my starting point,' I warned them, 'is that the killer, or killers, was somebody of status. They are permitted to use the King's bath house – and last night Pomponius accepted their presence when they joined him in the caldarium. That rules out the labourers.'

'Ruling us in?' concluded Magnus wryly.

'Yes.'

'I object!'

'Out of order, Magnus. Pomponius will receive the same consideration as anyone. Being a bad team leader, even a highly unpopular one, does not excuse violent removal. Brutus and Cassius realised that.'

'So you would have offered a crown to Pomponius, Falco?' Magnus scoffed.

'You know what I thought. I loathe that type – it changes nothing,' I said tersely. 'He still gets a funeral, a *Daily Gazette* obituary – and a courteous report on his demise for his grieving parents and the old friends in his hometown.'

I nearly said *and for his lovers*. But that meant Plancus, for one. He was a suspect.

Plancus had already handed in his tablet; I glanced at it, looking casual. He claimed he was dining with Strephon. Strephon still held his own tablet, but I knew it would confirm the tale. There was supposedly no love lost between the two junior architects, yet they had somehow produced cover for each other last night. Was it true? If true, was it pre-arranged? And if so, was taking a meal together normal or exceptional?

People had noticed me looking at the Plancus offering. There was a general move to collect and deposit the other statements. I publicly declined to look through the tablets. Camillus Aelianus, still laid up with his bitten leg, could play with these fabrications for me. I had no patience with their obstructiveness.

Magnus was still trying to force issues. 'Surely your concern, as the Emperor's man, is how losing Pomponius causes yet another hitch in the project?'

'The project will not suffer.' I had worked this one out while I lay awake in bed last night.

'Shit, Falco – now on top of everything, there is no project manager!'

'No need to panic.'

'We need one –'

'You have one.' My tooth gave a twinge, so I may have sounded curter than I meant. 'For the immediate future, I myself will take over.'

Once the words were out, it made me gulp myself.

As their outrage boiled up, I interrupted levelly: 'Yes, Pomponius was an architect, which I am not. But the design is good – and it is complete. We have Plancus and Strephon to take forward the concept

195

– they will be assigned two wings each to supervise. Other disciplines and crafts are controlled by you people. You were chosen as leaders in your field; you can all cope with autonomy. Report to me on progress and problems.'

'You have no professional training –' gasped Cyprianus. He seemed truly shocked.

'I shall have your competent guidance.'

'Oh stick to your brief, Falco!' Magnus roared. I had suspected that Magnus would seek control himself. Maybe I would recommend it – but not while he was, with the rest, under suspicion for Pomponius' death.

'My brief, Magnus, is to steer this project back on target.'

'I concede you are a tough auditor. But do you think you have the expertise to *supervise*?'

'That would be nonsense.' I kept my reply gentle. 'In the long term Rome has to appoint a man with standing and professional skills.' Plus man-management and diplomacy, if I had any say. 'It will not necessarily be another architect.' Magnus cheered up. 'In the interim, I can supply common sense and initiative – enough to stitch things together until we appoint a replacement.'

'Oh this needs approval from the governor, Falco –'

'I agree.'

'He won't allow it.'

'I'll be pushed out then. But Frontinus is renowned for technical nous and practicality – I know him. I've worked with him. I came to Britain because he asked for me.'

That silenced most of them. Magnus did mutter, 'Someone else seems to have a lust for power!' I ignored that. So he sought to bamboozle me with 'We're held up by some major indecisions, Falco.'

'Try me.'

'Well, what is to be done about incorporating the old house?' he demanded with ill-concealed truculence.

'The King wants it. The King is an experienced client, prepared to endure any inconvenience – so go ahead. Raise the floor levels and bring the existing palace into the new design. Had you already looked into this?'

'We did a feasibility study,' Magnus affirmed.

'Let's define that,' I offered light-heartedly. '*Feasibility: the client proposes a project, which everyone can see will never happen. Work is held in abeyance. Some disciplines do carry out independent preliminary work, failing*

196

to inform the project manager that they are doing so. The scheme then revives unexpectedly, and is thrown into the formal programme with inadequate planning . . .'

Magnus finally had the grace to soften up.

'Strephon!' I disturbed his dreams. 'I said we'd divide the blocks between you and Plancus. You take the east and south wings, including the old house. Consult with Magnus over its incorporation, then bring your conclusions to the next meeting, please. Anything else?'

'My bloody collection tank!' put in Rectus gloomily. He was a man who came to site meetings expecting to be thwarted.

'Present your docket and I'll sign for it. Anyone else?'

'The King requests a large formal tree in the central garden,' ventured Timagenes. 'Pomponius had vetoed it – well, it ought to be a pair of trees –'

'Trees agreed.' I had not envisaged that this trip to Britain would include arboretum planting. Hades, I was game for anything now. 'Trees, feature quality, two of same. Agree a species with the client, please.' Next I glared at Cyprianus. 'Did you ever obtain a chief stonemason?' I could hardly remember who had mentioned it. Lupus, perhaps.

'Well . . .' For once I had caught out Cyprianus, who looked startled.

'Has your mason been assigned or not?'

'No.'

'Bull's balls – your footings are in, you need to start – I'll courier Rome and plead extreme urgency. Give me the name you want and his current location, plus a second best in case.'

'Rome has already been told all the details, Falco –'

'With Rome,' I snapped, 'I always tell the full story every time I communicate. That way, no snooty clerk can thwart you with the old *incomplete documentation* trick.'

There seemed no point continuing the meeting so I called a halt. Magnus leapt for the door first, tight-lipped and clutching his instrument satchel as if he wanted to swipe me with it. I signalled to Alexas that now was the time to deal with the bath-house corpse, but Verovolcus stopped me leaving. I could hardly sweep the others out with a besom, so they all hushed and listened in.

'Falco, the King suggests that perhaps Marcellinus –'

'Could be called back here to assist?' I was as brisk with Verovolcus as I had been with the rest. I had expected his plea. Instinctively I was opposed to allowing the old menace to return. It was time someone stopped him agitating in the background as well. 'It is an attractive solution, Verovolcus. Leave the idea with me. I must talk to the King – and Marcellinus too . . .'

I was being diplomatic in the first instance. From the mutters it caused, the rest of the team failed to grasp that. With Verovolcus mooning at us, I could hardly expound my position. I summed up the previous architect as a difficult autocrat. I wanted him to stay in his retirement villa. But first I would persuade Togidubnus that Marcellinus had served his turn. Then I would have to explain this to Marcellinus himself – in strong terms.

While the King's representative hovered unhappily, I took myself off to avoid further arguments. Strephon, who had been in whispered conversation with Cyprianus, detached himself and followed me out.

'Falco! What should I do about that man?'

'Which man?' I was anxious not to hang around in case Verovolcus grabbed me again. But I was also waiting for Alexas.

'The statue-seller.' Strephon dodged aside as Cyprianus pushed past him and stomped off hastily somewhere.

'Sextius?'

'Pomponius would not see him. Shall I bring him to you, Falco?'

I would be swamped with petty decisions unless I trained this crew to take some responsibility. I grasped the young architect by one shoulder. 'Is there a statue budget?' Strephon nodded. 'Right. Your scheme must allow at least one colossal full-length portrait of the Emperor, plus high-quality marble busts of Vespasian and his sons. Cost in family likenesses for the King. Add a bunch of classical subjects – bushy-bearded philosophers, unknown authors, naked goddesses leering back over one shoulder, cute animals and pot-bellied Cupids with adorable pet birds. Plan enough to ornament the garden, the entrance hall, the audience chamber and other major positions. If there is anything left in your money chest, then you can play with it.'

'Me?' Strephon went white.

'You and the client, Strephon. Take Sextius to the King. See if Togidubnus likes the mechanical toys. They may be technically astounding, but the King is trying very hard to be cultured and he may have more refined taste. Let him choose.'

'What if –'

'If the King really wants some plaything with hidden waterworks, be firm about costs. If he's not interested, be firm with Sextius. Clear him off the site.'

There was a slight pause. 'Right,' said Strephon.

'Good,' said I.

Neither Verovolcus nor Alexas had emerged from the plan room. Since I had Strephon's attention, I collared him. 'How was your dinner with Plancus last evening?'

He was ready. 'Decent pork, but the shellfish starters make my guts gurgle.' It sounded rehearsed.

'Regular event, was this mutual dining?'

'No!' He thought I was implying his sexual tastes were all masculine.

'So why last night?'

'Pomponius used to lose interest in Plancus. Then Plancus would throw a despairing fit; I had to take him in and listen.'

'How despairing was he yesterday?'

Strephon could see where I was aiming. 'Just enough to drink himself under the serving table and lie there snoring until dawn. My house slave will confirm that we were stuck with him all night. And that Plancus snores so loudly, *I* stayed up playing board games with the boy.' An intelligent bit of self-defence had surfaced there.

'I'll have to check with your boy, if you don't mind . . . Why had Pomponius dumped Plancus yesterday?'

'Same reason as always.'

'Oh buck up, Strephon. What reason is that? Since Pomponius was done in yesterday, yesterday's cause of distress seems relevant!'

Strephon, in whom I had begun to see a glimmer of accomplishment despite his gawky air and his revolting way of copying Pomponius' hair pomade, drew himself up: 'Pomponius was a self-centred bastard who easily got bored. Whatever you think of Plancus, he was a true devotee. But Pomponius almost hated him for being so steadfast. When it suited, then Plancus was his darling. When being horrid was more fun, then he avoided poor loyal Plancus.'

'Right,' I said.

'Good!' Strephon retorted sparkily, picking up my own repartee. Well, he was an architect. He should have a feeling for elegance and symmetry.

The door opened behind us. The team was coming out. Foremost in the gaggle, Lupus was joshing Blandus, the chief painter. 'Hope you did an alibi submission for that assistant of yours! He gets around. Whoever knows what he's up to –'

Alexas squeezed out among them. I nodded to Strephon and we left smartly.

XXXVIII

A LEXAS SENT for a stretcher to collect the corpse. We walked back to the old house and waited in my suite for the bearers. Alexas thought he might as well take a look at Aelianus' leg. I was impressed by the meticulous care he applied to the cleaning and rebandaging processes. The wounds looked foul now, and the patient had grown feverish. That was bound to happen. It was where my worry started. Many a mild dog bite has turned into a will-reading. Aelianus, clearly feeling rough, said little. He must be worried too.

Alexas spent additional time advising Helena on how her brother should be cared for. He really was thorough.

'Where's Maia?' I asked. 'I thought she was helping to nurse him?'

'She probably wanted to bathe,' Helena said.

'Not today. You've forgotten the corpse. I had the bath house closed.'

Helena looked up sharply. 'Maia will be annoyed!' I could see she was concerned about the safety aspects, with a killer haunting the place.

'It's all right. Alexas and I are just going there.'

'Ask Alexas to look at your tooth, Falco.'

'Problem, Falco?' he asked helpfully. I showed him. He reckoned the fiery molar needed to be removed. I decided I would live with it.

'You'll have less pain if it's taken out, Falco.'

'It may be just a flare up.'

'When the pain takes over your life, you'll think again.'

'Is there a decent tooth-puller in this area?' Helena was determined I should act. I must be more irritable than I had realised.

'I'm not complaining,' I muttered.

'No, you're trying to winkle it out yourself,' Helena accused me. I wondered how she knew.

'Well, let me know when you want help and I can find you someone local with a set of pincers,' Alexas volunteered. 'Or Helena Justina, you can take him to Londinium and spend a lot of money.'

'For the same brutal job!' I grumbled. Alexas grasped he had a difficult patient and offered to grind me a herbal painkiller instead.

I dragged him off for our unsavoury task. Passing another room in my suite, I spotted our nursemaid obviously about to try on one of Maia's dresses in my sister's absence.

'It suits the real owner better,' I announced loudly from the doorway. 'Put it back in the chest and mind my daughters, please, Hyspale!'

Hyspale turned round to the doorway, still unashamedly holding the red dress against her body. She would probably have uttered some surly rejoinder, but saw I had a male stranger with me, so that caught her interest. I informed her the medical orderly was married with three sets of twins – at which the simpering chit had the cheek to tell Alexas that she loved children.

'If you want her, she's yours,' I offered as we headed down the corridor.

He looked rightly scared.

With a sense that everything around me was going wrong, I set off through the internal corridor to the royal bath house. Alexas took a detour through the garden, looking for his stretcher-bearers, he said. He seemed to be avoiding this corpse with every possible excuse; it was odd, because when he showed me the body of Valla, the dead roofer, way back on my first day here, he had been perfectly composed.

I went on ahead to the baths, where a shock awaited. I could appoint myself the project manager and imagine that I now ran this site – but Fate took a different view. My precautions had been thwarted.

The entrance should have stayed roped off. My instructions last night had been clear. The rope was there all right. But it had been slung aside in an untidy heap, on top of which lay two battered tool baskets that contained a few chipped chisels, flagons and half-eaten loaves. Squatting in the doorway were a pair of slack-mouthed hopeless workmen. They were holding a wooden spar across the threshold, which gave the impression they were levelling or measuring. They did neither. One was deep in argument about some left-footed gladiator, while the other stared into space.

'This had better be good!' I roared at them. My imitation of Mars the Avenger had all the effect of a warm-up act at a run-down theatre in the off season.

'Keep your curls in, tribune.'

'You moved that rope?'

'What rope? You don't mean this one?'

'Oh yes I do. But you're right – why not untie the thing? It will be a lot easier to use the rope to hang the pair of you!'

They exchanged glances. They were treating me like any wild-eyed client at the end of his tether – with utter indifference.

'What are your names?'

'I'm Septimus and he's Tiberius,' the spokesman informed me, implying that such a question was bad manners. I took out a tablet and pointedly wrote down the names.

'Stand up.' They humoured me. 'What are you doing here?'

'Spot of work required, tribune.'

'I don't see you doing it!' I snarled. 'You're loitering at a crime scene, interfering with my security measures, allowing unauthorised access – and irritating all Hades out of me.'

They pretended to look impressed. Big words and a bad temper were a novelty. I had plenty more of both to call on. And they had plenty of stubborn defiance.

'Have you entered the baths since you took off the rope?'

'No, tribune.'

'You had better hope I believe that.' I did not, but there was no point nit-picking. 'Has anyone else been in?'

'Oh no, tribune. Not with us sat here.'

Wrong. At that moment my own sister marched out from the changing room behind them. She was carrying her personal oil flask and scraper and was livid. 'This is a complete disgrace – there is no hot water and no heat at all in the steam rooms!'

'My orders, Maia.'

'Well, I might have known!'

'There's a dead man in the hot rooms – not to mention a killer preying on lone bathers. Did you go in past these two brazen layabouts?'

'Well, I stepped over them,' Maia sneered.

Septimus and Tiberius just smirked.

Maia was storming off, but I held her back. 'Is anyone else inside?' I asked.

A guarded look crossed her face. 'Not now.'

'What do you mean? *Was* there someone?'

'I thought I heard movement.'

'Who?'

'No idea, Marcus. I was undressed as far as my undertunic, just exploring the cold room – what a waste of time! I didn't know who had turned up, so I kept quiet.' Maia knew what I thought about her visiting a mixed baths alone. She didn't care. Being Maia, she might have enjoyed the frisson of risk.

'Next time, drag Hyspale along to stand guard. You may like being leered at by lads looking for women in wet breast-bands – but being spied on by a strangler would be a different beaker of maggots.'

'I might just have heard these two messing about,' Maia returned, cheerfully implicating the workmen.

'Oh surely not,' I responded sarcastically. 'Septimus and Tiberius would never spy on a lady, would you, lads?'

They gazed at me, not even bothering to lie. Given the dopey way they were hanging about in the entrance when I turned up, playing at voyeurs probably never occurred to them. Besides, my sister exuded the air of a woman who would savage peephole spies.

With a whisk of her skirts, Maia darted away back towards our suite. I let her go. I could ask more questions later, with Helena in support.

Alexas finally turned up. When he saw the two workmen, I thought he looked slightly awkward. They were quite unabashed and greeted him by name.

'You know these scoundrels?' I demanded angrily.

'They work for my uncle.' Septimus and Tiberius watched our confrontation with the bright eyes of happy troublemakers.

'Your uncle is the King's bath-house contractor?'

'Afraid so.' Alexas sounded rueful. Well, I knew all about awkward relatives.

'So where is this uncle?'

'Who knows? He won't be on site!' A true professional.

'What's your uncle's name?'

'Lobullus.'

No one I was after, then.

I led the way indoors, heading a convoy that consisted of myself, Alexas, a couple of whey-faced lads carrying a pallet to remove the body, and the two workmen, both suddenly nosier about the corpse than they had professed to be about Maia.

'And where were *you* last night, Alexas?'

'It's on my tablet.'

'Tell me anyway.'

'I went into Noviomagus to see my uncle.'

'Will he vouch for you?'

'Of course he will.'

I never like family alibis.

The vaulted rooms were colder than last night. Even with the furnace out of action, it takes a while for the fabric of a bath house to cool. A slight clamminess was creeping through the steaming suite. We reached the final chamber. The dead Pomponius was still lying as I left him, as far as I could tell. If anyone had been in here and tampered with the body, I would never prove it.

Initially, there was no reason to think anyone had done that. Everything looked the same. After my companions finished exclaiming over the way the architect had been mutilated, they hoisted his corpse onto the pallet. I adjusted the small towel to cover his privates. Then I heard a rattle and something fell on the floor.

'Oh look!' cried Tiberius helpfully.

'Something was caught up in the poor fellow's towel,' added Septimus, bending to capture the object and hand it obsequiously to me. Everyone else watched my reaction. A cynical informer might have thought it was a planted clue.

It was an artist's paintbrush. Tightly bound pigs' bristles with carefully shaped tips for delicate work. Traces of azure on the short handle: was that blue frit? There were letters handily scratched there too. 'LL'.

Comment from me was unavoidable. 'Well, that's a curious hieroglyphic.'

'Would it be the owner's initials?' enquired Tiberius with almost intellectual interest.

'Hey,' murmured Septimus, suddenly shocked. 'You don't think one of the site painters was responsible for the murder, Falco?'

I had to hide a smile. 'I don't know what to think.' But somebody was trying *very* hard to tell me.

'An architect wouldn't bring a paintbrush when he came for a bathe, would he?' Tiberius asked Septimus.

'That painter in charge is called Blandus,' his mate answered. 'So he's not LL.'

'You know, I believe it must be his assistant,' I broke in. Septimus, Tiberius and even Alexas, whose role in this fiasco seemed the most subdued, all looked at each other and nodded, impressed by my deductive powers.

I held the brush in the palm of my hand, looking from the silent Alexas to his uncle's two workmen. 'Congratulations, Septimus. This seems to be an important clue – and you just helped me work out what it means.'

I could see what it really meant. Someone was being framed.

I seized the towel and shook it out, in case any other offerings had been deposited. Negative. I replaced the linen rectangle neatly over the dead architect's loins. I signalled to the bearers to carry off the body.

'So! It looks like that young painting assistant has killed Pomponius. There's only one way to be sure. I'll ask him to be a good boy and own up.'

XXXIX

IT WAS natural to retrace my steps down the corridor, via my own quarters. I needed to calm down. I found Helena, and told her what had happened.

'That paintbrush had arrived there since last night. Opening the baths so anybody could get in was deliberate, not just negligence by workmen. I've spent a morning allowing myself to be detained and delayed by Alexas – and I think by Strephon earlier. Half the project team must have been rushing about behind my back.'

'To cause confusion? As a set-up it's not very subtle, Marcus. If the young painter is innocent –'

'His innocence is not the point,' I said.

Helena pursed her lips, her great eyes dark with concern. 'Why do you think he has been set up as the culprit? He has offended someone?'

'Well, he drinks, flirts, gets into scrapes and hits people.' Mind you, Justinus still liked him, despite being punched. 'Then, too, I have seen his work. He is a strikingly good artist.'

'Jealousy?'

'Could be.'

'It sounds as if half the project team conspired to lay this false clue,' Helena said angrily. 'So did the project team – or some of them – kill Pomponius?'

'I'm not ready to decide.' My mood cleared slightly. 'But one thing's for sure, the project team really hates the *new* project manager.'

Helena knew at once what I had decreed at that morning's meeting. 'I see! You want your own chance to be dogmatic and overbearing?'

I grinned. 'And I'm ignorant of professional practice too, as was pointed out. I'm perfect for the job. With these talents, I could have been an architect!'

I had a quick word with Maia. She had little to add. Whoever she heard at the baths that morning had walked past the cold room briskly, then returned to the exit soon afterwards. That fitted. They must have gone into the hot rooms, dumped the brush and done a flit.

Now Maia had reflected on how she would have felt if she stumbled on the dead man. She confessed that she regularly lurked in the bath house alone, at hours when she hoped no one else would be around. She had gone there last night, for instance, she told me guiltily.

'This was after I left for Novio?'

'After dinner.'

'Stupid! Maia Favonia, your mother brought you up to know that bathing on a full stomach can give you a seizure.'

'It can give you a lot of thinking time too,' Maia growled. I preferred not to know what she was thinking about. Exploring the dark elements of my sister's soul would have to wait.

'Strangers might assume you are making assignations.'

'I don't give a damn what anyone thinks.'

'You never did! So you were at the crime scene last night, Maia. Tell me about that. Tell me every little detail.'

Maia was now prepared to help. 'I knew someone had gone through ahead of me. When I arrived there were clothes in two of the bunkers.'

'*Two?*'

'I can count, Marcus.'

'You can be rude too! Describe this clothing.'

Maia had worked for a tailor in her youth. 'Bright stuff in one – expensive cloth, untidily crammed in. Unusual; jacquard cloth, maybe with silk in the weft. In another row of bunkers, there was a plain white tunic – wool, a common weave – folded neatly, with a man's belt on top.'

'Was the expensive material dyed brown and turquoise?' She nodded. 'Pomponius. So who was the other man? Could it have been Cyprianus, who discovered the corpse? Was your visit just before I came home from Noviomagus?'

'No, quite a lot earlier.'

'Before the crime was committed. Anyway,' I remembered, 'Cyprianus was wearing blue last night. You never saw these men?'

'I decided not to stay,' said Maia. 'I reckoned they were in the hot rooms, but they could have stayed there hours.' The three hot rooms lay in sequence, normal procedure for a small suite. People had to come out the same way they went in, meeting anybody following. A woman alone would not want to be relaxing in a tiny towel when men strolled back through.

'So you decided not to wait?'

Maia confirmed her reluctance. 'I'm perished in this province. I could not face shivering in the cold room, applying my oil at a dawdle, while I waited to hear them leave. I thought I would go back this morning – but I'm still thwarted!'

'Sweetheart, just be glad you didn't trip naked into the last caldarium while Pomponius was croaking on the floor.'

'He was a man,' said Maia grimly. 'One who thought he ran the world – I expect I could have borne it.'

I was leaving when she added in an offhand tone, 'The one with the white tunic had hung a bag on the cloak hook.'

She was able to describe it, with the accuracy of an alert girl who took a practical interest. She described it so well, in fact, I knew whose bag it was.

As I set off to go to the painters' hut, I saw that studies were afoot for incorporating the previous palace into the new design. Strephon and Magnus were in deep discussion, while the surveyor's assistants stood around meekly with measuring equipment.

It looked a busier version of the scene I saw a few days ago. Magnus, distinguished by his smart outfit and grey hair, was setting up his elaborate *diopter* while more junior staff had to settle for the basic *groma*. Some were responsible for raising twenty-foot-high marked posts that helped in taking levels, while others were awkwardly deploying a huge set square to mark a right angle for the initial setting-out of the intersection of the two wings of the new palace. As they struggled to work close up against the building, hindered further by its cloak of scaffold, I overheard Magnus telling them to dispense with the cumbersome square in favour of simple pegs and strings. He had straightened up and caught my eye. We exchanged cool nods.

First things first. A fresh breeze riffled through my hair as I marched off to the hutments outside the west end of the site. I had crossed the great platform, striding over the flat area which would one day be the great courtyard garden and picking my way over the dug trenches of the formal west wing and the first blocks laid for its grand stylobate. There was action on site, but it seemed subdued. I could hear hammering from the yard where I knew stone blocks were shaped and faced, and from a different direction came the rasp of a saw slicing marble. Sunlight, bright but in Britain not glaring, gently warmed my spirits.

Ahead of me scavenging seagulls wheeled above the wooded area where the carts were parked. I could smell woodsmoke again from the camp. I walked up the track quietly, passing the mosaicist's hut, which seemed devoid of life. I stopped at the adjoining home of Blandus and his lad. Its door was open; someone was inside. It was not Blandus.

He had his back to me, but was standing at a slight angle so I could see he was working on a small still life. It was fresh fruit in a glass bowl. He had created the arrangement of apples and was now adding delicate white lines to represent the ribs of a translucent comport. Unsure whether he had heard me, I stood still, admiring the flushed rotundity of the ripened fruit and the exquisitely hinted glassware. The young painter seemed absorbed.

He was a big lad. I could see one protruding ear, half covered by unkempt dark hair which would have been improved by a serious trim and work with a teasing comb. His clothes were covered with multicoloured paint splashes, though the rest of him looked clean enough, given that he was about eighteen and a thousand miles from home. He worked steadily, adept and confident. His design was already live in his head, needing only those thoughtful, rhythmic brush strokes to create it on the wooden panel.

I cleared my throat. He did not react. He knew I was there.

I folded my arms. 'Creativity for your own pleasure is a high ideal – but my advice is, never waste effort unless you persuade some halfwit client to pay for it.'

Most painters would have spun about ready to thump me. This one only grunted. He kept going. The glass bowl acquired a thread of painted light to indicate a handle.

'The project team plotters have decided who eliminated Pomponius,' I said. 'They've settled on the smartarse from Stabiae. A stippling brush with some incriminating initials has been dumped on the body – just where I was bound to find it and shriek *Ooh, look at this!* So tell me, smartarse: did you kill him?'

'No I bloody well did not.' The artist stopped painting and turned around to face me. 'I was screwing a girl from a bar in Noviomagus – she wasn't as good as I hoped she would be, but at least I can tell Justinus that I got there first!'

I gave him a long cold stare. 'The only good thing about that story is that you were screwing the floosie, not my brother-in-law.'

'Plus another good thing.' He scowled, as unabashed as he had always been. 'You know the story's true, Falco.'

I knew him, so I did believe it. He was my nephew Larius.

XL

I TOSSED HIM the brush from the bath house. He caught it one-handed, the other hand still holding the finer one he had been working with, plus his thumb palette. 'That's your pig's bristle?'

'LL. That's me. Larius Lollius.'

'Thank Juno you were not born under a laurel tree,' I scoffed. 'A third L would have been obscene.'

'Two names are sufficient for me and Mark Antony.'

'Listen, bigshot, when you've finished aligning yourself with the famous, you are to get yourself to Novio and ensure that your luscious Virginia is not bribed to forget your romantic alibi.'

Larius looked coy. 'She'll remember. I said *she* was a disappoint-ment. I didn't mention my own performance.'

I reined in my reaction and merely answered quietly, 'Ask somebody sophisticated to explain about two-way pleasure. Incidentally, how is dear Ollia?' Ollia was his wife.

'Fine when we parted company,' Larius said tersely.

'You parted? Is this a permanent phase? Had the union of you two fresh hopefuls produced offspring?'

'Not as far as I know.'

'Still, I hate to see young love waning.'

'Skip the family talk,' he chided me. He did not ask after Helena, though they had met. While he and Ollia had been assuring the world they shared eternal devotion, the world had prophesied that the teenagers were doomed – then also decreed that I was a philandering louse, destined to abandon my woman. Assuming I could manage it before Helena ditched me first . . . Larius cut through my wandering thoughts. 'We need to know why people want to frame me for Pomponius.'

'They are not framing you,' I told him. 'They are implicating me.'

He brightened up. 'How's that?'

'I bring my nephew on site and he kills the top man? That's bound to diminish my status as the Emperor's troubleshooter!'

'Status bollocks!' Since I last saw him when he was fourteen Larius had coarsened up. 'I'm not connected with your work. Blandus brought me here. I've come to do miniatures – and I do not want to be dragged into any of your slimy political stews.'

'You are already neck deep in fish-pickle sauce. Have you told people you are my nephew?'

'Why not?'

'You should have told me first!'

'You were never there to tell.'

'All right. Larius, how did anyone else acquire this paintbrush?'

'From the hut while I was out, I suppose. I leave everything here.'

'Any chance Pomponius himself might have borrowed it?'

'What, to tickle his balls at the baths?' mocked Larius. 'Or cleaning his ears out. I hear it's a new fashion among the arty fraternity – better than a plebeian scoop.'

'Answer the question.'

'As for pinching a brush, I don't suppose that snooty beggar ever knew where our site huts were.'

'What happened when you wanted to show him a proposed design?'

'We carried sketches to the great man's audience chamber and waited in a queue for two hours.'

'You did not like Pomponius?'

'Architects? I never do,' scoffed Larius offhandedly. 'Loathing self-important people is a churlish habit I picked up from you.'

'And why are you so ripe for incrimination, happy nephew? Whom have you upset?'

'What, me?'

'Is Camillus Justinus the only man you've beaten up recently?'

'Oh yes.'

'Have you slept with anybody other than Virginia?'

'Certainly not!' He was a real rogue. A total hypocrite.

'Has Virginia another lover?'

'Famous for it, I should say.'

'So is she attached to anyone who bears grudges?'

'She's a girl who gets herself attached. No one regular, if that's any help.'

'And what about you, Larius? Everyone knows you? Everyone knows what you're like nowadays?'

'What do you mean – *what I'm like?*'

'Start with layabout,' I suggested cruelly. 'Try a wine-swigging, fornicating, quarrelsome byword for trouble.'

'You're thinking of my uncle,' said Larius, as ever surprising me with sudden caustic repartee.

'True.'

'I get around,' confessed the lad. I remembered him as a shy, poetry-loving dreamer – the single-minded romantic who had once spurned my dirty profession in favour of high ideals and art. Now he had learned to hold his own in rough company – and to despise me.

'You'd better come along to my quarters,' I said quietly. 'On reflection, I'm taking you into custody until this is sorted out. Let's get this clear – I have young children and polite nursing mothers in my party, not to mention the noble Aelianus withering away from his doggie bite, so we'll have no drinking and no riots.'

'I see you've gone staid,' sneered Larius.

'Another thing,' I ordered him. 'Keep your damn hands off my children's nurse!'

'Who's that?' he asked, full of rosebud ignorance. He knew who I meant. He did not fool me. He was born on the Aventine, into the feckless Didii.

To be honest, his attitude gave me a nostalgic pang.

XLI

I WAS WORSE than staid. I was suffering like any householder whose domestic life had filled up with crying infants, sex-crazed nephews, disobedient freedwomen, unfinished business tasks and jealous rivals who wanted him dismissed or dead. I was like the harassed foolish father in a Greek play. This was no milieu for a city informer. Next thing I would find myself buying pornographic oil lamps to leer at in the office and giving myself flatulence as I worried about inheritance tax.

Helena shot me an odd look when I deposited Larius in her care. He seemed startled to see her. He had once adored her. This was awkward for the new man who trifled with women for a bet then breezed off, callous and untouched.

Helena greeted him with an affectionate kiss on the cheek, a refined gesture that upset his equilibrium further. 'Oh this is splendid! Come and meet your little cousins, Larius . . .'

Horrified, Larius shot me a baleful glance. I returned an annoying grin, then left to investigate who really killed Pomponius.

Magnus was still supervising his assistants near the old palace. They had extended the lines for foundations where the two huge new wings would meet the existing buildings. When the dug trenches currently petered out, strings on pegs now showed the planned links. Magnus himself was scribbling down calculations for the levels, his instrument satchel lying open on the ground.

'This yours?' I asked casually, holding something out to him as if I had found it lying around on site. Absorbed in his work, he was fooled by my indifferent tone.

'I've been searching for that!' His eyes came up from the long string that I was proffering and I saw him freeze.

I had deliberately asked the question so his student helpers would hear. Having witnesses put pressure on. 'That's a five-four-three,' one of them informed me helpfully. Magnus said nothing. 'It's used to form a hypotenuse triangle when we set out a right angle.'

'That right? Geometry is an amazing science! And I thought this was just any old length of twine. May I have a private word, Magnus? And bring your instruments, please.'

Magnus came to my office without a quibble. He realised his setting-out string was what had strangled Pomponius. Now I had to decide, did he know that before I produced it – or did he simply work out why the knotted twine was in my possession today?

We walked the short distance to my office. Gaius the clerk prepared to leave, but I signalled him to remain as a witness. He sank back on his seat, undecided whether this was to be a routine interview or something more serious.

'You've declared your movements last night, Magnus.' For a second the surveyor looked at Gaius. There was no doubt about it. The glance, involuntary and cut short, was enough to make me wonder if my clerk was his pretty boy. Did everyone on this site have unmanly Greek tastes? 'One of my team is working on the witness statements, so I've not seen them yet. Remind me, please.'

'What team, Falco?'

'Never mind what bloody team!' I snarled. 'Answer the question, Magnus.'

'I was in my quarters.'

'Anyone vouch for that?'

'Afraid not.'

'Always the clever witness answer,' I told him. 'Avoids what sounds like easy collusion, after the event. Genuinely innocent men quite often lack alibis – that's because they had no idea they needed to fix one.' It would not clear Magnus – but it would actually not condemn him either.

I took the satchel from him and flapped it open on a table. In silence we both studied the neatly ranged equipment, all secured under stitched leather loops. Spare pegs and a small mallet. A pocket sundial. Rulers, including a fine, well-worn folding one marked with both Roman and Greek measurements. Stylus and wax tablets. And a hinged metal pair of mapping compasses.

'Used these today?'

'No.'

I carefully released the compasses from their restraining strip of leather, using only my fingertips. I teased them open. Barely visible along one pointed prong was a faint brown stain. But under the leather band into which the instrument had been pushed more staining was obvious.

'Blood,' I decided. It certainly was not cartography ink.

Magnus was watching me. He was intelligent, forthright and highly respected on this site. He also hated Pomponius, and had probably clashed with him as many times as anyone except Cyprianus – who seemed a close ally to Magnus. I thought two people had combined to murder the project manager. Those two, perhaps.

I spoke quietly. We were both subdued. 'You've worked it out, Magnus. Your five-four-three was unravelled from around the dead architect's neck. That and your set of compasses are the murder weapons. If Pomponius had been impaled on the bath-house floor with your *groma*, you couldn't be in more trouble.'

Magnus said nothing.

'Did you kill him, Magnus?'

'No!'

'Short and sharp.'

'I did not kill him.'

'You're too shrewd?'

'There were other ways to get rid of him from the project. You were here to do that, Falco.'

'But I'm working with the system, Magnus. How long would it have taken me? Incompetence is a persistent weed.'

Magnus sat quietly. He had chosen an X-shaped stool, one that must once have folded, though I knew it had seized up. Grey-haired and controlled, he had a still core that would not be easily broken into. His grim expression and tone of voice almost suggested it was him testing me, not the other way round.

I put my palms on the edge of the table and pushed back, as if distancing myself from the whole situation. 'You don't say much, for a prime suspect.'

'You do enough talking!'

'I shall act too, Magnus, if I have to. You always knew that.'

'I thought you capable,' Magnus agreed. 'You had assessed the situation. You would have tackled Pomponius – and not necessarily by removing him. You have the ear of high authority, Falco; you even summon up a kind of tact sometimes. You could have imposed workable controls, when you were ready.'

I gazed at him. This speech of his was a compliment, yet sounded like a condemnation.

'Well, that's what I thought until this morning, when you came up

216

with the damned idea of bringing Marcellinus back on site,' Magnus added. He now spoke with pent-up fury.

'He's the King's darling,' I replied curtly. Magnus had just told me why the project plotters were against me. They had loathed Pomponius, sure enough – but they did not want him replaced by another disaster. A worse one, maybe. 'This morning we had Verovolcus listening in, Magnus. The King, his master, is the client. But don't suppose the client will be allowed to impose a no-hoper on this scheme. If I have to thwart him, believe me I'll do it – but I'll do it with sensitivity if possible. If you don't know my views on Marcellinus, Magnus, that's because you never asked.'

We glared at one another in silence.

'So if I believed you could handle Pomponius,' Magnus muttered at last, 'why would *I* take the personal risk of killing him?'

I let the Marcellinus issue go, though clearly it needed sorting, and fast.

The surveyor was right. I could just about believe a scenario where he came upon Pomponius at the wrong moment and then snapped suddenly – but premeditated killing, when there were other solutions, contradicted this man's natural restraint. Still, self-control would not impress a court as evidence, whereas the murder weapons – his possessions – could.

'Risk is not your style,' I agreed. 'You're too fastidious. But you don't tolerate bungling either. You are vocal and you're active. You are a suspect for this murder precisely because you don't stand back.'

'What does that mean?'

'You have strict standards, Magnus. That could make you lose your temper. Yesterday we had all endured a long, irritating day. Suppose you went to bathe, very late, to relax and forget the Mandumerus fiasco. Just when you were calming down, you came to the last hot caldarium. That fool Pomponius was there. You flared up. Pomponius ended up dead on the floor.'

'I do not take my five-four-three string inside the baths, Falco.'

'Somebody did,' I answered him.

'I use a strigil, not a damn set of compasses.'

'What's your tool for excavating eyeballs?'

Magnus breathed hard and did not reply.

'Did you see Cyprianus yesterday evening?' I demanded.

'No.' Magnus looked at me sharply. 'Does he say I did?'

I gave no answer. 'There are some half-baked workmen at the baths this morning. Are you part of that?'

'No. I gave Togidubnus an estimate, way back. Anything after that is his affair.'

'Is much work needed?'

'*Needed* – none at all,' Magnus opined acidly. '*Possible* – as much as a rich client, urged on by a shameless contractor, wants to waste his money on.'

'So you say you are not connected with the wastrels on site today?'

'No.'

'Let's get to the main point. Did you go to the bath house last night, Magnus?'

Magnus held back his answer. I waited stubbornly. He continued to maintain his silence, trying to force me to break in, to take back the initiative. He was desperate to know whether I had any firm information.

After an age, he decided what to say. 'I did not go to the baths.'

Overcome by the tension, the clerk, Gaius, let out a gasp. Magnus kept his eyes on me.

'You're lying, Magnus.' My arm gave a wild sweep. I dashed the satchel of instruments right off the table. I then yelled out at full pitch, '*Oh shit in Hades, Magnus!* Just tell me the truth, will you?'

'Steady, Falco!' Gaius squeaked in great alarm. He spoke for the first time since we came in. His eyes flickered, blinking too rapidly.

I really let my temper rip. 'He was at the baths!' I roared at the clerk. 'I have a witness who says so, Gaius!' I would not look at Magnus. 'If you want to know why I'm raving about it, I thought he was a man of superior quality. I thought I could trust him – *I did not want the killer to be him!*'

Magnus gave me a long hard stare. Then he simply stood up and said he was going back to work. I let him go. I could not arrest him – but I did not apologise for implying he was the murderer.

XLII

A s soon as the surveyor left, I dropped the charade.
I sat quiet. Too quiet, anyone who knew me would have said.
The clerk had worked with me, though not long enough or closely
enough. Even so, apprehension pinned him to his stool.

'That tooth of yours still playing up, Falco?' he asked in a nervous
voice. It could be a joke, real sympathy, or a frightened mixture of
both.

Too busy to deal with it, I had forgotten my aching tooth until that
moment. Informers don't collapse at mere agonising pain. We are
always too busy, too desperate to finish the case.

'Where were you last night, Gaius?' It sounded like a neutral
question.

'What?'

'Place yourself for me.' He had attended my project meeting this
morning. He had filed a witness statement but I had had no time yet
to look at it.

'I . . . went into Novio.'

I scrutinised the bastard with a thin half smile.

'You went into Novio?' Repeating it, I sounded like a careworn
lawyer dragging out his weakest rhetorical manoeuvre. I was hoping
that the witness would cave in out of sheer anxiety. In life they never
do.

'Novio, Falco.'

'What was that for?'

'A night out. Just a night in town.' I still gazed at him. 'Stupenda
was dancing,' Gaius maintained. A nice touch. Detail always makes a
falsehood sound more reliable.

'Any good?'

'She was brilliant.'

I stood up. 'Get on with your work.'

'Is something wrong, Falco?'

'Nothing that I don't expect every day.' I let him see my lip curl. I had liked Gaius. He had made a good show of harbouring the right attitude. But it had been an act. 'In my job,' I elaborated grimly, 'I run into lies, fraud, conspiracy and filth. I expect it, Gaius. I encounter mad people who kill their mothers for asking them to wipe their feet on the doormat. I deal with lowlife muggers who steal half a denarius from blind army veterans in order to buy a drink from a thirteen-year-old barmaid whom they subsequently rape . . .'

The clerk was now looking as puzzled as he was petrified.

'Get on with your work,' I repeated. 'Let me know when you decide to revise your story. In the meantime, don't distress yourself about my feelings. Your contribution to this enquiry, Gaius, is just a routine pile of muleshit – though I can say that being betrayed by my own office backer-up hits a new low for me.'

I left him, striding out as if I had to go and hold a bridge against a wild horde of barbarians.

He did not know that I had been in Novio myself last night, also hoping to see Stupenda. Which of course I had not done – because last night in Noviomagus Regnensis, the woman called Stupenda did not dance.

XLIII

'MAYBE THIS clerk got his nights mixed up,' Aelianus suggested. Whatever draught the medical orderly supplied had perked him up enough to take an interest.

I disagreed. 'Be practical. You don't confuse yourself over *yesterday*, especially when being in the wrong place could make you the killer.'

'Might he have been a bit fuddled? Does Gaius drink a lot?'

'Doubt it. I've seen him pour away half a cup of *mulsum* just because a fly looked in the cup.'

We were in my suite, the invalid sprawled on a padded couch. Aelianus had created a crude sketch of the new palace on which to mark witness positions in red ink, together with a box (headed by a lopsided graffiti winecup) where he listed those who claimed they went to town last night.

'They are *all* involved,' I raved. 'So tell me your results, Aulus. Can we prove anything?'

'Not yet. Some seedy character called Falco has failed to report in.'

'Novio,' I muttered. 'Vouched for by your dear brother, plus a retainer of the King's. Come to that, you know perfectly well I refused dinner and trotted off on a pony . . . Is there any of your medicine left?' My tooth was on fire.

'No, Larius swigged it.' Larius was now flaked out in a wicker chair that Helena normally used, white in the gills and semi-conscious. 'Exhausted by his wild life,' Aelianus opined piously. 'Or poisoned off.'

My elder daughter Julia was using her little wheeled cart to play chariots around Larius, with him as a circus *spina*. The baby slept, for once, in her two-handled travelling basket. There were faint indications that Favonia's loincloth needed changing, but I was managing not to notice. Fathers learn to live with guilt.

'So what do we have, Aulus?'

'These tablets are a joke. Believe them, and the site was deserted and nobody could have done it. It's amazing the corpse was ever discovered. Most of the project team claim they were in town.'

'Gaius?'

'Yes, he says he was in town.'

'With any of the others?'

'Not specific. He's put down Magnus as a witness.'

'What did Magnus write?'

'In Novio too. Gaius is supposed to vouch for him.'

'That's wrong. Magnus just told me he was in his quarters.'

'Must have forgotten his official excuse under the stress of your questioning!'

'Don't be rude,' I rebuked him mildly. 'So, was anybody left here?'

'The two junior architects, vouching for each other.'

'Strephon and Plancus – heart-searching, swigging and snoring. I am inclined to believe them. It's too touching to be a bluff.'

'Also the clerk of works.'

'Cyprianus, mooching round the site on his own, hoping to forestall trouble – then heading for the baths and an unpleasant discovery. I think I trust him. He has family on site; if he was building a false alibi, he would make them say he was at home.'

Aelianus dipped his pen and marked a blob at the baths for Cyprianus. 'Isn't the person who claims to find a corpse sometimes the obvious suspect?'

'Rightly so, half the time.' I considered the man's demeanour when he came to find me. 'Cyprianus was in shock when he rushed here with the news. He seemed genuine. He was sickened by the gouged eye. It looked like genuine surprise.'

'Still, it could be a ruse,' Aelianus replied. He had second thoughts: 'But if he had been the killer, would he have run out naked?'

'I see why you ask.' Inactivity was doing Aelianus good. A bandage on his leg seemed to improve his brain. He surprised me with his logic, in fact. 'The killer stayed calm. He cleaned and replaced one of the weapons in Magnus' satchel . . .'

We both paused.

'He took it out; he put it back. Curious,' I said.

Aelianus mimed the actions. 'The instrument satchel must have stayed on the clothes peg throughout the killing . . .'

'. . . So where was Magnus?'

He could be the killer. Then there were two possibilities that left him innocent. 'Either he was in the tepidarium taking a slow cold plunge and oiling up – or he was fooling about with Gaius.'

'Likely?'

'Neither seems the type.'

'How can you tell?' asked Aelianus. 'I've known people who poked anything handy, whatever the sex.' It was Roman tradition, especially in high places. But it raised interesting questions about some of his own friends.

Reluctantly, I tackled the other possibility: 'Why ever Magnus went to the baths, he could still have been one of the killers.' I screwed up my face, still resisting the thought. 'I caught him out when I showed him the string this morning. He owned up to it openly. But if he had *known* it was used to strangle Pomponius, he would at least have played down his ownership.'

'Let's face it, Falco – Magnus would have known better than to leave something that could be identified as his property on the body.'

'Too disgusted to remove it?' I argued.

'No, no!' Aelianus had really entered into the spirit and his response was fierce. 'If you hate someone enough to strangle them, and to gouge their eye out, you can remove the evidence.'

'Agreed.' I reflected. 'It's interesting that whoever did it thought that the compasses should be replaced – but apparently they thought the string was just anonymous twine. Were they trying to implicate Magnus, or had they just never seen – or never *noticed* – a five-four-three being used to make a right angle? That means it was *not* a surveyor, and most likely not the clerk of works.'

Aelianus shrugged. This was my theory. He would not argue, but he would not become excited by it either.

'If there was more than one man involved,' I suggested, 'it could reflect different personalities. One removed the compasses, the other simply did not bother about the twine.'

'Neat and Slapdash?'

'Even if they were Neat and Tidy the killer, or killers, could have been interrupted. Maia arrived at the baths,' I pointed out. My sister was tough, but I tried not to dwell on her near encounter with the killers. 'Cyprianus too, if we accept he was an innocent participant.'

'It just won't work,' Aelianus rebuked me, typically frank. 'Maia Favonia never ventured further than the changing room. And we can discount even Cyprianus. You know bath houses have dead acoustics. Nobody in the final caldarium would have heard anyone outside until that person was on top of them. Then it was too late to escape.'

'So,' I began, pursuing a new line, 'do we reckon the killer or killers went to the baths on purpose, did their deed and quickly fled?'

'If they went there especially, Falco, how could they be certain that Pomponius was all alone and that nobody would interrupt?'

'They kept the baths under observation until it was safe to strike.'

'It's rather horrible,' mouthed Aelianus. 'Pomponius is inside lazing with his strigil set . . .' He tailed off for a moment. 'Well, that's clear premeditation anyway.'

'No doubt a good barrister, untroubled by conscience, would argue them out of that . . .' I thought little of lawyers.

'But Falco! He was cornered like vermin. Once you get in the bowels of a bath house, you're trapped.'

'Don't dwell on it, Aulus. Or next time you're slaking off the grime with your lavender oil, you might get jumpy.'

Aelianus whistled through his teeth.

After a moment he perked up and decided, 'So we think it's a conspiracy by the entire project team.'

He and I had been so absorbed we had forgotten our companions. At that, there was an upheaval from the wicker chair. Larius bestirred himself, wriggled himself upright and let out an extraordinary belch. Aelianus and I looked pained. Julia Junilla sat down on a rug with her fat legs in front of her and tried to copy the disgusting noise.

'Myths!' exclaimed Larius. 'You two mad buggers are indulging fantasies. Why say it's the damned project team?'

I raised an eyebrow. 'You're defending them?'

'They are a bunch of wet-arsed, boneless sea anemones,' Larius growled. 'Jelly throughout. Not one of them could fight his way out of a cushion-case. The whole team together couldn't work out a plan to open a latrine door – even if they all had the squits.'

'You give us a fine assessment of these noble men,' Aelianus congratulated him sarcastically.

'Let's have your assessment then, Larius.'

'Uncle Marcus, the place is swarming with angry parties who all hated Pomponius for much better reasons than any of your suspects. The worse the project team had against him was that he was overbearing and horrible.'

'I concede that if being unpleasant were enough to get a man slain at the baths, Rome would be an empty city.'

'Try these,' Larius listed. 'The marblers. Who needs bloody marble veneers anyway?' he complained professionally. 'I can paint better veining, without any expensive breakages . . . They had some ruse, which has been stopped.'

'The over-cutting scam. Milchato was told to prevent it,' I said.

Larius pulled a face. 'No, it was something much more lucrative, not just the old coarse-sand trick. Don't ask me what. I don't gossip with marble-men.'

'Standards!' scoffed Aelianus.

'Get stuffed.' Larius grinned. 'Next, how about Lupus or Mandumerus?'

'Both?' I was surprised.

'Of course.'

'Mandumerus had a fake labour fiddle. I exposed that.'

'So Falco is next for strangling with the tight necklace?' asked Aelianus, rather too keenly.

'Oh he has you and your brother to look after him!' Larius laughed. 'Anyway, it's known all over the site that Pomponius wanted to crucify Mandumerus but Falco vetoed it. So Mandumerus still doesn't like him, but he knows my dear uncle has a sensitive side.'

'Tell me more about the Mandumerus racket,' I said. 'And why you include Lupus.'

'Mandumerus has been working this trick with the false numbers for decades. He probably cannot even remember how to operate honestly. Lupus has his own scheme.'

'What? I've gone through the labour records with the fine side of my comb, Larius, and found nothing suspicious.'

'You wouldn't. The overseas labour has to be paid for by the Treasury. They pay Lupus; Lupus provides the men. But what Lupus does is *sell* the jobs to the highest bidder.'

'How does it work?'

'To be employed in the overseas gangs, men have to bribe Lupus. Once they come out here, full of hope, it's a long way home if they don't get taken on. So he sets his own terms. Mostly they give him a cut of their pay. Some manage to produce wives or sisters whom they pimp to him. He's not fussy. He'll take payment in kind.'

'Beats three sacks of barley and a basket of garlic,' I sighed.

'The Treasury is getting what they pay for. Does it matter?' Aelianus asked.

'It does to an emperor who wants a reign famous for fairness,' I explained.

'That's a bit idealistic!'

Larius and I, both plebeians, stared at Aelianus until he moved uneasily against the arm rest of his couch.

'That you think so is no surprise,' I told him coldly. 'I would have hoped a man of your intelligence would know better than to say it.'

Helena's brother shifted again. 'I thought you were a cynic, Falco.'

I clasped my hands over my belt. 'Oh no. I'm constantly expecting good in the world, believe me!'

XLIV

A T THE prickly silence which ensued, my daughter Julia became unhappy. As always, she yelled her head off. Larius shoved her toy cart about with his toe. The distraction failed. Julia woke Favonia, who joined in the noise. I bestirred myself and picked up the baby, causing Larius to pinch his nose with disgust. 'She stinks, Falco!'

'Reminds me of you at this age,' I retorted. 'Where are all my domestics anyway? What have you two done with the women of my household?'

'Helena Justina went to talk to the King. She took your sister as a chaperone.'

'Now you tell me! There is supposed to be a nurse. Where's that idle miss Hyspale?'

'No idea.'

'Aulus?'

'I would have said she had dressed herself up and gone off to swoon over Larius – but Larius is here.'

'She'd be disappointed anyway,' scoffed Larius. 'I have some standards.'

'Anyway, you're too worn out by the bar girl,' I jibed. 'Why is Helena talking to Togi?'

'He sent for you. You were not here. I volunteered to replace you,' Aelianus complained, 'but my sister overruled it.'

I grinned, deducing that Helena had been her forceful self. 'She's just a girl, you know. Try standing up to her.'

He shot me a scornful look and did not deign to respond.

Leaving the lads in charge of the infants (with little hope of them changing the loincloth), I hotfooted round to the royal apartments. The few plaid-clad attendants on duty seemed surprised that I should feel the need to bother to appear on my own behalf when someone so competent as Helena was already representing me. Still, they let me in.

'When I was in Rome –' began the King as I entered. I could see him as the forerunner to a long tradition of British visitors to foreign parts who would never get over the experience. Looking at what they had here at home, how could anyone blame them? A hot dry climate (or even a hot humid one), a leisured pace, a generously comfortable lifestyle, warm wine, brilliant colours, not to mention exotic food and tasty women, would seem like a philosopher's ideal republic to the hairy *homunculi*.

I felt homesick again.

This was a colourful symposium. Everyone was sitting around in wicker armchairs like snobs at a music recital. The room itself, elegantly coved and dadoed, was a sophisticated mix of purples and contrasting shades, mainly ochres and whites, against which the King made a different kind of contrast, dressed today not in his Roman wear but local garments in a whole fruit basket of berry dyes. Helena was in white, her formal choice, and Maia in pink, with green bands. I was now down to the last tunic in my chest, which happened to be black. Not my shade. In black, I look like a third-grade undertaker, a slapdash halfwit who will lose your beloved grandma and send you the ashes of a dead ass instead. In the wrong urn.

Togidubnus saw me and stopped. Perhaps Maia and Helena briefly showed relief. They looked as if they had been sharing his regal anecdotes for too long.

'Sorry to interrupt.' I smiled. 'I heard you wanted me. Of course Helena Justina knows what I have to say better than I do, but she may let me listen while she recounts my views.'

'I hope you are not being sarcastic, darling,' Helena commented. She rearranged her stole on one shoulder, with a faint jingle of silver bracelets. A decorous ringlet shook against her ear, causing a near-indecorous reaction in me.

'Actually, no.'

We all smiled. Helena took command. 'His Majesty wanted to talk to you. He is concerned that with Pomponius dead, lack of supervision may disrupt his new building.'

'Awfully bad luck for Pomponius,' broke in the King. He had not yet learned to allow Helena her full number of waterclocks when she made a speech.

'His Majesty,' said Helena directly to me, not giving the King a look-in, 'was with Marcellinus yesterday. The architect's wife held a birthday party at their villa. On his return, King Togidubnus was shocked to learn what had happened to Pomponius. Now he wants to ask you, Falco, whether Marcellinus could assist professionally.'

If he was at his wife's party miles away, Marcellinus was in the clear. He had not helped himself back into power by strangling Pomponius. Well, not unless he could be in two places at once like that myth about Pythagoras.

Of course, somebody else could have killed Pomponius for him.

'I know Marcellinus will volunteer,' murmured the King – with just sufficient gloom to cheer me up. I had a welcome impression that he was being leaned on over this. Thirty years of the same architect could wear any client down; Marcellinus should have been thrown out for good the last time the cushions were changed.

'There is official protocol,' I hummed. 'Pomponius was a Rome appointment and I cannot anticipate what Rome wants done next.' This overlooked the fact that it was my role to *tell* Rome what Rome wanted.

'Verovolcus says you intend to discuss the situation with Marcellinus.'

'I do.' I could say that with sincerity. 'But you will understand it is rather low on my action list. My priority is to discover who killed Pomponius. For one thing, we don't want to lose anybody else the same way!'

The King raised bushy white eyebrows. 'Is it likely?'

'Depends on the motive. Strangely,' I said, 'I find no sense of anxiety amongst people here. There is a marauding killer: the normal reaction should be acute fear that others are at risk.'

'People believe Pomponius died as a result of a purely personal animosity?' suggested the King. 'That would make the rest of them safe.'

'Well, they know how many people hated him.' In my new role as a staid man of sense, I did not ask whether Togidubnus was afraid for himself. Nor did I query his feelings towards Pomponius. I had witnessed them in furious disagreement on design issues, but you don't use emotive words like 'hate' about landscape gardening and room layouts.

Or do you? King Togidubnus cared a lot about such matters.

'He and I had our disagreements, Falco, as you are aware.'

'Personal?'

'Professional!'

'Public too . . . Still few clients actually kill their home makeover man.'

The King smiled. 'Given how much bad feeling refurbishments can cause, there could well be more who do! Luckily I can say where I was yesterday,' he assured me, rather dryly. 'Should you ask.'

'Well, I like to be thorough, sir.' I made it a joke. 'I'll put down a formal note: all day at the Marcellinus villa?'

'Yes. Have you been there?'

'No, but I have an invitation.'

'A beautiful place,' said Britain's foremost connoisseur. 'I gave Marcellinus the land, as thanks for his work on this house . . .' He tailed off slightly. Had the gift gone wrong subsequently? 'I feel you would be interested in the property, Falco.'

He sounded like a realtor. I was not planning to buy within nine hundred miles of here. Not that that stops them.

'Internal viewing recommended, is it? *Must be seen . . .*' Why would the King assume I had a special interest in property, self-build or otherwise? Rome's official brief would have covered my status and talents, not my living arrangements.

Perhaps I had imagined any significance in the comment. The King merely resumed his tale of south-coast society: 'The birthday party was due to last all day, concluding with a banquet – but I retire early nowadays, so could not undertake the long journey home at night.' Surely after their long years of collaboration and friendship, the Marcellinus couple could have provided a royal put-you-up? 'I went for lunch only and drove back at dusk after a pleasant afternoon. I stayed overnight in my house in Noviomagus, returning here this morning. I was then told what had happened.'

'I thought you were here last night,' I mentioned. 'I sent someone to ask your permission to close off the baths.'

'Verovolcus or others in my household should have dealt with that.'

'Yes they did . . . though it did not deter some labourers this morning, unfortunately.' No reaction from the King. 'Verovolcus was not invited to the birthday party?'

'No.' The King now looked embarrassed.

'Verovolcus is organising the contractors at the bath house,' Helena broke back in. 'He stayed behind to deal with them.'

'You need not be shy about the refurbishment,' I reassured the King. 'The new palace is your gift from Vespasian, but you are perfectly entitled to make additional improvements. You are a wealthy man,' I told him. I wanted to hint that if he added to the approved scheme, he must commit his own funds – at least while I was auditing. 'Lavish spending is the duty of a wealthy Roman. It demonstrates status, which glorifies the Empire, and it cheers up the plebs to think they belong to a civilised society.'

This time nobody asked if I was being sarcastic, though they probably all knew.

'You should ask about the architect's party,' Maia put in suddenly. She had a morose expression, fired by a dangerous glint. I tipped up an eyebrow. 'There was food and drink all day – then in the evening, after the King left, there was to be a grand formal dinner. That was to be accompanied by music and hired entertainment, Marcus.' I sensed what was coming. 'The highlight was a special dancer,' my sister announced.

It came as no surprise. Maia would hardly look so grim over a light poetry recital or a troupe of fire-eaters. 'Let me guess. That would be a professional dancer, some exotic import all the way from Rome? Sinuous and expert?'

'Expert in a lot of things,' Maia snapped. 'Her name is Stupenda.'

'Her name is Perella.' I now had no doubt. But what would Anacrites' agent want with the retired ex-architect?

Nothing good. Nothing that I could afford to ignore.

XLV

T HE MARCELLINUS villa was supposed to be about twelve miles
away – that was probably as the crow flew, and in my experience
British crows were tipsy old bunches of feathers who could not use
maps.

The King realised I would not contemplate breaking off the murder
enquiry to make such a journey unless I feared danger. He provided
fast horses and a small escort of keen warriors. We were seen leaving
by Magnus, who somehow found a mount and attached himself.
Verovolcus also tagged along. So did Helena. While I protested, she
made me carry her on my horse behind me. This was a fine example
of Roman nursing motherhood – because yes, we had to have Favonia
with us too. Helena had quickly run to fetch her, then turned up with
the baby secured to her body with her stole. Not many informers go
about their business accompanied by a madwoman and a four-month-
old child.

Maia stayed behind, with Nux and a human bodyguard. 'I'll look
after little Julia. I'm not taking on those other two you fostered. They
look nasty blighters.' Aelianus and Larius pretended not to hear.

Larius wanted to come. 'You're a murder suspect,' Aelianus
rebuked him. 'Just sit tight.'

'I've been assisting Uncle Marcus since you were a two-foot-high
whiner dribbling over your gold amulet –' Larius scoffed.

'You were brought to Britain to paint sprays of pretty flowers. I am
on official attachment –'

'Stop arguing, both of you,' Maia scowled. Surprisingly they did.

We were offered a boat. It could have been quicker, for all I know.
But I wanted to see if we met anybody coming back to Noviomagus
from the villa. It did not happen. Still, you have to check.

The Marcellinus spread lay a couple of miles inland. We certainly
knew when we got there: its size and grandeur compelled attention
the same way he did, with his dramatic clothes and haughty bearing.

As soon as we galloped up to the monumental entrance, my fears about last night were confirmed. The great place was in turmoil. The slaves were either running about like startled mice or cowering, all terrified. We soon found the architect's wife, whom I put about twenty years younger than him – maybe it was her fiftieth birthday she celebrated yesterday. Scream after scream told us where she was. She must have been screaming helplessly for a long time, because she had grown completely hoarse. None of her staff dared approach to soothe or comfort her.

The hysteria was caused by finding her husband dead. I did not need to ask her whether he died from natural causes. They had a bath house – but unlike Pomponius, Marcellinus had died in his bed.

Helena took charge of the poor woman. Striding through elegant suites full of ornate furniture, I soon came on Marcellinus. He and his wife had separate bedrooms – the sophisticated system that enables couples to ignore each other. He was in his bed, still lying where he had slept, as the wife had said. Somebody had cut his throat. It was expertly done, through both jugular and windpipe, so deeply the knife must have scraped his vertebrae.

The room stank of last night's wine. There was a great deal of blood. I had been half prepared for this; well, I had seen such handiwork before. It still turned my stomach. Magnus, who followed me, failed to make it from the room before he vomited. Some of the Britons who came with me looked queasy, though they all managed to stay upright and nobody fled. Verovolcus came right up and inspected the scene at close quarters. A head half sliced from its body held no terrors for tribesmen whose nation decapitated enemies as war trophies. The young men could never have joined in much action, but Verovolcus gave the impression he had seen sights I would not like to hear about.

It was a ghastly sight. I tried to remain professional. Marcellinus may have been asleep when he was set upon. From the way he lay high against the pillows, with the top portion of his body outside the bedspread, I thought it more likely he had sat up and been slashed from behind. Someone had been allowed to get close enough for that. If a woman did it – and I knew who I meant – any cynic could speculate as to how she wound herself so far into the man's confidence – on his wife's birthday too.

Most of the blood was on the bed. There were no footprints. The door handle was clean. The perpetrator cannot have escaped the gore entirely, but had left no trail. A professional job. Little could spoil it except that my presence in the locality was real bad luck. I had seen enough handiwork like this to name Perella outright as the killer.

There was no weapon at the bedside, but we could tell it had been a highly sharpened, thin-bladed dagger. Sharp enough to fillet fish, bone meat – or for any other butchery. It would be well cleaned by now, pushed tidily back in its sheath, and tucked into the belt of the quiet, dowdy-seeming woman whom I had once seen pare an apple probably with that very knife. A cloak would cover any blood splashes.

'Man from Rome, what do you think?' croaked Verovolcus. I thought he showed far too much eager curiosity, for one thing.

'If people continue to die at this rate, nobody will be left as suspects . . .'

Verovolcus laughed. I did not join him. 'Two great architects in the same night!' he marvelled.

'Intriguing coincidence.' Or was it? 'Pomponius and Marcellinus had a professional rivalry. Since they were killed the same evening, all this distance apart, neither killed the other. Mind you, we could still find the same motive – and the killers could have been organised by the same person.'

'A jealous wife?' Magnus suggested.

'You knew the couple,' I told Verovolcus. 'Did she have a reason to be upset with her husband?'

Verovolcus shrugged. 'If she did, she never showed it. She always appeared content.'

'She is upset now!' I commented.

We searched the house, discovering nothing significant. The slaves said that after prolonged festivities, everyone had slept in late. That included some guests who had stayed overnight; we found them huddled together in a dining room. Local dignitaries, not particularly dignified in this crisis, they had nothing to tell us. People had risen late, came to breakfast – which was by then at lunchtime – and were planning their departure. Marcellinus' wife decided to check on him, as he would normally bid farewell to any guests in person. After the screams started, the guests felt they should remain here, though nobody knew what form their assistance should take.

I asked about last night. They all said the party was a huge success; the dancer had been splendid. The musicians were provided by Marcellinus, not brought by Stupenda, as she called herself. This morning, both musicians and dancer left – and were seen leaving by a gateman – one responsible citizen had thought to check this. The strummers and tambourinists went first. The dancer emerged a little after them; by prior arrangement she had been fetched from Noviomagus and was to be returned there in Marcellinus' own carriage.

The carriage was still out. I asked Verovolcus if the warriors could ride around and scour the countryside at least in the near vicinity. They ought to find the conveyance. They would not to trace 'Stupenda', I was sure.

I went to talk to the wife.

No luck. Helena had calmed her down, but it had been necessary to sedate her. A woman in the kitchen had produced medicinal herbs for this purpose. Helena had wrapped the widow in a blanket. Now she simply sat weeping slowly as shock really set in. She was incoherent and oblivious to our presence.

Helena drew me aside and spoke in a low voice. 'I found out what I could. The party ended very late. People were exhausted, and most of them tipsy. Beds were found. Marcellinus and his wife slept in separate quarters . . .' I did not comment. Helena and I shared strong views about that. Still, this was an elderly couple and he was an artistic type. 'This morning the servants were all drowsy so the wife herself investigated his non-appearance. She just walked in, and came upon the horror.' Helena was shaken. Maybe she imagined how she would feel if she found me like that.

'What is she like?'

'Decent. Respectable if not cultured. Not his freedwoman; there would have been rank and a dowry, I'd say.'

'He would want a wife who brought him money — expensive tastes.'

'She has not yet absorbed what this means.' Helena herself in a crisis always saw instantly what it would involve. Helena conquered bereavement, fear, or any other tragedy by fiercely planning how to deal with it. 'I told her we think the killer will be long gone and there is no threat to others. She could not take it in. She is not even calling for justice yet.'

My voice rasped harshly. 'If the killer comes from Anacrites, he *is* justice — imperial justice executed sneakily and summarily.'

'Don't blame the Emperor.' Helena sounded tired.

'Oh let's pretend Vespasian does not know what his Chief Spy fixes — or his filthy methods. No. Be realistic: Vespasian does not *want* to know.'

I knew Helena would resist. 'Inform Vespasian if you want to, Marcus – but *he won't thank you!*'

Helena supported the Flavian regime, yet she was a realist. Vespasian maintained a pretence that he hated spies and informers – yet the imperial intelligence service still flourished. Titus Caesar had made himself commander of the Praetorian Guard, who ran the spies network (on the rationale that they were using it to protect the safety of the Emperor). From what I heard, rather than disbanding it, Titus was planning to restructure and expand the team.

Even my own work for Vespasian was part of this system. Being freelance rather than on the palace payroll did not absolve me from the ordure of undercover work. I had approached this mission openly – yet in the preparatory stages even I had considered whether I could accomplish more on site disguised as a fountain expert.

Any casualties in my work were unavoidable. I never sought to cover up my actions with executions. When tragedies happened, I hoped the dead deserved their fate. But Anacrites would say the same. Perella slitting throats in far-flung provinces was only a means to liquidate offenders with maximum efficiency and minimum public outcry – using cost-effective means.

'But why Marcellinus?' I had spoken out loud.

Helena and I moved to an anteroom together so she was able to speculate with me, unheard. 'For Anacrites to go this far seems very strange. Marcus, surely Marcellinus' only sin was being too cosy with the client? A cold letter from Vespasian should have dealt with that.'

'That was my reaction. I had intended to recommend recalling Marcellinus to Italy, whether he wanted to go or not.'

Helena was frowning. 'Perhaps it isn't Anacrites. Could Claudius Laeta be at the back of this?' She could be as suspicious as I was. Laeta was a senior bureaucrat who meddled in major initiatives of all kinds. He was a keen enemy of Anacrites and no friend to me. Whenever he could, he set the two of us against one another.

I could not reconcile myself to that suggestion. 'Laeta briefed me for this trip. While it's true I had suggested Anacrites to Vespasian as an alternative, I've never seen Anacrites working with Laeta – well, not since they started jostling each other for position – and I've never known Perella to work with anyone other than Anacrites either.'

'So this is just the Chief Spy and his overseas agent. Every time we come abroad, we have the same problem of Anacrites dogging our footsteps,' Helena grumbled.

'If he's done this, I'm assuming it's his personal initiative. Anacrites is not supposed to know that I am here.'

'Did you ask Laeta to keep it confidential?'

'Yes – because I thought Laeta would enjoy deceiving Anacrites.'

'Ha! Perhaps Anacrites found out?'

'That would make him a good spy! Don't wind my ratchet, lady.'

We sat quiet, perusing the décor while the situation sank in.

'Look around you, Marcus,' said Helena abruptly.

I had hardly taken in the layout and styling of this villa. That was partly due to the crisis, but also I felt I was in familiar surroundings. Now I saw what Helena meant. We had ended up in reception rooms that could be part of the 'old house' back at the palace. I suppose it was natural. Marcellinus was the architect. He would impose his personal style. Yet the similarities were eerie . . .

Its floor had multi-coloured cutwork stones . . . *a calm geometry of pale wine-juice red, aqua blue, dull white, shades of grey, and corn.* Well, well. There was a blue-black dado and a painted cornice with an effect just like plaster bathed in evening light. Glancing from the window (fine-quality hardwood with long-life workmanship) I could see that the exterior materials were all equally familiar too, especially the grey stone, close to marble, which I knew came from a fine British quarry on the coast. The huge bath house looked just like the one at the palace.

Helena stood at my shoulder.

'I presume,' she murmured, 'the aristocracy will have seen the King's palace and want their private homes to be just as grand. Friends and family of Togidubnus in particular.'

'Agreed. And Marcellinus was best placed to ensure *his* villa had positively the best of everything. So he shows Britain how to adopt Romanisation – right down to our sophisticated corrupt practices.'

Helena pretended this came as a surprise. 'Are we Romans so bad?'

'As in all things, sweetheart, Rome leads the world.'

'And are you saying Marcellinus *stole* these expensive materials from the palace?'

'I am not in a position to prove it – but until this moment, I was not looking for that kind of evidence.'

'And now the truth just met your eyes.'

'Very tastefully. In beautiful colour configurations, all skilfully worked.'

Maybe someone else had been looking for the necessary evidence. Outside a familiar white-clad figure moved in a courtyard. Magnus.

He had been very keen to accompany us, and after we discovered the corpse he had gone off alone to poke about. Finding an opportunity to explore Marcellinus' villa was his reason for coming with us, probably. I marched out to join him, *sinister, dexter, sinister, dexter*.

'Don't tell me you're looking for "lost" property!'

I had found Magnus frantically pulling covers off piles of stacked materials. In his triumph, he forgot our disagreement when I accused him of the other killing. 'Jupiter, Falco! He had some depot!' Excitement left him bright-eyed.

Marcellinus was storing all a home enthusiast could want – and these were not mere samples. Fine goods were assembled here in large quantities. A renovating handyman would have gurgled with delight at this collection of building sundries. Roof tiles, floor veneers, flues, drains – '*Ceramic water pipes!*' crowed Magnus.

'I keep a few things at home myself,' I mused. 'I follow the "it might come in handy one day" principle.'

Magnus turned to face me. 'Couple of spare tiles for when your annex loses that wonky patch in the next storm? Timber offcuts? Sack of tesserae to match your special floor in case some idiot kicks up a corner? Don't we all!'

'And architects do it on a grand scale?'

'Not all of them,' Magnus said grimly.

'Maybe this stuff has been paid for.'

Magnus only let out a harsh guffaw.

'I'd ask the grieving widow for a sight of the relevant invoices,' I rasped, 'but it seems heartless.'

'Now you're making me weep, Falco.'

Magnus was once again burrowing among stacks of marble sheets. 'The carts come in,' he muttered, his roughened hands pulling the heavy slabs forward to inspect them. 'We certify the delivery; the carts go out again. Cyprianus has taken to installing a gateman, who inspects every empty one.'

'And you have been checking them personally, while they are parked up!'

'You saw me, Falco – and I saw you checking me, for that matter.'

'You could have told me what you were doing.'

'*You* could have told *me*! I was trying to catch them using the rubbish removal trick – a layer of stolen goods is hidden under rubble. Anyway – *yes!*' He stopped. He had licked his thumb and washed it over a particular marble block. Under the dust showed a small, neatly scratched cross. Magnus let the block rest against its brothers, then stood back, sighing like a sailor who had glimpsed his home port.

'You marked a consignment.'

'And now I've found it here. Let him talk his way out of that one.'

'Slight problem with the interrogation, Magnus! I'm diligent – but Marcellinus may not co-operate . . .'

'Plus he had those pipes – they must be the ones Rectus is bellyaching over.'

'Rectus will be pleased.'

'He'll be *farting* delirious!'

'Will you arrange to fetch all this back to the palace?'

'I'm staying here to guard it. When you go back, Falco, will you ask Cyprianus to organise transport?' Magnus then gazed at me. 'By the way – I had back-up, you know. When Gaius couldn't explain his whereabouts yesterday, it's because he was helping me search wagons.'

'So you were never at the bath house last night?'

'Actually I was.' Magnus looked shamefaced. 'I really have to explain this, don't I?'

'It would be wise.' I now thought him innocent, but I answered coldly.

'It was like this: I *went* to the baths, took off my togs and then Gaius nipped after me to say there was movement by the wagons. I'd already seen that Pomponius had put his lurid kit in the changing room and I was not looking forward to leisure time with him. So I dragged on boots and a tunic, then left everything else.'

'So that's how your satchel was hanging there unsupervised, when the killers borrowed your five-four-three and compasses?'

'Right. It turned out there really was a cart leaving, but it was just that appalling statue merchant you brought on site.'

'Sextius is not my protégé!'

'Anyway, Strephon finally gave him the push. Sextius was skulking off to Novio and taking his junk. Have you *seen* it, Falco? Useless trash . . . We searched the cart, then I was so demoralised I really could not face strigilling down next to Pomponius. I fetched my bag and clean clothes and went back to my quarters. If anyone had meddled with my satchel, I didn't notice.'

'Did you see where Gaius went?'

'He didn't come back to the baths with me. He went off to bed. I didn't hang about, and I don't know whether Pomponius was dead at that point or not.'

'Why didn't you tell me all this?'

Magnus gave me a sneer. 'You're the man from Rome!'

'That doesn't make me the enemy.'

'Oh doesn't it!' he scoffed.

I ignored that. 'And you think Gaius is reliable?'

'He's been an enormous help.'

'How did he get involved, Magnus?'

Now it was the surveyor's turn to dodge the question. 'Gaius is a good lad.' I had thought so myself once.

'So you're a diligent site official, he's an honest clerk? And I thought you two were cuddling in the same bath robe!'

'Oh spare me! You know about Gaius?'

'I know nothing. No one talks to me.'

'Ask him,' said Magnus.

XLVI

$\mathbf{M}$AGNUS AND I continued thoughtfully to gaze at the Marcellinus house.

'Nice billet!' I commented. 'From the superb workmanship, he even used labourers and craftsmen from the palace site. It's a cliché, the architect doing up his own house at the client's expense.'

'It still stinks, Falco.' Magnus was disgusted. He was a straight dealer who on principle denied himself the perks that Marcellinus had taken so readily. He must have known already what had been going on. That did not make it easier for him to stand here staring at the proof.

'Did Pomponius take liberties too?' I asked.

'No.' Magnus calmed down slightly. 'One thing you could say for Pomponius, he owned about five properties, but they were all in Italy – none placed conveniently near a project. And I never knew him commandeer so much as a wood nail for any of them.'

'How do you think Marcellinus got away with it?'

'Probably started small.' Magnus forced himself to evaluate the fraud scientifically. 'Genuine unwanted stuff. Mismatched colours. Overbought items. "*Nobody will miss it; it will only go to waste . . .*" Labourers they were trying to keep busy during quiet periods in the contract would be despatched to help out here. As project manager, Marcellinus could certify anything. If nobody picked up the increasing costs, he was laughing. And nobody did.'

'Maybe.'

'Don't pretend you knew about it, Falco!'

'No.' But seeing what had now happened, I could name a palace bureau that must have Marcellinus on a file. There had to be some reason why Anacrites had sent Perella out here. It was typical that he would be acting on outdated information, when current problems on the new scheme made Marcellinus a mere side issue.

'Eventually, Marcellinus saw his source of supplies as a right?' I deduced. 'He saw nothing wrong in it.'

'Everyone here thought supplying the architect with goodies was routine,' Magnus confirmed. 'My worst problem has been breaking that attitude. I thought the King was in on it – still, he's a provincial. Marcellinus had a duty to set him straight.'

'I'm sure that, finally, he embarrassed the King.'

'Too late,' said Magnus. 'They had been too close. The King couldn't shake Marcellinus off. That was why Pomponius used to hate letting Verovolcus in on anything.'

'The long shadow of Marcellinus thwarted all attempts to keep the new scheme solvent? I've seen for myself,' I told him. 'Even with me right there on site, Marcellinus was quite openly leaning on people like Milchato to keep his free gifts coming.'

'Bloody Milchato takes a cut,' the surveyor growled. 'I'm damn sure of it.'

'We can sort that. He worked here on the previous building. Time he had a career move.'

'Oh – "for further development of his personal craft skills", you mean?'

'I see, dear Magnus, that you know how it's done!'

'Just move the problem on.'

'Move him to work on a military latrine at the bad end of Moesia.'

'They don't have marble,' Magnus corrected me pedantically.

'Quite.'

We reflected on the failings – and in the long run, the powers – of gigantic bureaucracy. When that became too solemn, I mused ruefully, 'It must have seemed so neat at first. Togidubnus has a refit – then so does Marcellinus.'

'Then spoilsport Rome sends in a brand new project manager.'

'Pomponius makes himself unpopular, so Marcellinus sees his chance to reposition. But the King has adapted to Vespasian's style; he definitely grows unhappy.' Despite their famous friendship, I was now sure Togidubnus had sent me to see this villa on purpose. I was to discover the fraud. 'Togidubnus wants to see the corruption end.'

Magnus stared at me. 'Just how badly does he want that, Falco? This murder seems rather too convenient.'

I was startled. 'You're surely not suggesting he had a hand in it?'

'He made damn sure he had left the scene before it happened.'

'I don't fancy explaining back on the Palatine that a favourite of Vespasian's is a murderer!' I groaned. 'But did he organise it? I do hope not.'

'The Palatine may not be entirely clean, Falco. I bet this starts a whole way further up than Novio.' Magnus was sharp. Too sharp for his own good, maybe. He might not have heard of Anacrites or Laeta by name, but he knew what went on.

I tried to disagree. 'It's a menace. Murder draws too much attention.'

'But this way, there won't have to be an embarrassing corruption trial,' Magnus pointed out.

'True.'

Was avoiding political embarrassment enough to justify this murder in Anacrites' eyes? Yes, his wheeler-dealing, double-standards section at the Palace would certainly see it that way. And they would not like Magnus and me deducing what they had done.

Helena Justina came out to the courtyard to join us. She looked from me to Magnus. 'What have you found?'

I indicated the mass of stored materials, then waved an arm at the house. 'Marcellinus had a lovely home – kindly supplied to him at government expense.'

Helena took it calmly. 'So the man was somewhat unscrupulous?'

'Why avoid libel? He was utterly corrupt.' Helena sighed. 'This will be a hard blow for the wife,' I said.

At that my own flared up angrily. 'I doubt it! In the first place, Marcus, they lived together here for a long time. The stupid woman ought to have noticed what went on. If she didn't suspect, then she closed her eyes purposely.' Helena was hard. 'Oh she knew! She wanted her fine house. Even if you tell her now, she will deny any wrongdoing, insist that her husband was wonderful and refuse all responsibility.'

Magnus looked startled by her virulence.

I put my arm round her. 'Helena despises meek little women who claim they know nothing of the business world.'

'Parasites – who happily enjoy the proceeds!' Helena growled. 'When she wakes up, that woman's first thought will be whether she can keep the house.'

'If it's all hushed up,' Magnus replied bitterly, 'then she probably can.'

'Expect comprehensive hushing. The Emperor,' I told him dryly, 'won't wish to be seen as a tyrant who harasses widows.'

Helena Justina had had enough. She pointed out briskly that if we were going back to Novio that evening, we should set out now. 'Leave the corpse. Let that woman deal with his remains.'

'You're brutal.'

'I'm angry, Marcus! I hate corrupt men – and I hate women who let them get away with it.'

'Settle down. The widow may in fact be shocked and apologetic when she learns her husband was a crook.'

'Never. She'll never see it.'

'She may turn everything over to the grateful Treasury.'

'She won't.' Helena had no doubt. 'That wife will cling to this villa ferociously. She will give Marcellinus an elaborate funeral. Neighbours will flock to celebrate his life. There will be an overscale monument with fulsome carved tributes. This pilfering grandee's memory will be cherished for decades. And the worst of it is – she will speak of you and Magnus as mundane interferers. Men of lesser vision, men who *did not understand*.'

'My lady is upset,' I told the surveyor. I sounded proud of her, I'm proud to say. 'I'll take her home.'

'She's bloody right!' proclaimed Magnus.

'Oh I know that.'

XLVII

THERE WAS no sign of Verovolcus and his men, and I had no great
hopes of results from their search. I found our horse and set off
back to Noviomagus with Helena myself. We were already tired.
Anger made it worse. We travelled the long road almost in silence, yet
being together apart from others was refreshment for us both.

At one point, Helena began dozing against my back so for safety I
stopped and took charge of Favonia. Swapping a baby between two
drowsy parents on horseback, when the baby is wide awake and wants
to throw its weight about, takes time and courage.

'Maybe we should swaddle her, after all,' I muttered. Helena had
vetoed this for both our children. She believed in exposing the girls to
exercise and danger; she called it training, so they could one day deal
with men. On the other hand, she said if we had boys, she would keep
them in straitjackets until they left home on marriage.

'Swaddling *you* wouldn't keep you out of mischief,' she told me.
'Have you got her?'

I had somehow tied Helena's stole around the baby and knotted it
to hang around my neck.

'She's got me.' My offspring was now gripping the front neck of
my tunic hard. Half throttled, I rode on.

When we reached Noviomagus, I decided we would follow the
King's example from yesterday: we would rest here and stay overnight
at Helena's uncle's house. Another mile to the palace might not seem
too much, but it was a mile along a road frequented by men from the
site. I was exhausted and ill-placed to tackle trouble. Besides, I was in
no mood to restrain myself with any fool who tried to take me on.

Helena wanted to see her brother Justinus too. Rather to my
surprise, he was actually at home; I thought hard living must have
paled. But I was wrong; his hard-living cronies had merely come to
him. Once it was clear that Helena and I were not in transit but
staying, Aelianus and Larius both sneakily emerged.

'It's been a long day, with some bloody episodes,' I warned them.

I was past even berating them for breaking the rules and leaving base. I could not face a noisy group discussion about recent developments. I had thought things through on the long ride here, but still had some pondering left to do – the kind I could accomplish best when fast asleep.

All three young men volunteered with great courtesy to go out for the evening. They might be home-loving types, but felt they could amuse themselves at some respectable venue so Helena and I might have some peace. The trio promised to return to the house with extreme care and quietness.

'And don't be late,' ordered Helena. They solemnly nodded their heads. 'Who is looking after Maia Favonia?' she then enquired. The lads assured her Maia Favonia was well able to look after herself.

We had to hope it was true.

XLVIII

NO, WE didn't.
I caught the lads as they were skipping out the door. With Perella still on the loose, Maia needed guards. 'Aelianus and Larius, you are to go back to the palace now. Make sure my sister is all right.'

'Maia is perfectly safe –' Aelianus began stroppily. After his sojourn in the woods, he wanted a treat.

He might be right. Perella's sole target might have been Marcellinus. But he could be wrong.

'If anything happens to Maia while you have bunked off partying, I shall kill you, Aulus. That's as in disembowel you with a meat cleaver.' He was still looking rebellious so I said curtly, 'Marcellinus had his throat slit by that dancer we thought was tailing Maia.'

He did reconsider. 'And now the woman is on the loose again?'

'Stupenda?' Justinus joined in, with a quick glance at his crony Larius. 'She won't have energy for Maia. She will be resting. She has a long night ahead of her tomorrow.'

Larius explained: 'Tomorrow night is billed as Stupenda's farewell appearance.' As I stared at him, he added lamely, 'Virginia tipped us off.'

Tomorrow was nearly here. 'You're done in, Falco,' Justinus said quietly. 'Aulus and Larius will certainly go back now and guard Maia. I'll try to find out from the management at the bar if they know where the dancer stays. If they don't know, we can all join the audience for her final show.'

'What, and arrest her in front of a baying crowd?' I knew nothing works out that easily. But I was so tired I was powerless. 'She won't appear.'

'She had better,' Justinus replied grimly. 'The men are all keyed up for it. If she fails to arrive there will be a riot.'

I grinned wanly and said well, none of us would want to miss that.

IXL

I SLEPT BADLY. My tooth hurt. And when you most need rest, it refuses to come.

I felt events were either running towards a climax or, more likely, shooting out of my control. The palace project was well in hand. I had identified enough of what had been going wrong for officials to screw things back in line. It could be done painlessly. With both Pomponius and Marcellinus dead, the two architects could jointly be blamed in reports for inefficiency and the theft of site materials. Magnus' part in trying to trace losses would support my recommendation that he be given greater authority. A new title might help, say prefect of the works. Cyprianus would act as deputy. Strephon could be given a chance to lead the designers; he might develop well. If Magnus was correct that the clerk, Gaius, was honest, he could be made the senior; the others could be smartened up or replaced, so cost control and programming would then be pulled back on target. That was fine.

I still wanted to identify for sure who killed the two dead architects and why. Other deaths on site were either natural events or safety issues; firm management would help stop unnecessary accidents.

I still wanted to safeguard my sister, in a way that would deter Anacrites permanently.

I still wanted to find Gloccus and Cotta.

Shocking death stays with you. Bloody sights affect your dreams. When I did drift off to sleep, nightmares that sprang from the killings here, oddly combined with low moments from my own past, leapt from my tired imagination. Waylaid by terror, I woke, needing to sit up and detach myself. Helena, unused to riding long distances, slumbered deeply at my side. I had to stay awake, knowing the nightmares would stalk me if I relaxed again. By the morning, I felt grim.

Justinus appeared as fresh as a bird during my late breakfast. He was even sober enough to notice my silence.

'I've been out on reconnaissance. Everyone thought "Stupenda" was lodging in a dive near the Calleva Gate, Falco. Not so, apparently. I searched, but she was not there.'

'How do they contact her about bookings?'

'She comes to see them.'

'So are they confident that she is still on for tonight?'

'Apparently.'

I ate my bread gloomily. Helena, who was feeding the baby while seated on a leather box-backed couch, looked over. 'What's wrong, Marcus?'

'Something's not right. Perella does not act this way. If she was sent by Anacrites specifically to eliminate Marcellinus – who knows why? – then her normal behaviour pattern would be: stake out the ground; move in for the kill; then vanish.'

'Well, she has disappeared,' said Justinus, though Helena stayed silent.

'I meant, vanish from the whole area. Probably from the province.'

Justinus pushed back his dark floppy hair. 'You suspect that Perella has not yet carried out her full mission?'

'That's one theory,' I replied cautiously. 'One I don't want to think about. Let's stick with the hope that promising she will dance for the boys tonight is just a ruse to give her time and space to make a getaway.'

'She must be stuck. People can only leave this province by sea,' Justinus pointed out. 'You're at the mercy of tides and sailing ships for a fast exit.'

I managed a grin. 'Sounds as if you've thought about this.'

'Every minute since we arrived, Falco!'

I drained a cup of lukewarm flavoured wine, checking with Helena that she was ready to leave for the palace. 'I'll spend a day at the site, Quintus. You can come if you like, if you've nothing on here. There's not much to lose now if people realise you're on my team.'

'I would like to see the palace, after travelling all this way.'

'We can take it easy, then return to Novio this evening, when the floor show is due to begin.'

'Wonderful.'

I grinned at Helena. 'Your brother, who has graceful manners, manages to pretend he'll be happy chaperoned by a chaste older man.'

'Oh who's that, then?' asked Helena dryly. 'I thought he was going with you, Falco.'

Justinus, who knew how to look innocent, roused himself as if to

249

go and fetch his travelling gear. Then he paused. 'Is this the moment to mention someone you're looking for?'

'Not Gloccus and Cotta?'

'No. You told me about that supervisor, the hard man I was not to approach alone.'

'Mandumerus? The gang leader Pomponius wanted to dangle from a man-made tree?'

Justinus nodded. 'I think I saw him. I'm sure it must be him. He fitted your description – he was among the Britons from the site, heavily patterned with woad and a real ugly brute.'

'When was this, Quintus?' Helena put in.

'The same night Marcus came over and mentioned him.' That would be the night Pomponius was killed.

'Why not tell me earlier?'

'I haven't seen you since. I went out for a drink, after you had left.' Justinus managed to sound casual. And he was conveniently forgetting that he saw me last night. My assistants were growing casual. This could all go wrong.

'A drink?' asked his sister. 'Or mooning at that bar girl?'

'Oh she just reminds me of my own dear Claudia,' he lied.

Then he described what had happened. As he sat supping what he alleged was a modest beaker of diluted beverage, a man who resembled my description of Mandumerus had entered the bar.

'Is this your favourite joint? Where Virginia gives the men the eye, and more, while Stupenda issues promises of what life is like among the gods? What's it called – the Maggot's Arse?'

'The Rainbow Trout,' said Justinus primly.

'Very nice. I do love fish.'

'Do you want to know about the Mandumerus lookalike or not?'

'Absolutely. What are you waiting for?'

'He seemed to have just come from out of town – I can't say why exactly I thought that. Something about the way he plumped himself down as if he was either exhausted or really fired up.'

'What – "*Give me a drink, I'm desperate!*", you mean?'

'More or less his words, Marcus. The other men huddled round him. I won't say they lowered their voices, because they didn't say much; they just exchanged rather significant glances.'

'Were they keeping things from you as a stranger?'

'General caution, I would say.'

'And is this the bar where the Britons drink?'

'Yes. It's none too pleasant.'

'But you and Larius fit in!' I sneered. 'So had you seen this man before?'

'I think so. What caught my attention this time,' Justinus said, 'was one quick gesture he made to his cronies as he sat down.'

'Go on?'

'He put one hand around his throat and imitated somebody choking – eyes bulging and tongue out.' Justinus copied it: the universal mime for being throttled or suffocated.

Or strangled, as Pomponius had been that night.

BACK AT the palace later, I detected an uneasy atmosphere. Verovolcus and his men must have returned last night, having found no sign of Perella. Naturally word snaked around the site huts that Marcellinus had been slaughtered in his bed. No doubt those who had benefited personally from his constant home refurbishments were looking now to other scams to enhance their income. That would take up some of their time. The rest was given over to shinning up the scaffold on the old house, whence they leaned over showing their underwear, or in most cases their lack of it, while they whistled at passing women.

They were targeting one in particular: my nursemaid Camilla Hyspale. 'Oh Marcus Didius, those rude men are insulting me!'

'Try minding Julia indoors out of sight, then.'

'Of course, Marcus Didius.' That was strangely obedient. Had Maia taken the girl in hand?

'Beyond my scope,' Maia reported in an undertone. 'She's being nice because she hopes you will let her go out and spend this evening with a friend.'

'What friend?'

'No idea. She keeps running off to flirt with a man. Larius swears it isn't him.'

'Should I let her go out tonight?' I consulted Helena.

'Of course,' she returned mildly. 'So long as the friend is a matron, free from any hint of scandal, who will send her own chair for Hyspale!'

That seemed unlikely.

Julia was too busy to go indoors. Too young to be worried by men on scaffolds, she had her entire toy collection spread in the courtyard: ragdoll, wooden doll with one leg missing, fashionably dressed ivory doll, push-along cart, clay animals, dolls' dinner set, rattle, beanbag for throwing games, balls in three sizes, nodding antelope, and – dear gods – some swine with no care for her parents' eardrums must have given her a flute. I won't say my daughter was spoiled, but she was fortunate. Four grandparents doted on their dark-eyed toddler. Aunts vied with one another for her love. If a new toy was created in any corner of the Empire, Julia somehow acquired it. You wonder why we had brought every one on a thousand-mile journey? Sheer terror of her reaction if she discovered we had left any treasure behind.

Now our acquisitive two-year-old was absorbed in some well-ordered play.

Helena grabbed my arm and hissed with mock-excitement, 'Oh look, darling! Julia Junilla is taking her very first inventory!'

'Well, that's next Saturnalia sorted. Her present can be an abacus.'

'The child has expensive tastes,' Helena replied. 'I think she would rather we supplied her with her own accountant.'

'Be more useful than her nurse!' scoffed Maia.

Maia had been standing in the open doorway to our suite, supervising Julia – or rather applying a jaundiced eye to Hyspale's encounters with the men on the scaffold. The fellows would have had more to comment on if they could see Maia, but she stayed the wrong side of the threshold so was out of sight. One member of my household knew how to behave modestly, if she wanted to.

She did, however, have a male follower. She had been talking to Sextius the statue-seller. Well, she had been letting him talk, without making her replies too objectionable. Sextius, still with the wary look he had always given Maia, had been telling her he had sold his cartload of statues.

At this news, Aelianus stuck his head out; he and Larius must have been lounging indoors. 'Olympus, who bought them?' demanded Aelianus with professional interest.

'One of the contractors for the King's bath house.'

Aelianus shot me a private smirk; apparently he thought little of the statues. Installing them in the royal changing room would be a huge joke.

'There should be plenty of water on hand for the works!' I commented. Unnerved by our presence, Sextius shambled off. If he had returned to the site hoping to inveigle himself into Maia's confidence, it had failed.

Maia was only interested in hearing from me. She dragged me indoors. Having reassured myself that in our absence there had been no incidents, I gave her a brief update on Perella. I had to come clean about the Marcellinus death before my sister heard it from others. I played down the details. I stressed that this indicated Perella's mission to Britain had been quite unconnected with us.

'Oh really!' scoffed Maia.

I went to my office. There I found Gaius, working on a batch of invoices and sipping *mulsum*. We had not spoken since I stormed off after accusing him of lying to me.

'Oh I see, Iggidunus waives his ban on serving this office, so long as I'm not here!'

Gaius grinned warily over his beaker rim. 'You have to know how to handle him, Falco.'

'That's what I was always told about women. Applying it to the drinks boy never cropped up before.' I gazed at him. 'Magnus says I got you all wrong. Apparently you are honest, helpful and an all-round model of probity.'

'Well, I am on the right side,' he claimed.

I told him what we had discovered at the Marcellinus villa. The missing supplies that we would be fetching back today should improve chances of balancing the site account. Gaius cheered up.

'So tell me about helping Magnus. In particular, explain why you never told me what you were up to.'

Gaius looked shy. 'Not allowed to, Falco.'

'*Not allowed*? Look, I'm tired. Murder depresses me. So does blatant corruption, actually. Magnus said I should ask you what's what.'

The clerk still kept mum.

'Gaius, I like hearing that you are straight, but it is not enough. Explain your role. I won't allow mystery men to meddle in this project.'

'Is that a threat, Falco?'

'I can dismiss you, yes. Dalmatia's a long way to trundle home in disgrace, with no transport and your pay held up.'

Dalmatia was where he had said his mother lived.

Somebody else in this province had a Dalmatian birthplace: a highly placed British official. '*Your father's highest position was as a third-grade tax inspector in a one-ox town in Dalmatia*' was how I once put it to the man defiantly. I was stroppy in those days. '*No one but the governor carries more weight in Britain than you . . .*'

'Flavius Hilaris!' I exclaimed. How could I have forgotten him? After all, he had lent us his town house in Noviomagus. Once my mission was completed, Helena wanted us to visit him and his wife in Londinium.

Gaius had flushed slightly. 'The financial procurator?'

'A fine man. My wife's uncle, did you know? He was born in Narona.'

'Is that so?' murmured Gaius.

'Skip the bluff.'

'Lots of people come from my province, Falco.'

'Not so many end up here. What are you – twenties? What did you work on before the palace, Gaius?'

'Forum feasibility study.'

'Not the forum in Novio? I've seen that; it must have been planned on the back of a whelk bill – one that someone then lost. *Where*, Gaius?'

'Londinium,' he admitted.

'Under the nose of the provincial governor – and of his right-hand man! Hilaris is fair. He knows how to select staff. He's not given to favourites. But being from Dalmatia would endear you, I bet. And if he thought you showed promise – well! His speciality, for your information, is the rare one of weeding out graft. That was how I met him; it was how I met my wife, so I'm unlikely to forget. So tell me, are you working undercover here for the procurator in Londinium?'

'He would have told you, surely?' The clerk, who would have been sworn to silence for his own safety, tried one last gambit.

'I'm sure he meant to keep me fully informed,' I answered starchily.

'Administrative hitch?' murmured Gaius, starting to reveal his amusement.

'Absolutely. And Helena Justina's uncle in his curule chair is a mischievous swine!'

We seemed to understand one another, so I left it at that. Gaius was well placed to observe what happened on this site, but he was fairly junior. He was doing good work. I would tell Hilaris that. To enhance future control, it was best to leave the planted clerk here if possible, maintaining his cover. So I winked in a friendly manner and continued with my own work.

I spent a couple of hours drafting a report on the site problems, and my thoughts on their future resolution. From time to time people came in with dockets for me to sign as project manager, though things seemed quiet. Cyprianus was off site of course, taking transports to collect Magnus and the materials we were retrieving from the Marcellinus villa. Not much was happening here.

When I wanted air, I took a walk around. The place today was full of abandoned barrows and half-dug trenches. I could either regard it as a site where everything had gone into limbo because of a real emergency – or as a perfectly normal building scheme where, as so often, nobody had bothered to turn up.

Investigations acquire their own momentum when they start going well. Discover enough, and new connections then quickly become apparent. It *may* even help to surround yourself with well-chosen, intelligent assistants.

First Gaius softened up enough to try ingratiating himself. 'How's the tooth, Falco?'

'It was all right until you just mentioned it.'

'Sorry!'

'I tried to tweeze it out myself, but it's too deep. Have to ask Alexas to recommend a painfree puller.'

'There's a new sign up showing a dogtooth, down by the Nemesis. It must be a barber-surgeon, Falco. Just what you want.'

'Could you hear any screams?' I shuddered. 'Is the Nemesis a drinking dive?'

'Owner with a sense of humour,' Gaius grinned.

I had lost mine. 'Informers are famous for their irony – but I don't want my gnasher wrenched out next door to a hovel called after the goddess of inescapable retribution!'

'Her wrath is averted by spitting,' he assured me. 'That should be easy during deep gum dentistry.'

'Spare me, Gaius!'

I carried on scratching away with my stylus. I was using a tablet that had a rather thin wax sheet. I must remember that my words might show up on the backboard. However lucid and elegantly phrased, I did not want them being read by the wrong people; my discarded tablets must be burned after use, not tipped into a rubbish pit.

'About that other problem of yours, Falco,' said Gaius after a while.

'Which of many?'

'The two men you want to find.'

I looked up. 'Gloccus and bloody Cotta?' I set down my stylus in a neat north–south line on the table. Gaius looked nervous. 'Speak, oracle!'

'I just wondered about that uncle Alexas has.' I stared. 'Well, he might know them, Falco.'

'Oh is that all. Know them? I thought you were about to say he *was* one of them! Anyway, Alexas has always said he's never heard of Gloccus and Cotta.'

'Oh well, then!' There was a small silence. 'He could be lying,' offered Gaius.

'Now you sound as cynical as me.'

'Must be contagious.'

'His uncle is called Lobullus.'

'Oh that's what Alexas says, is it, Falco?'

'He does. However,' I said, with a wry smile, 'Alexas could be lying about that too!'

'For instance –' Gaius made a great point of proffering the reasonable solution – 'his uncle may be a citizen, with more than one name.'

'If he builds bath houses, I bet his clients call him a few choice ones. Or he might be using an alias to avoid lawsuits . . .' I put down my stylus, considering the proposition. 'Do you know Alexas? Apart from his own job, is he from a medical family?'

'No idea, Falco.'

'And you don't know what part of the Empire he hails from?'

'No.' Gaius looked crestfallen. It was temporary. 'I know! I could ask my pal who keeps the personnel lists. Alexas should have filled in a next-of-kin record. That would give his home city.'

'Yes – and it will say who wants his funeral ashes, if I find out he has fibbed to me!'

By an odd quirk, in an earlier conversation with Alexas about deaths on site, I might even have nudged him into supplying these details myself.

Camillus Justinus stuck his head into the office at about mid-morning. I introduced him to Gaius; they acknowledged each other suspiciously.

'Falco, I've just seen a man I recognise,' Justinus informed me. 'I've come to tell you immediately this time. Larius says he is the King's project representative.'

'Verovolcus? What about him?'

'Thought you might like to know I've seen him before – he was drinking with Mandumerus,' Justinus explained.

'Oh those two have always been thick as ticks,' Gaius contributed. He looked smug – until I tore into him for not mentioning their alliance earlier.

'Mandumerus and Verovolcus are best friends?'

'From the cradle, Falco.'

'Is it a lead?' asked Justinus meekly.

'It is – but I'm not thanking you!'

I ran both hands through my hair, feeling the curls coarsened and sticky after exposure to the salty coastal air. I wanted a three-hour bath, with a full technical massage, in a first-class establishment – in Rome. One with manicure girls who looked like haughty princesses, and three kinds of pastry-seller. I wanted to exit onto travertine marble steps, in early evening, when hot sun still ripped off the paving slabs. Then I wanted to go home for dinner: in my own house on the Aventine.

'Hades, Quintus. This is tricky. Suppose Verovolcus and Mandumerus murdered Pomponius.'

'Why would they?'

'Well, because Verovolcus is loyal to his royal master. He knows all about the King's design rages with Pomponius. He probably thought the King preferred working with Marcellinus. It's even possible there was some exchange of benefits between Verovolcus and Marcellinus. Unaware that someone else was planning to kill Marcellinus, let's say Verovolcus decided to eliminate Pomponius – remove the new incumbent so the old one can be brought back. His crony Mandumerus would be happy to help; he had just lost a lucrative post on site, and Pomponius had wanted to crucify him. No doubt about it, Mandumerus would be after revenge.'

'Do you believe the King connived at this, Falco?' Justinus was shocked. For one thing, he could see it was a stupid thing for anyone to have done. For another, the whimsical boy liked to believe in the nobility of barbarians.

'Of course not!' I snarled. 'My thoughts are strictly diplomatic.'

Well, that could be true.

'So killing Pomponius was an unsophisticated manoeuvre by two misguided henchmen that was doomed to exposure?' Justinus demanded.

'Not quite,' I told him sadly. 'If the surmise is correct – only idiots would go ahead and expose it.'

A short time later I made a formal request for a private interview with the Great King.

258

LI

Tᴉᴍᴇ ꜰᴏʀ a professional statement.

A problem arises when working with clients who demand confidentiality clauses: the investigator is required to keep silent for ever about his cases. Many a private informer could write titillating memoirs, full of slime and scandal, were this not the case. Many an imperial agent could produce a riveting autobiography, in which celebrated names would jiggle in shocking juxtaposition with those of vicious mobsters and persons with filthy morals of both sexes. We do not do it. Why? They do not let us.

I cannot say I ever heard of a sensitive client calling up a court injunction to protect his reputation. That's no surprise. Faced with public exposure by me, many of my own clients would take action privately. A father of young children cannot risk being found lying in an alley with his brains spread around his head. And working for the Emperor involved even more constraints. This subtlety was not spelled out in my contract because it did not need to be. Vespasian used me because I was known to be discreet. Anyway, I never managed to obtain a contract.

Want to hear about the Vestal, the hermaphrodite, and the Superintendent of Riverbanks? You won't get a sniff of it from me. Is a nasty rumour running around that horses' wet-weather shoes, all left-footed, were once ludicrously over-provisioned by the army at enormous cost? Sorry; I cannot comment. As for whether one of the imperial princes had a forbidden liaison with . . . No, no. Not even to be condemned as tasteless speculation! (*But I do know which of the Caesars . . .*) I myself will never reveal who really fathered the baker's twins, the current location of that girl with the massive bust, which cousin is due to inherit from your feeble uncle in Formiae, or the true size of your brother-in-law's gambling debts. Well, not unless you hire me and pay me: fee, plus costs, plus full indemnity against nuisance claims and libel suits.

I mention these points because *if* there were any scandals involving the building scheme, I was there specifically to suppress those scandals. One day the great palace at Noviomagus Regnensis would stand proud, every gracious wing of it fulfilling the vision of which Pomponius had dreamed. My role was not simply to get the monstrosity built, within a realistic margin of its completion date and budget, but to ensure it never became notorious. Magnus, Cyprianus, the craftsmen and labourers could all move on to other projects, where they might well curse the palace as an old bugbear, but their moans would soon be lost amid new troubles. Otherwise, its sorry design history would die, leaving only sheer scale and magnificence to excite admirers.

Here would be the palace of Togidubnus, Great King of the Britons: an astounding private home, a tremendous public monument. It would dominate its insignificant landscape in this forlorn district of a desolate province, possibly for centuries. Rulers would come and go. Further refurbishments would succeed one another, according to Fate and funding. Inevitably its fortunes would wane. Decay would triumph. It roofs would fall and its walls crumble. The marsh birds would reclaim the nearby inlets, then call and cry over nothing but waterlogged hummocks and tussocks, with all grandeur forgotten.

All the more reason for me to sit one day in some gimcrack villa of my own, to gaze across a low river valley, while rowdy descendants of Nux barked at shrieking infants in some struggling provincial garden where my ancient wife was reading on a sunny bench, intermittently asking her companions to keep quiet because the old fellow was writing his memoirs.

Pointless. There would be no scroll-seller willing to copy such a story.

I could take the private route. Any head of household hopes to become someone's interesting ancestor. I could write it all out and shove the scroll in a casket, to keep under a spare bed. My children were bound to minimise my role. But maybe there would be grandchildren with greater curiosity. I might even feel the need to limit their noble pretensions by reminding the rumbustious little beggars that their background had some low, lively moments . . .

Impossible again, due to that invariable brake: client confidentiality.

You can see the problem. When I reported home on these events, the Noviomagus file was swiftly closed. Anyone who claims to know what happened must have heard it from someone other than me. Claudius Laeta, that most secretive of bureaucrats, made it clear that I was forbidden ever to reveal what Togi and I discussed . . .

Mind you, I never had any time for Laeta. Listen, then (but don't repeat it, and I mean that).

I had asked to see the King in private. He honoured this, not even producing Verovolcus: a nice courtesy. More useful than he knew – or was supposed to realise.

I myself had more stringent rules; I took back-up. 'Clean, smart, shaved,' I told the Camillus brothers. 'No togas. I want this off the record – but I want you as witnesses.'

'Aren't you being too obvious?' asked Aelianus.

'That's the point,' Justinus snapped.

The King received us in a lightly furnished reception room, which had a dado with sinuous tendrils of foliage, its colouring and form exactly like one at the Marcellinus villa. I admired the painting, then pointed out the similarity. I began by discussing diplomatically whether this use of labour and materials could be coincidence – then mentioned that we were retrieving the building supplies that were currently stored at the villa. Togidubnus could work out why.

'I had every confidence in Marcellinus,' commented the King in a neutral tone.

'You must have been quite unaware of the nature and scale of what went on.' Togidubnus was a friend and colleague of Vespasian. He might be mired in fraud up to his regal neck, but I formally accepted his innocence. I knew how to survive. Informers some-times have to forget their principles. 'You are the figurehead for all the British tribes. A corrupt site regime could have damaged your standing. For Marcellinus to place you unwittingly in that position was inexcusable.'

The King wryly acknowledged how delicately I had expressed it.

I acknowledged the acknowledgement. 'Nothing should ever take away the fact that Marcellinus designed you a worthy home, in splendid style, where you were comfortable for a long period.'

'He was a superb designer,' agreed Togidubnus solemnly. 'An architect with a major talent and exquisite taste. A warm and gracious host, he will be much missed by his family and friends.'

This showed that the tribal chief of the Atrebates was fully Romanised: he had mastered the great forum art of providing an obituary for a corrupt bastard.

And how would he record Pomponius, loathed by everyone except his fleeting boyfriend Plancus? *A superb designer . . . major talent . . .*

exquisite taste . . . A private man, whose loss will greatly affect close associates and colleagues.

We discussed Pomponius and his affecting loss.

'There have been some rather feeble attempts to implicate innocent parties. So many people disliked him, it has complicated matters. I have some leads,' I told the King. 'I am prepared to spend time and effort on these lines of enquiry. There will be evidence; witnesses may come forward. That would mean a murder trial, unsavoury publicity, and if convicted, the killers would face capital punishment.'

The King was watching me. He did not ask for names. That could mean he knew already. Or that he saw the truth and stood aloof.

'I hate ambivalence,' I said. 'But I was not sent here to push crude solutions. My role is two-fold: deciding what has happened – then recommending the best action. "Best" can mean the most practical, or least damaging.'

'Are you giving me a choice?' The King was ahead of me.

'Two men were involved in the death of Pomponius. I'd say one is very close to you, and the other his known associate. Shall I name the suspects?'

'No,' said the King. After a while he added, 'So what is to be done about them?'

I shrugged. 'You rule this kingdom; what do you suggest?'

'Perhaps you want them dead in a bog?' asked Togidubnus severely.

'I am a Roman. We deplore barbarian cruelty – we prefer to invent our own.'

'So, Didius Falco, what *do* you want?'

'This: to know that nobody else working on this project is at risk. Then to shun domestic violence and to show respect for dead men and their families. In wild moments of idealism, maybe I want to prevent more crime.'

'The Roman punishment for the base-born would be degrading death.' The Emperor's judicial teachers must already have begun work. The King knew Roman law. If he was brought up in Rome, he would have seen condemned men torn apart by arena beasts. 'And for a man of status?' he asked.

'Nothing so decently final. Exile.'

'From Rome,' said Togidubnus.

'Exile from the Empire,' I corrected gently. 'But if your culprits here are not formally tried, exile from Britain would be a good compromise.'

'For ever?' the King rasped.

'For the duration of the new build, I suggest.'

'Five years!'

'You think I strike a hard bargain? I saw the corpse, sir. Pomponius' death was premeditated – and there was mutilation afterwards. He was a Roman official. Wars have been started for less.'

We sat in silence.

The King moved to practical suggestion: 'It can be given out that Pomponius was killed by a chance intruder, who had entered the bath house hoping for sex or robbery . . .' He was displeased, but he was working with me. 'What of the other death? – Who killed Marcellinus?' he challenged.

I told him a hired dancer, her credentials insufficiently checked. The motive, I said with a slight smile, must be robbery or sex.

'My people will search for her,' the King stated. It was not an offer but a warning. He might not know Perella worked for Anacrites specifically, but he had realised she had significance. And if the King found Perella, he would expect some kind of trade.

Since I was sure she would have left the area by now, I did not care.

LII

I WAS UNEASY. Aelianus and Justinus purred happily, thinking our mission accomplished. I had a dark sense of unfinished business waiting to disrupt my life.

The site was too quiet. Never trust a workplace where absolutely nobody is standing around aimlessly.

It was now the second half of the afternoon.

Even this early, many of the labourers went tramping off the site, heading towards town. Soon it seemed as if they had all gone to the canabae. None of the project team were visible, so while no one wanted me to officiate, I retired to my suite to invest in the project manager's privilege: thinking time, paid for by the client. Not long afterwards there was a clatter of horses and most of the King's male retainers mounted up then swept off at a canter in the direction of Noviomagus too. Verovolcus was leading them. I assumed they had instructions from the King to search for Perella.

They had not found her the last time they scoured the countryside. But Verovolcus might have more incentive, if he had spoken to the King since my meeting. He looked grim anyway.

Helena's brothers and my nephew Larius still believed the queen of dance would appear that night at the Rainbow Trout. To prepare for the entertainment, they all spent time at the bath house, throwing aside tools and other equipment left in the changing room by the contractors; the workmen, of course, had made a mess, then fled the scene. Nobody completes a bath-house contract overnight. Where would be the fun in that?

Helena complained our suite was like a home with a wedding in the morning. A loner myself, I was appalled by the spectacle of modern youth getting ready for a big night out. Petronius and I never primped ourselves like these three. Aelianus stubbornly shaved himself, with a meticulous vanity that seemed typical. I reckon he skimmed over his legs and arms too. The sight of Larius and Justinus simultaneously rasping at each other's prickly chins while Aelianus kept possession of one dim hand mirror was unnerving. Then Larius cut himself while pruning his horny toenails and improvised a styptic paste with Justinus' tooth powder. Soon extra lotions were being splashed into remote anatomical crannies for luck.

Our rooms filled up with conflicting masculine unguents; cardamom, narcissus and cypress seemed to be this season's favourites. Then Camilla Hyspale also started tickling noses as she tricked herself out in another room. Ringlets had been well scorched and her face was positively frescoed with a thick layer of white plaster and artistic paintwork. When her dabbing brought a reek of fiery female balsam, Maia ground her teeth then muttered to me, 'That's my Sesame Stink! It used to keep Famia off when he'd had a few . . . Have you actually agreed that Hyspale can go out with her paramour?'

'Curiously, I am still waiting to be asked permission . . .'

Determined not to volunteer, but to force Hyspale to seek me out with her request, I sauntered back to the lads' room. The sight of their three glistening torsos, now stripped naked while they began fervently trying to choose tunics, convulsed me. Any woman who agreed to grope one of these beauties would find he slipped from her grip like a wet mullet. They were resolutely serious. Even selecting the right undergarments required a symposium. Length, fullness, colour, sleeve style and neck opening all had to satisfy stringent criteria – and to look right with their favourite top layer. I could not bear to watch the belt stage. I went out for some air.

Thus, by chance, I came upon a small figure who had been knocking at our door unheard.

'Iggidunus!' I was still grinning over the scenes indoors. 'What do you want?'

'Message for you, Falco.' The *mulsum* boy was as unprepossessing as ever. Mud-stained, surly and dripping unhealthily from every orifice. At least he had not brought me a drink.

'Who wants me?'

'Your man Gaius.' I crooked up an eyebrow. Surrounded by idiotic youth, I was feeling wise, tolerant and mellow. Iggidunus viewed my kindliness with suspicion. Drawing in a huge sniff, he mumbled, 'He's found something at the secure depot. He asked me to come and get you quick.'

I had thought we had discovered all the frauds on this site, but if any were still undetected, Gaius was the man to weed them out.

Iggidunus was pressing me to hurry, but after all the times I had gone feet-out in a muddy slide, I nipped back inside to change my boots. Nobody was paying attention. I called out, 'I'm wanted at the depot; won't be long!'

Waste of time.

When I went out to the veranda, the boy looked surprised that I was wearing a cloak, slung over my right side and corded informally under my left arm. I confessed we Romans felt the cold. He sneered.

Iggidunus and I walked around the site by road. Thin sunlight bathed the huge expanse in light. We skirted the great open area that was to become the formal garden, then went around the corner. The perimeter road brought us to a gate in the high fence of the locked compound.

I stopped. 'Where are the guard dogs?'

'In kennels or gone walkies.'

'Right.' There was no sound of the ferocious hounds. Normally they bayed themselves hoarse if anyone passed by on the road. 'How do we get in?'

Iggidunus pointed at the gate. Quite rightly, it was locked. Cyprianus kept the keys and he had not returned from helping Magnus with the materials at the Marcellinus villa.

'So, Iggy, where is Gaius?'

'He was going to climb in.'

'I didn't know he was that dumb!' He was not the only one. I applied a toe to a crack in the fence and shinned up it. Once perched on the top rail, I could see Gaius inside, lying on the ground. 'Something's happened. Gaius is over there. He must be hurt. Iggidunus, run and find Alexas. I'll go in –'

I swung over and dropped down. It was stupid. I would be lucky to see Iggidunus again. Nobody else knew I was here.

For a moment I froze and surveyed the scene. The depot was a medium-sized enclosure, arranged extremely neatly with stores placed in rows, each wide enough apart to permit a small cart to pass between them. Wooden racks held large slabs of marble. Whole blocks of stone were supported on low pallets. Fine timber was arrayed in large quantities under a roofed area. Near the depot entrance, a stoutly built locked shack must be occupied by the special storeman in working hours. Rare luxuries such as the jewel bases for fine paint pigments and even gold leaf might be kept there in safe custody for the finishing trades. Nails and ironware – hinges, locks, catches and other fitments – would be locked up in the dry too. A row of rough low hutments next to the shack was probably the dog kennels.

Gaius was lying still, alongside the shack. I had recognised him by his clothing and hair. I cowered in the shadow, keeping in cover, watching. Nothing moved. After a moment, I ran lightly across to the prone figure. This area must have been used as a working marble yard at one time; white dust kicked up all over my boots.

'Gaius!' He was so still because he had been tied up and gagged. He seemed unconscious too. I crouched over him, quickly scanning the nearby area. Nothing. I stripped off my cloak and draped it over him. With the knife from my boot, I began to cut away his bonds. 'Gaius, wake up; stay with me!'

He groaned.

Talking in a low voice, I checked him over. He must have been thumped a few times. I had seen worse. The experience was probably new to him.

'What happened?'

'Came for me – but going after you,' he muttered groggily. It had a nice balance. I like a man who sustains his rhetoric even after a thrashing. 'Britons.'

I dragged his arm around my shoulder. 'They beat you?' I pulled him upright.

'I'm a clerk; I just gave in.' I started to manoeuvre him towards the fence. He let me push and pull him, not contributing much.

'How many of them?'

'About eighteen.'

'Let's get out of here, then.' I tried to hide from him my anxiety. That 'about' was conversational stuff; as an invoice clerk, Gaius was bound to have counted them.

We were at the fence. I had my back to the compound. This was bloody dangerous. I looked over my shoulder as much as possible.

'I can't make it, Falco.'

'Only way out, lad.' I was very tense by now. They had brought me here for some reason. I was surprised nothing had happened yet. 'Put your foot there, Gaius. Grab the fence and climb. I'll shove you up from behind.'

But he was desperate to tell me something. 'Alexas –'

'Never mind Alexas now.'

'Family in Rome, Falco.'

'Fine. I wish I was there. Well done.'

He was woozy. Getting him over the fence took a few tries. In fact, it felt like several hours of effort. I would not call Gaius an athletic type. I never asked, but I guessed he had no head for heights. This was like acting as a caryatid to several sacks of soggy sand. Once I had heaved him halfway up, he stuck his damn foot in my eye.

At last he was above me, clinging on, astride the top rail. I bent down to collect my cloak. 'I'm feeling faint,' I heard him say. Then he must have slipped off, because I heard him crash-land – luckily on the other side.

I had troubles of my own. Had I stayed upright, I would be dead. For just as I stooped, a heavy spear thudded into the fence, right where I had been standing. Retrieving my cloak had saved my life. In two ways: hidden under it, I had brought something useful. So when the villain who had thrown the spear now rushed me as a follow-through, I was ready. He came straight into my knife – which he clearly expected. As he parried the knife, I jerked out his innards with my sword.

LIII

Don't blame me. Blame the army. Once the legions train you to kill, any attacker gets what-for. He meant me dead. I slew him first. That's how it works.

I stepped away. My heart pounded so loudly I could hardly listen out for others coming. One down, seventeen to go! Stinking odds, even by my standards.

It was a cluttered compound. If they were here, they were well hidden. Some were outside: when I turned back to shin up after Gaius, gingery heads appeared above the fence. I grabbed a long piece of timber and thrashed at them. One fell back. Another seized the plank and yanked it from my grasp. I jumped aside in time, as he threw it down at me. Otherwise, if they were armed, they were keeping their weapons for later. Sensing that there were more men inside the depot with me, I broke away, ran down an aisle and dodged through some racks of marble. Yells from the fence were reporting my whereabouts. I dropped, and wormed my way very fast at ground level into a long tunnel of cut timber.

Suicide! My way was blocked. Trapped, I had to squirm backwards. Every second I expected to be attacked hideously from behind – but the watchers had not realised I was backing out again. Men were searching the far end of the timber row where they thought I would emerge. Flattened and sweating with terror, I inched under a trestle. One man came to investigate the place where I went into the timber. He was too close to leave alone. Crouched in my hiding place, I managed a backhand sword-swipe through his legs. It was an awkward piece of scything, but I hit an artery. Anyone who hates blood can now go into hysterics. I had no time for that luxury.

His screams brought others, but I was out of there. I leapt up on the marble sheets and went flying over the top this time. Slabs groaned and lurched beneath my weight. A spear whistled past my head. Another thudded harmlessly nearby. The third skimmed my arm. Then the marble slabs began keeling over. I had hit the ground again, but the row of tilted materials behind me slipped and crashed, each expensive slab grazing the surface of its neighbour, and some smashing into my assailants.

While they jumped and cursed and nursed crushed feet, I doubled back unseen. I had some fun trying to climb around a stack of water pipes. Then I banged into a small pile of lead ingots; that brought back bad British memories for me.

The custodian's shack was locked. The only open hideyhole was the dog kennel.

Bad move, Falco. The stench was dreadful. The hounds were out, but their mess remained. These were not lapdogs. They must be fed raw offal, without the use of fancy feeding bowls. Nobody had even tried to house-train them.

Through a crack in the kennel door I could see swarming figures. The searchers thought I had scuttled among the timber again. They decided to smoke me out. Great. I preferred to survive than to save this valuable stock. It may have been imported from all over the Empire to create skirtings, folding doors and luxury veneers, but my life mattered more. Fire damage would be a new excuse in my financial reports. Who wants to be predictable?

It took some time for them to make a light, then the hardwood refused to kindle. I could do nothing except lie low, while desperate thoughts coursed through my mind. If I tried to make a break for it, I stood no chance. The men were enjoying themselves. They thought they had me there, caught in a trap; at least one was prodding the stacked timbers with a long pole, hoping to puncture or spit me. Eventually they let out a cheer; soon I could hear crackling and smell woodsmoke.

The noise and smoke were localised, but the passing of time had brought help. Some of it was unwelcome; in the distance I could now hear the dogs. Still, they were locked out, weren't they?

Not for long. Suddenly someone was trying to break down the gates – with a huge wheeled ram, apparently. It was a sound I last heard on an army training ground. Deep crashing noises came at regular intervals, accompanied by cheers. Even from within my hide I could tell that the gates were weakened and about to give. I waited as long as I dared. As the gates of the compound crashed inwards, dragged open by a two-wheeled cart, I scampered out from the kennel before the guard dogs came home.

'Falco!'

Dear gods: Quintus, Aulus and Larius. Three incongruously well-dressed and coifed ram-raiders. My first hope was they were armed. No. They must have raced straight here without stopping to equip themselves. If they hoped to snatch me, they were thwarted by the assembled men who wanted to do for me first. These renegades rushed at us, whooping.

We all set to, biffing at anyone with wiry ginger hair. Smoke was choking us. There were too few of us. If we tried to make a break for it, we would be massacred. So as we fought, the lads using timbers, we stamped at smouldering wood or tried smothering flames. A great oak log finally caught fire; Larius and I tried to haul it free. A thick haze of smoke had filled the compound. It helped give the impression there were more of us than actually existed. We concentrated on putting in the boot in traditional Roman style.

Three of us had military training. I was an ex-footslogger. Both the Camilli had served as army officers. Even Larius, who spurned the army in favour of art, had grown up in the toughest neighbourhood in the Empire; he knew nasty tricks with feet and fists. Teamwork and grit soon showed our calibre. Somehow we cleared our opponents out of the depot. Then we blocked the gateway with the cart on which the lads had brought a large tree trunk as their improvised battering ram. They must have unhitched the beast of burden and combined as human mules to run the cart at the gates. Straight from the training manual. But with nothing in the shafts, they could not now use the cart to drive away. We were stuck here.

Larius was heaving up pieces of broken marble to make chocks under the cart wheels so no one could drag off our blockade.

'A ram!' I marvelled.

'We're well organised,' boasted Aelianus cockily.

'No swords, though . . . I didn't think you knew I'd gone –'

'We heard you say –'

'You didn't answer! Giving houseroom to you lot is like having three extra wives . . .'

With four of us, we could now take a side of the compound each. Justinus was flailing at heads as they popped up on the fence. 'If I were on the outside,' he shouted, 'my priority would be to rush the gates.'

I swiped a man who peered over at us. 'I'm glad you're in here with us, then. I don't want attackers who use strategy.'

The green timber had dried out enough to burn now, so we had to spare more time to beating out sparks or we would be roasted. Heat from the blazing tree trunk we had dragged free was making life really difficult. Rather than waiting to pick us off at leisure once the smoke increased, our attackers had the bright idea of setting fire to one of the fence panels. It took at once. A column of smoke poured skywards; it must have been visible for miles. We heard new voices, then the dogs baying once again. Aelianus sucked his teeth involuntarily. Shouts outside heralded some new phase of fighting. I waved at the lads, then we all scrambled over the cart and leapt outside the depot.

We found mayhem — a fist fight all over the roadway. I spotted Gaius, being carried around on a pony behind a small girl – Cyprianus' daughter, Alla. Maybe Gaius had fetched the help. Anyway, he was now riding in circles, letting out war cries. Dog handlers were patrolling the scrimmage, unable to decide where or when to unleash their charges. The men who had ambushed me were dressed indistinguishably in site boots and labourers' tunics, but they were mainly fair or redheads, favouring long moustaches, whereas the new crowd were dark, swarthy and stubbly chinned. These arrived in small numbers – most labourers had left earlier for the canabae – but they saw themselves as Roman support against the British barbarians. The rescue gang were Lupus' men, opposing those who had worked with Mandumerus. They could all fight and were eager to demonstrate. Both sides were viciously settling old scores.

We joined in. It seemed polite.

We were hard at it, like drunks at a festival, when we heard more shouts above the mêlée. Trundling and creaking, along came a row of heavy transports, from which Magnus and Cyprianus leapt down in astonishment. The carts had returned from the Marcellinus villa.

This took the passion out of everything. Those of the Britons who could still stagger made off sheepishly. Some of the rest and a few of the overseas group were suffering, though it looked as though there would only be two fatalities – the man I disembowelled first, and the other whose legs I had slashed; he was now bleeding to death in the arms of two colleagues. My party were all bruised, and Aelianus' leg wound must have reopened, adding colour to his bandages. As Cyprianus tore his hair out over the fire damage to the site depot – then growled even more when he realised what had happened to some precious stores inside – I recovered my breath then explained how Gaius and I were set upon. Magnus appeared sympathetic, but Cyprianus was angrily kicking a torn-down, smouldering fence panel. He was furious – not least because he now had the Marcellinus material to store, but nowhere secure to keep it.

I nodded at the lads. We made polite farewells. The four of us sauntered, perhaps rather stiffly, back to my suite at the King's palace.

Then, as we approached the 'old house', I saw a man I recognised, shinning up a ladder on the scaffold: Mandumerus.

Nothing for it: my wife, sister, children and female staff were inside that building. Anyway, I was well worked up for action. I reached the building at a run, grasped the wooden ladder and shot up after him. Helena would have said it was typical – one adventure was not enough.

'Go inside and comb your hair, boys. I'll be with you soon,' I roared.

'Mad bugger!' That sounded like Larius.

'Has he got a head for heights?' One of the Camilli.

'He gets squeamish standing on a chair to swat a fly.' I would deal with *that* rascal later.

There was a working platform at first-storey height, and another up at roof level. I felt perfectly safe climbing aloft to the first one – then deeply insecure. 'He's gone all the way up, Falco!' Aelianus was sensibly resting his leg – standing back at a distance so he could monitor events and shout advice. I hated being supervised, but if I fell off, I would like to think someone could make out a lucid fatality report. Better anyway than Valla's: *What happened to him? He was a roofer. What do you think happened? He fell off a roof!*

Grit rattled through the boarding overhead, showering me in the eye. I came to the second ladder. Mandumerus knew I was after him. I heard him growl under his breath. I had my sword. Faced with light fencing practice, twenty feet above the ground, I shoved the weapon into its scabbard. I wanted both hands free for clinging on.

I saw him now. He laughed at me, then ran lightly ahead, vanishing around the building. Beneath my feet the boards seemed far too flimsy. Gaps in the loose, elderly planks gaped. There was a guard rail of sorts, just a few roughly tied cross-pieces that would snap under the slightest pressure. The whole scaffold had been braced with mere scantling. As I walked, I could feel it bowing gently. My footsteps echoed. Bits of old mortar left unswept on the platform made the going treacherous. Obstructions jutted at intervals, forcing me out from the apparent safety of the house wall. Keeping my eyes fixed ahead, I knocked into an old cement-encrusted bucket; it went bowling off the edge and crashed below. Someone cried out in annoyance. Aelianus, probably. He must be tracking me at ground level.

I turned the corner; sudden sea views distracted me. A gust of wind slammed into me frighteningly. I grabbed the guard rail. Mandumerus crouched, waiting. In one hand he wielded a pick handle. He had hammered a nail into the end of it. Not any old nail, but a huge thing like the nine-inch wonders they use for constructing fortress gatehouses. It would go right through my skull and leave a point the other side long enough to hang a cloak on. And a hat.

He made a feint. I had my knife. Small comfort. He lunged. I swung, but was out of reach. I stabbed the air. He laughed again. He was a big, pale, swollen-bellied brute who suffered from pink-eye and eczema-cracked skin. Scars told me not to mess with him.

He was coming at me. He filled the width of the platform. With the pick handle flailing from side to side in front of him, I had no clear approach, even if I had dared close with him. He flailed at me; the nail point hit the house and screamed down the stonework, leaving a deep white scratch as it gouged the limestone blocks. I grabbed his arm, but he shook me off and viciously jabbed at me again. I turned to flee, my foot slipped on the boards, my hand grabbed for the rail again – and it gave way.

Someone had come up behind me. I was barged to safety against the wall. It knocked the breath out of me. As I scrabbled to regain my footing, someone stepped past, featherlight as a trapeze artiste. Larius. He had a shovel and an expression that said he would use it.

Justinus must have run along at ground level and climbed up by another ladder. I glimpsed him too at our height now, crashing towards us on the scaffold from the far side. He only had bare hands, but his arrival was at high speed. He grasped Mandumerus from behind in a bearhug. Using the surprise, Larius then smashed his shovel on the brute's shoulder, forcing him to drop the wood and nail. I fell on top of him and laid my knife on his windpipe.

He threw us all off. Dear gods.

He was back on his feet and now chose to run up the pantiles. He scaled the palace roof at a slant. The tiles began to suffer. Marcellinus must have provided inferior roof battens. (No surprise; the best probably went to his own villa.) Even climbing at an angle away from us, the steep roof pitch told against Mandumerus. He got halfway up, then lost momentum. With nothing to grab, he began to slow down. Then his feet skidded.

'Not a roofer – wrong boots!' chortled Larius. He was setting off to intercept Mandumerus.

'Watch yourself!' I cried. His mother would kill me if he killed himself up here.

Justinus and I inched warily past the section where the guardrail had gone, then followed Larius. The Briton slid slowly down the roof slope, in a vertical line towards the three of us. We captured him neatly. He seemed to give up. We were taking him back to the ladder when he broke free again. This time he managed to get his great hands on the giant hook on the pulley rope.

'Not that old trick!' scoffed Larius. '– *Duck!*'

The evil claw, made of heavy metal, came hurtling round in a circle at face height. Justinus leapt back. I crouched. Larius simply gripped the rope, just above the hook, as it reached him. Four years playing about on Neapolis villas had left him fearless. He took off and swung. Feet out, he kicked Mandumerus in the throat.

'*Larius!* You are not nice.'

While I contributed the refined commentary, Justinus rushed past me. He helped my nephew batten onto the man again. Clutching his neck, Mandumerus gave in a second time.

Now we had a problem. Persuading a reluctant captive to descend a ladder is no joke. 'You can go down nicely – or we'll throw you off.'

That was a start. We acted as if we meant it – while Mandumerus looked as if he didn't care a damn. I dropped my sword to Aelianus so he could stand guard at the bottom. Larius did gymnastics down the scaffold, then jumped the last six feet. The Briton reached ground level. The ladder must have been merely lent against the scaffold (or else he slipped its ties as he went down). Now he grasped the heavy thing and hauled it away from its position. I had been about to follow him down, so I had to make a jump for safety. He swiped Aelianus and Larius with the ladder – and left me dangling from a scaffold pole. Then he threw down the ladder and was gone.

I had no alternative: I sized up the distance to the ground, then as my wrists began to go, I dropped. Luckily, I broke no bones. Larius and I replaced the ladder for Justinus to descend.

The fugitive made it to the end of the garden colonnade. Then two figures appeared unexpectedly, discussing some abstruse design point in the fading light of dusk. I recognised the parties and feared the worst. Yet they turned out to be quite handy. One threw himself headlong in a tackle and brought Mandumerus down: Plancus. Maybe a low lunge to the knees was how he acquired new boyfriends. The other grappled with a garden statue (faun with panpipes, rather hairy, anatomically suspect; dubious musical fingering). He wrested it from off its plinth then dumped the armful on the prone escapee: Strephon.

We cheered enthusiastically.

Being captured by a pair of effete architects hurt Mandumerus' pride. He subsided, grizzling tears of shame. As he pleaded in crude Latin that he had meant no harm, Strephon and Plancus assumed the high-handed manners of their fine profession. They summoned staff, loudly complained about rowdiness on site, denounced the clerk of works for permitting horseplay on a scaffold and generally enjoyed themselves. We left them to supervise the miscreant's removal to the lock-up. Thanking them quietly, we continued to our suite.

LIV

MAIA WAS alone with my children.
    She was furious. I could handle that. She was anxious too.
'Where's everyone?' I meant, where was Helena.

The Camilli and Larius, sensing domestic danger, shuffled off to another room where I could soon hear them trying to repair the damage to their outfits. At least their bruises made them look like men to reckon with.

My sister's mouth was tight with distaste for yet another stupid situation. She told me Hyspale had gone off with her 'friend'; he had turned out to be Blandus, the chief painter. Hyspale must have met him when she was hanging around the artists' habitat, hoping to encounter Larius.

I was disgusted and annoyed. 'Blandus should not be entrusted with an unmarried woman – one with limited sense and no experience! Helena allowed that?'

'Helena forbade it,' Maia retorted. 'Hyspale sneaked off anyway. When none of you men came back for hours, Helena Justina went after her.' Of course; she would.

'You couldn't stop her?'

'It's her freedwoman. She said she couldn't leave Hyspale to her fate.'

'I'm surprised you stayed at home,' I scoffed at my sister.

'I would have gone to see the fun!' Maia assured me. 'But you have two babes in arms, Marcus. Your nurse is a complete wastrel and since their mother has abandoned them, I'm looking after them.'

I was making preparations. I called out to the others. There was a water flagon on a tray; I drained it. We had no time to rest. No time to wash off the sweat, blood and smells of the dog kennel. I checked my bootstraps and weapons.

'Where did Hyspale and Blandus go?'

'The Rainbow Trout. Hyspale wanted to see the dancer.' To be a woman in the company of the men 'Stupenda' aroused would not be clever. Helena would instinctively understand that. Hyspale had no idea. Hyspale had been nothing but trouble to the pair of us, but Helena made up for the other woman's complete absence of feeling for danger. 'He'll jump her,' said Maia bleakly. Nobody needed to tell me that. 'And the silly chit will be *so* surprised.'

'I'll go. Don't worry.'

'With you in charge?' Maia was now positively caustic. I told myself it was a form of relief since I would have to take the blame.

All my sisters liked to disrupt life with a complete turnaround just when plans had been made. 'I'm coming too,' Maia suddenly declared.

'Maia! As you said just now, there are two small children –'

But it seemed one crisis had forced her to speak out over another. The moment was inconvenient but that never stopped Maia. She gripped my arms, her fingers digging through my tunic sleeves. 'Ask yourself then, Marcus! If you feel like this about *your* children, what about mine? Who is looking after mine, Marcus? Where are they? What condition are they in? Are they frightened? Are they in danger? Are they crying for me?'

I forced myself to listen patiently. The truth was, I did find it odd that Petronius Longus had never sent a single word of what the situation was. He must have made arrangements for my sister's children – with Ma looking after them, probably. I would have expected a letter, at least one that was heavily coded, if not to Maia then to me.

'I don't know what is going on, Maia. I was not in on the plot.'

'The children had help,' Maia insisted. 'Helena Justina.' Helena had admitted it. 'Petronius Longus.' That was obvious. 'You too?' Maia demanded.

'No, really. I knew nothing.'

It was the truth. Maybe my sister believed it. At any rate, she agreed to take care of my two daughters, and she let me go.

It had been a long afternoon, but a much longer evening lay ahead.

LV

THE RAINBOW TROUT was a dump. I expected that. It stood at the junction of a puddled lane with a frightening alley, just two or three kinks in the road from the town's south gate. Calling its location a road is a courtesy. However, it did have a set of road-menders installing new cobbles at one end – and the inevitable workmen following them, tearing up the brand-new blocks in order to fiddle with a drain. Civic-amenity management in true Roman style had hit this province.

There was no streetside space where foodshops with marble counters could offer food and drink to passers-by. A grubby wall, mainly blank, offered a couple of tiny barred windows too high to see in through. The heavy door stood half open; that passed as a welcome. A petite signboard showed a sad grey fish who would be a waste of pan space. There was no graffiti on any outside the wall, which told us that no one in this neighbourhood could read. In any case, they had cleared the streets. Provincials don't dally. Why linger to socialise when your province has no meaningful society?

I had the Camilli and Larius with me. We stepped down a couple of uneven treads into a gloomy cavern. It had a warm rank smell: too much to hope this was caused by animals – the people alone were responsible. There was one interior drinking den, with misshapen curtains half concealing filthy anterooms that ran off to the sides like burrows. Quality customers were perhaps reclining in an upstairs gallery, though it seemed unlikely. There was no upstairs.

That was to be rectified. Like everywhere these days, the Rainbow Trout had a facility-improvement programme. It was being extended upwards; so far, percentage progress was zero. A gaping hole in the ceiling marked the spot where a stairway was to be opened up. That was all.

Downstairs offered sparse amenities. Lamps were kept to a minimum. One amphora stood propped in a corner. Covered with dust, it served more as an item of décor than a source of supply. From the shape, it had only held olives, not wine. A single shelf carried a line of beakers, in odd sizes.

The place was far too quiet. I knew exactly how many labourers worked on our project. Even allowing for stragglers, most were not here. Maybe we were too early for the dancer. Musicians were certainly due to play tonight: on a bench lay a worrying pipe with a skin bag attached, whilst a hand drum was being pattered lethargically by a long-faced laggard dressed in what passed around here for glamour (a dull pinkish tunic edged in unravelling two-tone braid).

Of 'Stupenda' there was no sign. Nor did she have a decent audience. The place should have been packed, with people sitting or even standing on the rectangular tables as well as squashed on every bench. Instead, a handful of men dawdled over their drinks in ones and twos. The most interesting presence was a three-foot-high statue of a Cupid, supposedly bronze, on a plinth in the corner opposite the amphora. The love god had chubby cheeks, a big belly and a sinister fixed expression as he aimed his bow.

'Save us!' muttered Aelianus gloomily. 'Sextius must have been touting his tat. The landlord must be an idiot to buy that.'

'Rather a ferocious talking point!' Justinus observed. Instead of an arrow, some wag from the site had provided the naked Eros with a long iron nail in his bow. I made an audit note that nails were disappearing from the palace stores. 'Don't anyone turn your back on this little blighter.'

'You're safe,' his brother assured him. 'He's supposed to shoot harmless blunt arrows, but we never could make him operate.'

'Why have a love god on the premises when there are no skirts in sight?' complained Larius. There were no women visible. No Hyspale; no Helena. 'No Virginia!' groaned Larius to Justinus.

'Avoiding you,' came the reply, with an edge which suggested Justinus did know Larius had already had some luck with the girl.

We tired of waiting for a greeter to seat us and positioned ourselves at a table. This took some doing as all the stools had wobbly legs. I managed to keep mine steady by wedging one knee under the table rim and bracing the other leg. A man with a grimy apron lurched from a back pantry to serve us. Aelianus asked, in his crisp aristocratic accent, to see the wine list. It was the sort of dump where customers were so locked up in their own misery, nobody noticed this crazy breach of etiquette. Even the waiter simply told him that there wasn't one. It was hard work causing a shocked silence here, let alone making people fail to see a joke.

We had what came. Everyone had what came. Ours was brought in a blackened flagon, which seemed to be a polite gesture to Roman visitors. The rest had theirs poured into their Celtic face-pots from a cracked old jug which was taken away after one quick slosh.

'Could you run to a dish of appetisers?' Aelianus asked. He was a joy to take undercover.

'What?'

'Forget it!' I ordered. I had just tasted the drink. I wasn't risking food. All my companions had parents who would blame me if they expired of dysentery.

A handful of trench-diggers sidled in, looking like first-timers here. After an age they were joined by a small group of more boisterous characters, determined to make the party swing. They failed. We all sat unhappily, wishing we had stayed at home. A couple of the lamps faded and died. Half the customers looked ready to follow them. The trench-diggers muttered among themselves for a while, then stood up together and snuck out like ferrets, giving the rest of us guilty smiles as if they wanted to apologise that they had left us suffering.

Things suddenly improved. A girl came in. Larius and Justinus stiffened but pretended not to notice her. Aelianus and I glanced at one another and chorused: 'Virginia!'

She heard us and came over. With a perfect young face and extremely neat dark hair, drawn back tight in a ribbon, she was old enough to be serving in a grimy bar, yet young enough to look as if her mother ought to keep her in at nights. She wore a simple dress, pinned on so it looked ready to slip off. It revealed nothing; she had less to offer than she hinted. The tempting teenager had perfected a gesture of realigning the sleeves on her shoulders as though she felt nervous about their stability. She got that right. It made us watch.

'Stupenda's dancing this evening?' Justinus checked.

'She certainly is,' Virginia assured him brightly. She indicated the drummer, who responded by fractionally speeding up his beat.

'Seems rather quiet here,' Aelianus put to the girl. I noticed Larius kept to himself. He was pretending to be the man who was onto a certainty, with no need to exert himself. What a fraud.

'Oh it will liven up.' The waitress was full of blasé assurance. I didn't trust her.

You can see them all over the Empire: little girls in bars who have big dreams. On rare occasions something comes of it, not necessarily a great mistake. Helena would say that the young men were responding less to the girl's beauty than her aura of expecting

281

adventure. This was all the more tragic if she was really going nowhere.

Her dreams made her fickle. Larius was history. She had already moved on. Justinus had never been in with a chance. Aelianus might suppose that as the newcomer he would be a strong attraction, but he was wrong. I drank my drink quietly and let the young men jostle for her. Virginia picked her favourite; she smiled at me.

'Who's your friend?' she asked Justinus.

He knew better than to show disappointment. 'Just an old codger in the family; we have brought him out for a treat.'

'Hello,' she said. I smiled faintly, as if I found being chatted up by barmaids embarrassing. I had the lads' six dark eyes staring with hostility, but I was old enough and had enough bad history to live with that. Virginia's patter was basic. 'What's your name, then?'

I replaced my beaker on the table and stood up. If she wanted a mature challenge, I could give her some surprises. 'Let's go somewhere more private, and I'll tell you, sweetheart.'

Then the door crashed open.

We were bathed in a flood of light from smoky flares. Verovolcus and the King's retainers poured inside with a flurry of bare arms, fur amulets and bright trousers. Shouting in several languages, they swept through the bar, shoving tables aside and elbowing customers out of their way as they searched the place like vicious myrmidons in bad epic poetry.

They were rough, though not a quarter as rough as the vigiles in Rome. When Petro's men took a bar apart, everything was wrecked. That was on a day when the red tunics were taking things easy. Other times, you would be lucky to be able to tell afterwards that it had ever been a bar. These fellows of the King's had amiable faces, apart from a few bent snouts, cut eyes and missing teeth. Their idea of raiding the canabae was pretty tame. They all looked as if they knew how to curse, but would be too shy to do so in front of their mothers. I moved Virginia to safe shelter among our group, lest the sweet thing should be accidentally bruised, then we waited patiently for the racket to subside.

They tired of playing bullies even sooner than I thought they would. Only Verovolcus maintained an ugly attitude. When he chose to give up his clowning and turn nasty, he could achieve it in stylish fashion.

'*You!*' He stopped right in front of me. I let him glare. 'I hear you say I killed someone.' The King must have told him.

'You'll do best to keep quiet, Verovolcus.'

The Britons were patiently waiting for their furious leader. I hoped they stayed so calm. There were far too many for us to take on, and if we fought with the King's men we were finished.

'Maybe I will kill *you*, Falco!' It was clear how much Verovolcus wanted to do that. He didn't scare me but I felt my mouth grow dry. Threats from fools are just as likely to go wrong as threats from thugs.

I lowered my voice. 'Do you admit killing Pomponius?'

'I admit nothing,' Verovolcus jeered. 'And you can prove nothing!'

I kept my cool. 'That's because I haven't tried. Force me – and you will be finished. Give in. You could have been kicked right out of the Empire. Be grateful that is not being demanded. You must have cousins in Gaul you can stay with for a few years. Remind yourself of the alternative, and learn to live with the same tolerance that Rome is showing you.' He was livid, but I did not let him bubble over. 'You could have jeopardised everything for the King – and you know it.'

Yes, he knew. I reckon the King had already made his feelings felt. With a snarl, Verovolcus turned and strode towards the door. As a gesture of contempt, he knocked the Cupid from its side-table plinth. It lay on the floor, its iron arrow still rigidly in place. All the Britons stepped over it politely as they made their way out. Perhaps they thought it might bite their ankles.

Something close to peace returned to the bar. Customers took up the same seats as before, finding their drinks again. Some had a slight air of sadness, as if they had hoped their drinks had been spilt in the commotion.

I turned back to the girl. Now I was in no mood for messing. She started to smile but I cut short the pleasantry. 'The angry man said it, sweetheart. The name's Falco. Marcus Didius Falco.'

Her blue eyes were appraising my new mood. She had heard the name. Like others before her, she was in two minds whether this was good or bad. 'You are the man from Rome.'

Larius laughed briefly. 'We are all men from Rome, Virginia.'

He would learn.

To Virginia I said sternly, 'So, tell me again – what time does the entertainment start –' my tone hardened – 'or does it?'

She knew what I meant. 'She's not coming,' Virginia admitted. 'She is dancing somewhere else tonight.'

My nephew and the Camilli were indignant. 'You said –' Justinus started.

I thumped his shoulder playfully. 'Oh grow up, Quintus. The

whole point of beautiful barmaids is that they lie to you.'

'So why did she tell *you* the truth?' he raged.

'Simple. We are all men from Rome – but Virginia knows that I am the important one.'

LVI

WE WERE all on our feet, to go hunting for Perella. Justinus was already at the door. As the stricken statue lay in their path, Larius and Aelianus cautiously picked it up between them and placed it back on its table. Aelianus jokingly lined up the bow, so it aimed at me.

I had been about to leave with the lads, but I turned back. 'Who owns your cheeky table-top art?' I asked Virginia.

'The builder – at the moment.' Clearly she did not appreciate the off-balance cherub. His peeping buttocks and his leer were wasted on this worldly girl. 'He gave us it as part of the decoration scheme for the new rooms upstairs.'

'Appropriate.' I confess I sneered. Upstairs rooms in places that sell drinks have only one purpose, everybody knows. I gazed at the girl. 'Will you be working there yourself?'

She was too young to be insulted so meanly, but perhaps it would make her think. The bar owner was bound to be planning a career move for her. Sophistication had hit Britain; disease and low morals had arrived.

'Certainly not!' Her indignation sounded real. The bar owner had not told her his intentions yet.

'Oh you will find it hard squeaking that you're innocent, once the stairs are built. Stairs in bars go up to private rooms – and customers think rooms above bars have only one purpose.' In Rome waitresses are officially designated prostitutes. It is among the infamous professions.

'That's libel!' snapped Virginia. The law tutors had been here too. Strange how quickly barbarian peoples learn to use the basilica courts as a threat. 'I am a respectable woman –'

I glanced at Larius and laughed. 'No. You've slept with my nephew, darling. He's married. Well, I'm married. We are all married – except for the snooty one.'

The Cupid fell over again.

'Shove a stick under it!' muttered Aelianus. Larius broke a splinter off a table edge and began to comply. Aelianus was fussing. 'It's playing up again. You have to get it absolutely level or the bloody thing tips up –'

'Not the best invention of Heron of Alexandria?' I jibed. The Cupid was too top-heavy.

'Pure Sextius,' Aelianus growled, giving it a sharp punch in the stomach. It reacted with an angry clang.

Delaying for art criticism had served a purpose. A man emerged from one of the side rooms looking to refill an empty beaker. He saw Larius trying to wedge the statue upright – and at once tried to sell it to him.

'Nice bit of bronze – feel that; absolutely genuine. Look at the lovely patina – takes years to acquire, you know.'

Larius stepped back, alarmed. He had seen enough fly salesman to know his purse was at risk. Aelianus scowled and jammed the Cupid's table into a corner of the room, where he somehow propped the bronze beast uncertainly upright against the wall. Justinus was still holding open the outer door impatiently, waiting for the rest of us. 'Name of the gods, Marcus – we have to go!'

But I was looking at the newcomer.

It had to be the building contractor. He was somewhere between forty and fifty; he had lost most of his hair. His manner was urbane enough to come from outside Britain. Like all builders he wore a scruffy oversized tunic, creased in the body and loose in the sleeves, with a wide neck. They live in old garments that won't be harmed by dust and heavy work – despite the fact they never lift a finger on a contract. The tunic was bunched untidily over a scratched belt. Only his boots were worth much and even they had been repaired.

He needed a shave and a haircut. He was one of those men who looks as if he never settled, but wears an outsize wedding ring. A wife probably put it on his finger, but whether she had stayed around afterwards was a different matter. He was well built, at least around the midriff; he could be prosperous. He had a direct, friendly air.

He had noticed me staring. 'Do I know you, legate?'

'We've never met.' I knew a great deal about him, though. I walked across, holding out my hand. He took it, producing a personable smile. He had a firm handshake. Not as firm as mine.

'*Falco!*' urged Justinus from the doorway. At my name, I felt the builder's grip slacken. He was trying to back off. I held on grimly.

'That's me,' I acknowledged with a smile. 'Falco. And you must be Lobullus?'

Lobullus returned a sickly grin. I stopped smiling.

'You're the uncle of Alexas, the orderly on the palace site, aren't you? He has told me all about you.' I don't mind lying. People tell me enough untruths; I deserve to even up the score. And Alexas was one who had lied to me. 'So you're working here at the Rainbow Trout – and starting the Great King's bath-house update?' Lobullus nodded, still distracted by my fierce grasp of his hand. 'You get around,' I commented. 'The last I heard, you were finishing a long contract on the Janiculan Hill in Rome . . . Are you using a false name, or is Gloccus just a cognomen you leave at home when you take off as a fugitive?'

Aelianus stepped away from the side table, so he could move in to support me. We pushed the builder onto a stool.

'Didius Falco,' I spelled out. 'Son of Didius Favonius. You also know my dear Papa as Geminus. He may be a rogue – but even he thinks that you stink, Gloccus. Helena Justina, who employed you for *our* bath house, is my wife.'

'A very nice woman,' Gloccus assured me. That was decent. I knew that on several occasions Helena had let rip at him in her best style. With cause.

'She will be delighted that you remember her. Pity she's not here; I know she has a word still left to say to you. Camillus Aelianus – that's him over there – had the pleasure of meeting your own wife in Rome. She is much looking forward to your return home, he tells me. Plenty to discuss.'

Gloccus took it cheerily.

'So where is your partner this evening, Gloccus? What chance of meeting the infamous Cotta?'

'Not seen him for months, Falco.'

'Alexas is *your* nephew – but I thought Cotta was the one with medical relatives?'

'He is. We're all related. Cotta is family.'

'So where is he?'

'We parted company in Gaul –'

'I shall want to know,' I growled, 'in which town, which district of the town – and which bath house you were both destroying when you did him in!'

'Oh don't say that! You've got it all wrong, Falco. Cotta is not dead.'

'I do hope not. I shall be very annoyed if you deprive me of the pleasure of killing him. So where did he go?'

'I've no idea.'

'Back to Rome?'

'Could be.'

'He was coming to Britain with you.'

'He may have been.'

'Why did you part? Surely not a falling out?'

'Oh no, not us.'

'Of course not – he's family! Don't you want to know,' I asked, 'why I thought you might have finished him off?'

Gloccus knew that.

I told him anyway. 'We found Stephanus.'

'Who would that be?'

He was sitting on a stool with his feet tucked under it. I lashed out. I hooked my right foot under, kicking out his legs. Aelianus grabbed him by the shoulders lest he fall. I pointed to the builder's feet. Gloccus wore worn but well-kept boots, with hob-nailed soles. They had three broad thongs across the arch of the foot, crossed straps around the heel and a couple more wide straps going up the ankle. These thongs were black; the one that had been repaired was narrower, with tight new brown stitching.

'Stephanus,' I announced clearly, 'was the last owner of these boots. He was well dead when I saw him. Word is, he went to work angry because he thought you had diddled his wages.'

'Yes, he was a bit put out that day . . . But I never killed him,' Gloccus insisted. 'That was Cotta.'

'And what will Cotta say?' jeered Aelianus. He leaned on the man's shoulder heavily. ' "*Gloccus did it!*" I suppose?'

Gloccus returned the fearless gaze of a man who has had to face sticky questions many, many times before. We would not find it easy to break him. Too many furious householders had tackled him, all determined not to be put off again. Too many customers had screamed their frustration when his labourers failed to turn up yet again, or mould grew in the wall flues, or the plunge bath was lined finally after months of delay – but in the wrong colour.

Maybe he had even had to face interrogation by the vigiles.

Nothing was new to him. He answered everything in that infuriating way – denying nothing, promising all, yet never coming good. All my fury about the bath house returned. I hated him. I hated him for the weeks of bad feeling we had endured, for the waste of money, for Helena's disappointment and stress. That was even before I remembered the scene when Pa and I set to with picks and unearthed that hideous corpse.

I said I was arresting him. Gloccus would be tried. He would go to the arena beasts. There was an amphitheatre in Londinium; Hades, there was even an arena here. Lions and tigers were in short supply but Britain had wolves, bulls and Caledonian bears . . . First I would make him tell me where to find Cotta. If that required torture, I would personally set light to the tapers and tighten the screws.

Maybe I laid it on too thick. He jumped up suddenly. Justinus and Larius were blocking his escape route to the street. He turned to make a run for it through the back exit. He barged Aelianus. Aelianus knocked against the corner table. The Cupid statue clanged against the wall. There was a loud retort. The bow twanged. Gloccus was shot by the great iron nail, straight through the throat.

LVII

IT WAS a freak accident. It killed him. Not instantly. He suffered. Not enough for me, yet too much for the humane to find bearable. I sent the lads off. I stayed.

There was no point trying to ask again whether it was him or Cotta who had killed Stephanus. Even if he had been able to speak, he would not have told me. If he had said anything, I would never have been sure I could believe it. To finish the business, to draw the requisite line in the sand, I waited there until he croaked.

All right. In the circumstances croaked is the wrong word. I can still hear Gloccus in his dying moments. I mention it purely to give comfort to those of you who have found raw sewage backing up a waste pipe in your new caldarium, three days after your contractors vanished off the site.

I was in a dark hole where life was brutal. The Rainbow Trout stayed open, whoever might be dying on their filthy floor. Customers did move aside to give me light and air as I crouched beside Gloccus. Someone even handed me a drink during the ghastly vigil. When Gloccus died, they just towed the body out through the back exit.

Once he had gone, I felt no more cheerful. At least we avoided formalities. In Britain you don't hear the vigiles whistle, then find yourself stuck with hours of questions all implying you are guilty of some crime. Given how I felt about Gloccus, his end lay lightly on my conscience. It was fitting. Best not to think that the arrow could have struck down one of us and we too would have been dumped in a narrow alley for the wild dogs. But the sense of unfinished business crippled me.

As I made to leave, Timagenes the landscape gardener came in with Rectus the engineer. They must be regular drinking pals. In shock, perhaps, I blurted out what had happened. Rectus took a deep interest and decided he would haggle with the landlord to acquire the fart-arse

Cupid. Its arm dropped off while he inspected it, but Rectus reckoned he could fix that.

They too bought me a drink. It helped my toothache, which had started up again.

'What are you two doing here? If you've come to watch the dancer –'

'Not us.' Rectus grimaced. 'We came here on purpose to avoid all that.' Quiet types, unimpressed by the twirling of elderly pulchritude. Still, Rectus was a man who noticed things. He knew what was going on.

'So where is she appearing?'

'At the Nemesis.'

That sounded like a place where any accidents would be neatly planned by Fate.

Rectus and Timagenes gave me directions. Starting to feel light-headed, I roamed off alone. Summer evenings in southern Britain can be pleasant enough (by their standards). If this had been a port there would have been noise and action, but Noviomagus lay slightly inland. It was partly surrounded by a river, nothing significant, not enough to encourage nightlife – or any life that would satisfy Rome. The town was only half developed, still with many empty plots lining the silent streets. Where there were houses, they displayed no lights. I found my way purely by luck.

This new dive lurked by the Calleva Gate, which was on the western edge of town. It was the approach road from the palace handiest for the site workers. I found the venue by the soft glow of lamps shining from the open doorway and the loud hum of men's voices. It was the only place in Novio that night with any real hint of activity. I was sure this was the right location, next door lay a darkened lock-up, where a large signboard showed a human tooth. Gaius had mentioned the adjacent tooth-puller. Had he been open for business, I would have rushed in, demanding that the mouth-mangler relieve my pain. Like everywhere else except the bar, it was closed for the night.

As I approached, I saw a tall woman, her body and head decently shrouded in a Roman matron's stole. She paused briefly outside, then made herself go in boldly. She was no mystery to me: Helena. I called her; she never heard me; I rushed after her.

Indoors was pandemonium. Helena could be determined, but she hated noisy crowds. She had stopped, nervous. I fought my way to her, breaking into my best grin.

'You wicked piece! Is this how you spend your evenings? I never had you for a barfly –'

'It's you! Thank goodness.' I do like grateful women. 'Marcus, we have to find Hyspale –'

'Maia told me.' Helena was covering her ears against the din. I saved my breath.

There seemed no chance of acquiring a table, then a group of Italian diggers decided they would leap up and knock hell out of some Britons. The management had organised a party of big Gauls to keep the peace; they were of course eager for a ruckus, so all three lots went outside in good order and held their fight there. Impressed, I manoeuvred Helena to a free space, just beating a friendly set of Spanish hearties. They tried chatting to my girl on principle, but took the hint when I lifted up her hand and pointed to a silver ring I had given her.

'My daughter,' Helena explained, miming heavily that she had a baby, 'is called Laeitana.' This went down well. They had no idea what she was saying; they were from the south. Baeticans don't give an *as* for Tarraconensis. That my child had been named for a wine-producing area near Barcino in the north had no effect. But Helena had made an effort and they made us share their flagon. Helena noticed I looked flushed. I blamed my tooth.

Drink was being sold at a furious rate, though there was no sign of imminent dancing. I climbed on a bench and looked over heads; I saw nobody I recognised.

'Where are my brothers and Larius?'

'Who knows? I found Gloccus.'

'What?'

'Later!'

'Pardon?'

'Forget it.'

'Forget what?'

There were so many men crammed in, it was hard to see what this bar looked like. I could tell how it smelt, and that we'd be lucky if the animal fat in the lamps failed to set the joint ablaze. If Noviomagus Regnensis lacked street lighting, there was no chance they had organised a patrol of firefighters. Once, when I was an efficient operator full of good sense and energy, I might have wandered through the back kitchens to locate a well and buckets in advance . . . No. Not tonight, after a death and several drinks.

A plate of grilled meat snacks passed itself to our table. It sat there a while. No one seemed to own it, so I tucked in. I could not remember my last meal.

The crowd heaved and reordered itself into new configurations. Through the press I glimpsed the Camillus brothers, squashed and red-faced. Helena waved. They started the long process of inching over to us, but gave up. I mouthed at them, '*Where's Larius?*' and they signalled back, '*Virginia!*' Then somewhere in the thick of the drinkers at the far end of the room a stillness fell. Excitement was transmitted through the hubbub, bringing silence. Eventually new sounds became audible through that silence: a shimmer of a tambourine, shaken with infinite restraint, and the faintest ripple of snare drum. Someone shouted to the people at the front to sit. Helena saw men climbing on a table near us. She flashed a glance at me. One minute we were both on our feet, the next standing up on the narrow bench.

That was how we stayed, clinging to each other for balance. That was how, in that dirty, noisy, disreputable hovel by a gatehouse in a half-built town, we were taken halfway to Olympus the night we saw Perella dance.

LVIII

A LL THE best performers are no longer young. Only those with experience of life, of joy and grief, can wring the heart. They have to know what they are promising. They have to see what you have lost and what you yearn for. How much you need consoling, what your soul seeks to conceal. A great mature male actor shows that although the girls scream after the ingenues, they are nothing yet. A great female dancer, in her prime, encapsulates humanity. Her sexual power attracts all the more because in popular thought only young girls with perfect limbs and pretty features are exciting; to prove that nonsense is a thrill for both men and women. Hope lives.

Perella revealed almost nothing physically. Her dress seemed entirely modest. Her severe hairstyle emphasised the bones of her pale face. She wore no jewellery – no tacky anklets, no twinkling metal disks sewn in her garments. When she entered that dire den, her casual poise almost insulted the audience. They thrived on it. Her matter-of-fact floating walk asked no favours. Only the respect with which her musicians waited for her gave a hint. They knew her quality. She let them play first. A double flute, eerie with melancholia; a drum; a tambourine; a small harp in the pudgy, beringed hands of an incongruously fat harpist. No clichéd castanets. She played no instrument herself.

At what point in her past history she had been taken up to dally with spies, I dared not contemplate. They must have approached her because she was so good. She would be able to venture anywhere. She had neither fear nor grand airs; she was dancing here as honestly as she must ever do. The only fault for her palace employers would be that she was so good, she would always attract attention.

She began. The musicians watched and responded to her; she tempered her movements perfectly to their tunes. They loved that. Their enjoyment fuelled the excitement. Perella danced at first with such restraint of motion it seemed nearly derisive. Then each fine angle of her outstretched arms and each slight turn of the neck became a perfect gesture. When she burst forth abruptly into frantic drumming of her feet, whirling and darting in the confined spaces available, gasps turned to stricken silence. Men tried to fall back to give her room. She came and went, within the free area, flattering each group with their moment of attention. The music raced. It was clear now that Perella was in fact clad alluringly – we could glimpse white leather trunks and breast-band under sheer veils of Coan silk. What she did with her supple body was more vital than the body itself. What she said through her dance – and the authority with which she said it – mattered most.

She came nearer. The entranced crowd parted for her. The smiling musicians slipped to their feet lightly, tracing her progress through the room so they neither lost sight of her nor left her insecure and unattended. Her hair came loose, a deliberate part of the act no doubt, so she swirled it free with a deep toss of her head. This was no slim and devious New Carthage beauty with a tumbling sheen of oiled, inky locks, but a mature woman. She might be a grandmother. She was aware of her maturity and challenging us to notice too. She was the queen of the room *because* she had lived more than most of us. If her joints creaked, nobody would know it. And unlike the crude offers purveyed by younger artists, Perella was giving us – because she had nothing else to give – the erotic, ecstatic, uplifting, imaginative glory of hope and possibility.

The musicians strove to a high climax, their instruments at breaking point. Perella twirled to an exhausted halt, right in front of me. Applause burst all around us. A hubbub rose; men called feverishly for drink to help them forget they had been overcome. Congratulatory grins surrounded the dancer, though she was left alone respectfully.

She saw who I was. Perhaps she had stopped here deliberately. 'Falco!'

Helena teetered dangerously on the bench edge; I could not leap down and seize the dancer, I had to hold on to Helena. A Roman does not allow the well-bred mother of his children to tumble face first on a disgusting tavern floor. Helena probably relied on that; she kept me with her on purpose. 'Perella.'

'I have a message for your sister,' she said.

'Don't try anything! Following my sister is a mistake, Perella –'

'I'm not after your sister.'

'I saw you at her house –'

'Anacrites sent me there. He realised he went too far. He sent me to apologise.'

'Apologise!'

'A stupid move,' she admitted. 'That was him, not me.' That was him dead then, I thought.

'And what are you doing here?' I demanded accusingly.

'Earning my fare home. You know the bureau: mean with expenses.'

'You're still following my sister.'

'I don't give two sleeve-pins for your bloody sister –'

A draft hit us. The noise dimmed for a moment as men sank their noses into beakers thirstily. The crowd in the outer door had moved to allow somebody admittance. It was someone whose manner always made men move aside for her. My sister walked in.

A woman screamed.

Helena was off that bench like a centipede fleeing the spade edge. Fighting through the press, she came to the curtained anteroom. It looked dark but we could see flailing limbs. A foul hole in which to deflower a fool.

Helena reached the couple first. She had slipped between the drinkers where my wider shoulders jammed. While I was discouraging those whose beakers I had jogged, Helena Justina broke in on Blandus as he attempted to rape the screaming Hyspale. I saw Helena tear down the hide curtain, heard her yell at him. I called out. Somewhere behind me, I was aware of her brothers shouting. Other men turned to watch the scene, impeding me more. As I battled on, Helena took hold of the inevitable amphora used to imply fancy décor; she heaved it up, swung it and crashed it down on Blandus.

He was tough. Now he was furious too. He threw himself off Hyspale and turned on Helena. He had grabbed her by the arms. I was desperate. Helena Justina was brought up to wear white, think clean thoughts, encounter nothing more exciting that a little light poetry read to her in a nice accent. Since she came to me I had taught her good sense on the streets and where to kick intruders so it hurt – but she was no match for Blandus. Raging, publicly thwarted, still aroused, he went for her. She struggled. I struggled to reach them. Someone else got there ahead of me.

Perella.

'I'll have no rape at my events!' she cried to Blandus. 'It gives me a bad name.' I choked quietly.

He was lucky. She did not knife him. Instead, she high-kicked one powerful dancer's foot in a fine arc straight to his privates. When he doubled up, she grabbed him, twirled him around bodily and showed him just how bendable his neck could be. Her strong hands reached down and did something horrible, once more to his nether regions. She thumped his ears, pulled his nose and finally sent him flying into the barroom. Blandus had suffered enough, but he landed in a space right beside the mosaicist, Philocles Junior. Now that was bad luck. Philocles had reached the point in his evening where he was ready to revive old family feuds . . .

'Juno, I'm getting too old for all this,' Perella gasped.

'Not as old as your caseload,' I taunted. 'Marcellinus was crooked, but long out of it. There was a time an emperor might well have had him removed quietly. It would have saved money and curbed his corrupt influence on the King – but that was another world, Perella. Other emperors, with different priorities. So is Anacrites still following up correspondence that's ten years out of date? Pointless, Perella!'

'I just do what I'm ordered.' Perella did look sick. For a skilled operator to be despatched on stupid missions by an inefficient clown like Anacrites must hurt.

Helena was rescuing our nursemaid. As Hyspale sobbed hysterically, I flung my arms around Helena. She was too busy to need it, but I had not recovered from seeing her in Blandus' clutches.

A glimmer of silk slid by. I looked up and saw Perella had sashayed through the bar. She came face to face with Maia. She said something. Maia obviously scoffed at it.

A violent flurry indicated new trouble. Verovolcus and his search party had worked their way to the Nemesis. Perella looked quickly at me. Instinctively I jerked my head. She needed no second warning. She was off through the crowd, who let her pass with gruff courtesy; then they closed in excitedly, hoping she would dance another set. Verovolcus had missed his chance. By the time he realised, Perella was hidden from view.

I would be livid tomorrow that I let her escape. Tough.

LIX

M AIA FORGED her way to us.
'What are you doing here?' I asked.
'Where are my children?' asked Helena.
'Safe, of course. Fast asleep here, in beds in the Procurator's house.'
Maia was storming up to Hyspale. 'Did he succeed?' she demanded of
Helena.
'Not quite.'
'Stop bawling, then,' Maia rebuked Hyspale. She tweaked the red
dress Hyspale was wearing. 'It was your own fault. You have been
stupid. Worse, you've been stupid wearing *my* best dress – which,
believe me, you're going to regret. You can take that off. You will
take it off this minute and walk home in your under-tunic.'
Women can be so vindictive.
I kept out of it. If terror of Blandus failed to educate Hyspale,
maybe embarrassment would.

In the main room, the men realised that Perella had left them. Uproar
ensued. Verovolcus and some of the King's retainers had found a man
I recognised as Lupus. They were punishing him for his feud with the
disgraced Mandumerus. His own men, to whom he had sold jobs so
dearly, watched in cynical silence. No one offered help. Once he was
pummelled into pulp, Verovolcus and the others disappeared through
the back exit, clearly not searching for the lavatory. They never came
back, so they must have galloped off. Others in the bar decided to vent
their frustration on anyone available. Deprived of the dancer for
entertainment, the different groups of site workers chose to thrash
each other. We cowered in our nook as fists thumped cheekbones.
Men were on the floor; others jumped on their backs punching
furiously. Some tried rescuing those who were down; they were
attacked by the men they thought they were helping. Flagons went
flying across the room. Beer was upended on the floor. Tables
overturned.

The trouble spilled out onto the street. That made space for more complex wrestling. We sat quiet and let it pass. I felt rough. I was cradling my cheek where my tooth now hurt so much I had to deal with it in the next few hours or I would die of blood poisoning.

On the far side of the barroom, I could see the Camillus brothers. They had opted out of the fight and were seated aloof at a table like minor deities, munching food and commentating. Aelianus held his wounded leg out stiffly. Justinus lifted up a dish to me, offering to share their victuals; refusing, I mimed dental anguish. The Camilli had been talking to a man at the next table; Justinus pointed to him with one finger, showing his own fangs. They had found the local tooth-puller. Deafened, harassed by the turmoil around me and in pain, I just wanted to die quietly.

Suddenly the row diminished. As quickly as they had flared up, all the fights finished. Someone must have brought news of a good torch singer at yet another bar. Next minute our den was empty. The landlord was clearing broken pots. A few stragglers had their heads down on tables looking ill, but something like peace descended. My womenfolk were gathering themselves to take us home. I could see the Camilli negotiating terms for late-night dentistry.

A group of travellers, unaware of the mad scene they had missed, now entered and scanned the amenities.

'Phwoar! This is a bad one!' cried a young boy's voice. He sounded cheerful. He had a large shaggy dog with him, which was untrained and very excited.

'It will have to do,' said someone else. I looked up.

Into the Nemesis marched a strange party. Behind the boy came a big, quiet man, dressed all in brown, who rapidly checked around the place. He wore a heavy cloak with a pointed hood and a triangular storm flap at the neck. Good travelling gear, it went with solid boots and a satchel slung across his chest. With him were four children of various ages, each warmly dressed in similar style, with woollen socks inside their boots, and each with a bag. They looked clean, fit, well cared for and probably enjoying life. The two boys needed haircuts but the two girls had neat pigtails.

Once inside, the youngsters clustered close to the man while all four children glared about, scanning the bar for undesirables exactly as he had done. He had them well drilled.

'*Whoops!*' They had noticed Maia. This was more trouble than they had bargained for. 'Look out, Uncle Lucius!'

Ancus immediately hurtled straight across the bar and threw himself into his mother's arms with a piteous cry. He was eight, but had always been a baby. Sensitive, she said.

Maia's eyes were slits. Carrying Ancus, she stepped towards the others and pointed to Petronius. 'This man is *not* your uncle.'

All four children stared at her.

'He is now!' decided Rhea. The brutal, forthright, open one. Aged almost five, she spoke her mind like a ninety-year-old matriarch. My mother must have started out in life just like Rhea.

'Let's face it, Maia,' Petro drawled. 'The very fact that they are yours makes the poor things uncontrollable.' He bent down to the three who were still beside him. 'Go to your mother, quick, or we're dead meat.'

Marius, Cloelia and Rhea trotted to Maia obediently then held up their faces to be kissed. Maia stooped and put her arms around all of them. She turned her furious gaze on Petronius, but he got in first. 'I did my best,' he told her quietly. 'I brought them to you safely, and as quickly as I could. We would have been here sooner, but we all fell ill with chickenpox just north of —'

'Cabilonnum,' supplied Cloelia, who must be the keeper of their travel notes. 'Gaul.'

Maia was lost for words, though being my sister this did not afflict her for long. Sick with wrath, she accused Petronius, '*You have brought my children to a bar!*'

'Settle down, Mother,' advised Marius (the eleven-year-old authoritative one). 'This is about the hundredth time. We're slightly short of funds, so we make do. Uncle Lucius has taught us how to behave. We never question the prices, we don't pull a knife on the landlord and we don't break up the joint.'

LX

T HE TOOTH-PULLER had a strange attitude. I thought he was
drunk.

I had gone with him alone. Had not Maia's children wanted
feeding – urgently, they all insisted – I could have escaped this.
I would have preferred to exchange news with Petro, but he and I
swapped a coded agreement to speak in private later. Since the tooth
man seemed willing to deal with a patient, everyone insisted that
while the children tucked in at the Nemesis, I had to submit to
dentistry. Playing brave, I rejected company. It is bad enough yelling
in agony, without a helpful audience. Helena wanted to come with
me, but I knew my ordeal would upset her terribly. I could cope with
pain, but not that.

The street outside the bar was oddly peaceful. Somewhere across
town, I could hear raucous voices as the site team progressed between
venues, but here by the Calleva Gate all was at rest. Cool air soothed
my temper. There was rain drifting in fine gusts. It could be nowhere
but Britain.

We entered the molar man's lair. It had wide doors, which he
opened a bare crack, as if scared I would admit muggers with me.
Inside, although he lit a lamp its dwindling flame scarcely reached any
distance. I felt my way to the seat where he would operate. I had to
put my head back against a block of something cold and hard.

'I heard you only opened up here recently?'

'That's right.'

'You bought the place? Had it been some other business?'

'Believe so.'

I wondered what.

He started to mix up a very large draught for me. Poppy juice in wine.
Just looking at it made me feel I was bursting for a latrine visit; I
managed to spill the beaker and avoid drinking most of it. He seemed
anxious about that. The strong herbal scent of his medicine reminded

301

me of the painkiller Alexas had prepared for Aulus with his dogbite.

'I'm tough. Just hurry, will you?'

He said we had to wait until the poppies took effect. I could understand that. He did not want his hand gnawed off.

I lay there in the semi-darkness, feeling myself relax. The tooth-puller was pottering somewhere behind me, out of sight. Suddenly he reappeared to take a look in my mouth. I opened wide. He seemed awkward, as if I had somehow caught him out.

'It's the old story,' he mumbled. 'Too much grit in food. Breaks down the surface and trouble gets in. If you came to see me sooner, I could have filled the hole with alum or mastic – but it never lasts.' Even though what he was saying was all professional, I felt myself losing confidence in him. 'Do you want a slow extraction?'

I gurgled, still with my mouth gaping. 'Quick!'

'Slow is best. Causes less damage.'

I only wanted him to get on with it.

Now my eyes were more accustomed to the Stygian gloom. The tooth-puller was a skinny stoat, with nervous eyes and thin tufts of hair. He had perfected a manner that must make his patients all terrified.

I remembered my great uncle, Scaro, who had once visited an Etruscan dentist whose skill impressed him enormously. Scaro was obsessed with teeth. As a small boy I had listened to many tales of how that man held his patient's head between his knees, rasping away with sets of files to remove the tartar – and how he would create a gold band to fit over surviving teeth, into which replacements carved from ox teeth would be pinned . . .

I would not acquire a cunning gold brace and a workable bridge in Noviomagus Regnensis. The man was barely competent. He prodded a gum. I cried out. He said he should wait longer.

The medicinal draught was taking effect. I must even have dozed off briefly. Time shrank, so a few seconds passed, filled with a wide-spanned dream in which I found myself reflecting on the new palace. I saw some fellow who was project manager. He costed the works, created the programme, negotiated supplies of precious materials and hired specialists. Around him a pall of stone dust hung over the largest mason's yard north of the Alps. He inspected marbles from every corner of the world – limestones, siltstones, crystalline and veined. Columns were fluted; mouldings were polished; cornices were run off from hard templates. In joineries, planes squealed, tenon saws rasped and hammers banged. Elsewhere, carpenters banging down floorboards whistled piercing tunes to overcome their own racket. In forges, blacksmiths clanged incessantly, turning out window catches, drain covers, handles, hinges and hooks. They produced mile after mile of nails, which in my dream were all nine-inch monsters.

I saw the palace complete, in splendour. One day the King's quiet corridors would be trodden by businesslike feet, amid the murmur of voices from elegant rooms. One day . . .

I woke. Something was wrong in my darkened surroundings. I saw it blearily. A large interior with a workplace. Fearsome gadgets hung on walls. Pincers and hammers. Was this tooth-puller a torturer, or just provincial and crude? He owned one tool that was familiar: a joined set of clamps with cutting edges. The last time I saw anything like that, it was the most precious possession of Maia's dead husband Famia. He used it for castrating stallions.

The man approached me. He was holding a set of enormous pliers. He had watery eyes, in which I discerned evil intentions. Through my numbed brain the truth rammed home. He had drugged me. He was now going to kill me. I was a stranger. Why would he do that?

I stirred. I jumped up. He must have thought I was unconscious. He fell back indignantly. I threw aside the cloth he had used to cover me; it resembled an old horse blanket. I discovered my head had been resting uncomfortably on a smithy's anvil.

'This is some wayside blacksmith's haunt!'

'He left. I bought it –'

'You're an amateur. And I fell for your story!'

This was not for me. I would make Cyprianus pull the damn tooth out with a set of nail-head pliers. Better still, Helena could take me to Londinium. Her uncle and aunt would produce some skilled specialist who could bore fine holes into abscesses and drain off the poison.

'What do you think you are doing here? What kind of pathetic loser wants to be a fake mouth-surgeon?'

The shrinking fraud said nothing. He pushed open the wide stable doors for me to leave. I was too angry for that. Anyway, I had realised who he was.

I gave him a shove and he fell to his knees. Even through the fug caused by his sleeping draught, I knew I had had a narrow escape. I grabbed his lamp and shone it near his face. 'I need a piss; I think I'll piss on you! Where do you come from – Rome?'

He shook his head. That was a lie.

'You're as Roman as I am. What's your true trade?'

'Barber-surgeon –'

'Cobnuts! You run a builder's yard. I'm Falco – now go on; pretend you have never heard of me. I'm a bounty hunter – but there's no money reward on my present quest – just pure satisfaction.'

I found an old rope, maybe an abandoned halter, and bound him tightly.

'What's this about?' he quaked.

'Have you got a brother who does something medical?'

'Barber and tooth-puller. Same as me,' he added unconvincingly.

'Father of Alexas, on the palace site, I take it? Or is he just a cousin? Alexas certainly tried to put me off finding you. Even your partner tried to pretend he had lost you in Gaul. But once I found him, I was ready for you too. So are you going to own up?' He trembled feebly. 'All right, I'll say it. You're Cotta. A builder. The firm Stephanus worked for. You come from Rome. You ran away because of how Stephanus died – who killed him?'

'Gloccus.'

'How curious. He said you did it.'

'It wasn't me.'

'You know –' now he was trussed, I sat him up playfully – 'I don't care which of you hit him over the head. You both hid the body and you both scarpered. You have to share responsibility. Gloccus died tonight – but don't worry, that was an accident. You will have longer in the world. Much longer. I'm going to make sure of it. I know just the punishment for you, Cotta. You are going to the silver mines. It's final, Cotta, but it's ghastly and slow. If the beatings, hard labour and starvation don't kill you, you'll be grey-faced and die of lead poisoning. There is no escape except through death – and that can take years.'

'It wasn't me! Gloccus killed Stephanus –'

'Maybe I even believe that.'

'Let me go, then. Falco, what have I ever done to you?'

'Something really criminal! You built my bath house, Cotta.'

It had been a long night, but a good one. Now I felt no pain.